NO
KILLING SKY

No Killing Sky

First published in English in 2017 by
New Internationalist Publications Ltd
The Old Music Hall
106-108 Cowley Road
Oxford
OX4 1JE, UK
newint.org

Edited by Chris Brazier
Front cover design: Andrew Kokotka
Design: New Internationalist

Printed by TJ International Limited, Cornwall, UK
who hold environmental accreditation ISO 14001.

British Library Cataloguing-in-Publication Data.
A catalogue record for this book is available from the British Library.

Library of Congress Cataloging-in-Publication Data.
A catalog for this book is available from the Library of Congress.

ISBN 978-1-78026-392-2
(ISBN ebook 978-1-78026-393-9)

NO
KILLING SKY

Rory McCourt

New Internationalist

For Kerry

To the south of Cronin's Yard stands a fragment of old stone wall.
It points the way to the head of the Carrauntoohil track.
On its pale face, but easily missed in the dawn shadows,
several modest memorial plaques bear witness to
the treacherous nature of the brooding mountain.
Near the rusting iron gate there is space for one more.

1

THE DROMDARRAGH locals would say, in that soft, song strong way of theirs, that Liam Doyle hiked out of his mother's womb wearing mountain boots.

His first visit to the summit of Ireland was achieved before he could walk, bounced along in a pack on his dad's back. His first uttered word was not dada or mamma but mahtun – mountain, delivered with a tiny crooked finger pointing unsteadily toward the jagged northern skyline. His first steps were taken on a gentle slope overlooked by the mighty Coomloughra Horseshoe. Not long after his fifth birthday he'd toddled to the summit unaided and by the age of ten he was doing it regularly, alone. At 12, he'd spent a solitary night high on Maolan Bui when a sudden summer snow squall took him by surprise. He returned home to his frantic mother the next morning as if he'd just been down to the mail box.

This morning, long before the first warming rays from the east stole across the damp earth between Drishana and Broaghnabinnia, he was out of bed and onto the mountainside. As the valley slumbered he climbed the steep slope past Curraghmore to the Caher ridge and tracked along the knife edge to the tall iron cross.

The weather remained perfect and unchanging during the hours on the mountain, but his life was to be transformed profoundly and forever, between ascent and descent.

The farmhouse was still a gable-topped sugar cube as he loped down to the level of the fast-dissipating smoke from his mother's well-tended hearth. On the track next to the stone wall was a stationary car. A figure, recognizable even from this distance, was emerging painfully from the driver's side. He could imagine Denny O'Rourke, the old gard, breathing heavily as he dragged the sagging gate from his path.

A sudden chill lifted the down on the back of Liam's neck. It was too early. The visit was too early. Something wasn't right. As the car crawled slowly toward the house, he started to sprint, his feet flying over the broken ground with unerring instinct. And yet the thundering of his heart came not from exertion but from an awful dawning dread.

He had half a mile of soggy slope to cover when O'Rourke started towards the front door. Margaret, his mother, appeared, wiping her hands on her apron, and took several steps towards the gard before being overcome by a shattering stillness. Liam, although he heard nothing, knew the gard was in the process of revealing some terrible secret and this was confirmed seconds later as his mother sank to her knees. By the time he'd leapt the crumbling garden wall she'd begun to wail. It was the sound of keening, an inconsolable lament as old as the hillsides from which it now echoed and it was more than his young ears could bear.

'It's your dad, son,' the old man said lamely, arms limp and helpless at his side. Liam leaned heavily against the gard's car, his body shrieking from every sinew. 'There was an accident, on the mountain. He didn't make it.'

'Dead,' Liam said flatly. It was a statement and a question. Enquiry and confirmation in one.

O'Rourke nodded. 'We had a call from the Pakistan Police early this morning.' He shrugged. 'Evening,' he added, 'based on their time,' trying desperately to restore some form of structure to this chaos of death and grief.

Liam knelt and cradled his mother in his arms. She seemed to be on the verge of collapsing further. Her keening had subsided into a soft series of moans and whimpers.

'I'll go on in and put the kettle on,' O'Rourke said softly, leaving mother and son stunned and alone with their anguish for a moment.

* * *

'Where is he? When will they bring him home?' Liam whispered, trying unsuccessfully to stop his voice from breaking.

O'Rourke had freshened up the fire and poured the tea. At another time the room might have been described as cozy.

'He's not coming home, macushla,' Margaret breathed tearfully. 'He's near the summit. In deep snow – they're not sure where. They told Denny they couldn't bring him down.'

'But Da is the best climber in the world,' Liam exclaimed angrily. 'How could that happen? He's never been hurt on a mountain in his life.'

'K2's a bigger mountain than Carrauntoohil, son,' O'Rourke ventured gently. 'Much more dangerous.'

'I know that, Mr O'Rourke, but Da could do the Reeks in his sleep. He's climbed eight-thousanders all over the Himalayas. It's what he does for a living.'

Margaret sobbed softly again.

'Have they found his... him? Have they seen him? Do they know for sure, absolutely, one hundred per cent?' A hint of hysteria was creeping into his voice and he checked himself abruptly. O'Rourke remained silent. His mother said nothing. His questions went unanswered.

Liam stood, stepped to the window and looked out at the mists now obliterating the nearby summits. 'They can't leave him up there.' He shook his head. 'It's not right. He needs to come home, to be buried here.' He wiped tears roughly from his cheek. 'He'll never have peace if he's not here,' he trailed off to a whisper. 'Among his lovely Reeks.'

'I must be gettin' back,' O'Rourke murmured, reluctant to desert his friends but at the same time keen to create some distance between himself and this private pain. 'Look after your mother, will you, son.'

* * *

'Lots of strange chatter in the air tonight,' the radio guy was saying with a full mouth, as Charlie Casement bent under the sagging lintel and came into what passed out here for a mess tent.

'Anything relevant?' Charlie grabbed an apple and a Coke and

9

slumped beside him. He'd been on assignment, combing the hills for days, and was starting to feel his 40 years.

'All far-away stuff. Scrambled like an army egg.' The radio guy belched. 'No time to try a decode now, leave that to the boys at Langley,' he said. 'Too much static, too much local shit to listen to. Still having trouble with some of my Pashto.' He stood and tossed his chocolate wrapper onto the packed dirt. 'Man, I'm bushed. Catch you later.'

Charlie sat alone, rubbing his fingertips across the grip of his pistol and staring at the pock-marked walls. In a few days they'd be back down at Chapman; well, what was left of it. He couldn't wait.

His had become a life without structure, without the clear-cut discipline and procedures of an air strike, without the unambiguous comfort of a recognized military operation. This was chaos: formless, shapeless and out of control.

Flying had been relatively simple. It had been detached. No matter how bad the things you were doing, they were done from a distance. The screen image was just that, an image. He looked down at the dried blood on his boots. This shit was real. Much too real. He wasn't sure how much longer he could handle it.

The blood had congealed to the color of Kansas mud.

Kansas mud. Now there was something he'd not seen in a long, long time. The final years on his father's farm had been all about dry dust, drought and failed crops. Explained why he was here really. If, year upon year, the drought hadn't turned the sweet young corn to rustling husk stubble, he'd probably still be flying crop dusters.

Charlie had always loved flying, but flying war planes had been more necessity than choice. A poor farm boy from the Midwest, with a destitute old man, didn't get the opportunity to fly commercial heavies.

* * *

A fossicking rabbit, startled by the sudden opening of the front door, bounced away over the grass as Liam banged out with

Margaret's bag. He dropped it onto the back seat of the taxi and turned to watch her tuck a rogue strand of hair under her beret. It seemed impossible but in just a few short hours she had become a different person. She looked older, less present, almost indistinct. It was like seeing her through a lens that was ever so slightly out of focus.

'There's enough food in the fridge for a week. If I'm not back by then, go over to Mavis Cooney's. I've told her I'm going. She's offered to…' She left the sentence unfinished, slid into the seat behind the driver and wound down the window.

Liam was tempted to say he was quite capable of fending for himself, but knew that, given his mother's fragility, it would start an argument. With her beside him for just a few precious moments, before she too disappeared off to Pakistan, it was the very last thing he'd choose to do.

She had been on the phone making arrangements even before the sound of O'Rourke's motor died away. Liam was desperate to go with her, to see, to feel, to try to understand, but the money wasn't there and Margaret refused to take the charity offered by the people of the valley and the town.

He was torn between wanting to know what had happened to his father and worrying about his mother's safety. The tabloids were filled with horrific stories detailing the atrocities unfolding along the Indo-Pakistani frontier. He'd lost his father; he didn't think he'd survive the loss of his ma as well.

'And stay off the mountains while I'm gone,' she called as the taxi pulled away.

* * *

The wet season had arrived early in the Australian north.

Nuggets of water the size of shelled peas pounded the tarmac and drummed deafeningly on the terminal's metal roof. The overflowing gutters made waterfalls of the wide windows and turned the world outside into a bizarre aquarium. Palm trees played the role of Gorgonian corals and the small buffeting aircraft became the pelagic fish.

11

Two men, waiting for two consecutive flights, sat apart from the small cafeteria crowd, heads together in muted conversation. One had arrived in Darwin just minutes before on a delayed SQ flight from Singapore and was booked to return on the same service.

'Pity your plane was late,' the other said quietly. 'They'll be calling the Alice flight any moment now. I can't afford to miss it. It's best if nobody knows I've been up here.' He checked his watch nervously. 'Why do we have to meet face to face like this? We can organize encrypted traffic, that's our expertise.'

His companion shrugged a pair of elegantly draped shoulders. 'It's corporate policy. Avoid leaving electronic signatures whenever possible. I don't make the rules; I simply ensure they're carried out.'

Mr Paul checked his watch again. 'Well, you'll need to be brief.'

The other man nodded. 'There's been an incident. People have been deployed but the object is yet to be located.' He slid a flash drive across the sticky table. 'The details. All there. You'll need to get organized more quickly. No doubt there'll be similar requirements as time goes by.' The small, bright red object lay on the surface, a punctuation mark emphasizing the space between them. Paul let it pulsate in place for moments. He seemed almost reluctant to touch it.

'You'll have to decrypt,' the other man said, indifferent to the tension.

Paul looked around furtively and then zipped the stick into his raincoat pocket. 'We've been looking at various options and processes. There are significant issues to address. It's very labor-intensive but there's no other option if we're going to get it to work seamlessly.' He spoke with the prim pride of a junior civil servant. 'It's just a matter of staying on top of it, which isn't always that straightforward. There are issues.'

The other man shrugged, not really interested in his associate's problems.

Paul craned in a little closer. 'I don't want to appear difficult…' He paused in an attempt to choose less bureaucratic language. 'But a few extra dollars would help to ease the load, grease the skids.'

A muffled announcement, inaudible against the roof-pummeling rain, struggled from the public-address system. The Singapore man looked up at the departures screen. 'Your flight is boarding.' He stood, making no attempt to take Paul's proffered hand. 'I'll see what we can do.'

He turned, strolled unhurriedly across to the newsagent and started to peruse the various headlines. It seemed, to the watching Paul, a deliberate act of dismissal and it annoyed him.

* * *

He was there, trembling… in the snow again, eyes wide, sliding… sliding… hands reaching desperately… frozen fingers… no gloves. 'Where are your gloves, Da, your gloves, Da… Da?' Somewhere deep in the smothering snow a phone was insistent. Liam jolted upright, calling his father's name. The nightmare phone was still ringing. He leapt down the stairs three at a time and clutched at the receiver anxiously.

'I'm sorry to wake you in the middle of the night, my darling.' She sounded small and frightened and so, so far away. 'I'm in Skardu. It's the only chance I've had to get to a phone. Are you all right?'

Liam hovered somewhere between the still-real dream and the dream-like reality of the call. 'I'm fine, Ma, fine… Did you find him? Can you, can you bring him home?'

For long moments the only sound was an electronic echoing murmur. It seemed other-worldly and very distant. In his mind's eye a lonely stretch of poles and wires marched across a ridge, somewhere high in the Karakoram. They trembled with gentle anticipation and hummed silently, waiting for the caller's voice to share their solitude once again.

'They can't bring him down, my love, they're not even sure where he is,' she said eventually. 'They searched for days, even tried a military helicopter, but then the weather closed in. All they're sure of is that his last contact was from way up high; they think he's near the summit. There's nothing more they, nothing more I, can do.'

Liam was silent so Margaret filled the quavering space.

'The Pakistani people have been wonderful, Liam. They took me up the glacier, to Concordia, in the helicopter. We couldn't get any closer because of the weather.' Her voice splintered for a second and he could sense her, feel the determination on the line, pulling it back together. 'I placed some flowers for your Da, from you... In sight of the mountain.'

In the Dromdarragh darkness Liam began to weep silently.

'There was another man with him, Liam, a local man. He didn't come back either.'

She waited for a response and then, realizing the reason for his stillness, continued. 'The policeman needs his phone now, love. I'll see you in a couple of days. Look after yourself.' The line went dead and Liam was left as bereft and desolate as the far-off mountainside on which his father's body now lay.

* * *

'Hello, morning there, how would you like a little drive out into the leafy suburbs?'

Cherry Davitt had been with *The Washington Dialog* for just a few weeks when she was asked by the newspaper's owner to cover the story. It involved the disappearance of a man in Arlington.

'It's not Watergate,' Saxon Melville chuckled. 'But it's a little more interesting than the usual bullshit from the Hill.'

The missing man, in his late forties, had allegedly gone off to walk the Appalachian Trail and not been seen since.

Walter Dyson was a childless bachelor and, according to the neighbors, spent the bulk of his time locked away with his computer. It was only when the same neighbors became aware of newspapers piling up unopened on the now-unkempt lawn that the alarm was raised. A few days later his car was found, concealed in a thicket at the end of a muddy track. It was hundreds of miles from any point of access to the Trail.

Cherry worked the case with the DC police and became more and more fascinated by 'the onion being peeled', as the officer in charge would say, always using the appropriate hand movements.

'Yo, Cherry,' it was Bob Schultz again. 'You join me for a drink round five and I'll give you the latest.' Schultz would never head up his own department; he was always going to be a bit of a klutz, but all in all he wasn't a bad sort.

Schultz seemed to make a point of finding cheerless, smoky bars and then leading her to the darkest corner in the place. At times she wondered if he planned to hit on her, but his propriety never wavered.

'Seems this guy's bank account was emptied. Cash, no transfers. His closets were all bare, all gone.' Schultz dispatched his second bourbon. 'Let's face it, you don't take your pajamas or your robe if you're going on a hike.'

'What about his workmates, buddies, family?' She refused the offer of a third drink with a hand placed firmly over her glass. 'Any of them turned up yet?'

'This is the weird thing. His computer was gone, no records anywhere, nothing to say who he was working for, who he knew – and nobody's come out of the woodwork to claim him yet.'

Cherry added a scribble to her shorthand. 'Have you tried the covert angle, CIA, FBI, NSA, DIA?' She tilted her head in the general direction of the Capitol. 'This is Washington, after all.'

'Nada,' he said shaking his head. 'Tried them all. Nothing. Never heard of the guy. Not on their radar apparently.'

Time went by and no trace of the man was ever found, nobody had seen or heard him. The trail, Schultz ventured on several occasions, was as dry as a Death Valley waterhole in July.

And so, just one more missing person's report found its way into the Cold Case section of the Metropolitan Police Department's overflowing vaults. At the offices of the *Dialog*, Cherry's file was tied up in black ribbon and consigned to the archives. Life moved on. Walter was forgotten.

✱ ✱ ✱

An emptiness had overtaken the small farmhouse. For a decade or more James Doyle had eked out a living photographing mountains and wealthy mountaineers and, as a consequence, was away, sometimes for months at a time. But this was different. This was a void that would never again be filled; a desolation that now made the solitary windswept ridges far more of a home for Liam than the little cottage. A lonely longing consumed his days and deep, nightmarish snowdrifts, from which his father's face peered sadly, filled his nights.

Three weeks from the day Gard O'Rourke brought the sorrow, a message arrived. It was as though, Liam thought with a shudder, it had come from beyond the grave. Not that there even was a grave, he told himself bitterly.

A postcard, soiled and stained with thumbprints, travel grime and what looked like engine oil, arrived with a Kathmandu postmark. The image on the front was of a faded K2, seen in the distance from the Baltoro Glacier. 'Mount Godwin Austen,' the caption read, in a font attempting, unsuccessfully, to emulate an Urdu script.

The brief scrawl on the back appeared to be in a feminine hand, which, although it had trouble forming the letters of the language, had managed the grammar surprisingly well.

'Laim must keep to doing what he does best,' it said simply.

Liam kept the card with him constantly, feeling its presence against his skin as he walked the high country and taking comfort from it as he slept. But it confused and disturbed him. What, if anything, could it mean? Who was it from?

* * *

Dashka worked quickly and nimbly to adjust the drive-chain tension on the snow-spattered vehicle; the cold tears on her cheek far more of an impediment than the thick mittens covering her hands.

Dashka Anasovna, the cod eaters would say, was the finest mechanic north of the Arctic Circle. And the only woman, some would add, with a sly wink.

Her earliest memories embraced a warm one-bedroom apartment above her father's Arkhangelsk repair shop. She performed her first oil change at the age of five and by the time she was seven she was stripping old carburetors and fitting head gaskets. As engines became more sophisticated, so too did Dashka's skills. She studied electronics and computers and was customizing hardware and writing software as a young teenager. By the time she was ready to leave home and head off on her first big adventure, there wasn't a motor or computer she couldn't repair blindfolded.

It was a bleak soulless place, this workshop she now found herself in. But then nowhere else on the planet could be quite as bleak as Severny Island according to Dashka, and the bleakest of the bleak was Cape Zhelaniya.

Initially the site had been operated automatically but after one breakdown followed another and caused the constant delivery of inaccurate data, Moscow decided it needed to be staffed. Only individuals strong enough to endure months on end in isolation were accepted and she was flattered when she'd been chosen. She was like a lighthouse keeper, she thought at times during her lonely vigil, keeping the darkness at bay.

Not only was Zhelaniya an Arctic-white desert that in winter dropped below minus 20 Celsius, it also shared the island with an assortment of abandoned nuclear test sites. God knew what that was doing to her health. But still, in remote Russia these days, a job was a job. And there was more to it than that. She had come to love the remoteness, the vast beauty of the wilderness. She explored the landscape in meticulous detail, both online and on the snow. Her days off were spent on the workshop snowmobile, wandering the wide desolation of a frozen world.

'Dashka,' the others claimed proudly over a vodka or two, 'knows more about Severny than anyone else on earth.'

The young mechanic had maintained the base's snowmobiles, ploughs, generators and, when needed, the computers for several years, enduring vicious winter weather, barely concealed misogyny and during long dark nights a solitary, lonely existence.

It was only when Dmitri arrived that things had changed.

A few weeks after the handsome young scientist's appointment, following a night of too much alcohol and years of too little affection, she'd made love to him on his laboratory desk.

17

The next few months had been the best of her time on the island. They had laughed and teased and had long conversations about every imaginable subject. They would take a snowmobile and ride together for hours, 'inspecting the base' as Dmitri would say. He had taught her the periodic tables and the basics of his monitoring activities and she had taught him the principles of fuel injection and how to retrieve information from a damaged hard drive.

The affair had gone on in secret for some time, the sex always discreet, either in his quarters, the rear of the workshop or the laboratory. The excuse they used, if ever the others began to wonder, was the need to repair the computers or discuss the maintenance of the station equipment.

On balance she was relatively happy here. Which was why, in spite of the radiation, the cold and the isolation, she was devastated when, without notice or even a little courtesy, she was told that Dmitri was being replaced and that, within days, somebody would be arriving to take over the station. She was welcome to stay on working for his replacement if she so desired.

Dashka was reasonably sure no one else at Cape Zhelaniya was aware of her indiscretion and yet now, out of the icy blue, with no explanation, Dmitri was being sent away, replaced as the senior analyst and station head. It simply wasn't fair. If it was because of their affair, why not replace her as well?

She was told on a Wednesday morning and by Thursday afternoon, Dmitri was strapped into the big Kamov Ka-62 on a flight back to the relative civilization of Arkhangelsk.

She had failed to admit it to herself, until right up to the very last minute, but as Dmitri shook her hand and bade her a formal farewell, she realized how much she loved him. She wanted to throw herself at him, wrap her arms around his strong neck and yell at the top of her lungs, 'I love you Dmitri... take me with you.' Instead she remained still and silent and Dmitri said nothing.

The big helicopter lifted, banked off into a darkening western sky and left her to return to her machines and the bleakness of her life on this bleakest of Arctic islands.

Weeks rolled on, autumn turned to winter and the mystery postcard continued to burn a hole in Liam's pocket. It was still there early one Saturday morning as he scrambled up Cruach Mhor. He had stopped on the first ridge to look across to the misted Dingle when he suddenly remembered the Rolex Oyster he'd found on a nearby slab of stone several years earlier.

'Sure, you have the eagle eyes,' James had said. And, flattered though he was by his father's compliment, he was aware it was true. They were eyes that roamed the landscape, observing constantly; interpreting and storing every detail no matter how seemingly trivial or how minute.

'He found a Rolex watch up there today,' James told Margaret proudly as they banged their exuberant way into the cottage. 'It's very valuable, the lad might even get a reward.' James walked over to where Liam was removing his boots and ruffled his hair. 'He's always discovering interesting things on mountains,' he continued. 'It's a great skill. It's what he does best.'

Liam dragged the battered postcard from his pocket. He read it for the thousandth time. 'Laim must keep to doing what he does best.' It seemed so very clear, at that moment, that he was being sent a message. 'Keep searching for interesting things on mountains.' But what did it mean? Who sent it? Was it from James somehow? Was this a message to come and search for him? For his father's body?

And, anyhow, what could a teenager, a schoolboy, possibly do when it was so vague, so uncertain, so far away?

There was no answer, no solution, no resolution and slowly, in a process as gradual as the high-country grasses changing their seasonal hues, normality crept back into Liam's life. Other than in the recurring nightmares, James was allowed to attempt whatever rest might be achievable for his frozen soul, high on that most distant and alien of peaks.

2

SEVEN SUMMERS of high-country melt had turned to valley torrent, and rushed and fussed beneath the stone bridges of Dromdarragh, since Liam's return from the mountain on that morning of sorrow. And now here he was with a different accent, a different passport, a different life; still pining for The Reeks and trying, once again to find something to do to fill the emptiness.

His mother, Margaret, had been unable to cope with the demands of the farm on top of the grief. She'd sold to a Dublin solicitor in late autumn and by winter's end they were living in a soulless horizontal suburb near her sister in Oklahoma. Being so far from his beloved mountains was like a second death and, early in the morning on the day after his graduation from school, he packed a small bag and took off to hitch a ride to Colorado.

A few months of steering spoiled brats onto ski lifts at Beaver Creek had been all he could stomach and within the year Liam had been in Alaska leading parties to the summit of Denali.

But even this had not satisfied his restless need for greater challenges and loftier heights, and so began an aimless, world-wide wander. After a season in Nepal, on the advice of a fellow climber, he headed off again, this time to San Diego to try his luck with the Marine Corps. Tired of living the life of an itinerant pauper, the idea of being paid good money to walk the high trails of Afghanistan, even if it meant getting shot at, held some appeal. His height, his powerful build and his mountain skills meant he was transferred to Special Operations early in his military career and in short order was spending his days between the Kesai Mountains and the Spin Ghar ranges of eastern Afghanistan; deployed from the skeletal remains of Forward Operating Base Salerno.

***

The American President's term in office had nearly two years left to run, but on The Hill and in State Capitols up and down the country, the jockeying, lobbying, name calling and horse trading were already under way.

The incumbent was not a popular man. He'd had difficulty coming to terms with a House and Senate split along party lines after the midterms and the smart money in the media was saying he had all the makings of a one termer. His arrogance, the major dailies were suggesting, his inertia and his questionable friendships, were having a seriously adverse effect on the nation's future.

Cherry Davitt read the opinion piece in her own paper as she waited for the next interviewee. It wasn't one she'd written herself, but she agreed with most of the sentiments.

Her deliberations were interrupted by an assistant knocking softly on the glass partition. 'Liam Doyle is here for his appointment,' he said.

'Send him in.' She swung her feet down from the desk, located her shoes with her toes and folded the paper.

The young man was taller, older and a lot better-looking than she'd expected and she was immediately aware of, or perhaps she simply sensed, something a little out of the ordinary. Perhaps even a little exceptional. She indicated the seat opposite.

'So why journalism?' Cherry slid her tortoiseshells a little further up her nose. 'You seem to be a wee bit old for a cadetship.'

He shifted a little awkwardly on the soft padded chair. 'I did some writing when I was in the military. Personal observations about overseas postings, operations, the local landscape, the people...' He tailed off. She watched him impassively. 'I enjoyed it. My buddies said I wrote well; reckoned I had a knack for getting to the guts of things. I've brought a few samples.' He reached into his backpack and brought out a fresh manila folder. 'I had an intelligence role, it taught me how to probe, to look for the truth below the surface.' He handed the file across the cluttered desk. 'There's a résumé in there too.'

'Born in Ireland, I see, gorgeous place. Whyever did you leave?' It clearly didn't require an answer. While the woman flipped through the pages, Liam took the opportunity to walk in the mountains of his mind, to visit his past. Since his father's long-ago death it had become an essential sanctuary; it had never become a foreign country.

'Served in Afghanistan, I see. Special Forces.'

'Yes,' he said. 'But late in the piece. When most everybody else had gone.'

* * *

What the résumé didn't include was 12-odd months as an involuntary and reluctant guest of a Taliban spinoff.

Not long into his second tour he'd been in a small observation post high in the ranges north of Khost. The enemy had come up from the rear on a moonless night, gliding across the terrain like ghosts. Liam had been the only one who had survived long enough to become a prisoner; a dubious honor, he'd thought while stumbling along over steep stony ground with a stinking bag over his head.

For what he estimated as around 30 hours they climbed and then descended intermittently. There was also a stint in the back of some sort of vehicle, hands tied, face pressed against hot rusting metal. When the bag was finally removed and his eyes adjusted he found himself in an ancient stone hut, with walls barely a meter high and a dirt floor that smelled of sweat, shit and piss.

At first they asked him questions and beat him when he refused to answer. It struck him as half-hearted; perhaps no more than an idle pastime. The questions seemed vague and irrelevant and even had he been able to provide answers they would have been of no practical or strategic value. For a while he tried to engage the men who delivered the slops that passed for a meal, but silence was the only response and, after a few weeks of unsuccessful effort, he adopted the same technique himself. Mutual muteness was the way forward, he decided with a grim smile. But there was no one with whom he could share the insight.

An attempted escape did not end well and he carried the cuts and bruises for some months. The passing of a year saw his life reduced to the most rudimentary of cycles. Sleeping poorly, eating very poorly, defecating and waiting for the inevitable.

From time to time he would be moved, always wearing a bag and always up and down across lacerating knife-stone gradients. He thought of these rare occurrences as treats, as a kind of busman's holiday. An opportunity to stretch his limbs and breathe deeply, even through coarse fabric, something other than the fetid air of the various huts and caves that contained his existence. At times he would listen to the Pashto of his captors as they sat outside his darkened cell, or came and went with messages and supplies. He soon tired of this: what little he gleaned of their conversations suggested a daily reality as monotonous and impoverished as his own had become.

A few days after yet another move, he crouched behind the barricaded entrance to a cramped cave. Peering through the cracks between the rough-hewn timbers it appeared to be sited below a rock outcrop to one side of a high mountain saddle. His captors began a conversation nearby. The subtly lowered tone of their voices, an unfamiliar gravitas, made him crane forward, ear to the door. Something was muttered about using a video camera and the name of an unfamiliar town was mentioned. One or two more issues were discussed quietly and then he heard a skittering of rocks and the crunch of sandals receding down the slope. Two people, he estimated. The odds were that this left just one guarding him. The reference to the production of a video could only mean one thing. A contrite confession to camera for being an agent of the great infidel, followed by some sort of messy execution, probably a beheading.

There was no point in being passive; a lamb awaiting slaughter, Liam decided. Better to die trying. He peered out through the crack. The one he had heard called Ali was tossing dung onto a small fire, an AK 47 slung loosely from his shoulder.

Good.

What looked like becoming a major problem had in fact become an opportunity. Not only did Ali seem slighter and slower than the others, he was also more punctual. The gruel, with a sliver of stale naan, arrived each evening as the sun's last thin rays filtered into the cave. By Liam's reckoning that was an hour away. He sat calmly, cleared his head, relaxed every muscle and waited in a near-meditative state. When the light illuminating the dancing dust motes was all but horizontal, he coiled himself against the rear of the small space and waited, hands at the ready. He heard the scraping of a plate on the stones near the fire. This was it. While Ali's attention was on the rickety door, his hand held a plate and his eyes adjusted to the darkness, there would be a millisecond in which to act. The door scraped open. The man's neck was snapped before his pupils were given time to dilate.

Ali's shalwar kameez was filthy and rank, but no more so than Liam's own tattered rags. He stripped the man's corpse, dressed himself in the still-warm garments and relieved him of his cheap watch and weapon.

He touched the silent shape lightly on the shoulder. 'Sorry, my friend – you or me,' and then started to jog away. Not downhill to the south, the west, towards his base, which they would expect, but deeper into the mountains, up towards the high peaks, to the north and east, towards what he imagined would be Pakistan.

He used the sun, the stars, the wind, the shapes of the terrain, the contrails of the aircraft high overhead, all the skills that James had made sure, long ago, were his second nature as they had climbed together in the Reeks. This was landscape he'd studied endlessly on map and screen. The lay of the land, the structure of peak and valley made him fairly certain he was somewhere to the west of the Spin Ghar range, home of the notorious Tora Bora. He felt confident that if he survived the trek he would eventually find his way across into Peshawar. He knew there was a US consulate there and he was fairly certain he could locate it.

He holed up during the day, his outfit indistinguishable from the faded colors of the surrounding sand and rock, and walked or ran through the night. These peaks and ridges weren't Ireland but they felt like home.

On the third day he dragged himself from sleep around an hour after starlight had relieved the sunlight of its role. As his vision adjusted he became aware of what appeared to be cold celestial light glinting, intermittently, from a pair of dark eyes. They were watching him from just a few feet away. He sat rock still and stared into the gloom. Gradually he made out a shape, an animal of some sort, big but not too big. He heard a soft snuffle followed by a single soft bark. A dog. Hopefully not rabid. Still, it could be worse. There were wolves and leopards in these mountains. Not many, but they were there.

His appearance, to a local animal, would not be strange, probably not pose a threat. The scent too, from the clothes he wore, would be familiar. But a dozen sharp barks from the beast could be disastrous. It wasn't worth the risk. He reached out with a closed hand to simulate food, whistled softly and whispered in Pashto, as he'd heard the local children do, and coaxed the animal across. It approached tentatively, head and tail down. Beneath its powdering of grey Nangarhār dust it was probably a mangy black. Even the faint light from the stars was sufficient to reveal the starkness of rib against wasted flesh.

Liam took the trusting head between his two hands, drew the animal toward him, lifted his knees to create a pincer and with a deft shift of weight, snapped its neck. He held it in his arms for some minutes, stroking its dying head and then gently shifted the corpse to one side, gave it a quick pat, wiped tears from his eyes with a filthy sleeve and loped off into the night once more.

The hunger was bearable but the thirst was a killer. Below the snow line he sucked what moisture he could from the almost non-existent morning dew and chewed the roots from the scattering of bitter plants. Above the snowline were enough pockets of dusty summer drift to keep him alive. Early one morning, when the light in the east was little more than a vague promise, he brought down a still-drowsy hawk with a well-aimed stone and within scant seconds had consumed raw flesh and warm blood and left nothing but a sad residue of bones and feathers.

After several nights of stealthy progress over the barren, featureless mountains, dawn found him concealed among rocks on a high bluff overlooking what he was fairly certain was the Jalalabad to Peshawar highway. But whether he was at the eastern or western end of the Khyber Pass he wasn't sure and so he stayed high above the road, concealed among the crags and crannies, as he plodded off toward the east again that night.

Within 24 hours he had come down out of the high country, skirted the vast refugee camps on the outskirts, negotiated the back streets of the town and at midnight was rattling the consulate gate. His feet had been torn and bruised, he was around 70 pounds lighter but other than that, according to the local doctor, in 'emphatically good shape'. Despite his protestations, they were not as sure about his mental condition. Three weeks later he was on his way home to the States.

* * *

Cherry Davitt's voice dragged him back to the present.

'Some promise there,' she said, indicating the slim A4 document in her hands.

She found a space for his file on the desk, nodding her head. 'Okay, you're a little older than our usual trainees and generally we prefer graduates but I'll give you a shot. We'll pay you a pittance and work you until you drop.' She tapped the folder with a manicured fingernail. 'But then, that shouldn't be anything new.' She stood and reached across to shake his hand. 'Welcome to *The Washington Dialog*. Let's see how you get on.'

* * *

A return from the extravagances of foreign espionage to the insipid safety of the DC streets, Liam knew, was never going to be easy but he wasn't quite ready for the mountains yet. Although he was happy with life as a trainee journalist, the trivial nature of his modest assignments made him restless, irritable and desperate to do something, anything, that had a little substance, anything that would keep the beast at bay. This, he knew, was a residue of his time in captivity in Afghanistan. So he put it behind him and addressed his mundane daily tasks with as much good grace as he could muster.

Then two things happened in quick succession and his life changed, suddenly and dramatically, once again.

On a Monday his mother was diagnosed with cancer. Margaret appeared to take the news of her illness in a far more measured way than did Liam and he was still reeling with shock when, just two days later, an early-morning call shattered a deep but troubled sleep.

'Liam, my name is Greg Carter. I am… *was* a mate of your dad's.' The accent suggested Australia, perhaps New Zealand.

'Hi,' was all Liam could offer, but his heart, for some reason, skipped a little beat.

'I apologize for calling out of the blue like this but I have something I thought you should know.'

Liam waited, dreading what might come.

'I'm calling from Pakistan, the Karakorams.'

Not about Margaret then. Thank Christ. Liam exhaled silently.

'I've just come down off K2. I didn't summit but it's been a particularly hot, dry season and the melt has been early and extensive.' He paused for several seconds. 'I guess this is going to dredge up stuff that you might prefer to be left alone but I, well I just thought you needed to know. We sighted a body, the thaw had uncovered it… him.'

Liam's pulse was gathering speed, but he waited, silent.

'He's around 26,000 feet. There was a bloody great serac between us. Weather coming in fast, couldn't attempt the extra traverse in the time we had, but through the binocs I could get a pretty good look at his gear, his outfit. I've climbed with James countless times and I'd put my bloody house on the fact it was him.' His voice quavered momentarily. 'Sorry, mate.'

'Fuck,' Liam said. Not knowing how to react. He was exhilarated, angry, relieved and grief stricken all over again.

'Ah,' he tried to calm his voice. 'Would you still be there if I flew over? I've been above 26,000 a few times myself. I'd like to try getting up there to see him.'

'Sorry, old mate, I have to fly back to Nepal, to my office in Kathmandu. Been away too long.' Liam thought he could hear genuine regret in the man's voice. 'I can probably help you find

the Balti high-altitude porters who were with him on that final...
on that climb. I can also send you the co-ordinates of, you know,
the location, they'd be within just a few meters.'

'Fine, I understand... and thanks for the call, I appreciate it.'

'No worries, sorry to be the bearer of more bad news. Let me
know if there's anything I can do.'

Carter gave Liam his number then clicked off and Liam was
left in the early twilight with a fast-fading image of a smiling
James striding confidently up a scree slope in O'Shea's Gully
long ago.

* * *

Cherry Davitt was perplexed. 'C'mon, Liam, I know it means a
lot to you but you've been with us for no more than six months.
I can't give you special treatment – time off that I wouldn't give
the others.'

Liam shrugged. 'It's my *dad,* Cherry.'

'It's *The Washington Dialog*, Liam. There are policies, rules.'
She sat back and laced her long fingers behind her head. 'I don't
make them. Besides, it'd cost a small fortune and the company
certainly wouldn't be footing the bill. Who's paying?'

'My military pay is sitting in the bank virtually untouched.'
He smiled for the first time since knocking tentatively on her
office door. 'We live a very frugal life, we climbing folk.'

He walked to the window of her cluttered office on Vermont
and looked past Freedom's statue crowning the Capitol dome and
off to the distant east. K2, Godwin Austen, his missing father;
out there round the other side of the earth and just three degrees
to the south.

'All these years I've spent wondering; never knowing where he
was. Now I know.' He turned to face her. 'I don't have a choice, I
have to go. If you want my resignation, I'll understand.'

Cherry sized him up. There was something about the young
man that made her hesitate; something that suggested he was
one of a kind. And, besides, she smiled, she was a sucker for his
wonderful Irish-American accent.

'I'll see what I can do. But there had better be a damn good story in it.'

* * *

Margaret was far easier to persuade than his editor had been. 'I'm not planning to die any time soon me darlin',' she smiled through her pain. 'Besides, I wouldn't try to stop you even if I were. You and your da and your precious mountains.'

She seemed a little more frail, a little more translucent, the veins a little more blue each time he visited and he wondered out loud, yet again, whether he should go and leave her there, battling her illness alone.

'I'll do a deal with you,' she said, leaning forward and reaching for his hand. 'You go find your dear dad and then, when you return, you can take *me* back... to Ireland, to Kerry.'

'But your health, Ma,' he started.

She stopped him with a raised palm. 'Ireland's my home. It was your father's home. I've not ever settled in here. Ireland's where I belong. Where I want to be buried.'

She beckoned for him to bend and kissed him lightly on each cheek. 'You go and find him and, if it's at all possible,' she brushed away the beginnings of a tear. 'If it's at all possible, do something for me: bring him home, to his *own* mountains.'

3

A BEGGAR approached Mahmood Khan as he entered the terminal at Benazir Bhutto. He handed over a couple of crumpled bank notes and made his way to the chaotic arrivals area.

The Pakistani pilot's friendship with Liam hadn't been a long one but, for all that, it had become remarkably intense. The skin-and-bones young fellow he met on a visit to the US consul in Peshawar had just endured a year in Afghan captivity which still haunted his pale blue eyes. But his quiet stoicism, his almost ingenuous directness, together with their shared military backgrounds, had crafted a bond very quickly. This friendship, they both sensed, would endure, regardless of time or distance.

'Mahmood!' The young Western man appeared head and shoulders above the locals loitering about the gate. He negotiated the waiting throng deftly and enveloped his slightly built Pakistani friend in big arms. Mahmood stood back, grinning widely. He surveyed Liam with satisfaction. The gaunt, troubled young escapee of the past had been transformed into a powerful, healthy and beamingly confident fellow.

He pumped Liam's hand vigorously. 'Very good.' His smile threatened to engulf his ears. 'Come, I have a car waiting.' He commandeered the overloaded luggage trolley and used it to cut a swathe through the crowd. 'The rest of your equipment arrived a week or so back; I have it in a warehouse near the hotel. I've organized to have it sent on up to Skardu as soon as you check through it.' He grinned. 'Let's hope it will still be there when you arrive.'

As they drove, Liam became increasingly aware of the military presence almost everywhere he looked.

Mahmood read his thoughts.

'Things are changing very quickly. It has escalated since you were here. The government is fighting insurgents, terrorists on both sides, west and east. In Azad Kashmir our troops are fighting not only India but also so-called Mujahideen. They are coming from here there and everywhere.'

'What's the situation up north, the Karakoram?'

'This war is gradually spreading along the length of most of our borders and much of it is not being fought by our army.' Mahmood shook his head. 'Nowhere is immune any longer, but the isolation, the difficulty of the terrain up there helps. The irony is that, at the moment, K2 might be one of the safer places for you in Pakistan.'

The driver pulled up and waited as the armed guard lifted the boom gate at the entrance to the hotel grounds. 'I booked you into the Marriott.' Mahmood indicated the hotel logo. 'It's more expensive but it's the only accommodation in Islamabad that's relatively secure nowadays. Even the anonymous guest houses in the suburbs are being targeted these days.'

'The Western press is saying our old enemies now have new friends and are angling for a Caliphate that stretches the entire length of south Asia,' Liam said, eyeing a group of fierce-looking, bearded tribesmen conversing earnestly in the porte-cochère.

'It's more complex than that,' Mahmood said quietly. He walked around to the trunk and lifted one of Liam's bags. 'Most revolutions, when all is said and done, are about bread.'

* * *

'Mister President…'

Cherry Davitt was seated among several dozen media people in the White House Rose Garden. The President stood behind a podium, the presidential seal thrusting importantly from its center. It had taken Cherry a good 15 minutes to get a question in and she wasn't planning to let the opportunity slide.

'There is currently a conflagration brewing across more or less the whole of the Middle East and southern Asia; it will soon extend, they keep telling us, from Syria to Saigon.'

The President listened patiently; an aide alongside twitched once or twice.

'You are on record as saying that this is entirely the work of ISSA, the Islamic State of South Asia terrorist group. Would you not agree that there are many other more local geopolitical events contributing to the conflicts as well? In India, for example the Ganges…'

'I'm sorry, Cherry,' one of the President's brisk young media advisers cut in. 'We'll have to leave it there. The President has a plane to catch.'

Cherry strolled along to Pennsylvania Avenue and gave Richie a call. He was curbside in ten minutes.

A further ten minutes and the peak-hour traffic on Vermont was moving at around the same pace as the old man negotiating the sidewalk with the aid of a walking frame.

'So what's the fourth estate thinking today? Who's gonna be our next great leader?'

Even after ten years, an ex-Bronx cabbie working in Washington still sounded like a Bronx cabbie.

Cherry Davitt smiled. 'This time it's tricky, Richie. A bit early to tell and too close to call. Depends on the candidates, I guess.'

Over several years she and the garrulous driver had developed a symbiotic relationship. When she needed a taxi, she'd usually ask for him by name.

Richie got the hot news from her, sometimes before it hit the news-stands, and occasionally she gleaned some very useful material from him. In Washington all sorts of people used cabs and a smart, tactful cabbie with good personal radar picked up the odd snippet of some very interesting secrets. For Cherry, once she had the seed, the rest was just hard graft, investigative journalism.

'I'm going for Donna Stone this time, I'm thinkin'. They don't got the House, but they do got the Senate, maybe if they at least get the President up, some stuff gets done. I dunno. At the moment the Congress is pullin' this way, the Senate's pullin' the other way and the President, well, he's just pullin'…' he chuckled. 'Nah, I won't go there wit' a lady in the cab.'

'It's kind of hard to shock me, Richie. You work on a Washington paper long enough, the inside of a cab's one of the more genteel places to spend time.'

He chuckled again and inched forward.

'One thing's for sure,' she said. 'I've never seen such a gulf between the two sides before. Economy, health, welfare, environment, the military. All the big-picture stuff. This country and, I guess, the world is going to go in one of two very different directions, depending on who's calling the shots here in the next few years.'

The smile on Richie's face disappeared. 'So you're worried?'

'Some,' she said. 'Some.'

* * *

Short notice had meant that none of Liam's climbing buddies were too positive about joining him for the crack at K2. The fact that he wasn't planning to tackle the summit made for even less enthusiasm among the few he approached.

He would try to find climbers once in Pakistan and, if not, perhaps hitch up with a group already at the mountain. If worst came to worst, he was anxious and impatient enough to tackle it solo. No one knew the risks better, but then, he thought, no one was better equipped to handle them.

'You must climb with an experienced team,' Mahmood said. 'You, of all people, know how dangerous this mountain is. It is crazy to try this unless you are totally prepared.' He looked at the pile of equipment that had been steadily growing in the small warehouse. 'I can be your military liaison officer but I can't climb with you. I wouldn't get past Camp One. I spend most of my time sitting on my butt in an aircraft.'

'Necessity must,' Liam said. 'The year is well along already. I need to get up there while there's a window.'

He sorted gear into orderly groups. Lengths of six-and eight-millimeter rope were placed neatly together. 'The longer I leave it, the more chance there is that his body will move again and I may never find him.' He lifted his shoulders in a shrug and raised open palms. 'Besides, a small team means less food, less gear to transport, less ferrying to and fro.'

As Liam spoke, snow pickets, ice screws, dead-men, pitons and aluminum chocks were all counted and separated carefully into individual collections. 'I hear there are some local climbers up there these days who were virtually born on K2. With luck I can find people like that. If it all goes pear shaped, I'll have no choice, I'll have to come back next spring.'

Mahmood was not convinced. 'You'll have no doctor, no medical back-up. No back-up of any kind, in fact. I suspect you will be joining your father on that mountain.'

Liam grinned and clapped a big hand onto Mahmood's shoulder. 'You fancy a little wager?'

He bent down and ran his thumb along the sharp blade of an ice ax. 'Even way back in the 1930s, hampered by all their heavy, old-fashioned gear, two Sherpas, Pasang Kikuli and Tsering, climbed from Base Camp all the way to Camp Six. They climbed just shy of 7,000 feet of ice, rock and snow in a single day. Incredible. It can be done.'

'As I recall,' Mahmood answered drily. 'They were attempting to rescue a climber called Dudley Wolfe.'

'Right.' Liam nodded his head.

'As I recall,' Mahmood continued. 'Two of the three died up there.'

* * *

Within weeks of arriving in Islamabad, Liam had his permissions in place. Having Mahmood along to wrangle the local bureaucrats was a big help. Finding climbing companions had not been nearly as easy. The end of week three saw him on a crowded ATR 42 twin-turbo prop bouncing across tropospheric potholes above the peaks and valleys, en route to Skardu. In his pocket were the names of the Balti porters who'd been with his father all those years ago and the co-ordinates sent by the Antipodean Carter. He was, still, alone.

The little town was usually bustling with would-be mountaineers at this time of year. But here, again, there were significantly fewer climbers and hikers than he had expected and the possibility of joining somebody else's expedition was quickly fading.

Rumors of increasing intensity and brutality in the battles being waged to the south and east, just beyond the high peaks, were everywhere.

'This, this war, is what is causing the *pardeesi* to stay away.'

The man was normally busy organizing porters, equipment and supplies but today he sat outside his dusty office drinking chai and chattering to anyone who was willing to stop by.

'They do not want to risk losing their heads just to climb *Kechu*.' He wobbled his own head vigorously, no doubt in an attempt to indicate how easily an infidel's might be separated from its shoulders. 'The children in the villages will go hungry again.'

Liam waited respectfully for the melancholy of the moment to pass and then showed him the names of the two Balti porters from long ago. Tahir Shafiq and Shamim Ibrahim. He hoped Carter had the spelling right. He hoped they were still alive.

The local man finished off his chai. 'Askole,' he said, indicating the northeast with a thrust of his chin. 'In Askole. But Shamim Ibrahim very old now. I get you young, strong porter, here.' He pointed at the dirt between his feet. 'Right here in Skardu.'

Liam declined politely and returned to his room. A battered Land Cruiser pickup stood outside the modest dormitory ready to tackle the wild track up to Askole for whoever was first to produce the required number of rupees. For the moment he had no competition. He'd get as much gear as possible trucked up to Askole and take his chances with his dad's old porters up there.

* * *

Askole turned out to be a green pocket handkerchief of a village folded into a narrow space between monochromatic massifs. Liam walked its length in a few minutes and both men were located without effort. Tahir was significantly younger than the now-wizened Shamim Ibrahim, but the older man had the advantage of several strapping sons.

A death on K2 was of little consequence to these wiry, life-toughened people; it was not an infrequent occurrence. But, for whatever reason, their memory of the events surrounding James's loss were remarkably fresh in their minds. They seemed, in fact, to have entertained a genuine fondness for him and deeply regretted his dying.

'Yes,' they all said eagerly. At the end of a poor season, the opportunity for a little late income was a pleasant surprise. They were happy, Tahir said in his broken English, to carry Liam's gear as far as base camp, perhaps even advance base, but they didn't climb, wouldn't climb. Especially this close to season's end.

'You get Hassan Baig,' Shamim said, giving him a toothless grin. 'Good for climb.' He lifted his arm towards the sky to indicate the mountain tops near the end of the glacial valley to the east.

Hassan Baig, it turned out, was a very experienced high-altitude porter and climber hailing from Sadpara a few miles south of Skardu. He had waited around Askole longer than usual, in the daily-diminishing hope of getting at least one climbing job this summer. Hassan had two brothers, also experienced climbers, but the paucity of expeditions had forced them to look for work in the city. Liam's arrival was the answer to his prayers. And he to Liam's.

Hassan was a strongly built man of few words; his only remarkable feature being a large, glossy and deep black moustache. They negotiated his daily fee and agreed that departure would be within two days. There was no time to waste, he indicated, with a couple of spare sentences and simple hand movements, with winter waiting in the wings.

Liam nodded in agreement. Weather, he knew only too well, would, ultimately, call all the shots and decide the success or otherwise of his mission.

* * *

With pale light promising from upriver, but the sun still hours away from breaking over the seemingly endless Karakoram peaks, Tahir had the porters in an orderly line and heading briskly towards the beginning of the Baltoro Glacier at a cracking pace.

Hassan strode along easily a little way ahead – it was clear that this was his natural element. Liam watched his rhythm with some satisfaction. The prospect of just the two of them making a quick and lightweight attempt to find James on K2, while it would have its dangers, made Liam feel remarkably at ease. The bigger the group, the more likelihood of possible problems. 'The greater the number, the greater the risk,' James would say as they attacked a steep pitch alone. James as lead, the teenage Liam belaying studiously from below.

The Balti porters seemed eager to reach their goal. Perhaps with a sense of wilder weather to come, they were keen to earn their fees, put this poor season behind them and return to the relative comfort of their valley homes.

Five long days saw what was normally a seven-day journey completed and as darkness fell the weary men dropped their loads on the stony glacial moraine, lifted their gaze heavenward and looked up in silent reverence at the towering monolith that was K2.

'The Savage Mountain,' Liam said, with a hint of awe in his voice. Hassan Baig grinned and spoke softly. 'One week, maybe ten days, up and down, up and down.' He indicated a number of imagined ascents and descents with his moving hands. 'Enough for acclimatize.'

Given the limited window of time and the scarcity of numbers, their climb would be a hybrid of Alpine and expedition style. Fixed lines up House's Chimney and the Black Pyramid, a few trips up and down to camp sites with a bare minimum of gear, but other than that, just two climbers and self-sufficiency. And the weather.

Liam had nothing to prove. There was no summit to 'conquer'. This would be a purely pragmatic exercise with just one goal; locating his dead father.

He studied the mountain in rigorous detail, watched the clouds as they swirled ceaselessly through valleys and boiled over summits. He scrutinized each avalanche, no matter how small and seemingly insignificant, in concentrated silence. He scoured the mountain up and down and left and right through a pair of powerful binoculars and spent hours poring over online weather forecasts, climbing records and historical charts. On a mountain like this you couldn't afford to make careless mistakes.

After a few days working to acclimatize, the initial lethargy and mild high-altitude headaches he'd suffered since arriving at the mountain's base had diminished significantly. Hassan, Liam sensed, perhaps because of his regular visits to the mountains, seemed to have no issues with altitude.

Seven days passed, then eight, and the following day's forecast was for clear skies.

'Okay, tomorrow at dawn, we get started,' Liam said simply to the ever-patient Hassan Baig.

* * *

The wet road shone with the cloud-reflected light from the last of the sun's rays. Apart from a lone cyclist, the pock-marked bitumen was empty. Zhang Jia let the tired lace fall back into place across the window. She looked at the clock above the simmering noodles. He was an hour late. It wasn't like him. He was a man of science, of mathematical precision, a man of orderliness and regular habits. He would not be late without letting her know, without calling. She stood watching the silent telephone for several long minutes, expecting at any moment to be relieved of her vigil by its clamoring bell.

Silence. The rhythmic click of the kitchen clock, the soft hiss of the gas and silence. She lifted the receiver, tapped in the work number and asked to speak to her father.

'He's not here,' a man's voice said. 'He left a few hours ago. With friends.'

'Do you know where he, where they were going?' She began to breathe a little faster. 'He should have been coming home.'

'I don't have any idea,' the man said. Given his tone of voice, he might just as well have added, 'And I couldn't care less.'

Jia lifted the noodles from the small ring, shut off the gas and carried her bicycle out onto the road. A fine rain was falling as she rode off. His office was a ten-minute cycle away. As she went, she scoured the verge for some small sign of her father. His health was generally good, but since her mother's sudden death there had been the business with his heart. There was no sign. On the return trip she checked the bars, the shops and the only restaurant. Still nothing. Nobody had seen him or his friends.

She sat in the orange glow of the incandescent light spilling into the kitchen from the roadway. The hands on the ancient clock seemed locked in a single moment of time but, painfully, inevitably, they reached midnight.

'My father hasn't come home from work,' she blurted tearfully to the voice coming down the line from the local police station. 'He should have been back hours ago. Something must have happened.'

The patient man took down her details slowly and carefully. 'There's nothing we can do tonight. We are only two here. Come along to the station in the morning if he's not back and we'll see what we can find.'

A week later, in spite of their best efforts, he was still missing. It seemed possible, the distraught Jia now conceded, that he might never be coming back.

* * *

Liam's plan was to move up through the higher camps as quickly as was prudent, fixing new lines where necessary and using existing lines when not. In many places the fixed lines left behind by earlier climbers were still in fair condition. Where the rope looked damaged or on the more challenging sections, where the pitches above were bare, they either set about installing their own or climbed without protection.

Camp Two would be located on a pocket handkerchief of sloping snow above House's Chimney, Camp Three near the apex of the Black Pyramid.

A few days setting up Camp Two and then Three and adjusting to the increase in altitude would be followed by a return to Camp One at the foot of the Abruzzi Ridge to rest up, collect a minimal quantity of supplies and await the right conditions for an ascent to Four on the shoulder. This would, he hoped, be followed by a quick diagonal traverse beneath the Bottleneck, to locate his father's co-ordinates somewhere beyond the looming ice cliffs.

In spite of their initial reticence, Tahir had talked the porters into carrying all the necessary gear from Base Camp across the riven glacier and up to Camp One, which meant a saving of several days and significant effort.

The temptation to have a crack at the summit was always there but with just the two of them and winter approaching it would be taking unnecessary and unplanned risks. And besides, Liam reminded himself, whenever his gaze shifted to the seductive peak, that was not what they were here for.

Hassan Baig, he quickly decided, was worth ten times his meager fee. The altitude seemed to have no effect on his physical capacity and he put vertical space behind him with apparently very little effort. While even Liam found the sheer ice-crusted rock funnel of House's Chimney required all his concentration, the Sadpara man appeared to handle the scramble with remarkable equanimity. Normally, in a location like this, the chances of the lead climber dislodging dangerous rocks onto the climber belaying below were fairly high. Hassan, however, was as sure footed and delicate as a cat. His hands and feet seemed to fly over the harsh surface of stone and ice and not a pebble had been dislodged when he finally made it over the top ledge of the precipitous gap.

A day later they were confronting the near-perpendicular base of the Black Pyramid, a vast, bone-chilling triangle of glossy, ice-polished rock-face that soared to above 25,000 feet; a sheer 2,000 feet of the most dangerous and challenging climbing on the mountain.

They moved up at a snail's pace, where necessary, fixing rope as they went. Handholds were small and hard to locate and

40

boots had to make do with purchase sometimes no more than millimeters wide and often made more treacherous by a lacquer of hard ice. Hours passed with no place to pause, to rest, save on these precarious perches. Liam, in the lead, found no ledge or outcrop on which to sit and rest his aching legs and arms until he had added a thousand feet to their altitude.

Hassan once again seemed to handle the challenge with almost meditative calm.

He was always where he should be and appeared instinctively to know what Liam wanted, sometimes several seconds before Liam himself knew.

They worked together without words. And they worked fast. If Liam needed to add a line to a fresh section of face, Hassan was instantly there, ready to belay without being asked. He knew exactly where to be, when to provide slack and when to take in.

Around four weeks from their arrival at Base Camp they had pitched their tent at Camp Four. A tiny sanctuary, high on the shoulder below the summit at nearly 26,000 feet. Around them lay the mournful detritus of climbers past, successful and unsuccessful, who had shared this forbidding site. Nearby, a collapsed tent, ripped by the merciless winds long ago, channeled the fury of a building gale and howled incessantly throughout the first night.

For a week the weather had been more serene than even the greatest optimist could possibly have hoped. But the first dawn at the high camp, with the mighty Godwin Austen glacier small and insignificant far below, began in a shroud of low cloud and blizzarding snow. They passed the hours in the tent, melting snow to drink and waiting in a relaxed and easy silence for the violent gusts to abate. The fates were on their side once again and by late afternoon the Jetstream had carried the storm away. As night drifted towards them across the eastern peaks the air was clear and still; an incredible stroke of luck, at this altitude, at this time of year. Liam looked to the heavens one more time and then down into the dizzying void. The words of the great Italian mountaineer Fosco Maraini spilled softly from his lips as he secured the tent flap.

'...just the bare bones of a name, all rock and ice and storm and abyss. It makes no attempt to sound human. It is atoms and stars. It has the nakedness of the world before the first man – or of the cindered planet after the last.'

The words, from a book James had given him for a long-ago birthday, distilled, in an instant, the reasons for his constant yearning for the mountains.

He had told Hassan early in the evening that tomorrow's remaining climb would be handled solo. There was no need to explain the momentous nature of the coming encounter, the need for even more solitude than this vast, sky-vaulted space already provided; the need, simply to be alone with his father, so long lost, and his rekindled grief. Hassan understood intuitively and simply nodded his head. He would wait.

* * *

Cherry Davitt was preoccupied. She sat watching an interview with a new entrant to the presidential race but her mind was somewhere else. Liam Doyle had been in her life for a relatively short time but he had made an impression. There was a connection. Common sense told her she was being fanciful, but still, it was there. Perhaps, she thought, it was some sort of belated mothering instinct – he was, after all, nearly young enough to be her child. But, no, it was more than that. She felt tied to him in some way. She was loath to even admit it to herself but she had the vaguest sense that they somehow shared some form of common destiny.

Cherry shook her head and tried to redirect her focus to the big screen on the wall.

She'd been vaguely aware of the candidate, over the past couple of years, as a low-profile member of Congress from New Mexico.

She studied the man's face as he spoke.

Jason Arnott would never be described as the presidential candidate from central casting. He was neither tall and broad shouldered nor handsome. His teeth were his own, his hairstyle clearly left to the scissors of a suburban barbershop and the frames housing his thick lenses, much more prosaic than their expensive Italian counterparts beloved of the lobbyists on Capitol Hill.

Cherry liked him instantly. He was blessed with a radiant and natural smile and appeared to have a gift for taking the voters with him, appealing to people on both the street and the land.

He spoke earnestly to the male interviewer in his home state. 'I believe that as a nation we're at a crossroads, Mike. I think, without wishing to be melodramatic, that this next election will determine the future nature of our great nation and, indeed, our existence. If the right decisions are not made by the next President, whoever he, or she, may be, then we're in deep, deep trouble.'

The television reporter was looking for less rhetoric and more conflict, more drama, and used the opening.

'She?' he asked rhetorically. 'At this early stage it is looking like your stiffest competition for the nomination will come from Californian Senator Stone. What's your impression of her?'

Cherry drifted away again to thoughts of Liam. She imagined him somewhere in the wilds of Baltistan, high on a mountain, perhaps in danger. She'd read somewhere that K2 – Godwin Austen some called it – was considered the most dangerous mountain on earth. She slid her cellphone from the coffee table in front of her and punched in his number. The call rang out.

She tried, once again, to focus on the interview.

'Donna, Candidate Stone, is an extremely bright, competent woman, Mike,' Arnott was saying, an engaging grin illuminating his plain features. 'No doubt she'd make a good President but I thought we were here today to talk about my campaign...'

As she watched distractedly, it occurred to Cherry, with a sudden chill, that Liam could be dying in deep snow, somewhere cold, lonely and merciless, as she sat there.

She tried his number again. No answer. She sighed, turned off the set and poured another tall glass of Rioja.

4

ACCORDING TO the co-ordinates provided by Greg Carter, the body of James was around 26,000 feet, somewhere to the east of the K2 Bottleneck, a little beyond and above the point at which the Northeast Route intersected with the Abruzzi. None of the Balti men had been able to recall which route James had taken and Liam could only guess he'd climbed the Northeast Ridge, either planning to join the Abruzzi Spur at the Bottleneck or to tease out an alternative route to the summit.

Long before the first glimmerings of dawn stirred the yawning porters from their tents, tiny specks on the glacier cleaving the distant valley, Liam was moving diagonally to the east of the Bottleneck, across a faintly glowing surface. With each labored step his foot would plunge, sometimes knee deep, sometimes thigh deep, into the freshly fallen snow. On a slope this steep, a fresh fall increased the likelihood that at any moment a slab avalanche could send him tumbling thousands of feet, to be smashed to pieces on the rocks below. Approaching the death zone now, he was having to work hard for every breath, and he struggled constantly to shake off a debilitating lethargy and intermittent nausea.

The Bottleneck loomed off to his left, chilling in the predawn twilight, as he secured himself to a small outcrop and paused, breathless, to assess the daunting, vertical ice-wall in his path. As the dawning light turned the indistinct dream shapes of the night into hard-edged reality, a phalanx of jagged seracs began to stir and crackle ominously not far above.

Slowly, with extreme care, he inched out to his right across the perpendicular ice, self-belaying as he went; each ice screw placed with exquisite precision, each foothold scraped and gently kicked into position. After hours of this excruciating traverse he was almost within reach of a patch of steep but solid ground, when a loud blasting sound detonated directly above. With a freight-train roar, a chunk of ice the size of a small bus crashed down the face, splintering as it went and taking out a section of his fixed line. The sudden impact on the rope caused a zipper fall and Liam found himself dropping fast before being jerked to a sudden stop and smashing like a wayward pendulum into the wall. The final link, the fixed protection immediately to the left of his unsecured point above, had stayed true.

The ice face here sloped slightly inward and he found himself dangling in space fighting to breathe and contemplating a thousand feet of nothingness below.

He unclipped jumars and aiders from his harness, snapped the ascenders onto the rope and gradually, painfully, hoisted himself back to the secured anchor. Using ax and crampons, with muscles aching and knuckles white with cold and tension, he kicked his way across the last gap of sheer ice and dragged himself to safety on the narrow solid ledge. He lay, panting and spent for several minutes, before staggering to his feet and setting off again.

An hour later he checked the co-ordinates for the umpteenth time. Greg Carter had calibrated a GPS to match his own and left it for Liam in Islamabad. So he must be close, he was now right on them. And then, with a rush of blood into every extremity that sent him to his knees, there he was.

A dozen shaky paces through knee-deep snow brought him face to face with his dead father. Years of grief, years of that inexplicable emptiness, long nights of endless wondering had come down to this: an oh-so-familiar figure in familiar gear, so tiny now, insignificant almost, and dwarfed even further in death by this monstrous mountain.

The tears froze on Liam's lashes before they had a chance to fall. He removed his gloves and, with outstretched fingers, brushed away snow and touched his father's shriveled face tenderly.

James appeared to be almost sitting, wedged between two small outcrops, on a narrow ledge above a long sharp drop. His goggles were on his forehead and his eyes were closed. He might even have been described as peaceful, but for the hole in his chest the size of Liam's fist. Around it, frozen into the fabric, was a mass of dark blood. Liam had seen the results of enough firefights to know it was a wound that would have killed him instantly. He bent in close – deep in the cavity he saw snow. The thing appeared to have gone right through his father's body. It could only be a bullet wound; from a very large gun.

Liam knelt and spoke for the first time. 'What the fuck happened to you, Da?' He brushed the salty crystals from his cold cheeks.

Apart from the hole in his father's chest, everything seemed to be in its place. The watch on his wrist had what looked like a sliver of bone through its face and had stopped forever shortly after four in the afternoon. His mitts were clipped to his harness but he still wore a pair of light windproofs and the old Canon that Liam recognized from his childhood was still gripped in his stiffened hand; the strap wrapped tightly round his forearm. Liam left the shattered watch where it was but prised the fingers gently and turned the camera over, the little gate at the base hung open and the memory-card slot was empty. He looked around automatically, studying the surrounding snow, before realizing how absurd the action was. With great care he unwound the camera strap, clicked the card aperture shut, wrapped the camera in a spare pair of mittens and stowed it in his pack. This small, innocuous and outdated item had now become a memento mori of immeasurable value.

He sat with his dead father for some time. 'Who the fuck would want to shoot you up here? Why no card?' The responding silence from the mountain was absolute. But then he heard it – the soft roar of a distant wind. He looked to his right, towards Xinjiang. A telltale lenticular cloud hovered high over the summit of Skyang Kangri. A massive weather front was moving in at speed. Even in the unlikely event that it didn't carry snow, it would definitely hammer these exposed heights with its gale-force winds.

In an instant Liam had switched from grieving son, to soldier in survival mode. James wasn't going anywhere right now. The

46

rescue stretcher would remain, unused, at base camp. Trying to traverse it across the vertical ice wall with just two sets of hands would be suicide. Going straight down was impossible. Two men, however capable, would never get him down past the Pyramid or House's Chimney. Another route would have to be found, plus extra bodies, and that would take more time than the fast-approaching winter would allow.

Liam looked again at his father's deep wound. An ember of childhood rage was fanned and started to glow. Someone had murdered this precious, harmless man and he wanted to know who and why.

The idea of someone having so destructive a weapon so high on the mountain didn't make sense. Terrorism didn't fit. Who else had been there? He needed to think it through. Somewhere beyond the seemingly endless peaks lurked a killer. After all these years whoever it was had probably relaxed, secure in the knowledge that his crime had gone undiscovered. Liam's jaws tightened. 'Time for them to start worrying again, Da,' he said into the wind.

For now, he decided, keeping all this to himself seemed to be the wisest option. Knowing something that the killer didn't, meant that at present he had the edge.

He hammered a pair of pitons deep into thin cracks on either side of James's frozen body, threaded a short section of line through the gear loops on his cold harness and lashed him securely to the rock-face. With his ax he worked at the ledge, scraping together enough snow to create a thin covering layer. The approaching storm would do the rest.

'I'm coming back to get you, Da.' He lifted his hand in farewell. 'In the summer. I promise.' The sound of his quiet voice was instantly consumed by the all-encompassing silence.

He double-checked the map co-ordinates carefully one more time and then began his perilous descent back to Hassan, who was waiting patiently at Camp Four.

* * *

A small bird of prey fluttered overhead, avoiding the cold Moscow air currents. Lionel Rigby had no idea what it was – he had no interest in birds of any kind. He tightened his coat collar and hurried along Gruzinskaya Ulitsa towards the cathedral. He'd become a regular at the Neo-Gothic brick edifice some years before, mainly because Mass and confessions were conducted in English.

Lionel – to his contemptuous associates Eleanor, but only behind his back – was a Catholic, a conservative and a loner. Today, Saturday, was the day for his weekly visit to his confessor. But this confession, this act of contrition, would be different.

The majority of Lionel's waking hours were spent either within the elegant white confines of the Immaculate Conception's nave or deep in the bowels of an innocuous building behind a high wall; in the Organization's computing section.

When nightfall made time away from his work station unavoidable, he'd secrete himself in his small apartment and bury his head in arcane algorithms, in procedures so complex that even his mathematically literate colleagues would have found them incomprehensible. The results were invariably the same and they were troubling.

Lately, the years of stress had been starting to take their toll. He was eating very little, was irritable, nervous and had taken to bursting into tears at the slightest provocation. He was desperately concerned. Things were going very wrong, the processes weren't working the way they should.

Then he made his penultimate mistake. He broadcast his concerns to his colleagues. His final mistake was the decision to bare his soul to his confessor. This, sensibly, he kept to himself. But Lionel, for all his genius, would have made a lousy poker player and anyone observing him couldn't help but notice that something was about to fracture, to go awry.

'I really need to get away for a few days, Claude,' he told his superior late one Friday afternoon as the snow buffeted and rattled the room's only window.

'Not starting to have doubts, are you, *Eleanor*?' His sardonic

French superior used the word as a weapon. 'A *crise morale*? A moral crisis?'

'I have to confess I'm having serious ethical difficulties. I just need to clear my head. I've been at this a long time.' He ran trembling fingers through the sparse remnants of his straw-pale hair. 'I'm tired.'

Nothing had been resolved by the time Lionel departed for the weekend but he'd left behind a ticking time bomb. Paranoia in facilities of this nature, Claude knew only too well, was an occupational hazard. But Lionel's words, possibly innocuous, kept drumming away. 'I have to confess, I have to confess.'

Several hours passed; several laps cutting through steam rising off a heated pool, a massage and a second glass of Grand Cru did nothing to still the voices in Claude's head. 'I have to confess.'

Better to be certain.

She punched in a number not included in her cellphone memory. 'That fellow Rigby,' she said briskly. 'The crazy Catholic guy. He attends confession at the big church over on Malaya Gruzinskaya. Every Saturday round ten, regular as the steeple clock. I suspect the only person he ever confides in is the damned priest.' She finished off her wine in one large mouthful. 'Find out just exactly what he is confessing.'

* * *

A day into their long slog back to Askole, Liam was suddenly appalled by his own insensitivity. 'Christ.' In his obsession to locate his own father he had totally forgotten his mother's message from long ago.

'A local man died too.'

Liam jogged forward to the fast-striding Tahir and called for him to stop. 'Sorry,' he said, his breath shortened more by anxiety than by exertion. 'There was another man who disappeared with my father, I think. Was he one of your brothers, your family, Hassan's?'

Tahir, who had paused momentarily, headed off quickly again. Liam strode alongside. 'No,' the Balti man said. 'He was Sherpa, stranger, good friend of your father.' He walked for another 50 yards. 'Kathmandu man, I think.'

Kathmandu!

Liam thought immediately of the ancient postcard, still buried deep in his backpack.

'Laim must keep to doing what he does best.'

'Does anyone know if he died for sure?' Liam asked anxiously.

Tahir gave an indifferent shrug, adjusting his load at the same time. The Kathmandu man had been a stranger, a *pardeesi*; his survival or otherwise in this brutal trade was of little consequence.

At the first rest stop Liam retrieved the faded, dog-eared message from beneath the soiled clothing in his pack. 'Laim must keep to doing what he does best.'

And yes, the postmark was definitely Kathmandu.

He strolled over to where the porters were gathered, leaning on their heavy loads.

'Does anyone remember the name of the Sherpa who died with my father?' He asked in imperfect Urdu.

There was a general chuckling and chattering in Balti, some shrugging and the odd bit of head scratching.

'Maybe Da...' Tahir said eventually. 'Da...' He shrugged again.

One of the others said something quietly in Balti. There was a quick exchange between several of them and then Tahir turned to him again. 'He says a stranger, a foreign man, came in a helicopter, asking about them, your father and the Sherpa.'

'When?' Liam asked quickly.

Another discussion followed.

'He says maybe a few days, a week after they were lost.'

What did he tell the man?'

'He told him they were dead, on the mountain.'

There was nothing further forthcoming. The porters started hoisting their loads. They were bored now and eager to get home.

By week's end the group was back in Askole. The Land Cruiser's motor throbbed erratically in the background as Liam said his farewells. The porters had been paid and tipped; Hassan had received the most handsome gratuity on top of his fee and had agreed, with a grin and a tilt of his head, to climb with Liam in the summer.

They shook hands warmly and, without warning, Hassan leaned forward and gave him a spontaneous hug. Liam turned quickly to the waiting vehicle. Tears were a strong possibility.

✳ ✳ ✳

The weather had deteriorated further throughout a sleepless night. With dawn still well beyond the eastern outskirts of Moscow, Lionel Rigby gathered the material into a single file and burned a compact disc.

At first light he stole into the kitchen, created a slim crack between the curtains and looked out at the snow-laden landscape. The man in the dark raincoat stood under an awning across the road, the river at his back. He seemed to be looking directly up at the window. Lionel jerked his head back quickly, then, without moving the curtain, peeped out between the small holes in the lace. The man was still there. He knew what this meant – he'd seen it happen before. His time was up.

He scrabbled through a cluttered drawer and located the old newspaper clipping. The yellow highlighter had faded but was still obvious. He scrawled a hasty few words onto a sheet of notepaper, attached it to the news clipping and stuffed them urgently into an envelope along with the compact disc.

Dressing quickly, he slipped out through the service door at the rear of the apartment block. He lingered in the swirling shadows for a moment, made sure the man was not around and then hurried off through the tumbling snowflakes. There was just one thing on his mind now. He must confess. His mortal soul depended on it.

The cathedral echoed emptily as Rigby pushed in through the heavy doors. Claude's reaction the previous day; the man across the street; his every instinct told him he was running out of time. He made directly for the confessional, stepped inside and knelt in the cramped space. The panel between the two cubicles slid back, leaving only a dark screen between them. He could feel the priest's presence, hear his soft breathing.

'Bless me, Father, for I have sinned. I have something very serious to confess today, Father.' He hesitated.

'Go on,' the voice behind the screen urged gently.

'At work, I have been involved in some very morally questionable activity.'

'What sort of activity, my son?'

Lionel paused again, trying to find the words. 'It's complex, Father, but basically we have been…'

There was a soft hiss and a thud as a single silenced bullet tore through the screen, penetrated Lionel's skull neatly and embedded itself deep within his remarkable brain. He was clinically dead before his forehead crashed against the confessional door.

The man in the ill-fitting cassock checked Lionel's body quickly and then left via the sacristy, the way he'd entered just minutes earlier. The corpse of the elderly parish priest was located in a closet in his residence an hour or so later.

Claude took the call on the heated tennis court.

'Merde!' Replacing Lionel would be difficult, but regrettably the deed had to be done. In truth the little American had been a pain in the arse. *'C'est la guerre,'* she breathed as she returned to her doubles partner.

Claude's contempt for Lionel meant it had not occurred to her that the ineffectual little *andouille* might have been to the post office on Tverskaya to dispatch a small package before he made his final journey through the rain to the Church of the Immaculate Conception.

5

ALEXEI GAVRILOV arrived to take over the Cape Zhelaniya station just a few weeks after Dmitri left for Arkhangelsk. At first he'd been courteous but distant; perhaps even a little secretive. His relationship with Dashka Anasovna had been formal and, on the rare occasions that conversations took place, they related only to the station business at hand.

Dmitri had moved to Omsk and Dashka learned by way of the supply ship's captain that he'd married a local girl 18 months back and was already the doting father of twins.

As one indistinguishable season was replaced by the next, Dashka embraced the return of her solitary status, her remoteness and her loneliness and, with true Siberian stoicism, immersed herself in her work.

For some time things continued much as they had when Dmitri had been in charge. She was left to her own devices, as far as her work was concerned, which came as some small compensation for her wounded heart.

There was, after all, always her computer and her books and, of course, the primordial majesty of the savage island. The winters were hard to bear, eternally dark and bone-crushingly cold, but the summers. Ah, the summers. They made every sacrifice, great and small, worthwhile.

By June, she no longer needed her heavy parka outdoors, the snow around the base had melted and small tufts of resolute green appeared from beneath the frozen stones. It was no less than a tiny miracle, Dashka declared to anyone who'd listen.

Come July, even a small migratory bird would flutter down occasionally, to perch on a rusting machine. On an island so decimated by atomic testing, she worried that the delicate creatures might be damaged by radiation and was torn between shooing them off and letting them rest. She was sure, at those times, that the tiny traveler was en route to a faraway land like Australia, Brazil or some other sultry and exotic place. And, for a moment, she would be overtaken by a wistful longing.

The daylight hours were long and sunshine was not unknown even close to midnight. Nobody at the base appeared to care what she did or where she went, as long as all the machines were in good repair, and so she roamed deep into the island's center, ignoring the possibility that the radioactivity might be more intense further to the south.

As the new management continued to respond indifferently to her overtures of friendship, another long winter set in. She began to consider, for the first time, the possibility of moving on, finding work somewhere warm. Her nights were her own. She would use them productively, she decided, to learn English.

* * *

The latest polling was not looking good for either Jason Arnott or Donna Stone.

Cherry Davitt watched the results on the big boardroom screen as the details unfolded. For much of his first term the President had been a man on life support, the battles between the House and the Senate had taken their toll and his popularity levels were rarely out of single figures. It seemed unlikely there would be a second term, but, with what appeared to be remarkably good fortune on his side, things were gradually beginning to turn around and Arnott and Stone, the opposition frontrunners, were both gradually falling behind. With the Iowa Caucuses just a few months away, bad polling this early could throw the race wide open again.

Cherry perused the figures carefully, trying not to reveal her frustrations. 'There can only be one or two reasons for this,' she said to her assembled journalists.

Her deliberations were interrupted by an assistant poking his head around the door. 'Sorry to butt in, Cherry, but there's a call for you from Pakistan – Islamabad.'

'Okay, we'll pick this up later,' she said, hurrying towards her office.

'Cherry, hi. It's Liam here. I'm back in Islamabad. I should be back in a few days.'

'Should or will?' Cherry was deeply relieved to hear his voice but in no mood for word games. Liam was silent.

'Well?' she said.

'Well, okay, I *will* be back in a few days.'

An editor had to be good at reading subtext, Cherry knew, and the subtext here wasn't good. She decided to give him the benefit of the doubt. Perhaps it was grief.

'Okay, we'll see you next week. Did you... did you find your dad?'

'No,' Liam lied. He watched the anarchic street life of Rawalpindi from a far more modest hotel than Mahmood's choice in Islamabad a month or more before. Mahmood had not been happy but Liam knew his bank balance would be.

'Big snowfalls. Must've buried him again I guess. I searched a fair bit round the co-ordinates I was given but nothing. The weather stopped me from searching any further.'

'Oh, Liam, I'm so sorry to hear that. You must be devastated. Too bad. Anyhow, have a safe flight and we'll drink to him when you get back.' She rang off.

'Shit,' Liam said into the unresponsive mouthpiece. He hated lying to a woman he admired and respected but there was no choice. If he admitted he'd found James, Cherry would want a story, something to justify his time away. A human-interest piece for the magazine section was the most likely choice. He had no idea what kind of trouble that might buy him and he didn't really want to find out. Without a body there was no story.

'It couldn't be helped,' he told an emaciated dog scavenging in the dust outside his window.

* * *

'We have no news for you,' the police officer said, making no effort to hide his frustration. 'If he had an accident or was hit by a car or robbed on his way home we would have found him by now.' He looked down at the paperwork on the desk in front of him 'As I've said many times before, if we find any evidence of your father we will tell you. You will be the first to be informed.'

Zhang Jia knew the man behind the desk was becoming exasperated but she was past caring. 'But he left with friends,' she said in her near-perfect Russian. 'The man at his office said so. How is it that in all these weeks you have not found one of these friends?'

He shrugged. 'Perhaps this man was mistaken. Nobody else saw these friends and we haven't been able to find the man you say you spoke with.'

'I *did* speak with,' Jia corrected forcefully.

'Perhaps he went back to China, your father, to Beijing.' He tilted his head to the east. 'Maybe he's run off with a woman.' He picked up a pen and started writing. It was a dismissal.

'He wouldn't do that without telling me. He wouldn't.' Jia could feel the tears building and she was determined not to give this man the satisfaction of seeing her weep. She left the front door open as she went, allowing the bitter north wind to sweep in and scatter his papers.

She bent into the icy grit-charged air and struggled back across the alien landscape. Apart from the meandering Irtysh River, Pavlodar had very little to recommend it. The bleak, flat terrain extended to a haze-softened horizon in all directions, with not a single topographical feature to punctuate the monotony; the only vertical shapes the endless sad blocks of Soviet-era apartments and a few dust-shriveled trees.

Jia had been happy with her life in Beijing – her work, her home – but her mother's unexpected death had brought a crushing end to all that. Her father Zhang Liu had been near catatonic with grief and she was convinced the decision to take the position in Kazakhstan had been a form of running away; running away from everything that resonated with his wife's previous existence.

As a dutiful daughter she had felt obliged to go along, to care for him, to assuage his sadness; if only a little.

From the moment of their arrival Jia had found the town confronting. While her father was by her side she could tolerate it but, months after his failure to come home that night, he was still missing and her desperation grew in parallel with her loathing of the place. She was sorely tempted to run, to return to the familiarity of Beijing, but she could never desert her father. Without knowing his fate she had no choice but to stay and wait, to keep the faith that one day he would walk back in, sit down at the kitchen table and, once again, smile as he polished a pair of chopsticks in anticipation.

What was becoming increasingly clear was that the local authorities had no interest in finding Zhang Liu. It was time to stop waiting for them to solve her problem and address it herself. The comment about another woman had stung. She knew her father – he wouldn't do that to her. But what if? What if? The seeds were sown. Perhaps, she thought, his office emails might reveal something.

She steered her bicycle onto the long straight road that led out to the refinery. The grass along the edge was grey and brittle. At the front desk she asked for somebody from Zhang Liu's department.

'It seems likely now that my father won't be coming back,' she said to the woman who eventually arrived from the laboratory. 'I'd like to collect his things, his computer, his phone, anything else. I think he had a picture of me on his desk.'

'Wait here,' the woman said. 'I'll get them.'

She returned after five minutes with a cardboard box. 'This is all there was. He must have taken his computer and phone with him when he left.' She turned and walked away then turned again. 'I'm sorry that he's missing. Nobody here knows what happened. I hope you find him.'

Jia pedaled home, carried the box indoors and placed it on the kitchen table. She was almost afraid to delve into its contents. Afraid of what she might find; or what she might not. She looked up at the scroll on the otherwise bare wall, illuminated by a shaft of street lighting.

Lao Tzu's words sent a silent challenge across the lonely room.

'If you are depressed you are living in the past.

If you are anxious you are living in the future.

If you are at peace you are living in the present.'

They contained a kernel of truth, she knew. But they gave her no comfort.

* * *

The mayhem surrounding Benazir Bhutto International was as absolute as ever. Liam stood in the long queue waiting to check in for the flight that would eventually return him to Washington, the office and some sort of normality.

A decision was needed and it had to be quick. After nearly an hour of equivocation he was nearing the head of the line. He scanned the departure screen above his head. A direct flight to Kathmandu was leaving in two hours. He left the queue, found a relatively quiet corner and called the number Greg Carter had given him.

'Hi, It's Liam Doyle. Just wanted to let you know I found my dad; I wanted to say thanks.'

There was a pause. 'Not sure what to say,' Carter paused again. 'Sorry you had to go through this shit. You safe and well?'

'I'm okay,' Liam said, trying to sound casual. 'Thanks for giving me the opportunity to, you know, see him.' He had decided that for now, at least, there would be no mention of the nature of James's death.

'Least I could do. He always spoke about his little Liam in glowing terms.'

'Something I wanted to ask you,' Liam said, ignoring the indirect compliment. 'The Balti guys said Dad was climbing with a Sherpa friend. Didn't remember his name exactly. They thought Da... something maybe.'

'Well, the only bloke I imagine that could have been was Dawa Tindu. Dawa, he was a local Sherpa. They climbed a lot together. I didn't know he was on that climb, but then I was back in Christchurch at the time.'

'They say he died on the mountain, with Dad.' Liam covered

58

his free ear to hear Carter over the racket of the tannoy. His Washington flight was being called.

'No way, I don't think so. As far as I know Dawa's alive and relatively well. Rumor was he retired from climbing though.' Liam was about to speak when Carter broke in again. 'Actually, from memory, I think he may have retired not long after your old man got killed.'

'But he's alive?' Liam's heart beat a little faster. 'Could Dad have been climbing with another friend, another Sherpa?'

'I guess so. Not impossible,' Carter said. 'But I don't think so. Locally, yeah maybe, but not all the way over in Pakistan. Nobody springs to mind. Those two were good mates.'

Liam fingered the postcard in his pocket. 'This may sound like a crazy question, but did you ever write to me when Dad died, you know, like a postcard?'

'No. Why?' Carter sounded puzzled.

'I got a card from Kathmandu a couple of weeks after he died. Strange message. Like from someone who knew me well.'

Carter was silent.

'Do you mind if I come on over and see you?' The decision finally made.

'No, perhaps you'd better.'

'I'll be there later today. I'll give you a call.' Liam rang off and headed for the ticketing counter. 'Single to Kathmandu on today's flight,' he said.

* * *

The vibrant colors and generous greens of the Nepali capital were almost confronting to someone still coming down off the monochrome highs of the Karakoram. Liam sat squeezed into a small taxi on the short ride into town and wondered again why he'd not made a trip, a pilgrimage perhaps, to K2 during the year he'd spent in Nepal. The climbing had kept him busy, it was true, and being based in Pokhara didn't exactly lend itself to a quick dash to the Karakoram, especially when a constant stream of climbers and hikers were champing at the bit to be spoonfed their Himalayan adventure. But the real reason was deeper; a fear of the emptiness of the experience, a fear of tearing at old wounds, the knowledge that there would, in the end, be no resolution.

And now, he had been to the mountain, seen James, found him, but until he knew why there was a gaping hole in his father's heart, there would be, still, an emptiness; a lingering wound in his own.

The taxi rattled to a stop at the address Liam had scrawled on a paper serviette in his wallet. A commotion of color and sound assaulted him as he dragged his bags from the trunk. A restless river of humanity scuttled and hurried, surrounded by the garish brightness of flowing Devanagari script. Proclamations for every conceivable service and trade beckoned loudly from every wall. Exhortations to part with hard-earned rupees filled the space above every door, every side alley and every pillar and post.

The one exception seemed to be a sign in English, over a small corner shop. 'Kea Climbing and Hiking' it said simply in a dreary grey sans serif, contrasting sadly with the extravagant swirls and flourishes of its neighbors. Below was a badly painted picture of a New Zealand parrot wearing boots, goggles and a rakish-looking Khunga hat.

In the doorway, Greg Carter waited with smile and outstretched hand. In the other hand were two bottles, caps already removed.

'I lived here for a while a couple of years back,' Liam said as he savored his first icy cold beer since Washington. 'I'm surprised we never crossed paths, given you were Dad's friend.'

Carter was clearly several years younger than James, but came across, in a very few minutes, as a man wise beyond his years. Liam decided quickly that he'd be willing to climb with him any time.

'I had some months back home round then. Younger brother had a bad fall on Aoraki, down on the South Island. Mum's getting on, needed help, so I spent a wee while with them. May have been then.'

Liam nodded.

'Sorry to hear that. Is he okay? Your brother?'

'Yeah, fine now.' Carter waved a dismissive hand. He clearly wanted the subject closed.

Liam examined the label on his beer bottle. 'Just wondering, did you tell anybody else that you'd found Dad?'

'Ah, yeah, I think I did, a couple of blokes, they knew him a bit from climbing. Most of his mates have moved on though.'

'I don't guess you gave them the co-ordinates?'

'Hell no, no way. I wouldn't do that. He was *your* dad.' Carter was momentarily offended. 'Nobody wants fuckwits or mountain trash taking sick souvenirs or bloody selfies and posting them on Facebook. You were the only one who needed to know where he was as far as I'm concerned. That's private stuff.'

'Thanks, I appreciate that.' Liam slid his passport from a shirt pocket and carefully removed the now-faded postcard from between its pages. 'There's this one other thing.'

He was keen to broach the subject of Dawa the Sherpa. Carter beat him to it.

'You want to hear about Dawa Tindu.' A statement not a question.

Liam nodded again.

'One of the best. They reckon he could walk up a greasy pole in bare feet without using his hands. Anyhow, seems he was working in Pakistan, out of Skardu I think, when your dad...' he left the sentence unfinished and moved on. 'So it's quite possible he was there. I doubt whether anybody around here would know.'

He pointed at the ancient bakelite phone next to the credit-card reader on the counter.

'I've made a few calls since we chatted. Dawa seems to have disappeared.' He held up a hand to pre-empt Liam's inevitable question. 'No. Not on K2. He was almost certainly back here later than that. But the local Sherpas reckon he was a changed man. Said bugger all to anyone and then, within days, mumbled something about retiring and disappeared.'

Liam passed him the postcard. 'Do you think he could have written this... sent it?'

Carter read it a couple of times, turned it over, turned it back, examined the stamp and postmark with care and then handed it back. 'Quite possibly. Can't think who else it could have been.'

'Do you, did you, trust him? Was he a trustworthy guy?'

Carter's response was to look puzzled. 'Hell, yes – as straight as they come. Your dad trusted him with his life on a dozen climbs. Why?'

'Looks like the trust didn't work on the last one. Seems he may have left Dad on K2 and just walked away…'

'No way,' Carter said forcefully. 'Dawa was one of the best. He'd never do that. If he was there he'd have his reasons. I'd bet my business on it.'

Liam felt bad about questioning the integrity of his father's Sherpa friend and upsetting Greg Carter, but it was too soon to talk about the way James had died.

'So is there some way…?'

Liam's question was anticipated once again. 'Yeah. There is some suggestion that he may have gone back to his home, his village. Saldang. It's way up in the Inner Dolpo region. "Snow Leopard" territory.' He smiled as Liam frowned. 'And, yes, I've radioed the nearest authorities I could find and, no, they say they don't know him, but if you really want to be sure…'

'Get myself up there,' Liam finished the statement for him.

'Yep. That's right.' He indicated a set of steep stairs, almost obscured by stacked climbing equipment, at the rear of the crowded shop. 'We'll get something to eat, then you can have a kip and decide how you want to play it tomorrow.'

* * *

A sharp rap on the door woke Liam from a deep sleep. The first he'd had since leaving home. Carter handed him a cup of steaming tea.

'You're in luck. There's a chopper heading up to a village called Dho Tarap later this morning. Medical evacuation I think. The chopper at Pokhara is grounded apparently, so they're having to go up from here.' He blew on the surface of his own tea.

'I've wangled you a ride if you've got a few bucks. Saldang's two or three days' trek from there, depending on how fast you walk.'

He sized Liam up for a few moments. 'Two days.' He tilted his head toward the grimy window. 'Out there, at this time of year on the high passes, you'd normally be up to your waist in snow, but this year there's very little.'

'Most of my gear is in storage in Islamabad,' Liam said, dragging himself from the warm cocoon of his down bag. 'I don't know that I can be ready that quick.'

'I'll lend you what you need,' Carter checked the corner of the room. 'You've got your own boots. I can organize the rest.' He paused then added apologetically, 'I'd be happy to come with you, but I'm taking a group into Tibet. We're doing Shishapangma in a few months, southwest face, and with all the unrest in China and Tibet, organizing the paperwork is driving me nuts.'

He bent to exit under the low lintel. 'I'd take the chopper ride if I were you. You're up for a bloody long walk otherwise. A couple of weeks at best, depending on where you can get to. And you never know, it may finally snow.'

He took two steps and turned again. 'If you're real nice to the pilot and you make him a reasonable offer, you may even be able to talk him into bringing you back. They're always roaming around up there somewhere. You may have to wait a few days but they'll do you a detour as long as it's not too big a one.'

* * *

It was like a return to the Karakoram; as though he'd never left and the stay in Kathmandu had been no more than a fleeting verdant dream. Liam had taken the advice offered by Carter and been extra friendly with the pilot, handing over many dollars more than he required. As a result he'd flown Liam a couple of extra miles up the Saldang track before putting him down and backtracking to pick up his patient.

Carter had loaned him a satellite phone.

'Give me a call in a few days,' the pilot shouted as Liam climbed out onto the hovering skid. 'I'll see what I can do for you.'

The day was warm and windless and he made good time

across the rugged terrain. He passed a couple of herders returning with their flocks as he climbed through a mountain wilderness but other than that he had no trouble imagining he was the last person left alive on earth.

As day two turned into overcast evening he approached the outskirts of Saldang. Not so much a town, he thought, as a toy box full of dun-colored children's blocks spilled carelessly across a parchment landscape of near-identical hue. Compared to Saldang, Skardu and Askole were, on reflection, the greenest of green oases.

He located the small village school. The kids had gone for the day but a lone teacher sat poring over a stack of books.

'*Namaste*,' Liam said, bowing slightly, his palms pressed together. 'My apologies, I do not speak Nepali very well, do you speak Urdu?'

The man smiled at Liam's effort.

'I speak some English,' he said, glancing down at Liam's dirt-caked boots and gaiters. 'You have come a long way; how can I be of assistance?'

'I'm trying to find a gentleman by the name of Dawa Tindu. My name is Liam Doyle. I believe he was a good friend to my father, James Doyle. I have heard Saldang is his home.'

The teacher held his eyes without speaking for a few seconds. 'I am new to Saldang, from over there.' He pointed to the northeast, to the steep ground across the valley, towards Tibet. 'I will ask in the village to find if this man is here. Meanwhile, where will you sleep?'

'If I can find a spot against a little wall in a field somewhere, something to act as a windbreak, I will be fine.'

The teacher shook his head vigorously. 'You will be my guest, please. I have a modest home but you will find it more comfortable than the stony ground.'

They walked together to a small cube made from roughly hewn local stone and pointed with local mud. It stood in a walled compound. The flat roof was fringed with what looked to be dry grey twigs and grass and a few irregular openings in the walls played the role of windows.

The interior furnishings were sparse but spotlessly clean, the room had a bed, a table and a rudimentary kitchen area with an open fireplace for cooking.

The young teacher indicated a space near the fire. 'You may sleep here, if that is agreeable to you. I will make the enquiry for your friend in the morning.'

'Thank you,' Liam said. 'That will be perfect.'

6

PERHAPS IT WAS a result of the brutal Maryland winter. Perhaps not. Perhaps the stress of the past few years had finally taken its toll. Either way the dementia had progressed far more rapidly than anyone had expected and old Mrs Rigby was becoming increasingly dysfunctional. Even though she kept very much to herself, the neighbors were beginning to notice how forgetful she'd become and were fearful for her future. But they knew of no way of contacting her family. Some thought they'd heard her mention a son living somewhere in a distant country, but weren't sure. They were sure, though, that if he existed he would have no knowledge of the swiftness of his mother's deterioration, given he was thousands of miles away and possibly even somewhere foreign. What the good neighbors didn't know was that Lionel himself lay dead, with a bullet in his brain, in a police mortuary in Moscow, victim of a still-unsolved crime.

The letter informing Ruth Rigby of her son's death had been mailed just days after the package sent by Lionel as he was on his way, unwittingly, to meet his maker. Both arrived, with their exotic Moscow postmarks, in the same delivery.

Lionel's frail mother stared, uncomprehending, at the plastic case that fell from her son's padded envelope and landed in her lap. She put the envelope to one side, fumbled the case open, removed the disk and held it in trembling arthritic fingers for a moment before it dropped onto the grimy linoleum. She watched in some confusion as it rolled under an old sideboard, then reached again for the envelopes and regarded them blankly.

Moments later they were consigned by the confused old woman to a growing pile of newspapers, magazines and mail in a kitchen cupboard. The news of her son's death remained unopened; the message from Lionel unread.

With each passing week the neighbors became increasingly

anxious. Ruth Rigby started to have regular falls and didn't seem to be eating. Mr Altmann, next door, called the police, the police called a social worker and the social worker alerted the doctor. Each attempt to locate the old woman's family drew a blank until, eventually, a police friend of the doctor's managed to establish that Lionel had been killed while living in Moscow.

In the absence of any family with whom to consult, the decision was made to have Lionel's mother taken into aged care.

The conscientious young assistant, charged with the task of clearing out the cluttered apartment, found the unopened mail with the Russian postmark, thought it might be important and added it and Lionel's exotic envelope to the small pile of trinkets and family photographs that Mrs Rigby was permitted to take with her to her new home.

* * *

'How are you?' a child's voice trilled.

Liam opened his eyes to see a small boy beaming in from the open doorway. He sat up in his sleeping bag, grinning back at the radiant child.

'How are you?' the boy called again, mightily pleased with his excellent command of the English language. Although the sun was still some hours from making its appearance above the Saldang ridges, he was already neatly dressed in a brilliant white school shirt and dark, pressed shorts. His feet were bare.

Liam, in comparison, looked like a disheveled vagrant as he clambered fully clothed from his sleeping bag and pulled on his boots. 'I'm fine, thank you, how are you?'

He stepped over to the doorway and the little fellow leaned forward and took his hand.

'Come,' he said, pulling Liam outside.

The teacher was already up and dressed and perched on a stone wall sipping *po cha*. He smiled, said 'Good morning,' and indicated with a move of his head that Liam should go with the youngster.

The boy kept his tight hold on Liam's big hand and led him

towards the far end of the settlement; they were followed at a safe distance by a gaggle of giggling fellow pupils.

The house they approached stood on a slight rise, removed from its neighbors, and appeared to be a little grander than the teacher's. A woman, perhaps in her late twenties, stood in the doorway. She bowed gracefully. *'Namaste.'* Then beckoned him in. The children remained loitering and tittering expectantly.

As his eyes adjusted to the interior darkness he was aware of a large young man standing, arms folded just inside the door. He glowered at Liam but said nothing. Another man, perhaps in his fifties, was seated in the far corner.

'Come closer,' he said quietly.

As Liam approached, the older man reached out and placed a palm on each cheek, then explored his features momentarily with quick gentle fingers.

'You are his son,' he said simply. 'I am Dawa Tindu. I have been waiting for you.'

He made a sign in the direction of the large man who, without a word, bowed under the low lintel and disappeared.

Dawa Tindu's eyes seemed near sightless. But they were moist.

'Snow blindness,' he said in English, with just a hint of an Irish lilt. 'A gift from Gondogoro La.' He chuckled drily, but there was no malice in the sound.

'I found him, found my father, James. On the mountain,' Liam said.

Dawa waited; silent, so Liam went on 'I was told... I think... you may have been with him, perhaps even when he died.'

There was an almost imperceptible nod. 'Yes.' Then silence again.

It was time to believe this man, trust him, Liam decided. Besides, if he was going to learn anything more he had no choice. 'I saw the hole in his chest. It looked like a bullet.'

Dawa made a sign to the young woman who had been hovering on the far side of the room. She said something in Nepali and left the house.

He touched his own head softly, pointed to his unseeing eyes with two fingers and then reached across and placed his palm on

Liam's chest. 'James spoke of you many, many times; of your mind... your eyes... your heart.'

To avoid weeping in this man's serene presence and to give himself breathing space, he fumbled with several of his pockets, before removing the postcard from the one he had known, all along, held it. He handed it to Dawa without a word.

He ran his bent fingers round the edge, then stroked the stamp. 'Yes,' the old Sherpa said, seeming almost pleased with himself. 'I sent it. I speak English, your father taught me, but I cannot write it.' He lifted a finger toward the space the young woman had just vacated. 'My daughter was in Kathmandu, I gave her the words, she wrote them down.' He held the card up close to his eyes but then, with only the merest hint of exasperation, handed it back to Liam.

'James told me often about your sharpness of mind, your sharpness of eye, the valuable watch you found on the mountain, He was very proud.'

'But why...' Liam began and then trailed off.

'It was all I could think to do, I knew no one else I could trust, or turn to. I wanted to send you a message that nobody else would understand, I believed you would be wise enough to understand, then maybe, one day, you would come, come and find me.'

He too now seemed on the verge of tears, his voice trembled. 'Maybe you would come, because I had something I needed to give you.'

A shadow darkened the room and Liam turned. Dawa's daughter had come in carrying two cups of chai. Behind one, in her closed palm, she carried something small. Without speaking, she handed a cup and the object to Liam.

It was a memory card and Liam knew intuitively and instantly that it was the one from his father's camera.

'You know what it is.' It was a statement.

Liam nodded. 'Yes, I know what it is.' The card looked to be in near-perfect condition; it had clearly been handled with great care in the years since its time on K2.

'Can you make it work?' Dawa's question was seeded with as much doubt as it was hope. 'Find the pictures?'

'We'll know soon enough, the camera it came from is here in the village. In my pack. I got fresh batteries and a service in Rawalpindi last week. It was working then.'

'Can the boy fetch it?' Dawa indicated the sunny smile still illuminating the doorway.

'Of course, it's in my bag, in the teacher's house.'

Dawa said something in Nepali and the boy was off like a startled hare, with the inevitable entourage galloping along not far behind.

They waited in silence sipping their chai. Within minutes the little messenger stood panting in the doorway, camera held tightly in his outstretched hands.

The first few pictures were scenics, shot in late light, early light and back light and framed by his father's unerring eye. Another, of a younger, leaner Dawa, smiling through bright, seeing eyes, clicked onto the small screen.

The following image made Liam's heart almost jolt to a stop. An aircraft, trailing a long golden plume of flame dissolving into black smoke, hurtled low overhead. It looked to Liam, for all the world, like a B2 Spirit – an American Stealth Bomber – and it was in serious trouble. Liam flicked quickly through four more shots, not all in sharp focus, as the aircraft receded and plummeted closer, with each frame, to the many massive peaks immediately beyond.

His shock at the next frame was even greater. This image was truly blurred, but it appeared to be some sort of fighter plane coming straight at camera, flying close to the steeply sloping terrain. In the next shot both wing cannons were firing.

There were no more.

Dawa's daughter watched him closely to gauge his reaction. What she saw was a pale, slightly trembling young man with a tightly clenched jaw.

'Have you told anyone else about this?' he asked softly.

Dawa shook his head. 'Not in the past. Not in the future.'

Even the kids at the door had fallen silent.

Dawa's voice trembled as he spoke. 'They killed your father but not me. I ran, I fell and rolled maybe 50 feet, I did a self-arrest

70

between tall rocks, I lay very still. Playing dead. Some of your father's blood had splashed on me, I smeared it on the snow. They came around one, maybe two more times and then flew away.'

'What direction?' Liam asked.

'My face was in the snow, I did not see.' Dawa answered without irony. 'I climbed back, there was nothing I could do for James. I moved him, gave him…' Dawa searched for the word.

'Some dignity,' Liam offered. Dawa nodded.

'I think they must be America, or Pakistan or China planes. If they want to kill us so much, they will want the pictures, they will not stop until I am dead too.' In his rekindled agitation he had switched unconsciously to the present tense. 'So I take the camera card, I run, I hide, I run. No base camp, no Askole, no Skardu. Many days of walking, hiding, eating snow, roots, leaves.'

'How did you get home, all this way, without being noticed?'

'It is a long story of a long journey.' He was calmer now. 'When I came off the mountain I was very shocked, very sad and afraid, afraid to return to base camp, to let them see I was still alive.'

He stopped and turned his sightless eyes from Liam, perhaps to the unseen mountains, beyond the walls and far to the west. 'What could a simple Sherpa do? The Pakistan police? Nepali police?' He gestured helplessly.

'Better for people *to think* I had joined your father in death on the mountain than to join him in death soon after,' he murmured almost inaudibly.

'So I kept near to the edge of the glacier, out of sight, and started walking. From Concordia I did not return to Askole, where I was known. I kept going south; south up to the Vigne Glacier and then over the high pass at Gondogoro La. It was closed by the Pakistan government that year so no climbers. Just me, alone in the snow and the bright light.'

He laughed and pointed at his lifeless eyes. 'No goggles. Lost on Kechu.'

'Another few days and I was in the Hushe Valley. Nobody noticed me, just another crazy Sherpa walking in the mountains. In Khaplu I found a truck driver going south to Shyok Valley

71

and I paid to ride with him. At Shyok, I climbed back up into the hills again and at night I walked across the border into Ladakh. Nobody there to see me. No passport problems. I walked on to Turtuk, then I got another ride to Leh and took a plane via Delhi to Kathmandu. And here I am.'

He made it sound like a Saturday evening stroll in the park.

A small table stood next to Dawa's chair. He felt around on its surface, found what he wanted and handed Liam a battered wallet.

'Your father's. He no longer needed it. I used some of the money to pay my way home. The rest is still there.' Liam peered briefly at the worn rupees in the familiar leather pouch. A milky photograph stared back at him from behind a rectangle of yellowing plastic. He was looking at his teenage self.

Liam slid the dog-eared photo into his pocket and then folded the wallet and handed it back to Dawa. 'You keep it,' he said quietly.

The tea cups were cold, the hearts of the two men heavy; there was no more to be said. Dawa placed an open palm on Liam's chest again. 'He was my close friend, he taught me English, he taught me Alpine, when his heart burst, mine broke too. You are his son. You must find who did this. I cannot.'

* * *

Jia glanced out momentarily at the dismal Pavlodar skyline, drew the thick curtains and returned to the simple and now lonely kitchen table. The possessions retrieved from Zhang Liu's laboratory were spread across the oilcloth in front of her as they had been for nearly a week. She carefully examined each of the contents individually yet again. Still nothing from the battered cardboard box held any interest; no inkling of where he might have gone or why. She set aside an abacus, her photograph and an expensive calculator then repacked the rest of the contents and dragged a kitchen chair into Zhang Liu's bedroom, intending to store the box at the top of his cupboard.

As she lifted it into place her wrist brushed an old rug to

one side and revealed a thick manila folder on the high shelf. It was tightly bound with a red ribbon. She lifted it down, took it to the kitchen table and unpicked the ribbon. The folder sprung open and a wad of pages spilled out. Jia's first response was disappointment. They were production notes, accounts, balance sheets and statements; a mass of figures that made her mathematically challenged head spin. As she flicked from page to page, not really knowing what she was looking for, or even at, she began to notice that, at regular intervals, particular entries had been circled in red pencil. These files seemed to be breakdowns of component quantities of refined fuel that went back several years. The fuel, according to its designation, appeared to be common gasoline but in the margins, again and again, going back two years before his disappearance, Zhang Liu had written 'additives' followed by a large question mark in bold red text next to each circle. On each page he had underlined what appeared to her unskilled eye to be large quantities of alkanes, cycloalkanes, iso-octanes and aryl hydrocarbons.

In another section Jia found several pages which he'd headed 'synthetics?' and scrawled in the margin nearby 'JP-8 and Syntroleum FT?' At the base of the final page in the section he'd written in the same urgent red: 'Fraud? Yuri?'

She put the bulky folder to one side and stared out at the waste ground behind the house. In the bleak distance she could see the flares from the refinery towers. 'Fraud.'

Her hand, as she reached for a cup, trembled slightly.

For two days she agonized over what to do next. Taking the documents to the police seemed the logical step, but she had no doubt it would mean just another brush-off. Finding Yuri and confronting him seemed to be the next option but Zhang Liu's notes troubled her. She was confused, not sure what it all meant. If Yuri was involved in some sort of illegal activity, perhaps this was why her father was missing. Perhaps simply watching Yuri for a while might be the wisest option.

* * *

The deceptively peaceful body of a female kookaburra punctuated the crab tracks in the sand. In the grey grass nearby a fat cane toad lay on its back, its corpse eviscerated by the bird's powerful beak. Her hunger, perhaps greed, had overcome her customary caution and taken her too close to the lethal parotoid gland behind the amphibian's eye and she had paid the inevitable price.

Toxic toads; poisonous spiders the size of your fist; venomous snakes that kill in minutes. And that was just on the land, in the all-encompassing bush. In the sea lapping at his terrace it was box jellies that stung so bad you died pretty quick from the pain, thumbnail-size Irukandji that could stop your heart, crocodiles the length of a small pick-up and, of course, the sharks.

'What kind of a goddam country have I moved to?' Charlie Casement asked himself with a satisfied grin. 'At least they don't carry rocket launchers,' he said to one of the Swedish backpackers challenging the melanoma gods beside the pool.

She registered his smile and returned it without having any idea what he had just said.

'Let me know if you want any help with that suntan lotion,' he offered, as he walked back into the gloom of his office.

He sat at the computer and, fingers flying across the keyboard, punched in a line of code. He was worried about indefinable things. He flicked from screen to screen, clicking and typing intermittently. He felt apprehensive. A tiny seed of anxiety had been planted in his gut and some indeterminate instinct was nourishing it. Something wasn't quite right with the pervasive geopolitics of the planet, something had shifted surreptitiously but he couldn't quite put his finger on what it was all about and it worried him.

And then came the call from Nepal.

7

ANNAPURNA loomed to his left, stark against yet another cloudless sky, as the chopper thudded its way towards Kathmandu. It was decision time again. He doubted he could stretch his absence from Washington and his job any further but, with the images on the memory card exponentially expanding the mystery surrounding James's death, it seemed to him there was just one choice.

There had only ever been two men that Liam was willing to trust with his life. One of them was dead. That just left Charlie Casement.

A first contact, standing over a couple of bloated Pashtun corpses, hadn't augured well for the beginnings of a beautiful friendship, but in the case of Liam and Charlie this was an exception. The 20-odd-year age difference, the markedly different interests and the diametrically opposite personas seemed to matter very little. Liam loved mountains, nature, tranquility. Charlie lived for the smell of avgas, fast machines and excitement.

The meeting took place on active duty in Afghanistan and the unbreakable bonds were quickly forged. From then on, whenever they could snatch a few minutes, even though there was distance and danger between the Chapman and Salerno bases, they'd grab some beers and some time together. Liam would talk climbing, Charlie would talk flying. But it worked fine.

Liam wondered at times whether he was unwittingly turning Casement into some sort of James substitute, but was quick to dismiss the possibility as Freudian nonsense. Still, he'd been pretty cut up when Charlie had retired from the forces and retreated to some remote corner of Australia.

While the pilot refueled in Pokhara, Liam made one last call on Carter's satellite phone.

Casement lifted the receiver. 'Charlie, India, Alpha speaking.'

It was his own private little gag.

'It's Liam Doyle, Charlie. How's the hermit getting on?'

'Recluse perhaps,' Casement glanced out at the two young women, still lying poolside. 'Hermit, never.'

'I was wondering if I could come on down and see you. Something pretty interesting to discuss. I'll leave the details till I get there. If you're available.'

'Couldn't think of anything I'd sooner have happen, son,' Charlie drawled. Liam could just imagine his shit-eating grin.

'Buy yourself a ticket to a little town in north Queensland, name of Proserpine. Call me when you know your arrival details and I'll come get ya. I'm a ways out and the limousine service is none too regular.'

Two days later Carter had his phone back and was satisfied with the story Liam and Dawa had confected while Liam had awaited the chopper's return. It was a simple story of shock and trauma on Dawa's part and a hike across the country to escape a deeply felt anguish and grief. No mention was made of bullets or B2 bombers.

A ticket to Australia had been purchased and now, before the flight departed, there was the small matter of alerting Cherry Davitt to the further postponement of his return.

* * *

Out on the Washington sidewalks, the air, for the time of year, was remarkably mild. Inside the *Dialog* editor's office it was becoming decidedly frosty.

'Another few weeks?' Even on a bad line from a noisy airline terminal, he could tell Cherry sounded ice cold. 'You are kidding me.'

'Sorry,' Liam said meekly.

'Sorry? Not good enough. I have Primaries starting in just over a month. I need people on the ground.' She flicked the phone off speaker and lifted it to her ear.

'If you didn't find your dad, what's this all about? You're not going back, are you?'

'No, I'm not going back. There's just something I have to attend to.'

Cherry prided herself on her intuition and a well-tuned ear and it was clear from Liam's unconvincing attempt to be matter of fact that something was very wrong.

She stood and started pacing, making an attempt to keep her voice more composed than her mood. 'I've really tried to cut you some slack, Liam. I think I've been more than fair, but if you won't tell me what's going on, I can't help you any further.'

'I can't tell you. I wish I could but I can't.' He considered his next words carefully. 'All I can say is I think I may have a big story for you.'

'When?'

'I don't know.'

He sounded unhappy but she'd run out of patience and compassion. 'I think you have a good future in journalism, Liam, but it won't be with the *Dialog*. If you do ever get this big story of yours perhaps you'll have to submit it as a freelance piece.'

Cherry dropped the handset into its cradle with a sigh. She should have been angry but all she really felt was miserable.

* * *

Drought seemed a permanent feature of the rural Queensland landscape these days, Charlie thought as he waited for Liam's flight from Brisbane to land. The sparse grass that played the role of lawn around the sun-baked terminal was grey with death and the scraggy melaleucas were no better.

The plane appeared out of the glare at the end of the runway, with a roar followed almost immediately by the whine of the engines in reverse thrust. This time Liam was traveling light, with no checked baggage, and they were on the road in minutes.

'Got to take it slow through here,' Charlie said, trying to cover up those first moments of awkwardness that bedevil even the closest of reunions after long separation. 'These pesky little rock wallabies love to play chicken with the traffic and they never win.' He turned to Liam. 'Damn fine to see you, buddy.

It's been a long time.'

A short stop at a small supermarket was followed by around an hour heading north on a sealed road, before Charlie bounced off onto corrugated dirt. Through the dust-coated trees to the right was a wooded island thrusting steeply from stunning turquoise waters. To his left, the bare hillsides with their bleached crags and stony defiles were as much like the hills of Afghanistan as any he'd seen. Liam wondered idly if this had influenced Charlie's choice of location. Perhaps, given all those years living with the bleak Afghan landscape, it had finally found its way into his soul.

Twenty minutes later, without passing any further sign of human habitation, they were pulling up outside an imposing two-story house in a large compound. Surrounded on three sides by a seven-foot wall, the fourth was open to a narrow beach and more of the calm bright water. An impressively large powerboat lay at anchor a little way off the sand and a helipad was tucked into one corner between wall and shore. On the roof an array of solar panels, aerials and discs glittered in the afternoon sun.

'Don't use a chopper much,' Charlie said, seemingly as an apology for the long rough ride. 'Tends to attract too much attention.'

He took Liam on a quick tour of the big house, showed him to his room and wandered off towards the distant kitchen. 'Drinks on the pool terrace in ten,' he said over his shoulder. 'No bathing beauties this week, I'm afraid. The Swedish gals left for Cairns a couple of days back.'

The sun was settling slowly over lazy hills across the bay, somewhere just south of west Liam estimated, as he took the icy beer from Charlie and pulled up a sun-lounger.

'So what's this all about?' Charlie asked.

The Canon was on Liam's lap. He handed it over without speaking.

'Holy shit,' Charlie said eventually. 'What the fuck is this?'

'You remember me saying my dad disappeared on K2 when I was a kid?'

Charlie, nodded, scrolling through the images again.

'Well, I found him. Near the summit.'

Charlie looked up.

'Found him with a great big hole in his chest.' Liam indicated the images on the camera. 'Put there by that lot.'

Charlie stood. 'You get more beers, I'll get these onto the big screen.'

By the time Liam returned with the beers the images had been loaded onto the giant Mac and Charlie was flicking through them once again.

'We know the Russians and the Chinese were trying to build their own stealth bombers a while back, but none of our intel had them looking anything like this.'

He tapped his big finger at the image on the screen.

'This looks a lot like a B2; the Spirit, but there are differences. It seems bigger.' He took a mouthful from the bottle and belched softly. 'See, here and here, the payload area seems to have been augmented.' He moved on to the next frame. 'And here, where it's banked, those engines look like they could be bigger too.' He clicked on the mouse and another image filled the frame. It was a US Air Force Spirit. He positioned them side by side on the large monitor. 'Otherwise it sure looks like the B2 – look here, wing configuration, cockpit placement, all pretty similar.'

'So where does that leave us?' Liam asked.

'Dunno, no markings, no nuthin'.' Charlie sat back on his chair and spun it around. 'Flying in that part of the world it could belong to almost anyone. Our guys, China, Russia, Pakistan. India.' He turned back to the screen for another look. 'Possibly not Pakistan. Bit rich for their tastes. Like I said, China started developing stealth a few years back, but they were fighters not bombers, the Chengdu J20 and the Shenyang, the J31, I think it was. There are rumors of a bomber, the Xian H-20, but that's still on the drawing-board as far as I know. No, dammit, this here looks a lot like a B2.'

Liam shifted a pile of paperwork and perched on the edge of the desk. 'The real question is: why would they blow my father to bits just because he saw them?'

'The answer to that, young Liam, is almost certainly "just because he saw them".' He sipped from the bottle again. 'The other question is why nobody at base camp ever reported seeing or hearing anything.'

'This thing looks like it was tracking along behind the Northeast Ridge on the China side.' Liam ran a finger along the bottom of the screen, below the stricken aircraft. 'That wouldn't be visible from down on the Godwin Austen. Maybe from way back at Concordia, but it's quite possible there was nobody there at the time.'

Charlie nodded. 'Anyways, the real question is what are you... we, planning to do about it?'

'Could you maybe talk to your buddies in the Air Force, see if they know anything?'

Charlie gave him a skeptical look. 'This happened how many years back? And nobody's heard a squeak about anything like it since. Whoever's behind it, this is likely deeply covert stuff. If they were willing to top your old man on top of a fuckin' mountain in Pakistan, they really don't want *anyone*, including me, to see their shit.'

He stood and walked outside. Liam followed.

'Personally I'd keep a very low profile on this one until I knew a little more. You're too young to end up like your dad.'

Liam watched the last fiery droplet of liquid gold disappear behind the haze-dulled hills. 'Maybe the whole thing is in the past – a prototype or something that crashed and that was the end of it.'

'Maybe,' Charlie said. 'Maybe best forget all about it.' Then, knowing Liam as well as he did, he waited. He didn't have long to wait.

'But they murdered my father, Charlie. How can I forget about that?'

'Well sure, okay. But what are you planning to do?'

'I'm fucked if I know.'

The nuns had done their job on Liam early and well and Charlie knew that on the rare occasions the young feller used an expletive, serious things were going to happen.

'I can do a bit of fossicking around online,' Charlie offered. 'Raid the odd secure site, see if I can turn anything up. I got firewalls coming out of my ears and all sorts of anti-hacking, anti-spying stuff in that Mac but once I start snooping there's no hundred-per-cent guarantee I won't be pinged.'

'I'd prefer it if you didn't take risks on my account,' Liam said.

They sat in silence as the light faded and the first stars arrived, in the company of a squadron of mosquitos. Charlie seemed oblivious to their intermittent whine.

'There is one other remote possibility, but it's a pretty crazy idea,' he said. 'A ten-year-old needle in a big, white, frozen haystack.'

'It's not quite ten years,' Liam corrected him quietly. He had an inkling of where Charlie was going.

'I've got software on that thing that can calculate trajectories and impact points if I can feed in enough data. Time of day, date, shadows, all that stuff. If we can identify two or three of the peaks in those shots and have a stab at the airspeed. I can do that by estimating the distance traveled between frames and having a crack at how quickly your dad fired off shots. Call it very sophisticated, fly-by-the-seat-of-the-pants triangulation.'

'That camera has a built-in motor drive, he'd have been using that for sure. We can estimate how quickly that's triggered without too much effort.'

'Good. I can get a pretty fair handle on the angle of descent working with the perspective on the aircraft. It's not going to be pinpoint but it'll give you a pretty good idea of where it came down. What you do with that information is up to you.'

'I don't suppose you fancy a short walk in the Hindu Kush?' Liam asked with a smile.

'I hope to Christ it didn't get that far,' Charlie answered. 'I'll get onto it tonight. Do not disturb.'

* * *

An 18-carat, solid-gold Rolex Oyster peeked from the man's sleeve as he skewered the remains of the Beluga caviar with the glowing end of his cigar. He screwed it aggressively to and fro for a moment and then tossed it into the curdling residue of a poached egg.

'Coffee,' he barked at the waiter hovering nearby, indicating, with a dismissive wave of the hand, that the soiled breakfast plate should be removed immediately if not sooner. 'And get this shit out of here.'

The half-dozen minions, who'd been summoned to the boardroom table for a sunrise meeting, faced the same bleak prospect regarding coffee that they had during the man's breakfast. They were simply not offered any. They sat like docile cattle and watched the solitary display of general bad manners and appalling table etiquette, in acquiescent silence.

'Right, we're done. Fuck off and do some work.'

The man's behavior came as no surprise to the initiates. He was the most unpleasant person most of them – none of them saints themselves – had ever met. He was also the most charismatic.

As they stood submissively to leave, he pointed an aggressive finger at the Filipino man holding the coffee pot. 'You too. And leave that thing.' He waved him impatiently from the room.

'Not you.' He stabbed the same fat index finger at a middle-aged man with bad burn scars down one side of his face. 'We're not finished.'

The scarred man paused at the door then stepped across to the sideboard, took a cup and helped himself to a coffee from the pot on the boardroom table. The seated man watched him; a mongoose watching a cobra.

'So there's been another fucking setback. Are those fuckers incompetent or what?'

The man took an insolent sip of his coffee before answering. 'These things are going to happen when you insist on constant fast tracking. It's a blip, that's all. A hiccup. We can handle it. There'll be no great delay.'

'Well, get over there and crack the fuckin' whip. Find someone. I have people who are putting pressure on me and I don't enjoy it.' Light glinted off the ostentatious watch as he stood and walked to the window. 'I don't pay you to drink fucking coffee.'

The scarred man studied his employer's back. He'd been a middleweight boxing champion in his youth and the breadth of his shoulders said he wasn't yet to be underestimated.

'Handle it personally.' His boss turned and pointed to the door. 'The longer this shit goes on the more chance there is of a major screw-up.' The scarred man ran a hand across his cheek and stood to leave. 'And that other business. Make sure that stitched-up Singaporean bastard has got it sorted.'

* * *

The waning moon stood high in his window, like something in a child's drawing. He woke in a sweat and turned to take advantage of the breeze rustling the open curtains. He looked out into the darkened passageway. A light still bled from the office and he could hear the soft protests of a chair as Charlie adjusted his large frame once again. Liam groped for his phone. Two-thirty. He rolled over and was asleep within seconds.

The fried eggs were almost ready to slide onto plates when Charlie finally emerged from the office, looking remarkably fresh.

'Get any sleep?' Liam asked as he adjusted the heat.

'I don't sleep,' Charlie answered with a grin. 'You never know if you're gonna wake up. Eat your eggs, I'll grab a quick shower and we'll have a look at this thing.'

Ten minutes later, coffees in hand, they were back at the computer. A yellow pin graphic marked a spot on a high-resolution satellite image of desolate-looking mountains.

'About 30-odd miles east of a tiny hamlet name of Shimshal, if my calculations are right. Other than that, there's nothing "within cooee" as these Aussies say. Very, very isolated. It's almost due northwest of K2, still in Pakistan but close to the Chinese border; one of the many areas of disputed border. I'm not sure whether India, China or Pakistan reckon they own this bit, this week.'

He sipped at his coffee. 'But here's the thing. I did a bit of trawling. Seems there was some sort of incident in the area not a week after your dad was reported missing. Pakistani troops responded to reports of an incursion. By the time they got there all they apparently found were a few illegal nomads, sans flock.

I don't know that they did any searching for a downed aircraft.'

He turned back to the screen and enlarged the area identified. 'I've been staring at this in extremely hi-res for hours. If there was an aircraft there it's either under a mountain of snow and ice or someone managed to spirit it away under the Pakistanis' noses.'

Liam craned in close to the screen. 'That's interesting. Seems to be more snow around than there was when I was there. Is that imagery current?'

Charlie checked the date on the screen. 'Yep, two days ago.'

'I'm going back,' Liam said. 'I know it's a long shot but otherwise I hit a brick wall. I have a buddy in the Pakistani Air Force. Met him while I was in Peshawar. He may be able to swing a chopper if I give him a little notice. If I can find something, anything, symbols on a piece of fuselage, anything, it may take me somewhere.'

'Nothing ventured,' Charlie drawled, but Liam could tell from his expression that he didn't think there was much point to it. 'Still, anyone who can do this sort of stuff probably has a shitload of power and influence. My advice to you, young Liam, is be very careful.'

* * *

Jia had been observing Yuri for a month.

Since arriving in Pavlodar, Kazakh had become her fifth language, along with Mandarin, Russian, English and French. With these skills, finding employment at the refinery had been relatively easy. She'd made it clear that she now believed her father had run off with some woman and that she consequently needed to support herself financially. The management seemed to be genuinely sympathetic and found her work in the refinery's busy reception area. Her role was to take any incoming calls from people who were unable to speak Kazakh or Russian.

Yuri's role appeared to be multi-faceted and she was unable to work out exactly what he did. He seemed to roam the refinery at will and through the floor-to-ceiling glass she would often see him in conversation with the departing tanker drivers. Nothing in the time she'd been watching him had given her the smallest clue as to what might have become of Zhang Liu.

Rain was spattering onto the packed earth as she made for the bicycle racks. The timid young girl with whom she shared a daily smile was there again, bent over locking her bike chain to the rack. She worked in the evenings as a cleaner and was often arriving as Jia left. There was usually a quick exchange of pleasantries as their paths crossed and nothing more. Although Jia had sensed that once or twice the girl had been planning to speak but had hesitated at the last moment, colored up, dropped her chin and gone on her way.

'You are the lady whose father has gone,' the girl said from beneath her lowered rain hood. A question and statement simultaneously.

Jia was taken aback for a moment then swiftly recovered her composure. 'Yes, I am.' She smiled. 'We think – the *police* think – he went off with a woman.'

The girl stood and looked round nervously; there was nobody about. She shook her head. 'No, I saw him.' She surveyed her surroundings again. They were still quite alone. 'Two foreign men pushed him into one of the big trucks and the three of them drove off. I thought your father looked frightened.' The girl herself looked frightened.

Jia's heart gave a little flutter. She pointed at a fuel tanker parked nearby, its red-and-silver surface gleaming in a momentary shaft of sunlight. 'What, in one of those?'

The girl shook her head again. 'No.' She pointed into the distance. 'The grey ones, without the writing.' She dropped her head again. 'I must go now, I'll be late.'

'Thank you,' was all the breathless Jia could manage to say to her departing back.

She stood and stared blankly for several minutes at the distant tanker. Unable to think. Unable to know what to think. In the months of watching and wondering she hadn't even noticed that there were two types of tanker. One lot were shining silver cylinders with the company's logo emblazoned along their length in bright red with a touch of blue. The others were painted a drab non-reflective grey with no identification marks. Even the registration plates, she now noticed as she wheeled her bike closer, were difficult to see.

It occurred to her that she had only ever seen Yuri talking to the drivers of the plain tankers as they left the refinery. The more she dredged through the recent past the surer she was that he'd never shown any interest in the gleaming company vehicles.

The following day was her day off and she spent it close by the cloverleaf junction on the main highway that bisected the city from east to west. Several tankers approached the intersection during the course of the day. The liveried vehicles turned southwest towards the Kazakh capital Astana; to Almaty in the south; took the road to the river port or into the city. Only the dull grey ones swung their heavily laden bulk to the left and headed off to the southeast. Jia rode to the southern edge of town and waited. At irregular intervals the innocuous vehicles trundled by, dropped a gear for a slight incline and accelerated out into the snow-sprinkled countryside.

Asking particular questions and trying to make them seem innocent was, Jia decided, not a skill she had learned. She had no idea whether her father's disappearance had anything to do with Yuri or his tankers. She had no idea which of her fellow employees were trustworthy, if any, or whether her curiosity was being observed and, if so, what the consequences might be. The only thread she had linking the grey tankers to her father was the hurried statement from the shy young cleaner, who now made a point of avoiding her. If she went to the police with the girl's claim, Jia believed the girl would almost certainly deny it.

She spent an anxious week trying as casually as possible to discover the destination of the mysterious fleet of trucks. Nobody in her immediate circle seemed to know or care, or if they did they were certainly not willing to share the knowledge. She risked staying back after her shift ended and searched the refinery computer network, but found nothing more. It seemed clear that if she wanted to know where they were headed, then she had just one choice. She would need to follow them.

8

'BACK SO SOON,' Mahmood said. The hotel foyer was crowded as usual, with conspiratorial whisperers, and Liam had to wend his way across from the elevator to shake his friend's hand. What he was about to request would challenge the oldest of friendships and this one was more or less in its infancy. Liam was almost certain it would pass the test.

'That hotel you stayed at in Pindi,' Mahmood said, as they walked into the lounge. 'It was hit by a car bomb, just days after you left. Nearly destroyed. Things become worse and worse.'

'I heard.' Liam nodded. 'That's why I'm back here. Not the sort of place my budget normally runs to.'

They ordered tea and Liam began his pitch. 'Mahmood, the favor I'm about to ask of you is going to sound totally unreasonable, crazy perhaps. And then, to make it even worse, I'm not going to tell you why I'm asking. If you're willing to help me out it will have to be because you trust me.'

Mahmood waited while the tea was delivered. 'Try me,' he said at length.

'I need a ride in your chopper. I know it's against military regulations but I also know you can swing it. I need to do a bit of a recce in a location in the mountains. If I find what I'm looking for you'll know what it is. If not you can remain blissfully and safely unaware.'

'I am already intrigued,' he searched Liam's eyes, in the hope they might give something away. Liam revealed nothing. He removed a printout of the location image from his bag. In the center was a penciled cross and a set of map co-ordinates.

Mahmood studied it for a while. 'This is the middle of nowhere,' he said at length. 'What could you be looking for here?' It hung in the air as a rhetorical question. 'But, of course, no matter. I will help you, my friend. It will take a few days but I can arrange things. I'll need to organize a fuel drop in Shimshal in case your 'search' burns up more fuel than you planned. Let's say Wednesday. I'll collect you in the morning at seven.'

* * *

The search was conducted on a rectangular grid. Northeast on one stretch, quick turn, southwest on the next. They had been over the location for some hours on the second day and seen nothing but a vast wilderness of snow, ice, rock and more snow. The white mantle appeared to be significantly sparser than it had been a week or so prior, when the satellite images were made, but there was still sufficient, it seemed, to turn their search into a futile exercise. Even the invariably composed Mahmood's patience seemed to be tested.

'I'm getting weather warnings,' he yelled into his intercom eventually. 'I think we'd better break off for now. Perhaps we can try again tomorrow. I'll take her in to Shimshal while we can still see our hands.'

Within half an hour Liam found himself, for the third time in as many months, in a narrow valley village, hemmed in by a wall of 20,000-foot peaks.

The icy weather front, once it arrived, had no intention of leaving the next day and they had no choice but literally to cool their heels for three days more. They were no more than 30 miles from Charlie's selected site and Liam knew that the locals traveled this harsh landscape at will, so he made a point of roaming around the tiny green oasis. Whenever he managed to waylay one of the villagers, he would ask if, during their wanderings, approximately seven years before, they remembered seeing, hearing or finding anything strange. For the most part they regarded him as a *pardeesi* lunatic to be pitied, and ambled politely away. One old man, however, regarded him strangely for several seconds before shaking his head and retreating through his modest front door.

'These are poor people,' Mahmood said on the second afternoon. 'They're not venal, but perhaps if you offered them something, a small reward for information, you might achieve a little more.'

The word spread quickly throughout the small community and, on the third afternoon, as the weather cleared, the old man approached Mahmood while he was checking his engine oil. He indicated shyly that the pilot from the big city should follow him back to his home.

Liam was sitting in the half-light of their guesthouse corridor just minutes later, when Mahmood came in lugging what was clearly a heavy bag and dropped it unceremoniously on the stone floor in front of him.

'This is going to cost you 10,000 rupees and one hell of an explanation.' It was the first time Liam had seen Mahmood angry.

He drew back the soft handles and took a tentative look into the bag. Covered though it was by an accumulated coating of dust and grime, the bright orange object was unmistakable. It was a flight data recorder, imprecisely described in aviation parlance as an aircraft's black box. A surge worthy of a quick double caffeine hit struck somewhere in the region of his solar plexus.

'You tell me why you were looking for it and then perhaps I'll tell you how it was found.' Mahmood was still smoldering.

There was no choice now but to come clean. Liam lifted the heavy device and examined each aspect closely before commencing his long and complex explanation. As his story unfolded, Mahmood reverted, gradually, to his more affable self. 'I am sorry to hear about your father, Liam, but why did you not trust me enough to share this information with me before?'

'It *wasn't* a lack of trust,' Liam said forcefully, returning the device to the flagstones. 'It was about protecting you. I don't know who or what's behind this. All I do know is they were ruthless enough to blow a stranger's heart out just for looking at them. I didn't think I needed to expose you to that type of risk. Even all these years later.'

'I am a soldier too, Liam,' he responded quietly. 'I live with risk. I can look after myself.' He pointed to the object standing on the floor beside the bag. 'I don't suppose I can persuade you to hand this to the authorities in Islamabad?' He didn't bother to wait for an answer. 'I am assuming you will try to get it out of the country.'

Liam nodded.

Mahmood shrugged and said nothing. He walked to the open doorway and looked across towards the distant dwelling. 'It was the old man,' he said eventually. 'He's had it for years. In the past he hunted in those high valleys to the east; wild sheep, goat.'

He indicated the seemingly innocuous object at Liam's feet again, without looking round. 'This one is definitely from a military aircraft, it's a deployable recorder. It has an ELT, an emergency locator transmitter, it should have been sending signals for weeks. The fact that they didn't retrieve it is strange. It could only be because they couldn't reach it. I think it may have dropped into a deep, inaccessible crevasse up on a glacier somewhere and then worked its way down the valley gradually. Your friends may have found their aircraft but the glacier kept your black box safe for you. The old man found it where it had been released from the ice at the edge of a moraine. It's very lucky it wasn't crushed. It was not that far from where you were searching. He's had it in his house ever since. His one indulgence really: a little color to brighten up his monochrome life.'

* * *

Ivor Petrovich was like sunlight come to a Stygian world. He was a young man not yet 20, still suffused with the mischief and enthusiasm of childhood.

But he was not to be trusted.

The son of a prominent politician in Arkhangelsk, he had been drawn into what the world's tabloid journalists liked to refer to as the 'undercurrent of the drug culture'. When his father's patience ran out and the largesse finally dried up, Ivor took to a career in petty crime. He was convicted on several counts of housebreaking, and the old man was obliged to use his considerable influence to avoid a jail sentence and criminal record for his son by sending him to the bleakest place he knew of: Cape Zhelaniya.

Alexei Gavrilov had no interest in wet-nursing the young criminal and so it fell to Dashka Anasovna to ensure he did something constructive with his time.

Dashka's initial response was annoyance. Her years of isolation on the island had brought about an emotional metamorphosis. She had changed, at a pace imperceptible even to herself, from a vivacious social animal to a skittish, solitary creature, no longer comfortable with the herd. The unwillingness of Alexei and the other replacements to treat her with anything beyond bare civility had only served to exacerbate her journey into introversion.

In spite of all this she was drawn to the newly arrived young villain. Ivor, much to Dashka's surprise, turned out to be a quick learner. He showed no lack of willingness, was always cheerful and, she discovered, fun to be around. But there was a darkness to him too. Something a bit secretive, perhaps even sly.

It was nothing she could put her finger on, so she chose to ignore it and gradually the old Dashka returned.

They worked and laughed together most days and he soon knew almost as much about the machines as she did. On days off he would often join her on her jaunts around the island. Everything seemed to be going along nicely and her thoughts of moving on gradually eased themselves from her mind.

It was really only after the flying visit from the Moscow people, she later concluded, that things began to change quite dramatically.

* * *

'You can't follow a fuel tanker on a bicycle,' Jia said to herself, seemingly for the thousandth time, as she watched yet another 18-wheel enigma lumber out of town to the southeast.

Deciding to follow was one thing; finding a practical way to do it and the courage to put it into practice was quite another. For a month she had been paralyzed by uncertainty and indecision. It seemed absurd, a young woman in a foreign, male-dominated country playing detective. As a child she had practiced her English by reading dog-eared Nancy Drew stories, found at a Beijing market stall, but this was different: this was reality. Then again, she had lost all confidence in the local police and had no reason to believe that sharing her observations with them was a wise, or even a safe thing to do. And so she completed the full circle and arrived back at her original conclusion. If she was to discover where the tankers might have taken her father, she would have to follow them. She could not know whether her journey, like Lao Tzu's, would take her a thousand miles or not, but, like his, it must start with a single step.

Old Ruslan's sight had finally deserted him completely. He was, Jia estimated, in his late eighties and the blindness had been progressive. Over the past few months their shared loneliness had forged a simple bond between them. His ramshackle timber home stood just a few doors away from hers and she would walk over some nights with a bowl of noodles or some freshly made dumplings. He, in return, would listen patiently while she unburdened herself of her fears about her father.

For almost a year the small Suzuki had stood unused under a canvas awning at the rear of the property. Ruslan was incapable of driving it, but he saw selling it as one more blow to his fragile independence and so it sat, gathering bird droppings and dust. From time to time Jia would start the engine to charge the battery but she had not driven it.

Ruslan felt his way to the front door in response to her knock. The scent of a steaming soup preceded her into the dingy kitchen. She prepared a bowl and handed him a spoon and watched while he slurped and murmured.

'I have a small favor to ask, Ruslan,' she said at length.

He looked up, although he saw nothing. An unconscious action dictated by a lifetime of habit.

'I need to go away, perhaps for a few days, and was wondering whether I might borrow the car.' She indicated the location of the car over her shoulder. Another gratuitous but instinctive act.

'The car?' Ruslan seemed a little vague. It had been a while – perhaps he'd forgotten it was there.

'Your little white Suzuki,' she said. 'Out the back. I'd take good care of it.'

'But yes, of course. Take it, take it. With pleasure.' He smiled, relieved no doubt that he was able, now, to form a mental picture of the car. 'Mind you, it may need some fuel. When I worked at the refinery I got my gasoline cheap but not now, not now.'

'I will pay for the fuel,' she said softly. 'And thank you. Thank you.' She took both his hands in hers, slopping a little soup from the spoon onto the scrubbed table top. He was unable to see the silent tears trickling down Jia's cheeks.

* * *

'You will not get it through customs, Liam.' Mahmood was becoming frustrated with Liam's obstinacy. 'Not only will you ruin the very small chance you might have of finding who did this thing, you will end up in a Pakistani prison.'

Liam stared, exasperated, at the now-clean data recorder secreted amongst the ropes, harnesses, axes, pitons, crampons and carabiners stowed in one large bag. The equipment had been left behind in Islamabad during his detours to Dolpo and Queensland and now he was hoping to use them to disguise a big, brightly colored piece of aviation equipment.

During a late-night call, Charlie, in his circuitous way, had made it reasonably clear that if Liam could get his 'machine' to Australia, he had 'friends in Canberra' that could do the rest. Liam was aware that Australia's Transport Safety people had an FDR laboratory in Canberra. It was one of the few in the region that had the necessary capabilities. The trick would be getting the thing into the country.

'So what do you suggest?' Liam looked up from the packed bag.

Beyond the Marriott Hotel, the smoke of 10,000 cooking fires hung low in Islamabad's still evening air. Mahmood stood facing the window, silent for long minutes, then turned back into the room.

'In a month or so we have a joint training exercise with Indonesia. It's a part of our Defense Co-operation Agreement. I'll be flying into Bali, Denpasar. I can probably replace the FDR on my aircraft with this one.' He pointed without enthusiasm at the item of contention in the bag. 'That's the best I can do. You'll have to get it from there to Australia.'

'But that's not safe for you,' Liam said.

'Not if I crash,' Mahmood smiled. 'But in that case it would likely be academic.'

'Are you sure about this?'

'I'm sure. But you owe me a bloody great big drink.'

Liam stepped over to him, embraced him tightly without speaking and then punched in the Queensland number again. Several seconds passed before Charlie answered.

'Goddam, Liam, I just got back to sleep.'

'Sorry, buddy, need a quick answer. If we get ourselves to Denpasar is there any way we can get to your place?'

'I'll think of something,' was all Charlie said.

'It'll be around a month. I'll keep you posted. I need to get home for a while. Move my mother back to Ireland. I've kept her waiting too long as it is.'

'How is she?' Charlie asked.

'She seemed a little better last time we spoke.'

'Well, give her my best.' Liam heard the line go dead at the other end.

* * *

The warm breath from his old lungs vaporized into cold steam as it made contact with Oxford's dawn air. He'd closed his front door gently at precisely 5.30.

Oskar Frederik was a creature of habit.

By six he was striding past William Morris's first garage on Longwall Street. The neat two-story brick building had a large central carriage door in a dark, gleaming green. The location had, as he never tired of informing visitors, produced Morris's first-ever motor car just two years before the start of the Great War.

This morning found Oskar uncharacteristically anxious. The paper he was planning to deliver late in the afternoon was set to put the cat well and truly among the pigeons.

He turned left onto the High Street at Magdalen College, right onto Rose Lane at the Botanical Gardens and passed the TS Eliot Theatre. The sudden crunch of his steps on the pale gravel startled a deer, which skittered off into the mist concealing Christ Church Meadow.

There would be people attending the seminar who could have serious issues with what he was about to suggest.

Right again took him past the Merton College playing fields and, a little further along, another right had him heading back home along the narrow Grove Walk.

He had thought long and hard about the content, his provocative conclusions, the wisdom of his decision to go public, but in the end the principled citizen had trumped the cautious scientist.

He was about to enter Magpie Lane when, as he negotiated the spiked iron gate before crossing the cobbles of Merton Street, he noticed a black Range Rover just to his left. The vehicle had deeply tinted windows but more unusual still was that its engine was idling so early in the morning. As the gate swung to behind him, he glanced up again. Two disturbingly emotionless men in dark anoraks had emerged, one from each side of the car, and were walking swiftly towards him. One appeared to be concealing a syringe in his right hand.

9

'IN A FEW MINUTES we will be landing at Denpasar International Airport,' the Indonesian flight attendant began.

After three days in transit he'd stopped listening to the endless directives from generally incomprehensible public-address systems.

In Bali it was sometime around midday Wednesday. He'd left Margaret at Shannon, with tears in her tired eyes, on Monday afternoon.

As a child, the neighbors had always said, little Liam was his dad's son, a man's man. There was, if he was honest with himself, some truth in all that. But it did nothing to simplify the divided loyalties: being torn between the desire to find his father's killers and the need to be there for his mother. It did nothing to ease the remorse.

He felt as guilty as hell leaving but comforted himself with the fact she seemed far better than she had a few months back.

'The doctors will arrange for me to continue my treatment in Cork,' she said, trying to be cheery. 'I'm feeling much better and they tell me I have years to live.' It may have been a lie, he couldn't tell, but he chose, in order to assuage his guilt, to accept it as the truth.

Besides, he consoled himself, she was now in a bright little cottage a few minutes from the village of Glengarriff and right next door to a close lifelong friend.

It had seemed prudent, given the fact he was about to go poking the bear, that she return to Ireland under another name. Without alarming her too much, he had persuaded her to revert to her maiden name and to keep her distance from the Dromdarragh community for the time being. While linking an anonymous Margaret Doyle back to him would be difficult, finding him via a Meg O'Brien would be nigh on impossible.

Two sets of gleaming teeth greeted him as he appeared from customs at Ngurah Rai. One set in a naturally dark face, the other in a freckled face made dark by too much Queensland sun.

They'd both been in Bali for a couple of days when he arrived. He'd been pretty sure that Mahmood and Charlie would hit it off and given the easy way they stood together waiting he had, clearly, been right.

Charlie stepped forward and grabbed Liam's hand. Mahmood hung back just a little.

'This guy's almost as good a pilot as I am,' Charlie said, tilting his head toward the still-smiling Mahmood.

'I challenged him to a dogfight,' Mahmood laughed, as he too shook Liam's hand. 'But he claims he left his aircraft at home.'

'True story. This is a boating holiday.' Charlie pointed over his shoulder in the direction of what Liam assumed was a marina. 'A fishing trip.'

'How did it all go?' Liam tossed his bag into the trunk of the waiting taxi.

'Thankfully I did not crash,' Mahmood said. 'And so had no need of the equipment.' He paused while the driver walked back to his seat. 'Charlie now has it safe and sound.'

The boat waiting for them was the one Liam had spied out the front of Charlie's Queensland place two months back. This time he was close enough to see the name 'Escapade' painted on the bow. It wasn't in a marina, as he'd imagined, but stood at the long commercial wharf that was Benoa Harbor and was tied up behind Greenpeace's Rainbow Warrior.

'Piece of luck, that,' Charlie said, indicating the gaily painted ship. On the dock nearby were several small marquees crowded with people buying T-shirts and signing petitions. 'So much excitement over there they're not the least bit fussed about us. I could be loading Sumatran tigers on board and nobody would notice.'

'What are they here for?' Liam asked.

'Dunno,' Charlie shrugged. 'Polar bears, tigers, whales… they're all in deep shit…'

'They're not the only ones,' Mahmood added quietly. He took

Liam's hand again. 'I need to get back to my base, my friend. Bon voyage and good luck.' He turned to Charlie and pointed to the boat. 'Keep our precious Karakoram catch fresh.'

'In Australia they'd call it an Orange Roughy.' Charlie winked at Liam as Mahmood turned to walk away.

'Thanks again, for everything,' Liam called. 'I won't forget the big drink.' Mahmood waved without looking back.

* * *

They clambered on board and Charlie prepared to cast off.

'Where's the flight recorder?' Liam surveyed the deck as if he half expected to see it sitting there glowing bright orange in the late afternoon sunlight.

Charlie indicated a tightly sealed compartment amidships. 'It's underneath the freezer. I've knocked up a bit of a false bottom. She's all wrapped up snug in foil and foam. If anyone wants to find it they'll be squishing through a lot of frozen fish.'

He walked over to the freezer, flicked open the latches and lifted the heavy cover.

'Nice-looking fish,' Liam said. 'Where'd you catch them?'

'Jimbaran markets,' he said grinning. He thrust his hand in between the shining scales and rearranged the catch. 'Red snapper, mahi-mahi, grouper, a couple of yellowfin. Some fine eating there.'

The sun retreated behind their departing backs as Charlie took the boat slowly through the busy channel off the Nusa Dua peninsula and then set a course to the south of Sumba Island across the Timor Sea.

'Should take us three or four days to Darwin, dependent on conditions. We'll have to do customs there, given I've been ashore in Indonesia. The Aussies patrol these waters regularly, big numbers of refugee boats coming from up north these days. But it shouldn't be a problem for us. I've been in their waters fishing before.' He lapsed into a bad Australian accent. 'I'll just tell 'em I picked up a mate from Bali.'

The days were hot and still and they made good time but the

updates from Australia's bureau warned of the likelihood of a high-category cyclone forming somewhere in the Coral Sea to the east.

'I've made arrangements to leave her in Darwin until the season's over,' Charlie said, looking up from his glowing screen. 'Too much time and unnecessary risk taking her all the way around to Gloucester Passage, at this time of year, particularly with a big blow coming in. I've had a couple of those since I moved down there. They're bad enough onshore. Don't need to test my fortitude with them at sea.'

He stowed the computer, came back on deck and took the helm from Liam. 'I've got the pick-up, the drive home will take us another three days if we share. We need to get back. I've got a guy coming up from Canberra. Knew him in Uruzgan a few years back. We still do each other favors.'

In spite of Charlie's assurances on the first afternoon out, they were not required to wait until Darwin to encounter Australian officialdom. Early on the third day as the Escapade bisected an imaginary line between Ashmore reef and Rote Ndao, a patrol boat appeared over the horizon to the south; it was traveling fast and was within a few hundred yards very quickly. The skipper eased off on the engines and a sleek, black Zodiac was deployed with impressive speed. In a minute or two they had slipped alongside and were politely but firmly asking for permission to come aboard.

'Sure thing,' Charlie said, seeming remarkably relaxed. He took the boat's painter and tied it off expertly. 'I'd offer you guys a coffee but I don't have enough cups.'

The senior officer smiled thinly. 'That's quite all right, sir.' He stepped across the low gunwale. 'May I see your papers?' He turned to Liam. 'And you, sir, your passport.'

He spent longer than necessary examining each passport in turn then spoke, without looking up. 'Do you mind if my people look around?'

'Not at all, go for it,' Charlie was still very much at his ease.

Liam hoped the guys couldn't see his heart pumping away through his shirt.

The search below deck took long enough to suggest it was thorough. Both men were sufficiently well schooled not to make nervous small talk and the three of them kept a polite silence while the others were below.

Eventually, inevitably, the officer indicated the fish box. 'Freezer, is it, sir?'

'That's right, I've had a lucky run this time out.' Charlie pointed to the neatly stowed rods.

'Can you open it for me please, sir?'

Charlie obliged. 'Help yourself.'

The man began to dig deeply into the ice between the catch. His sleeve was rolled to the top of his bicep but, even so, it was on the verge of submerging when the only crewman remaining on the inflatable took a radio call.

'They're asking us to check on a possible illegal south of Ashmore, sir.'

'Right, on my way.' He dragged his dripping arm from the box, called to the men still below and then turned to Charlie. 'Thank you for your co-operation, sir. You will still need to register with customs and immigration when you make landfall in Darwin.' He stepped nimbly onto the Zodiac. 'Have a safe journey.'

'You sure I can't talk you fellas into taking a nice fresh yellow fin for your dinner?'

The officer responded with the same thin smile as they sped away.

* * *

A low mist clung stubbornly to the early-morning surface of the Potomac.

'This river is like a metaphor for the conflicting needs of the planet,' Donna Stone was saying. 'West Virginia miners way up there near the source,' she pointed to the west as she ran. 'And down there to the east, tidewater Virginia and the watermen.'

She shook her head. 'And Washington is right here in the middle.'

Cherry Davitt jogged along comfortably beside her, listening without speaking.

Senator Stone, it seemed, hadn't achieved her current status as one of the party's preferred presidential candidates without having a strong competitive streak. She gave Cherry a quick sidelong glance then stretched her stride and pushed the pace. Cherry stayed with her. Stone kicked on a little harder. Cherry wasn't even breathing hard. They ran on, setting a punishing pace for the security detail following.

'You run well, Cherry,' Stone said, her breathing a little pushed.

'I was a college sprint champ,' Cherry's delivery was effortless. 'Coach believed I had Olympic potential if I stayed with it.'

They ran on past the playing fields toward the Lincoln Memorial. 'My major was journalism. "You chase Gold or you chase news," Coach used to say. "Not both." I chose news.'

Stone nodded, deciding not to expend lung power on unnecessary words.

'Speaking of news, I *am* here to interview *you*,' Cherry said.

Stone slowed to a relaxed jog. 'Right. Fire away.'

'Your toughest competition at this stage is Jason Arnott – in fact, if you believe the polling, he's probably about to take over the lead once you get to South Carolina.'

'Early days yet, Cherry,' Stone said, slowing to a walk.

'What do you think of Arnott? He seems to be the one to beat – very popular guy.'

'He's good, Cherry, I've worked with him on several committees. His heart seems to be in the right place and we agree on most things. I just believe I'd make a better President.' She smiled.

'Changing the subject, what you were saying earlier. Would you care to enlarge on that?'

The interview was interrupted by an aide carrying a cellphone.

'Call from California, Donna...'

* * *

'What do you want to know?' The man from Canberra asked. He'd turned Charlie's dining room into an impromptu workshop and his testing equipment was spread across the very large table. Over many drinks the previous evening they'd given him just enough information to reassure him that, while what they were doing might be a tiny bit illegal, it was in no way immoral or unprincipled.

'Ideally whose aircraft it was and where it originated,' Liam said.

'You don't want to know why it crashed? I assume it did crash?'

Liam shook his head. 'No, not really interested in that.'

'Well, the flight recorder still seems to be in reasonable shape. I can probably give you co-ordinates for its point of origin. I don't know if I can tell you who owned it. Normally I should be able to identify the aircraft from the serial numbers but they've clearly been tampered with. These all lead to a dead end.'

Liam watched him work for a few hours but it was slow, exacting work and he soon tired of observing an activity that he could hardly comprehend.

It took time but the Canberra man was as good as his word and, on a clammy morning, with yet another cyclone brewing somewhere to the northeast, the three men stood over a small complex instrument and stared at a single set of co-ordinates on the screen.

East 86°54'55.32' North 49°03'18.64'.

Charlie jotted them down, took them into the office and keyed them into the computer. The waiting satellite image of the earth skimmed across the monitor and came to rest in the north of the Xinjiang autonomous zone in the deep shadows of the Altai Mountains. Charlie positioned the mouse carefully and zoomed in until he was just a few meters above the surface.

'Nothing there. Empty valleys, barren mountains, snow everywhere, not a rock out of place,' he muttered. 'Goddam.'

He switched with deft movements from one online service to another, military, commercial and free access sites. The results were the same. A remote, hostile and deserted valley. No sign of life for miles around.

He looked up to the Canberra man. 'Is it possible you got them wrong?'

He shook his head. 'That data came directly from the FDR. I guess it might have a glitch, although I doubt it, but my machines? There's no way they're wrong.'

He seemed a little offended at the very suggestion.

'Anyhow, I need to get back, I've been away longer than I said I would. Afraid that's the best I can do for you.' He walked back into the other room and started to pack his equipment away, then paused and returned to the office.

'And remember, not a word about my being here to anyone, ever. If anyone knew what I'd been up to on your account, I suspect losing my job would be the least of my worries.'

He observed both of them thoughtfully, then turned to Charlie, laughed loudly and shook his head. 'The things I let you talk me into, mate. I must be bloody crazy.'

* * *

The black dog was snapping at Liam's heels again. Inactivity, inevitably, seemed to drag it from its dark lair. Whenever he sat still for too long, whenever there was no immediate journey to take, job to do, goal to reach, the dark emptiness would begin to close in. Being busy was the only way to keep the beast out of his head.

It had been this way since his service in Afghanistan. A result of his time there, the psychiatrists, psychologists, therapists and doctors were all happy to conclude. According to them, Liam's post-traumatic stress was an understandable product of his year spent in the merciless hands of terrorists. They prescribed a few pills, suggested therapy, closed his file and sent him on his way.

Liam sensed – no, he knew – that his melancholy went much deeper than that. He was able to trace the genesis of his desolation, his black despair, back to a long-ago morning on an Irish mountain when a teenage boy was hit by an avalanche thundering over him from the distant heights of the Karakoram.

'Just give me a little while,' Charlie had said when Liam

insisted, impatiently, that the only thing to do was to take to the trail and find the site for himself. 'There's something not quite right here. Let's wait and see if we can sort it before you go rushing off again.'

He was dozing in front of a late, late movie when Charlie yelled from the office. 'Hey buddy, get your ass in here.' He pointed at the screen with the remains of a cold spring roll. 'I've looked and looked, at the free sites, Google Earth, Flash, Bing, all of them. I've looked at the professional guys; the ones with a dozen satellites of their own. And there's nothing there.'

'But...' He popped the spring roll into his mouth. 'That doesn't mean there's nothing there. That just means it's not there on these *particular* images.'

He tapped the screen with a greasy forefinger then tried to wipe away the smudge with his sleeve.

'Even the high-priced professional services carry images that are sometimes years old. But some of NASA, Pentagon satellites, military and NSA satellite material should be virtually live feed. And I've looked at all of their stuff too. Nothing at these co-ordinates on any of them. No hidden hangars, no runways, impossible for an aircraft to take off. So either your co-ordinates are wrong or somehow all these services are showing us a landscape that simply doesn't exist any more.'

He turned to Liam and waved a finger in his direction.

'I've been looking at this stuff for days now and these guys have made one simple error.'

He returned to the monitor and indicated the edge; the seam at which the adjacent images were stitched together.

'See this. The photos of the areas all around our location keep changing a little with each satellite update. That's because the weather keeps changing; sometimes snow here, sometimes snow there, sometimes not. Our little location, on the other hand, is stitched in with images that don't change. The weather all around is changing, our site never does. These guys are camouflaging this one location with old images; you're not seeing what's currently there.'

He turned and gave Liam a high five then became suddenly very serious.

'But this is big. Very big.' He pointed at the ceiling fan rotating listlessly above his head. 'There are around 8,000 satellites up there and a lot of them have cameras. Somebody, somewhere, has either taken control of the incoming satellite data, all these sites, or is hacking into every supplier of earth imagery on the planet and substituting old images in this one location. You need to have a lot of pull to achieve that. And a very serious reason.'

'So even if there's something big there, we can't see it?'

Charlie nodded. 'Exactly right.'

'So therefore I need to take a trip to the Altai Mountains and see for myself. Kind of like I said a week ago.'

If he picked up the barb, Charlie chose to ignore it. 'Either that or we attempt to somehow hack the direct satellite feed and try to find the current images.' He shrugged. 'Your call.'

'So what do you suggest?'

'I'd take that trip to China, if I were you.' His customary grin was back. 'It'll probably be quicker and easier.' He nodded. 'And safer.'

'What about you?' Liam asked, knowing the answer already. 'Can't tempt you to come along?'

'I'm an aviator. I don't do walking.'

He sat at the desk, swiveled the chair toward the room and considered Liam carefully.

'But not that easy.' The grin was gone. 'Once you leave Urumqi,' Charlie warned, 'no more electronics. No phone, no fancy camera, no GPS, no EPIRB, nothin'. If this set up is as heavy as I think it may be, you won't want to be sending them signals to say you're visiting. You'll need to be a ghost.'

He returned to the monitor and zoomed out to a wider landscape. 'You'll have to navigate up from this lake the way we did in the old days. Hell, James Cook got two-thirds of the way around the earth with a goddam 18th-century compass, a sextant and a fob watch.'

He cast around in the bottom of a drawer and dragged out an old Nikon F2 camera, then opened a cupboard under a bookcase to reveal a small fridge. He gathered a handful of film canisters and placed them on the table in front of Liam. 'Possibly the last high-speed Ektachrome in existence, so don't waste it. We'll get ISO 1600 out of that if we push it. Try not to use it at night.'

'My dad had one of these before the Canon,' Liam said softly, holding the camera with near reverence.

'I still have contacts in the Middle Kingdom. I'll call in some favors. There'll be a small pistol and a couple of useful bits and pieces waiting for you in a locker at the Urumqi airport,' Charlie continued, all business now. 'The key will be in an envelope in the bar fridge of your Beijing hotel. The gun will be customized and made from a ceramic composite. It'll beat metal detectors but I'd try to avoid x-ray machines.'

Charlie left the room and came back a few seconds later with a metal briefcase.

'If there's anything or anybody way up there, doing things they shouldn't, then there's a good chance thermal imaging will be a part of their security set up.' He unlocked the case and lifted out a snow-white, hooded overall with what appeared to be some kind of thin plastic lining. 'This is something I used up in the Wakhan Corridor a couple of winters back.' He lifted his hand to deflect the question on Liam's lips. 'Don't ask.'

He held the garment up against Liam's torso to check the fit and then passed it across.

'It's a newly developed flexible polyimide aerogel. It's what the tech guys call super insulation. This is as new as the Nikon is old. In the snow the exterior of the fabric should stay cold enough to prevent any thermal imaging gear reading your body heat.'

He flipped the lid on the briefcase.

'That's the best I can do. Ditch the gun in the snow once you leave the area. There won't be a serial number on it.'

* * *

'Someone has been showing interest in our sites.'

The airport cafeteria table was the one the two men had been meeting at, on an irregular basis, for several years.

'It's still sticky,' the man from Singapore said, showing his distaste with a curled lip. 'All these years and still sticky.' He took a handkerchief from his suit pocket and wiped his fingers.

He replaced the handkerchief, sipped at his mineral water and then responded to Mr Paul's statement. 'Who is showing interest in our sites?'

'We don't know.' Paul corrected himself immediately. 'We don't know *yet*.'

His associate eyed him silently – the hair was decidedly more grey and there was less of it. Stress, no doubt. Mr Paul was obviously one to watch. 'When did you discover this was going on? How long could it have been happening without your knowing?'

Mr Paul realized his professionalism was being questioned and didn't react well. 'Not bloody long at all,' he said tersely, lowering his voice. 'We picked it up quite possibly within hours. Certainly no more than a few days.'

'A few days?' The man from Singapore made no attempt to disguise his irritation. 'And you still have no idea who you're dealing with?'

Paul, once again, was forced back on the defensive. 'Whoever it is knows their way around. They've been checking all the free sites, all the commercial sites as well as the official military ones, always the same precise co-ordinates. But they're bouncing around all over the place. We're not going to locate them in five minutes.'

'Could they have found anything, seen anything?'

'Nothing to see,' Mr Paul said proudly. In control again. 'We've stitched them together like a fine Persian rug.'

Paul mistook the other man's quick nod for encouragement. 'The relevant quadrant in this instance is managed from Diego, the Cape or the Gap, nobody else bothers to look at it. We make sure all the satellite data for the quadrant is fed to one central point. That's us. It's then distributed globally. Even the commercial services use our images.'

He smiled expansively. 'In an area as remote and irrelevant as ours, pre-existing data can be fed into the system over and over again and nobody is any the wiser.'

'I'm not interested in how you do it, Mr Paul,' the man from

Singapore said. 'I'm only interested in making sure the system keeps working and that's why you need to locate your nosey friend very swiftly.'

Paul exposed his exasperation. 'These things take time. My people are back at the Gap trying to track them down as we speak, but they're pinging about all over the planet, some of the best metadata encryption I've ever seen, impregnable fire walls, every trick in the book to throw us off the scent.'

'Is it likely to be an agency? Someone official? Or is it just some hacker snooping?'

'We don't know, but whoever it is, they're very slick.'

'Well, keep trying. We don't *have* time.' The man from Singapore reached into his briefcase and retrieved his airline ticket. For him the meeting was over. 'I'd prefer not to be exposed to the dubious attractions of Darwin every time you have a problem.'

'Those were the conditions under which I agreed to get involved. I had a good reason for making it Darwin,' Paul said defensively.

The photo of the two smiling children standing among coconut palms stayed snug in his wallet. 'I can justify Darwin. If I started going any further afield as often, Singapore, for example, it would soon attract unwanted attention.'

The man from Singapore ignored the remark. He stood and was about to leave.

'My people have raised the issue of money again,' Mr Paul said hurriedly. 'They know they are taking huge risks and think they should be remunerated accordingly. You promised to look into it, yet again, the last time you were down. But nothing ever seems to happen.'

'They're calling my flight,' the other man said. 'We'll discuss it next time we speak. When you locate the source of your security breach let me know. We'll need to send people.'

* * *

Baydala, Birlik, Komaritsyno, Yamyshevo. The exotic names

singing silently from the intermittent road signs were all that broke the monotony of the barren landscape. Jia knew the river was still somewhere off there to the right but, apart from the slightly greener tinge along the western horizon, there was nothing to suggest its continued existence. The back seat of the small car was laden with a cheap sleeping bag, a small backpack with her few warm clothes and a basket packed with a sandwich, a few pieces of fruit and two plastic water bottles. On the seat beside her were her camera, cellphone and a large-scale map of eastern Kazakhstan. The tanker she was tailing was around a hundred yards ahead.

After half an hour of frayed nerves behind the unfamiliar wheel, she had started to relax and was now actually enjoying what, for the moment, had become, simply, a pleasant countryside excursion. For the first time since Zhang Liu's disappearance she felt what might even have passed for exhilaration.

"'When I let go of what I am",' she quoted quietly to herself. "'I become what I might be".'

She had hatched a plan several days before she left. If the tanker destination was close by, then all well and good. If not, following one tanker for a significant distance meant an increased chance of being noticed. She would use the regular departure of the big vehicles to her advantage, following one to the far outskirts of a town before, peeling off, spending the night and then falling in behind another the following morning. That way there was very little likelihood that she would even be noticed. If, on the other hand, the tankers were heading out to several destinations, then she was in trouble.

By midday, she was, according to her map, approaching the turnoff to Kurchatov, once the center of operations for the Semipalatinsk Soviet atomic bomb test site, out on the lonely steppes nearby. Rumors of ongoing secret activity in the radioactive and forbidden ghost town of Akbota continued to circulate and this, Jia thought, might be a possible destination for the tankers. She moved up slowly to within a dozen meters, rather than lose touch with the truck ahead should it turn suddenly in towards the site.

The driver continued on down the road towards the town of Semey without giving the turnoff a second glance. Jia was momentarily disappointed and then immediately relieved. Even Semey, a significant distance from the epicenter, had suffered horrendous illnesses and birth defects as a result of the Soviet testing.

By the time the signpost announcing their arrival at the toxic town appeared up ahead, she'd been behind the featureless tanker for over 300 kilometers. She followed it across the river, stayed in touch until it began to accelerate away from the city's eastern outskirts and then pulled off and located a place to sleep.

An early frost still glistened from the roadside stubble as she fell in behind another tanker next morning. She tracked it for around another 300 kilometers as far as Kokpekty. Outside the tired little town the road forked. The main road continued southeast along the lower shore of Lake Zaysan while the other road struck off due east towards the ferry at Bukhtarma. The driver gave a couple of peremptory flashes of his indicator and took the left-hand fork. Jia was indulging in dreams of her Beijing childhood and sailed right past the intersection. She slowed and spun the car round; her balding tires spraying stones as she accelerated away and back onto the correct road. Way ahead she could make out the tail lights of her quarry and was about to settle in for the chase when she noticed a grove of trees on the banks of a small stream that crossed the road. She pulled in and passed an uncomfortable and anxious night sleeping in the icy car.

Day three brought light snow and the first tanker thundering by not long before midday. Jia pulled out onto the now narrow road and followed from a distance as far as the Kaznakovska ferry at the Bukhtarma River. She slid into place on the oily deck three or four vehicles behind the truck and stayed in the driver's seat for the voyage across the wide waterway.

A few minutes into the crossing the tanker driver opened his door suddenly and jumped down onto the steel plate, his heavy boot-soles making a resounding clang. He looked in her direction and then started walking briskly towards her. She hit the door lock button. She was trapped, cars in front and behind and water all around. Her fear was as cold as the glass through which she watched his approach.

He squeezed in beside her driver's window and indicated for her to open it. She wound it down no more than two inches.

'I'm out of smokes. I can't get any until Kurchum,' he said in heavily accented Russian. 'Do you have one I can borrow? Buy?'

She smiled and hoped he couldn't hear her drumming heart. 'No, I'm sorry, I don't smoke.' She watched him in the rear mirror as he tried the van behind her, then shifted her attention to the cars between her and his truck. In her anxiety at seeing him approaching she hadn't noticed that the drivers had left their seats. She was simply the first person he'd reached. Jia didn't know whether to laugh or cry and so chose to do neither. She waited patiently until the ferry docked and then followed the truck to Kurchum, hung back surreptitiously while the driver stopped for cigarettes and then fell in behind him as far as Terekty. The stress of following the tankers without being noticed was beginning to take a toll – the tightness in her neck was making her head ache – and so she called it a day, treating herself to a cheap bed in a modest guesthouse.

10

BY THE TIME Liam's papers for Xinjiang were all in place, the first cool breaths of spring were infusing Beijing's blossoms with watery color. As Islamic fundamentalists ranged ever further from their Middle Eastern dens, so the central government imposed ever greater restrictions on the freedom to travel to the country's west. It was, ultimately, only his press card and some cockamamie story about doing a feature on the natural beauty of the Kanas Lake that had swayed the carelessly indifferent public servant dealing with his file.

Two days later he was 30,000 feet above the bleached beige of the Gobi Desert en route for Urumqi. He wasn't sure who was seated behind him, but up ahead was a sea of glossy black hair. As far as he could tell he was the only Westerner on board. A pity, he thought. Impossible to keep a low profile when you 'stood out like dog's balls'. He smiled to himself. It was another Australianism Charlie had passed on with relish.

The key had been in the Beijing bar fridge as Charlie had promised and on arrival at Urumqi he located the locker and transferred the pistol to his hand luggage. The tour bus he'd booked for the ride to the bottom of the lake didn't leave for another 24 hours. The trip in from the airport did nothing to make him feel a need to explore the attractions of the city; the number of Chinese soldiers and angry-looking Uighurs prowling the streets suggested his hotel room was the prudent place to be, until the bus left.

He lay on the lumpy bed, stared at the ceiling and asked himself over and over again: 'What am I doing here? Why am I here?' The unanswered question traveled with him into a restless, fractured sleep.

On the bus he was, again, the only Western face. It was still very early in the season and there were no more than a half dozen others traveling. Thankfully, the group of tourists were so elated at the thought of their visit to the lake that, apart from a couple of curious glances as they pulled away from the Urumqi curb, they seemed completely indifferent to his presence. A flight, of course, would have been quicker but the thousands of small rag-tag bus operators were far more likely to fly under the radar.

Late-afternoon light filtered through the hilltop pines as the bus trundled its way into the first of the small settlements at the foot of the lake. He thanked the driver and started walking north towards the lake's southern shore, approaching a scattering of rustic timber cabins, tacky souvenir shops and a low-rise resort hotel with what, to Liam, looked like a couple of Swiss bell towers. Very few of them appeared to be open yet. Judging by the chill air lurking in the shadows, spring was clearly some time off in the high country and the area was all but deserted. He skirted the buildings, made for the track leading through the lakeside forest and, making sure nobody was about, melted into the darkness beneath the trees. He removed the battery from his phone, wrapped each piece separately in foil and buried them in shallow soil next to an unusual-looking conifer. He changed his tourist sandals for sturdy boots and set off at a quick trot along the western edge of the crescent-shaped lake. An hour in he made camp for the night under a rock buttress, a hundred meters above the pale teal water. Dinner for the next few days would be dried fruit, energy bars and a small serving of cold rice made almost palatable with the addition of a few unidentified vegetables, chili and soy sauce.

A low mist obscured the waters below as he set off in the pre-dawn hours. By mid-morning he'd reached the top of the silent lake and was climbing a desolate river valley towards the northwest. Apart from a cluster of deserted huts, probably used as shelter by nomadic shepherds seeking summer pastures, he seemed to be the only indication that humans had ever inhabited the planet. As the sun sped on ahead of him he reached the junction with another valley that carved its way through the peaks to the south. He crossed the broken river stones, climbed to a ridge 3,000 feet above, running north-south, and then found a sheltered place to spend the night.

Daylight saw him off the ridge and into a chaotic landscape of tumbled peaks and troughs that offered no topographical logic. They seemed to explode outwards to every compass point, determined to short circuit the sense of direction of even the most seasoned navigator.

In a high valley, with the tiny first blades of spring grass peeping through the snow, he came across a small, restive group of sheep. He scanned the area, looking for a shepherd, but the place was silent, deserted. And then he saw a shape, a small dark contour in the wet melt a hundred yards away. He walked over slowly, hand on the gun at his waist. There was no need for caution. The man's body, clad in the rags of a poor mountain shepherd, had a neat bullet hole in the center of its chest. Images of James came cascading back and Liam dropped to his knees and cried out involuntarily.

He looked around, but only the sheep had heard him. They watched him warily as they moved a little further away and then began fossicking for sweet shoots again.

'The fuckers didn't even have the sense to bury you,' he said to the dead man. 'Or the decency.' He pulled a small collapsible shovel from his pack. 'I guess I know what kind of animals I'm dealing with now.'

* * *

Nurse Beggs strode briskly into the darkened room and drew back the curtains with practiced ease. An early light filtered in and found the pallid grey face of the old woman framed on the pillow by wisps of hair of the same cold shade.

The sad, demented Ruth Rigby had at last joined her only child.

The final frail breath had sighed from her wasted body some time during the night but to Nurse Beggs this was nothing new. Within the hour the corpse had been made ready for disposal and the room was being prepared for its next transitory occupant.

Ruth Rigby's still-intact letter was found among her few possessions and finally torn open by the bustling woman. The letter was a simple official statement informing the old woman of the death of her son Lionel.

Nurse Beggs had a niece who was a philatelist; Beggs preferred the term 'philatelist' to the more common 'stamp collector'. The official letter had been mechanically franked so was swiftly consigned to the trash along with the family photographs. A second, padded envelope, however, featured two very attractive Russian stamps featuring traditional bucolic scenes. As she began to tear them carefully from the upturned envelope the contents slipped out and dropped, open, into her starched lap. A note was attached to a newspaper clipping.

The handwriting was decidedly wobbly and, to Beggs, appeared to be the effort of someone anxious and hurried. She studied the note, then folded it back and looked at the newspaper story. Her frown grew in intensity as she read. She returned the papers to the envelope with the stamps still largely in place, hesitated with it poised above the trash bag for a second or two and then, in a moment of uncommon altruism, slipped it into her handbag and made a mental note to detour via the post office when her shift ended.

* * *

As each episode of her self-imposed quest played out, Jia became more anxious. There were now no further Kazakh towns to the east. The Chinese border was at best just two miles away, but her map indicated no crossing anywhere nearby. Ahead, the road they had been following passed to the east of Lake Markakol and then forked. One route climbed into high mountains and returned north and then west to Bukhtarma. The other seemed to peter out no more than 50 miles ahead in the foothills of the range. She looked up from the map to see snow still clinging to the distant peaks.

Noon had been and gone before the next tanker ground slowly through the town on the following day. She fell in behind and stayed well back, afraid the driver would notice her on the now-deserted road. The wide, repetitive landscape she'd endured for days was being replaced, at first by low hills, but as they approached the lake they began to climb through heavily wooded range country and puddles of slush appeared scattered along the verge.

At the junction north of the lake the driver turned, once again, to the east. Ahead now was nothing but China and snow-capped mountains. The road surface was unsealed and, in places, hard going. Jia was pleased that the little Suzuki offered more clearance than a normal small car but was tempted several times to turn back and run for the sanctuary of home. Only the strength of commitment to her father stopped her. She estimated they were now no more than 20 miles from the track's end and stayed just close enough to ensure she could see the dust cloud from the vehicle up ahead. After four challenging days she was not about to lose him now. She passed one tiny settlement, the only sign of life a silent dog indifferent to her passing, and was then swallowed up in a wilderness of trees, streams and steep hills.

She crawled along now, fearing that the end of the track would present itself after every bend. The road made a sudden loop across a stream to the north and then headed southeast across a long straight section on the edge of a narrow valley. Ahead, through evening gloom, she could just make out the tanker as it pulled in at some sort of low facility. The driver climbed down, opened a gate and drove in.

Jia reversed quickly back into the sanctuary of the trees. She noticed an almost imperceptible track following the stream edge to the north. She bumped along it for a hundred yards and then, in a grove of thick trees, turned off and gunned the engine deep into the undergrowth, with small pine branches slapping at the windows from every side.

Driving, day after day, intent on the road around her and the trundling vehicles ahead, had given her little opportunity to reflect on what she was doing or what, in reality, she hoped to achieve. Now that she appeared to be at journey's end all the doubts and anxieties came rushing back. She'd been trying desperately to meditate, to settle her adrenaline-fueled nervous system, for no more than 15 minutes, when she heard an engine laboring back along the track. She stole across the clearing to the far edge and peered out into the long valley. The fuel tanker was on its way out, coming directly toward her, its lights cutting a swathe through sleeting snow. At least she now knew the destination of the endless stream of clandestine fuel deliveries.

She returned to the Suzuki and sat, alone, scared and shivering in the driver's seat. 'Why am I doing this?' she asked herself yet again. But the answer, of course, preceded the question. Zhang Liu. He was the answer. He was the reason.

She would wait until nightfall and then attempt to see if her long journey had revealed anything or had simply been one more impetuous and futile exercise. She didn't have long to wait. Winter, reluctant to leave, continued to cling to the valleys and it was fully dark within an hour of her arrival. She zipped herself into her wet-weather gear, laced the sturdy mountain boots and shrugged her small pack onto her now-bulky frame.

Snow drifted across her face and settled on her lashes as she crept slowly to the edge of the clearing. Ahead the track was silent, empty. At the far end she could make out a cluster of lights, but no sign of movement. Her boots crunched softly on the freshly fallen snow as she edged down the path, ready at any moment to melt into the woodland alongside. A hundred yards out she left the track and covered the remaining distance through the trees, with every nerve end tingling.

A peeling, grey, faded sign clung tenaciously to a single remaining upright at an angle that allowed Jia to read it in the glow from the nearby lights. A single word, 'Vladimirova,' had been smeared onto the warped plywood by a hand not schooled in the use of a paintbrush.

The settlement was tiny, poor and old and did nothing to justify the title of village or even hamlet. A few dismal dwellings crouched behind ramshackle fences. The reverberating silence suggested that the residents here were too deprived, even, to own dogs. One or two grimy windows were illuminated by either dim oil lamps or candles but the rest of the tumbledowns were in darkness. Jia slid silently past, intent only on the brightly lit fenced area ahead. Behind the high razor wire she could make

117

out numerous large fuel storage tanks. The compound still seemed deserted, silent, and it was only when she approached within a few yards that she noticed the man in the booth by the gate. She threw herself behind a stack of old palings. The scent of pine, still clinging somehow to the ancient timbers, filled her nostrils. She watched and wondered what to do next.

The decision was taken out of her hands. The growl of an engine, perhaps several engines, filtered through from somewhere to the east. Within minutes it grew into a deafening roar as a fleet of brightly lit all-terrain vehicles bumped through a narrow gap between the high foothills and rumbled up to the gate. The man left his booth and swung the heavy metal inwards. Jia noticed the rear of each vehicle was fitted with a large tray top and fastened to each tray were several bulky fuel drums. The drivers positioned themselves alongside nozzles attached to the storage tanks and began to fill the drums. As each vehicle was done the driver climbed into his cab, left the facility and waited on the track outside the gate. The final multi-wheeler pulled up to the rear of the waiting convoy and the driver climbed down and walked forward to speak to the man in the lead vehicle. Jia, without thinking, leapt from her cover and sprinted across the dark space between the timbers and the end vehicle. She was on the tray and under a tarpaulin before the drivers had completed their conversation.

She had no idea where she was now headed or what she would find when she got there. The process had developed a life, a momentum, of its own; she was a rider on a runaway rollercoaster. The ride was under way and she had no choice but to sit there clinging on desperately until the end. If only, she thought, she could scream.

The laboring of the engine and the roughness of the ride suggested they were climbing steeply over very rugged terrain. She managed to lift the edge of the tarpaulin momentarily to see nothing but headlights reflecting back from deep drift snow. An hour passed, then two. Jia was making a mental tally of her bruises when she was thrown forward against one of the drums as the vehicle stopped. She crawled to the edge of the tray on the far side, lifted the tarpaulin again and craned to see ahead. Another gate surrounded by high razor wire, another bright light making a small illuminated pool in the surrounding darkness. But this time, a difference. Two armed men in greatcoats were shining their flashlights beneath the tarpaulins up ahead. Once again instinct cut in. Jia dragged the canvas to one side, rolled off the tray into the snow and clambered off up a slope towards a small outcrop of rocks.

Hour after hour crept by, daylight came and went, and as another sunset approached she was still crouched, numb, frightened and freezing, in the same location. The fuel convoy had disappeared through the gate nearly 24 hours before and since then all had been silence. She had managed a few minutes of fractured sleep during the night and had dreamt, in the death hours before dawn, of a sky dark with hornets, swarming angrily back to their nests.

She was out of water. Her meager food supply was exhausted; so was she. She was out of strength, out of resolve, out of ideas. She had no idea how to move forward and no idea how to get back to where she'd left the car. She considered throwing herself on the mercy of the people beyond the fence but knew intuitively it would be suicidal. Better to die out here, behind this rock, of exposure, exhaustion, hunger and thirst – something that seemed more likely with every passing moment of indecision.

* * *

The map Liam carried was significantly less than 100-per-cent accurate, but it managed to provide an overview that he hoped would keep him on track to his destination. By early evening, on the second day, he was above the snowline, kitted out in his pristine white suit and slogging west across a saddle, beneath a series of serrated pinnacles towering to over 8,000 feet. Opposite, beyond a deeply shaded valley, another seemingly impenetrable wall of summits looked to be a thousand feet higher. A few final slivers of sunlight kicked off the western edges of the high peaks; all else was enveloped in early twilight. Liam had seen no sign of human activity since the nomad huts two days before and was startled when, as he approached the crest of a snow mound, he almost walked into a high fence topped with razor wire. Somebody had actually gone to the trouble of painting the woven metal white and, in the fast fading light, it was all but invisible against the surrounding snow. The barrier barred access to the edge of a steep drop-off a few yards ahead, making it impossible to see into the valley beyond. He retreated to a distance of around a hundred feet and then, crouching low, moved parallel to the fence, attempting, wherever possible, to keep all but the top of his head and his wary eyes below the ridgeline. Small, white painted boxes at intervals of a few hundred yards suggested some kind of camera surveillance. He burrowed into an icy crevasse between two stone buttresses and waited until it was fully night.

Liam's plan was to follow the fence to see if it would lead to anything of interest but, within minutes of the last, weak, westering light giving way to complete darkness, his nocturnal reconnaissance was interrupted.

The first indication that something was about to happen was a soft humming, the drone perhaps of a distant swarm of bees. The sound grew in intensity until, one after another, a series of sinister bat-like shapes, marginally darker than the surrounding night, leapt free from the valley, turned quickly to the north and disappeared over the unseen ranges.

Liam had the old Nikon out in an instant and had fired off two rolls, aperture wide open at a sixtieth of a second, before the sounds of the fleeing shadows had been consumed by the far tiers of their stone amphitheater.

There were no lights and the images, of course, would be next to useless, but he knew everything he needed to know about their source. They were aircraft, stealth aircraft, and several dozen had been disgorged, in mere minutes, from the deep valley below.

Now, more than ever, he needed additional information. He bent low to the crunching ice and continued along the looming fence line. The faint glow of starlight reflecting from the pale surface allowed him to keep the gleaming razor wire in view. After a mile or so the fence swung away to the right and followed a steep downhill slope. A mist was percolating in the valley and he was within a hundred yards of an imposing gate in the fence before he saw it. He dove for cover into a mound of snow, dug himself in, once again, and waited. Without a set of bolt cutters or a platoon of marines, there was clearly no way into the facility. The bolt cutters were in his bag; the marines, however, were unavailable.

He watched and waited, knowing from bitter experience that an hour or two after midnight was the only moderately sensible time to take senseless risks. An hour passed, then two. He was dozing fitfully when his body clock kicked in. He uncovered the illuminated dial on his wristwatch. Just after two. He slipped through the snow to a section of fence that appeared to be out of sight of the cameras on either side.

He checked the wires for electrical current. None there. One potential problem sorted. He was not aware, as he worked with the cutters on the lowest strands, of the camera concealed independent of the fence, standing sentinel on the ridge above him.

* * *

Apart from a bank of monochrome monitors on one wall, the interior of the cinder-block room was bare. It was also ineffectually heated. A group of men wearing heavy military-issue coats sat dozing on small, uncomfortable folding chairs.

One of the men, perhaps a little younger than the others, opened his eyes, yawned and looked sleepily up at the screens. As his eyes skimmed from one to the other he glimpsed a small movement near the bottom of a frame. He checked the number taped to the monitor. Camera 12. Not far from the main gate. He punched at a couple of buttons, grabbed a joystick on the desk and zoomed in to a tighter shot. The quality wasn't great but he was almost certain a ghostly pale figure was working at the fence with some sort of cutter.

His string of loud curses had the other men wide awake within seconds, one already on his feet, his hand on the firearm at his waist.

The younger man indicated the offending screen. 'Look at this shit. I think someone's out there.'

The senior man, a tall Russian with a grey moustache, took one look at the screen and then bellowed loudly. 'You two, get the fuck out there and find out what's going on. And be fucking careful – there could be more than one.'

Moments later Liam heard the growl of a diesel engine as a vehicle roared up to the gate on the other side of the fence. A heavily swathed figure jumped down and opened the gate, then returned to the vehicle. Someone else was driving, Liam realized, because the all-terrain was under way before the first man was fully back into the cabin.

It accelerated for a hundred yards and then skidded to a halt almost directly below him. He crouched lower, ditched the cutters, slipped the pistol from his pocket and flicked off the safety. A bright searchlight beam cut a razor line through the swirling mist below. It roamed left and right and then settled on the slope a few yards below Liam's location. One of the men began lumbering through the snow toward him while the other climbed down and stood next to the idling motor. To the first man's right and a little way above, a rocky outcrop created a darker patch in the pervasive gloom. Without warning, a small, pale grey figure broke from the rock cover and tried, with great difficulty, to escape up the snow slope in a direct line toward Liam. The leading man made no attempt to give chase; he reached for what was probably a holster and dragged out a hand gun. The driver dove into the cab and came out holding a semi-automatic weapon. The first man fired as the fleeing figure stumbled in the knee-deep slush and the bullet missed its target by just inches. Up on the ridge, Liam's soldierly instinct kicked in. The leading man was downed before he had time to get off another shot; the second had his weapon halfway to its firing position when he too began to leak bright blood onto the shadowy snow.

The grey hooded escapee glanced around, seemed uncertain for a second and then kept coming. Liam leapt from cover, threw his full body weight over the other much smaller figure and shoved it face down in the snow. His pistol was pressed hard against the head. He checked methodically through the anorak pockets and the small pack. There were no weapons. He removed a phone and a small camera and then he heard the sobbing. He flipped the body over to reveal a young and clearly terrified Chinese woman with a faceful of snow. She was about to scream when he clapped a big woolen mitten across her mouth.

'Do you understand English?'

She nodded, wild eyed.

'I'm not going to hurt you. I'm a friend.' It occurred to him that he was yet to establish whether he'd taken the right side in the altercation, but something about the young woman told him he had.

'This place is going to be swarming with angry people very soon. We need to get going quickly. Put some miles behind us before dawn. Okay?'

She nodded. He took his hand carefully from her mouth, she sobbed once or twice and then sat up.

'I must trust you,' she said tearfully. 'I have no choice.' She clambered to her feet and, as a light snow began to fall, started to lead the way up the slope and away from the fence. Without being told she seemed to know to walk on ice or rock wherever possible.

As he went Liam removed the cards and batteries from her camera and phone. He pocketed the camera card and hurled the remaining pieces into a deep cleft off to their right.

They'd been going for 15 minutes when he heard the sound of chopper blades cutting up the sky. He grabbed her, threw her onto the fresh snow and, once again, leapt on top of her, his big frame covering her entirely. Her natural instinct was to struggle violently.

'My suit,' he said to the wide eyes, petrified once again. 'My suit, it covers up body heat, infra-red. If I don't do this they will see your heat. Do you understand?' He wasn't sure she did but she nodded quickly and he could feel the tension in her body ease as a little of the fear left her eyes.

The helicopter came in low through the darkness, raking the falling snow flakes with its brilliant beam. It banked, came again, hovered a hundred yards away momentarily, then disappeared beyond a looming summit to their left. Liam waited for the drumming of the rotors to die away, helped the woman to her feet and urged her to move a little more quickly.

They loped on into the east until he saw the first crayon smudge of dawn define the ridge line ahead. The woman moved silently and without complaint but she was slowing him down; he sensed she was near exhaustion. He had enough food to last one person a few more days but with two of them one would go hungry. But then, he decided, he'd done that before. He found an overhang which concealed a deep bank of snow and, while she lay spread-eagled and panting, dug out a snow cave. 'We'll have to block the entrance once we're in. I hope you don't suffer from claustrophobia.' She forced herself upright. Her blank stare suggested 'claustrophobia' hadn't made it into her English vocabulary yet. 'We'll soon see, I guess,' he said, smiling for the first time in days.

Liam had the entrance sealed well before the cloud-scrimmed sunlight cleared the high country to the east and they sat silently, eating dried apricots and watching their snug sanctuary transform gradually into the interior of a dimly lit white egg.

'The first 48 hours will be the most dangerous,' he said to the stranger invading his personal space. 'They can't use snowmobiles over this terrain, but there'll be more choppers, people on foot and possibly dogs. I hope the snowfall will have covered our scent.' He turned awkwardly to look at her; she seemed to be listening closely. Her expression was grave.

'They'll be turning over every stone,' Liam continued. 'After that they'll conclude we've somehow slipped through, probably scale down the search. So the sensible thing for us to do is to stay put for a couple of days. They'll still have people monitoring our potential escape routes, airports, stations, but they won't be looking as hard.' He turned again to gauge her reaction to the concept of two days of extremely close proximity. She was asleep.

Liam turned to face the wall of soft snow and within minutes each was confronting their individual, but remarkably similar, dreams.

✳ ✳ ✳

'My name is Jia.' She was kneeling in the open entrance to the snow cave looking down at him as he opened his eyes. It was the first time she'd spoken in over 24 hours.

To Jia, the young Western man who towered over her was a strange, silent and exotic creature. To Liam, the delicate Chinese woman, with big expressive brown eyes, was a strange, silent and exquisite creature. But sharing thoughts and feelings was, for the moment, a way off and any exchange between them, even in this most intimate of circumstances, was formal and functional.

She indicated the snow opening. 'I did not do this until I was sure there was no sound. During the day I heard the barking of dogs but they were very far off. I needed to,' she dropped her chin demurely. 'You know.'

'Yes, I know. I need to go myself.' Liam flushed a little. 'Did you bury the...? We must cover everything with deep snow.'

She nodded. 'I did.'

Liam crawled from the confined space, stood, stretched, listened for a few moments and then disappeared behind the overhang.

'My name is Liam,' he whispered, as he reappeared. 'We must stay here until it's safer.' He held up two fingers. 'Two more sleeps.' He fired off the two remaining shots in the Nikon, removed the film, walked a dozen paces and dropped the camera into an icy crevasse. Jia watched him, bemused.

'If we're found and they find the camera on me there's less chance I can hide the film. There are places I can hide the film in an emergency.' He produced the ghost of a smile. 'The camera wouldn't fit.'

She continued to look bemused.

Inactivity for 24 hours would normally see the old black dog stalking him once again and this was inactivity in the extreme. But for some reason the young woman's presence appeared to act as an antidote. They consumed his meager rations. She refused to take any more than precisely half a share and by the third day they were surviving on melted snow. They slept, they peed,

125

they stretched their limbs when it seemed safe, and, eventually, they began to talk. The conversation, at first, was halting and fragmentary. It concerned, primarily, the people from whom they were hiding and what they were up to. Jia told him briefly of her search for Zhang Liu, his secret files and how she came to be courting death in such an unlikely location. Liam told her, less briefly, about James, about the aircraft, about his mother. It occurred to him that at no other time in his life had he spoken so candidly to anyone he'd known for just a few short hours; perhaps not to anyone, period.

From time to time a helicopter would circle over a valley nearby or the sound of distant dogs would fracture the stillness but as the hours passed the mountains returned, gradually, to their state of interminable silence.

As darkness settled in on night three they set off towards the lake. The respite seemed to have restored Jia's energy and she managed Liam's slightly modified pace fairly well. The decision to return via the lake had been made after some consultation. No other route offered any greater safety and, at the very least, Liam had an idea of the lay of the land. They moved only at night, holing up throughout the day. Once they'd joined the lake shore at the northern end they exercised even greater caution, staying off the path wherever possible and approaching any bend, rise or corner silently and with great care.

An hour or so before midnight as they approached a small incline, his finely tuned nostrils picked up a whiff of pungent tobacco. Liam, against Charlie's advice, had not disposed of the pistol in the snow and it was still in his pocket. He signaled for Jia to leave the lake's edge and they skirted around through the conifers, slightly uphill of the path. Through the foliage they could see a man sitting on a fallen pine trunk. He cradled what looked like an Uzi machine pistol on his lap. The small pinpoint glow from his cigarette wasn't enough to illuminate his features but, as Liam watched, his head appeared to droop from time to time. The forest ahead had been the victim of a strong wind and was a dense tangle of fallen trees and broken branches wedged against near vertical rock. The man had chosen his location well and the only way ahead was either a perilous high-country detour or along the path. Liam drew the gun slowly from his pocket and eased the safety catch. As he lifted it to take aim, Jia sensed a sudden change of mind. Liam handed her the gun and indicated without words that she should keep it trained on the nearby figure, then set off silently down the gentle slope, moving over the pine needles between the trees like a furtive ghost. The dozing man didn't feel the impact of the rock that glanced off his skull. Liam grabbed his collar and dragged him some way into the undergrowth; he was still breathing shallowly.

Jia, wide eyed again, arrived through the undergrowth. 'Did you kill him?'

'No,' Liam said shortly, binding the man with his own belt and boot laces and then filling his mouth with a large section of his shirt and tying it tightly in place with a sleeve. 'He may not survive anyhow but I don't kill people unnecessarily.'

She handed the pistol back to him and he buried it alongside the Uzi in a shallow hole a hundred yards further up the hill.

'We were too close to the settlement for me to risk a gunshot,' he said in a matter-of-fact way. 'We should be there in under an hour. We need to get away pronto. Once this guy is missed they'll probably be swarming all over us again.'

They covered the remaining distance quickly. In the darkness it took him a while to find the satellite phone, buried near the forest's edge, but, when finally located, it still held one bar and a signal and he used the last of the battery power to call Charlie's number.

'Goddam, what is it with you waking me up in the middle of the night.'

'If you have any favors left with your people in Urumqi, we need a ride out of here. Quicksmart.' Liam had no time for banter. 'Details later. My battery could go any time. Southern end of the lake. We'll be in the trees on the western shore behind the big hotel. Tell him to come to the edge of the forest and break off a branch.'

'I can do that,' Charlie said. The line went dead.

11

FOR THE PAST 24 hours, executive jets and commercial airliners had been disgorging men in dark suits onto airfields from Berlin to Belfast. Private choppers and limousines had then whisked them quickly away and now here they were – ensconced, anonymous and concealed – on a hunting estate near the Highland shores of Loch Glencoul. To any nosy locals they were simply an early group of wealthy stalkers, up for the deer, the antlers. To the rest of the world they were of no interest.

A row of supercilious, gilt-framed royals in period dress looked down their patrician noses, indifferent to the more contemporary power of the group below them, assembling round the banquet table in the great hall.

Ed Polson used his right hand to slide his sleeve back, revealing his outrageously expensive watch. He had ridden high as the arrogant, shameless CEO of one of the vast transnational investment banks, personally making a few fraudulent billions on the bubble that finally burst to become the Global Financial Crisis. He had followed this up with a second fortune made from selling short, betting against the securities he'd sold on the way up. If all went well with this bunch of turkeys, a third fortune of inestimable size was on its way.

He observed his colleagues carefully as they arrived, allowing himself a tiny smile of contempt. Names were not used, never spoken, but these were some of the most powerful individuals on the planet. And yet almost every one of them, each time they opened their mouths to lie, or became anxious, exposed their own little behavioral quirk. One scratched the right side of his nose; another tugged at an earlobe; another cracked his knuckles nervously; and a fourth coughed quickly into a closed fist.

The aristocratic British banker directly opposite was the exception, far too cool, too in control, to expose his hand. As

Polson watched the others, he watched Polson; in silence.

'We started our activities some time ago, as you all know,' the leonine banker began in an exaggerated Oxbridge accent, when the room had finally settled. 'You are also aware that they have been working remarkably well.' He stood and walked across to the portraits, his back to the table.

'However.'

He studied the assemblage of long-dead nobility above him for a moment or two then turned. His face would have been quite at home among those on the wall.

'Achieving the results we wanted, as quickly and effectively as we have, has come at a cost. We have seen a few small, unintended consequences.' There was a hint of military precision in his walk as he returned to his seat. 'We have also had a minor security breach at one of our many facilities; however, as is our approach to everything, we intend to address it with the utmost diligence. As a result we have been required to reassess the health of our financial status.' He held up a thin sheaf of papers, but made no effort to share them. 'Regrettably we will need another tranche of payments from all of you before the month is out.'

The sandy-haired man at the far end of the room removed his glasses. He placed them carefully on the table and scratched the right side of his nose. 'My people are not able to contribute any more, I'm afraid. We have already stretched ourselves to breaking point. If this thing has gone over budget, the money must come from others.'

The room was silent for long seconds. A sudden crack of knuckles echoed loudly around the cavernous walls.

'We have gone too far down this particular road to stall because of a few miserable billions,' the aristocratic man said softly. He raised his hand in a conciliatory gesture, but the movement somehow conveyed more menace than warmth. 'I suggest you try a wee bit harder. You will find the necessary amount, I have no doubt.'

Polson smiled grimly. Christ, and I thought I was a hard bastard.

Charlie was as good as his word. The first glimmer of dawn still hung back reluctantly beyond the lake's far shore as a van pulled up on an unmade track behind the hotel service entrance. A man climbed down from the driver's seat, flicked a cigarette onto the dirt and then ground it out with the toe of his shoe.

A true pro, Liam observed. Although, to the uninitiated, it would have seemed an innocuous act, Liam could tell that in those few moments, the man had conducted a thorough analysis of his situation.

Nobody was about, nobody yet watching. He strolled nonchalantly to the edge of the trees, appeared to relieve himself and then idly snapped a twig. Jia and Liam were out of the forest, into the rear of the van and covered in bolts of colorful fabric before the final ember on the man's discarded cigarette glowed out.

They traveled in silence until the scattered dwellings had been left behind. The road followed a fertile river valley not yet fully greened by the shoots of spring. Within an hour they were down from the mountains and crossing a wide parched plain. The driver spoke for the first time. Liam thought he caught the rhythms of Mandarin and proved to be right when Jia threw off their cloth covering and knelt up behind the vacant passenger seat. 'He says we can sit up now, but must watch the road ahead.'

Liam studied the slim, graceful lines of Jia's back as she conversed animatedly with the man up front.

'He is Uighur. From Altay. He is proud that he was able to respond to your needs so promptly. He says the call came from his friend in Urumqi at midnight and he was on the road in just a half of an hour.'

Liam nodded his thanks. 'Can you ask him if he has seen or heard anything unusual up near the lake, the mountains?'

Jia translated and the man replied with a shrug.

'This is the first time he's been north of his home town in 20 years,' she said. 'Local people don't go up there.'

Liam nodded his thanks. 'Can you tell him we need to get out of China very soon? We can't risk the airports.'

The two conducted another energetic exchange.

'It is best to go through Kazakhstan, he says. The PLA…
Chinese army, is too busy to think about one foreigner traveling
to the west. They are too busy sending the soldiers from Urumqi
to Tibet and the southeast. There is a lot of unrest there, along the
Yangtze River – maybe even civil war, they are saying.'

The Uighur driver chuckled and nodded his head. For him,
the departure of the Han troops was clearly a source of great
satisfaction. He continued his exchange with Jia.

'He says the Kazakh border is not more than one hundred
kilometers from Burqin, a town that is an hour ahead on this
road. If we can wait until tonight he is certain he can get us
a ride with a friend carrying goods to Kazakhstan. Sixty
kilometers over the border there is a town called Zaysan with
an airport.'

'What about visas? My passport has no stamp for Kazakhstan.'

Jia interpreted for their Uighur rescuer. He made a lofty
gesture above his head and spoke at length.

'This is a border crossing that carries a very great amount of
freight,' she translated back to Liam. 'They are very casual, they
search very little, especially on the Kazakh side. He says they
probably have, how would you say it, an 'arrangement' with the
drivers. Often Western travelers cross the border without getting
a chop.'

The Uighur man nodded and grinned into the rear-vision
mirror. 'No problem,' he said in heavily accented English.

'If there is a problem I can fix it for you, I'm sure. I speak
Kazakh language,' Jia said. 'I know how they operate in that
country.'

Liam looked doubtful.

'I live there,' she added brightly.

* * *

Dashka had never seen another woman on the island and, to be
honest, she'd never seen another woman, anywhere, like the one

who was being helped down from the large private helicopter by two men in tight suits.

It was a cool, late-spring day and the prospect of visitors all the way from Moscow gave Dashka the opportunity to add a little femininity to her outfit by tossing a bright cotton scarf around her shoulders.

The other woman's scarf was of shot silk; her coat, despite the relative warmth, of heavy sable. She wore tall patent leather boots to her knees, Thierry Lasry sunglasses and had long, unblemished, crimson fingernails.

Dashka stole a quick glance at her own. Short, ragged in places and, in spite of all the scrubbing, engine oil still clinging to their undersides. She hid her hands behind her back.

Alexei announced the staff names one by one, without bothering to name the arriving visitors.

'And what is your role?' the woman asked from behind her expensive shades, in what sounded to Dashka like a French accent.

'I'm the base motor mechanic,' Dashka said, producing a warm smile. 'I fix the machines.'

'How quaint,' the woman said. *'Charmant!'* The three visitors joined Alexei and his assistant Sergei and they disappeared into the laboratory, locking the door behind them.

'Who were they?' Dashka asked an hour later, as the helicopter lifted from the stony ground.

'Government people,' Alexei said evasively. 'They wanted to see the facility for themselves. They are considering an upgrade.'

The visit seemed to be a turning point and things on the base became progressively more dysfunctional with each passing day.

In the past, in Dmitri's time, when her work was up to date she would spend time with the men in the facility, talking to them about their activities and asking endless questions. Nobody ever seemed to mind. It was a friendly place. But no more. It was made very clear that she wasn't very welcome and whenever they left the rooms unattended Alexei or Sergei, his upstart minion, would lock the door.

With each passing week Alexei Gavrilov and his assistant

became more and more taciturn. Dashka was left with nobody but the adolescent Ivor to whom she could confess her distress, a workload she could keep under control with very little effort and an inclination to restart seriously considering the likelihood of getting employment somewhere else.

'What is this all about, Alexei Denisovich?' She asked one afternoon, after she had been the target of Sergei's contemptuous dismissiveness for the third time in a single day.

'My apologies, Dashka Anasovna.' He seemed momentarily discomfited at being confronted but returned to his role of impassive superior almost immediately. 'We have a great deal of work to get through each day and we can't afford to be distracted.'

'That's nonsense,' she laughed. 'There is no more work to do now than there was when Dmitri was here. There wasn't all this unpleasantness then. The place was welcoming to everyone.'

She gave another scornful laugh. 'What is it? Are you afraid of burglars all the way out here?'

He tried the conciliatory approach. 'Perhaps you need more people around you, Dashka Anasovna. That boy is not good company. You have been working out here in all this isolation for too many years, under very difficult circumstances. This is not a good place for a woman. You are lonely, tired maybe. I have been thinking it might be wise for you to consider moving on. We'll revisit the issue in a little while. Meanwhile there is plenty to keep you busy round the base.'

He unlocked the laboratory door and paused, key in the lock, for just a moment. 'There will be a supply ship towards the end of the year, I'm sure if you choose to leave, then head office will give you a good reference.' He entered the room, closed the door on her and Dashka heard him lock it from the inside.

* * *

The massive vehicle was the local equivalent of an 18-wheeler. The driver was reasonably happy to transport them across the border as far as Zaysan, but wanted payment for the risk he was taking. Their Uighur rescuer seemed embarrassed by the man's unseemly lack of graciousness and the two of them had loud words in the local tongue. He turned, eventually, to Jia with an apologetic shrug and muttered something quietly.

'He would like American dollars,' she said to Liam, pointing at the truck driver.

Liam dragged a small bundle of notes from his money belt, counted out several fifties and handed them to the man. 'That's all he gets,' he said firmly.

The driver nodded his satisfaction and the three men shook hands. Their gallant and gracious liberator bowed once to Jia, turned, climbed into his van and disappeared in a billow of diesel smoke.

Shuddering with the effort to be freed from its inertia, the big rig pulled slowly out of its Burqin parking bay as the sun disappeared below the distant Kazakh horizon. An hour or so later the powerful high-beams cutting through moonless darkness fell across the first line of nondescript Soviet-style buildings straddling the border.

Liam and Jia, huddled in a corner of the trailer behind high stacked boxes of cheap Chinese appliances, were unaware of their arrival at the border until the brakes began to grind the rig to a stop. They crouched in the darkness, listening to the muffled voices just inches away on the other side of the aluminum frame. Jia shrugged. She could not make out what was being said. The sound of a bolt being drawn back made her jump. A bright beam from a flashlight flooded through the opening door at the trailer's rear and sent sharp shafts between the stacked boxes. They heard someone grunt with effort as he heaved himself up onto the metal tray. The light probed the darkness around them, throwing huge rhomboid shadows onto the roof above their heads. A short discussion was followed by the sound of two men laughing and then the darkness returned as the bolt was shot. A few minutes later, the idling engine was thrown into low gear and the load moved ponderously off into Kazakhstan.

* * *

Jia's drab grey coat ended its useful life in a garbage skip outside a small department store in downtown Almaty.

The driver had apparently misunderstood his agreement, had bypassed the hamlet of Zaysan and its regional airport and carried them all the way to the sleeping city. Dawn was an hour away as the two fugitives stood sore and weary on the roadside and watched the tail lights of the big rig disappear into the murk. Almaty was a stroke of luck, Liam realized. The chances of scoring a trouble-free flight out of the country from a hectic international airport were greater than those from a small regional airstrip. These invariably meant few flights and bored officials desperate to alleviate the tedium of their day in any way possible; including closely scrutinizing foreign, stamp-free passports.

They sat side by side now, but already on different journeys. Liam was booked long-haul to Australia via Singapore. Jia's flight was a short internal hop.

In spite of his protestations she had insisted on returning to her home in Pavlodar. 'You have found your father,' she admonished him. 'I have not.' She explored the pockets of her unfamiliar red anorak unconsciously. 'What if he is somehow back in Pavlodar, hiding, sick, injured?' she asked unrealistically. 'I must return.' She found another label, unpicked the string carefully and tossed it into a nearby bin. 'Nobody saw my face, they know nothing about me. There is no reason for them to link me to Pavlodar or my father.'

'What about the car you drove?' He asked. 'Can they link that back to you if it's found?'

She appeared momentarily embarrassed. 'I borrowed it from an old man who can no longer drive, he has, what do you call it?' She tapped her eyelids with two fingers.

'Cataracts?' Liam offered.

She shook her head. 'No blind. He is blind.' She colored up again. 'He didn't need it so I took it. But that is another reason I must return. I must pay him for it.'

'But can he lead them back to you?'

She sat quietly, clearly contemplating the car issue. 'I don't think so, his memory is not so good. I don't think they will find it anyway. It is hidden very well in a forest near Vladimirova; the village where the tankers collect their fuel for taking up to that place.'

She paused, suddenly recalling the reason behind her unsuccessful journey.

'Perhaps my father is still there,' she added sadly. 'I will send you his papers. Maybe you will know what they mean. I am not a scientist, I don't really understand them very well. But perhaps they may show why he is missing.'

'At least get rid of the grey anorak if you insist on going back,' he had said earlier, as they had waited in a bus shelter for the airline offices to open. 'If there is a link back to your father then that's one of the things they'll be looking for.' She hadn't protested too much when he had insisted on paying for the coat, a pair of matching mittens and a new cellphone.

'This is my number. If you have any sense that things are not right, contact me immediately; get out of there. Try to get to Ireland. You'll be safe there. You can stay with my mother. Nobody would think of looking for you in Glengarriff.'

His flight was first to leave. They shook hands awkwardly and then Jia leaned forward quickly and brushed her lips against his cheek. 'Thank you,' was all she said before walking away, leaving him at his departure gate feeling strangely desolate.

* * *

The voice on the line was from long ago. Cherry Davitt recognized the broad cadence but was unable to put a face to it.

'It's Bob Schultz, you helped me out on a case some years back.'

Cherry retrieved the face belonging to the voice from storage somewhere in her cluttered memory. 'Oh Bob, hi, yeah. I did. It was that disappearance I think. Dobson, Dawson…'

'Dyson,' he said.

The voice was still familiar but it had changed. She remembered it as being filled with bourbon-fueled vitality but now it seemed tired, troubled.

'How are you, Bob?'

'Fine,' he brushed the pleasantries aside. 'My apologies for the weekend call. I've come across some stuff on the Dyson case. I've been doing some digging. I can't talk now. You remember where we met last time we spoke?'

She delved back in time again. 'Yeah, I think so, was it on...'

He cut across her. 'I'll see you there. Same time as back then.' The line went dead.

'Christ, Bob,' she said to the empty apartment. 'That was years ago.'

She dredged through all her saved emails but none were anywhere near old enough to provide answers. She scrabbled around in the bottom of drawers, old handbags and a long discarded briefcase. Nothing.

She poured a coffee, sat staring out at a bleak Washington Saturday and began a mental tour of the city. The name of a Georgetown bar on Wisconsin Avenue popped into her head. She opened Google Earth, went into Street View and found the place. It was familiar. Yes, that was it. Thankfully nobody had bothered with a paint job or renovation in years.

'Join me for a drink round six,' he'd said each time they'd met. The memories weren't flooding back, they were returning a few trickles at a time.

No not six, she corrected. Six would have been too long for Schultz to wait for that first bourbon of the day. Five. 'Join me for a drink round five.' That was it. Five.

Cherry spent the rest of the afternoon trawling the online archives, filling in the gaps in her imperfect recall of the Dyson story.

By a quarter to five she was in the bar at the same table in the same dark corner they had shared years before. She was reasonably certain that even the drink rings left on the stained timber in front of her had not changed.

She ordered a white wine and waited.

By 5.30 the glass had been drained and she was beginning to doubt the reliability of her memory. Maybe it was six. She waited until 6.30 and then called the precinct house.

'Officer Schultz isn't back on duty until Monday,' the desk sergeant said in response to her question. He refused to give her a cellphone or home number.

She checked her cell. His number wasn't in her directory. His call earlier in the day had been to the apartment landline.

At seven she left the bar and walked the few blocks back to her apartment. Her concern mingled with a little irritation. She'd been certain it was five. 'Why in God's name did he not just give me a place and time? Why the cloak-and-dagger stuff?'

The answer appeared to arrive with the nightly news bulletin.

'We have a breaking story right now,' the glamorous blonde newsreader said, feigning concern. 'A Washington police officer, Detective-Sergeant Robert Schultz, was killed earlier today in a hit-and-run accident in Georgetown.'

'Shit,' Cherry said, diving for the volume control.

'Detective Schultz was off duty at the time, around five this afternoon,' the newsreader continued. 'Eye-witnesses say a black SUV mounted the kerb, impacted Detective Schultz with great force and carried him for some yards before leaving the scene at high speed. Detective-Sergeant Schultz was pronounced dead on arrival at Georgetown University Hospital. Inquiries indicate that Schultz had no family. Police investigations are continuing.' The somber expression was replaced in a flash with a winning smile. 'And now it's over to Wayne for a wrap-up of all today's sports news.'

Cherry spent the following days trying to convince herself that Schultz being killed and the strange call he'd made to her were unrelated, that the two were simply coincidental. It didn't work: her attempt to reassure herself failed dismally and she quickly concluded that, for the time being, it might be prudent to keep his mention of the long-closed Dyson case to herself.

In the guise of a journalist simply demonstrating professional interest, she pestered the Metropolitan Police Department on a daily basis, but they had no information relating to their investigation of the detective's death. The plates on the SUV were false and there were no leads. None of his current cases, they claimed, suggested he might be in danger. 'Investigations were continuing.'

Her own discreet search for friends, partners or confidantes, anyone to whom Schultz might have spoken, hit a brick wall. If he'd discovered any new information about the mysterious Dyson, he had, it seemed, kept it very much to himself. There seemed nowhere to go with the story, nobody to ask, and so the Dyson file with its black ribbon was again put to one side as more pressing business piled up on her desk.

12

CHARLIE HELD his hand up to protect his eyes from the harsh Queensland daylight as he exited the darkroom.

'Well, you're not gonna win a Pulitzer for photojournalism for that little lot,' he said, using a thumb to indicate a group of still-wet pictures hanging on a line in the red photo-light gloom behind him.

'It was the middle of the night,' Liam said defensively, then smiled. 'And, besides, I was using a shitty old camera.'

'Yeah,' Charlie said. 'A very valuable shitty old camera that I no longer own.'

Liam entered the darkroom and examined the images through a magnifying glass. It was possible to detect a grainy outline of several aircraft against the sky. The shapes, once again, closely resembled that of the B2 Spirit stealth bomber, but they provided no detail.

On the bench beneath the poor images from the Nikon was a frame shot with the zoom lens on Jia's little camera. It had been taken some hours before the two men rushed from the remote compound intent on putting a bullet into someone's head. A board next to the gate on the white fence displayed a sign in Mandarin.

'According to Jia, the sign claims this place is a Global Seed Vault. You know, like the one at Svalbard in Norway.'

Charlie shook his head. 'You'll be surprised to hear there's actually something I don't know.'

'Svalbard is a big, permanently frozen, underground facility that's used to preserve as many of the planet's species of plant seeds as possible.' Liam said. 'They're basically duplicates, extra copies of seeds held in other gene banks around the world. The project was designed as an attempt to insure against the loss of seeds in other gene banks in case of major regional or global crises.'

'Yeah, sure,' Charlie said cynically. 'And this lot needs a fleet of stealth bombers to protect a few corn cobs. I don't think so.'

Liam tapped the photograph with an index finger. Picked out in red were the characters 未来的繁荣.

'Jia told me these symbols say *Wèilái de fánróng*,' Liam explained. '"Future Prosperity" in English.'

'Future prosperity for who and what?' Charlie muttered, still cynical.

Liam led the way into the other room. 'I guess the next question is, where does this leave us?'

Charlie shrugged his big shoulders. 'All we know now, that we didn't know before you took your little trip and lost my precious camera, is where the goddam things come from. We're still no wiser as to why. Right now I'm not sure what we do.'

He dropped heavily onto a chair and ran frustrated fingers through his unruly hair.

'What I do know is that you don't go to the trouble of creating a facility in a godforsaken place like that if your motives are innocent. You don't build a fleet like this if your motives are innocent. These things are almost certainly nuclear capable: they can drop bombs, nuclear bombs. If they're anything like the Spirit, they have an 7,000-mile range, they can fly at over 700 miles an hour. This location is swimming in a soup of nuclear powers. Russia, China, India, Pakistan. Whoever these people are, they've obviously managed to keep this thing below the radar.' He laughed without humor. '*Above* the radar, for Christ knows how many years. From a pivotal location like that they could be bombing every major city from Dublin to New York and beyond before the poor bastards'd had their Weeties.'

'If it's an Asian thing, maybe we should go to the Western media with it.' Liam didn't sound hopeful.

'Go to the media with what? What have you actually got?'

'Well, there's the pictures, the ones Dad took too, the aircraft black box, the tricked-up satellite sites, Dad's body with a fighter plane's bullet hole in his chest...' he trailed off.

'And what if it's not an Asian thing? What if it's bigger than that?' Charlie used his thick fingers to catalog the tenuous nature of Liam's evidence. 'The pictures you took are not worth the paper they're printed on. They could be anything, anywhere. The pictures your dad took are better but what do they prove? An aircraft crashed? Somebody claims they're doctored and how do you prove they're not? You could be dealing with very powerful people here.'

He headed for the fridge and collected two beers, slipping them into a couple of insulated rubber holders.

'You've been an Aussie too long,' Liam laughed.

Charlie ignored him, took a swig from his bottle and continued, his fingers still acting as props for his argument.

'The flight recorder could be from any goddam aircraft and if we front up to the press with that orange monster we're likely to end up doing ten years in maximum security. Christ knows how many aviation regs and international laws we broke with that little caper.'

He took another long draft from his bottle and stood it on the kitchen bench. 'Your father was obviously murdered and that, combined with his pictures, might raise their interest, but he's currently on top of the world's most dangerous goddam mountain and someone would have to go back there and bring him down.'

'Summer's not far off,' Liam said. 'I'd planned to do that anyhow.'

Charlie shook his head sympathetically. 'Frankly, young Liam, I'm not even sure that would achieve anything. Someone claims his buddy Dawa went berserk and murdered him with an ice ax and that's all the doubt the story needs.'

'It doesn't stop me needing to bring him down,' Liam said softly.

'Yeah, I understand,' Charlie nodded. 'Meantime the doctoring of the satellite data is probably your strongest point, but, even then, where does that leave you? If these people are as influential as they seem to be, you'll be told it's a technical glitch. Someone would have to get permission to visit the site to verify your claims. If the Chinese government are in on it, before they allow that, they'll create a stone wall, tell you it's a seed store, shift the evidence, update the aerials and you'll never find out anything. If they're not involved, don't know about it, then by admitting its existence they lose a tremendous amount of face. Unacceptable. So again you run up against a brick wall and, once again, you'll find out nothing.'

He helped himself to a second beer. Liam had hardly touched his.

'We need to know more, try to find out who's doing this and why,' Charlie continued. 'It's not smart to go public with it until we do. We tell the wrong people, we probably end up like your old man and they get on with whatever they're up to like nothing has happened.'

'What about Cherry, my ex-editor?' Liam suggested. 'I'm sure she's straight up and down. Maybe we can leak the story out there via her.'

'And risk getting her killed too? Bring her in by all means, but if she's as good as you say she is, she's not gonna take a chance on anything until you have your ducks in a row.'

Charlie walked over and gave the very despondent Liam an encouraging pat on his shoulder. 'Basically, we need more information. We need to find out who they are and just exactly what they're up to with these aircraft.'

He ambled across the room and stopped at the doors leading out to the abandoned pool terrace. There'd been no young women gracing it for weeks. He turned and pointed his beer bottle in Liam's direction.

'We follow the inevitable footprints in the sand. A project of this enormity, if it exists, would require a huge construction facility somewhere – they wouldn't have built the aircraft up there in that frozen, isolated valley. They'd need hi-tech materials for construction, computing technology, fuel. There must be a hundred ant trails out there. You can't keep something this big a complete secret, no matter how powerful your influence. Industry, military industrial complex, government, it doesn't matter, someone will make a mistake, there will be leaks. I know from sad personal experience. Find one of those and you have a thread back to their source.'

He belched loudly, then carried his bottle across to the kitchen bench and poured what remained into a glass.

'No matter how secure they are made, how well they are kept, eventually the secrets start to leak out. We find out where the secrecy is and break it and we're on our way. Eventually these things go wrong, they fall apart and the bigger they get, the more things there are to go wrong. Keep looking, you'll find a chink.'

He walked over and lowered his large frame onto the edge of the coffee table in front of Liam's chair. 'But it's not something to be done lightly, buddy. If we go after this we make sure we stay under the radar. No more calls from your own phone, buy burners and get rid of them regularly, no more using your own computer. Always use different IP locations, make sure there are firewalls, look over your shoulder continually. This place is pretty secure, but if we're on the road, we don't stay at any one address for too long. We let as few people as possible know where we are, only ever talk to people in the open wherever possible and, in the end, trust nobody. There is something very weird here and that suggests powerful forces at work.'

He rapped Liam's knee with his big knuckles. 'Above all, be careful. You're not old enough to end up dead yet.'

They sat in silence for several minutes.

'There is another way, of course,' Charlie said eventually. 'You post some of this stuff online, put it on your goddam Facebook page and then wait. That way they'll find you.'

He peered over the top of his glass and grinned. 'It does entail some risk of course.'

'Maybe I should just go see Cherry anyhow, before I do that,' Liam said. 'There's some legal stuff I need to tie up for my mom over there. Can't do any harm dropping in on her at the same time.'

***

Pavlodar had changed. No, that was wrong: she, Jia, had changed. In spite of the bravado she had shown when she and Liam went their separate ways, she now lived her life with fear always her silent companion. Whereas she had once tolerated the town, even as she despised it, now she feared it. The house seemed exactly as it had, the streets, the shops, even the refinery all still shared the same superficial blandness. But now, just below the town's surface something evil lurked. She knew she was being fanciful but there was nothing to be done. She had gone off on a naïve adventure, looking for her father the way Nancy Drew would have done and come back, finally initiated into real-world horror.

And, among all the strange occurrences of the past weeks, perhaps the strangest of all was that she missed the tall, quiet Irish-American. She missed Liam. They had not shared so much as a warm dumpling and yet there he was, almost constantly in her thoughts.

Nobody had missed her, on the other hand. Nobody had even noticed she was away. As far as the people at the refinery were concerned, she'd been at home with the flu.

Well, that wasn't quite true. Ruslan, when she arrived with his favorite noodle dish, said he had missed her. While he ate, she apologized profusely and paid him for the abandoned car.

The post office was not far from police headquarters, so, on her third morning back she mailed her father's files to the strange address in Australia Liam had scrawled on a coaster for her. She then spent the remainder of the day visiting the police, the neighbors, the people in the laboratory, but none were able to throw any new light on Zhang Liu's whereabouts. They shook their heads sympathetically and changed the subject.

Another brick wall and, not for the first time, she had no idea what to do next. There was no point accusing anyone at the refinery, no point in announcing to them where she'd been or what had happened. She was a Chinese woman in a foreign land; a Buddhist female in a land dominated by Muslim men; a woman tolerated politely but never totally accepted. She would be dismissed as hysterical; or worse, as insane.

Still, deep inside now was an ember, waiting to be fanned, ready to burst into flame. She knew something that possibly nobody in Pavlodar knew. Possibly not even Yuri. She knew about the strange site. The site that people were prepared to kill for. That was her glowing hope. If she was ever going to discover what had happened to her father, somehow she needed to find out what was going on in the remote valleys of the Altai and beyond.

With each passing day it became clearer. The site was in China and, if she was to find out anything, she, too, must be in China. She must, at some time soon, return to Beijing. She couldn't possibly know, as she bolted the front door, turned out the lights and snuggled down into the relative security of her warm bed, that she would be across the border again within 48 hours.

* * *

These days, mail that arrived via the US Postal Service rather than along a fiber-optic cable was becoming a rarity and, consequently, a novelty. Cherry spotted the large beige envelope on the desk as she entered her office and went directly to it. Inside was a faded, yellowing copy of the *Washington Dialog*'s front page. It was years old, dating back to the days of Walter Dyson's disappearance. The puzzling story had made headlines for a couple of days and this one had Cherry's byline just below the big, black, Times Roman capitals. She had referred to Detective Schultz in the text several times and in each case the name had been highlighted with a colored marker.

Cherry reached into the envelope and fished out two sheets of paper, one stapled above the other. She read the typewritten top sheet:

Cherry,
Enclosed is some material from a guy called Lionel Rigby. He was killed in Moscow the day it was mailed. I am looking into it at the moment. I will call you in a day or two to arrange a meeting. There's something very smelly about all this and so I'm sending a back-up copy to you. Just in case I go the same way as Rigby. Ha ha.
Schultz.
P.S. There was no disk in the envelope. More details when we meet.

Her heart stopped beating for a moment and then an instant later started thudding at a frantic rate. Nearly a decade had passed without a whimper since the Dyson story and then, out of the blue, Schultz's phone message followed by his deeply suspect death and now this; the belated delivery of a cryptic message in the mail.

She turned the page with a shaky hand. The second letter was written in a hasty scribble:

Dear Mother,

I am sorry to distress you. It is the last thing I would wish after having put you through so much. There is a possibility that something may have happened to me by the time you read this. You'll see the name of a detective in the attached newspaper story. If I am no longer around could you please locate him and give him this letter and clipping with the compact disk I have enclosed. It is vitally important.

Please tell him I know where Dyson, the man he has been looking for, can be found. He is a good man, I believe, and is in grave danger too.

'The disk contains the relevant material. I have made it as simple as possible. Mr Dyson can help with more detail.

Out of time.
Love always, L.

A number seemingly even more urgent in its scrawl had been added to the bottom of the page. *869372682027.*

Cherry re-read the letter then put it to one side and stared down at the photocopy of the discolored page. Dyson was a solemn, slightly harassed-looking man. His photograph had been sourced after some negotiation from a contact at the passport office. For Cherry, securing it had been the only modest success to come out of the entire sorry saga. And now this.

For once, the poised and professional editor of the *Washington Dialog* was at a loss.

A long online search eventually established that a Lionel Rigby had been murdered in Moscow some months before. And that was the sum total of her knowledge of the man, his cryptic message, his missing disk and his mysterious numbers.

* * *

Charlie watched the Sydney flight disappear into the late monsoon clouds. Even after all his years of flying he still marveled at the magic of aviation. At around the time he pulled into his driveway just up the way beside the Gloucester Passage, Liam would be landing in a city that his map said was over 1,250 miles away. Before the sun began to bake his Gloucester terrace early next morning, Liam would already be way over on the other side of the planet. He shook his head and smiled at the thought as he drove into town. 'Incredible.'

A bold red card in his post office box alerted him to the fact he had a parcel to collect. The queue at the counter inside was longer than he expected and, as it turned out, Liam was on the ground in Sydney well before Charlie arrived home.

The parcel was from Kazakhstan. It was addressed in a careful hand to Liam. Zhang Liu's files spilled out of their overstuffed manila folder onto the table as Charlie tore the wrapping. They were in Russian.

'Goddam,' he said loudly. Of course they were in Russian. It hadn't occurred to him when Liam said they were on their way but what other language would they be in?

'I hate Russian,' he said to Liam's now-vacant chair. 'Pashto, Urdu, Uighur, fine. Why did it have to be fuckin' Russian? This is going to take for fuckin' ever.'

By 24 hours later the table was littered with beer bottles, dictionaries and reams of screwed-up A4 sheets, but he had a translation for the bits he believed were important. Somewhere under the debris the phone started ringing.

'Goddam.' He swept the mess onto the floor, being careful to avoid the bottles, and found the cellphone among the pages of a book on Russian grammar.

'It's Liam. I had a layover in LA. My Washington flight leaves in a couple of hours. How's it going?'

'Your Chinese friend's stuff arrived. It was in goddam Russian. I hate goddam Russian.'

Liam's laughter sparkled down the line from the far side of the Pacific. Charlie smiled. It was a great laugh and it had been missing in action for a long while. And that was a great shame.

'A cunning linguist like yourself should have no trouble translating that.'

Charlie smiled again. 'You're sounding very frisky. Did you get lucky with a stewardess or something?'

'I wish. Have you done a translation, found anything?' Liam was all business again.

'There are no delivery documents, no paperwork from third parties, nothing like that, but there are component orders here that scream aviation fuel, there are invoice clusters that match in a lot of ways and that seem to be directed to the same unnamed clients, they all have common batch numbers. As my old mentor used to say, "Follow the money". I'm thinking that if I can find a way into their banking system I may be able to trace the payments made for this particular shit back to their source. A bit of a long shot but worth a try.'

'Sounds good. Good luck,' Liam said. 'I'll try to see Cherry in a couple of days.' There was a short pause. 'Okay with you if I come back then or do you want me and my crazy conspiracies out of your life?'

'No, no. Get your ass back down here ASAP. I'm beginning to enjoy this. Haven't had so much fun since... yeah, but that's another story.'

13

869372682027.

Cherry was trying again to make some sense of the number on Rigby's scrawled note. She'd jotted it down in big bright blue numerals and was gazing at it when a familiar face appeared around the office door jamb. 'Hi,' he said with a wide smile.

'Liam, what are you doing here?' She grinned back in spite of herself. 'I thought I'd fired you.'

'Just a social call,' he said. 'I had a few things I needed to finalize here for my mom.'

He was sun and wind burned, a little ragged around the edges and the superficial cheer on show wasn't able to conceal the troubled soul beneath.

'Come in, sit down.' She indicated the seat across the desk. 'How are you? Where have you been? What have you been up to?'

'Oh, here and there, this and that,' he said vaguely. 'After K2 I went off to see a buddy in Kathmandu, spent some time in Australia, Xinjiang… China.'

'So nothing much then,' she said, raising an eyebrow.

He was trying to decide whether he should fill her in on the events of the past months, share the conclusions he and Charlie had reached. But it all seemed suddenly so fanciful in this real-world city, so far away from the dreamlike wilderness of the Altai mountains and the dreamtime remoteness of Charlie's dry corner of Queensland.

He changed the subject. 'What about yourself?'

'This and that. This and that. A couple of interesting stories.' On a sudden impulse she spun the page of numbers across to him. 'Does that mean anything to you?'

He looked at the digits dubiously. 'I don't think so. Should it?'

'No, just wondered. Doesn't matter.' She reached over and retrieved the pad. He checked her with his hand and studied the number again. 'I think 86 might be the international code for China. I don't know if that's any help.'

'God, I'm stupid, why didn't I think of that?' she tapped her forehead with an index finger. 'Dummy.'

'Why don't I just ring it and see?' He reached for his cellphone. She leaned over and put a restraining hand on it. 'Not just now. Let's check with directories first.'

She reached for her computer and keyed in the information with flying fingers. 'International code, China, 86, right. 937, area code for...' She keyed again. 'Jiuquan. A place called Jiuquan.'

She looked up at him. 'Jiuquan. You said you were in China. Were you anywhere near there?'

'Not really,' he said. 'Jiuquan is maybe 500 miles away, in Gansu province, I think. I was in Urumqi. Xinjiang province.'

'What were you doing there? Urumqi?'

He frowned and, once again, considered the wisdom of entangling her in their seemingly bizarre exploits. She held his eyes with hers. They were wise, compassionate and without guile. He made a decision.

'It's a long, very unlikely story. If I tell you, I'm afraid you'll think I'm crazy and I'm also afraid by telling you I might be putting you in harm's way.'

'I'm a big girl,' she said. 'I can look after myself. Try me.'

Liam started with the discovery of his father on K2. He spread James's photographs from the mountain on her desk and watched as her face became progressively more stone-like. By the time he'd finished his story, the day beyond the glass had been replaced by the light-filled darkness of a Washington night.

'This is incredible stuff,' she said eventually. 'Unbelievable. I've never seen anything like it. Short of going to the authorities I have no idea what you do next. But I think you're right. You need to try to find out more somehow.' She sat back and shrugged. 'I can keep my eyes and ears open this end but I don't know where I'd start. Whatever is going on it's a long way from Washington.'

She stood and walked over to the coffee jug. 'Cold coffee?'

He shook his head.

She poured herself a cup and stood with her back to the night sky. 'I have a contact at Langley. I could do some poking about there I guess.'

Liam considered the offer for a moment. 'Thanks, but maybe not just yet. They looked like they could be modified American bombers. What if it's our own government that killed my dad? Maybe it's smarter for us to do a little more digging first.'

'I think so,' she said. 'But please, keep me in the loop.'

'We'll need to use prepaid phones from now on and ditch them at regular intervals. Are you okay with that?'

'I am, but the people who do my expenses may not be.' She laughed. 'I'll have to finance them myself.'

Liam stood and walked to the door. 'I'll be in touch before I leave, we'll need to swap numbers.' He paused and turned. 'Why are you interested in Jiuquan, by the way?'

'It's nothing really,' She demurred. 'Just some very old material that's come out of the woodwork. Nowhere near as interesting as your story.'

* * *

Ruslan was blind but he wasn't deaf.

Time meant nothing to him now as he sat in the dark. Midnight was no blacker than midday. He was sitting in the comfortable chair, lost in the roseate warmth of the past when the first scraping brought him swiftly back to the colorless present. A second scrape, then a click at the back door, was followed by two sets of footsteps entering the small kitchen.

'Christ,' a voice exclaimed in Russian.

No doubt he'd just been discovered. Perhaps, Ruslan thought, they've picked me up in a flashlight beam. He had no way of knowing.

'This is the guy,' the second voice said. 'He owns the car. Look at the license photo. That's him, younger, but him no doubt.'

'Well, it wasn't him driving, that's for sure. The old bastard's totally blind. Look.'

Ruslan imagined the light was being directed into his eyes, but once again, it was an educated guess.

'Who's been driving your car in the past few weeks, old man? Who's been driving the Suzuki?'

'I don't know,' Ruslan said. 'I didn't see anyone. As you noticed, I'm blind.'

'Don't give me lip.' The man's clenched fist sprayed blood from Ruslan's nose.

'Who was driving your car? Did you loan it to someone? Sell it?'

Ruslan had no idea what this was about. He was certain that it involved Jia in some way, but that was the extent of his knowledge and there was no way he was going to redirect these animals to his sweet, gentle and still-grieving friend.

'I loaned it to nobody. It was just sitting out there, anyone could have taken it.'

The man hit him several times. One blow smashing the socket above his unseeing eye. 'I don't believe you, you old fuck.'

'Believe me or not,' Ruslan gurgled through a mouth full of blood. 'It's the truth. Someone must have taken it.'

He endured two more blows and then the clearest thought he'd had in months filled his aching head. 'It's time for my heart to take its leave.'

And it did.

'They say he died of a heart attack,' the neighbor said to Jia next morning, her eyes wide with excitement. 'But the house was definitely broken into, they tortured him. Terrible. The police say it's likely what made his poor old heart fail.'

Jia said nothing, walked into the house and started to weep without restraint. She knew it was because of the car that he was dead. It could only be because of the car. There was no other logical reason. There had been no theft. Blind old men didn't get tortured in their homes for no reason.

She wept for her dead friend, she wept for her guilt, but mostly, she wept for his courage, his sacrifice. It was clear, now, that he had told them nothing, had not revealed that it was she who had borrowed the car; otherwise she, too, would now be on her way to the Pavlodar mortuary.

It was also likely that they would make the connection between

Ruslan and Zhang Liu's troublesome daughter fairly soon. She was, after all, a very near neighbor.

An hour passed, she wiped her puffy eyes, packed a small bag and locked the front door. She wheeled her bicycle around to the side of the house, collected a small fistful of the first spring daisies and took them across to Ruslan's doorstep. She placed them among several other modest posies. If there was someone watching she was simply another neighbor paying her respects.

By late afternoon she was on a flight back to Almaty. From there she would take a connecting flight to Beijing.

* * *

Breaking into the computers was a lot easier than Charlie thought it would be. The refinery's security software was amateurish and at least 12 months old. Their firewalls, with virtually useless IPs, were a joke, their encryption almost childlike. If you had financial transactions you needed to keep private, Charlie thought, this level of inefficiency was inexcusable. Somebody, either in the bank or the refinery accounts department, had been criminally sloppy. 'Then again,' he said to the unshaven image reflected back at him from the glowing monitor, 'as a conspiracy theorist from way back I have to recognize that leaving it accessible like this may just be a deliberate little trap.'

While the payee may have been lax, the payer was a very different story. A long, circuitous and complex search took him to every tax haven and dodgy banking establishment on the planet, some of them more than once, and had him pounding the desktop in frustration, with his dangerously large fist, and roaring at the night.

It took nearly 48 hours and the best part of a case of Hahn Premium, but around four in the morning he arrived at the location of the bank he was pretty sure was the original source. There were no more complex transfers, no tricky paperwork, just a simple and regular deposit each week. No matter what he tried, this was the end of the line – the name of the depositor was not about to be revealed. It was quite possible, Charlie considered, that these amounts were cash deposits. No paper work meant nothing to trace. Anything was possible in a frontier town and this bank was way out there on the western frontier of the Gobi Desert.

'How do you feel about another trip to China?' he asked Liam when they spoke later in the morning. 'There's something up there that may be of interest. It's not a million miles from our friends in Xinjiang and there's a very interesting satellite facility around a hundred clicks up the road, bang in the middle of a very empty desert.'

'Whereabouts?' Liam asked.

'Place called Jiuquan.'

Charlie waited for Liam's response. He was expecting excitement, congratulations, anything but silence. 'Well?'

'Jiuquan. That's incredible.'

'Thank you,' Charlie said. 'I thought so too.'

'No, no,' Liam said excitedly. 'Jiuquan. Jiuquan. Cherry was talking about it just yesterday. She was being cagey. She had this number, phone number. Look, it's complicated. I'm going to have to confront her and try to find out what's going on.'

'That's one hell of a coincidence,' Charlie said.

'Yes, I told her about...'

Charlie cut across Liam's attempted response. 'From now on we'll need to be a lot more careful when we're on the blower. This line should be fine but yours isn't. It's not a problem yet but it's likely to become one any moment now. We'll talk more when you get back.'

* * *

The moment Charlie had been fearing arrived with the 6.30 flight between Singapore and Darwin. Mr Paul's plane from Alice Springs had landed an hour earlier and he was waiting at the cafeteria table he had shared so often in the past with never a shred of pleasure.

The impeccably groomed man from Singapore lowered himself onto the plastic chair with a sigh and reached into a tailored pocket. 'There is a pattern emerging, Mr Paul.' He wiped the table as he had done a dozen times before. 'We are yet to locate whoever it was digging into our data, we still have no idea who was responsible for the breach of security, the people snooping about the site and now, in spite of what you reassure us is world's best practice, impregnable systems and all that, we have someone sniffing around our banks. Sometimes I wonder what we're paying you for.'

'Sometimes I wonder the same thing myself,' Mr Paul muttered. 'Certainly not for the hours we put in.'

'Be careful, Mr Paul. My capacity for tolerance only stretches so far.'

Paul ignored the caution. 'You'll be pleased to know that this time I have good news. We believe the source is right here.' He pointed to the east. 'In Queensland.'

'You *believe?*'

'We're almost certain. It's been a difficult one to crack. It's very isolated, off grid, well protected.'

'So are you saying I can deploy a team with confidence?'

'Well, yes, I guess.'

'You guess?'

For nearly a decade Mr Paul had found the man's arrogant sarcasm irritating. After all these years the bastard hadn't even deigned to provide his name. Lately it was becoming intolerable. 'Listen, you patronizing arsehole, I'm tired of putting up with your shit,' he said in a terse whisper. 'You don't pay me enough for this.' He looked around furtively to see if he'd been overheard. 'There is never 100-per-cent certainty with these things. Never.'

The man from Singapore ignored the outburst. 'How much certainty is there?'

'Ninety-nine fucking per cent, 98, that's the best I can do.' He dropped the small red flash drive onto the table. 'The location details are all there.'

He leaned forward and rested his hands on the table. 'And do you not think that after all these years you might at least have the courtesy to fucking well introduce yourself?'

The man glanced down at his Singapore Airlines boarding card. He smiled.

'Just call me SQ,' he said.

He slid the drive into a coat pocket, stood and, without a further word, walked away. When this was all over, he told himself, he would make this snotty little Antipodean pay for his insolence.

*＊＊

Cherry answered the buzzer, waited for the elevator to arrive and then, before Liam had a chance to ring the bell, opened the apartment door.

'Hello again,' she said. 'What's this about? What's wrong with the office? I'm not crazy about you bringing this stuff of yours into my home.'

'Sorry,' he said. 'I thought it was best we kept this private.'

'What's this?'

'You were looking at a Jiuquan phone number the other day.'

'Yes?'

'I was wondering why.'

'Why are you asking?' She seemed a little annoyed.

He shrugged. 'My friend's been in touch. He's pretty sure he's traced the bank the money's coming from. The money for the fuel the planes use.'

Her pulse rate increased. 'Go on.'

He gestured with his open hands, palms up. 'It's in Jiuquan.'

As warm as the room was, a sudden chill trickled down her spine. 'Holy shit.'

'The Chinese, it seems, have some sort of major facility near there. Very secret, apparently. Outsiders not welcome.'

As a teenager Cherry had read a novel called *The Celestine Prophecy*. It had been a little too new age for her at the time and its contention that there was no such thing as coincidence, that seemingly coincidental events always carried a message that should be interpreted and acted upon, had left her uncomfortable and skeptical. She had grown into an adult still armed with a healthy dose of skepticism, enhanced by her journalist's training, and the book had been largely forgotten. But now, here, this.

157

Within days. Liam and Dyson, China. Jiuquan, a place she'd never even heard of. One hell of a coincidence.

She walked into her bedroom, calling out as she went. 'Okay. I guess now I have something I have to tell you.' She came back in with a briefcase, took out a folder, opened it and dropped the photocopied *Dialog* page on the coffee table in front of him. 'Look at that. It came from a guy called Rigby. He was murdered a little while back in Moscow.' She headed for the kitchen. 'I need a glass of wine. *We* need a glass of wine.'

Liam read the newspaper story and had moved on to Rigby's letter when she handed him his glass. 'I need to sit,' she said.

They sank into the sofa's soft cushions and Cherry took him through the Walter Dyson story right back to the man's original disappearance.

'We were never able to establish what he did for a living.' She seemed suddenly excited. 'All we knew was he was in electronics of some sort.'

Liam looked puzzled. 'Why is that relevant?'

'It may not be, but you say these mystery aircraft look something like B2 stealth bombers, right?'

Liam nodded. 'As best we can tell. Bigger, but…'

'Well, Dyson disappeared from Arlington. That's no more than three miles from Falls Church.'

'So?' Liam said, still puzzled.

'Northrop built the B2 Spirit. Northrop are based at Falls Church and Dyson disappeared around the time your father photographed the thing that killed him.' She stabbed Dyson's photograph with an index finger. Now you tell me their money maybe comes from Jiuquan and according to the murdered Rigby, Dyson may be in Jiuquan too. Coincidence?'

Liam sat silently, sipping his wine. He shook his head. 'I don't know what to think. It could be just coincidence, but it's possible there's a link I guess. We don't have much else. Can I copy that phone number?'

She indicated the coffee table. 'It's on Rigby's letter. You can take that. I have another copy.' She took a pen from her briefcase and added some figures to the bottom of the letter. 'This is my burner number. I'll change it every few days.' She folded the sheet and handed it to him. 'Meantime I'll see what else I can find out about Rigby and Moscow.'

'Be careful,' he said quietly.

* * *

'I killed him,' Jia said, her tears obvious from thousands of miles away. 'He was kind enough to loan me his car and in return I led them to him. I had him killed.' She sobbed again.

She stood looking out at the Kazakh landscape beyond the runway, perhaps for the final time. She had no desire to return. Her father, she sensed now, if he was to be found alive, would not be found in Kazakhstan.

'You did everything you could, Jia,' he said gently. 'The car was well hidden, you said so yourself, and it was dozens of miles away from where we were seen. Some psychopath killed him. You're not to blame. They are. I'm just happy it wasn't you they killed.'

An inexplicable warmth grew out of the pit of her stomach in spite of her distress. 'Thank you,' she whispered.

'So what will you do now, are you safe?'

'Yes,' she said. 'I think so. I'm in Almaty again. I'm returning to Beijing tomorrow.' She hesitated. 'Where are you?'

'Washington,' he said. 'I had to finish off some legal things for my mother and see my old editor.'

An awkward silence followed.

'I may be in Jiuquan, in Gansu, in a few days,' Liam offered. 'Maybe I can come and visit you in Beijing when I'm through?'

The antennae that had become so finely tuned throughout her father's long absence locked in. 'Jiuquan? Why are you going there?'

Liam was silent.

'It's to do with this airplane business, the fuel, my father, isn't it?'

'Well, we have a possible lead we want to check, that's all. Nothing much.'

159

'It's on my way to Beijing. I can change my flight, meet you there.'

'No, Jia,' he said. 'It's not a good idea. It could be dangerous.'

Her soft eyes turned flinty. 'Oh, so for a small frightened Chinese girl it is dangerous but for a big brave American man it is not?'

Liam was taken aback by the power of her anger. 'It's not that. I just don't want to see you come to any harm, that's all.'

She softened. 'And I don't want to see *you* come to any harm. I have already been exposed to danger, very much danger and I have survived. I can be very useful. I speak the language and I am one of them, I will blend in. You will stand out like...'

'Dog's balls,' he said softly, off mike.

'Ruslan is dead because of me and my father is still missing. I must come. I *will* come, with or without your agreement.'

'Okay, okay.' He smiled. 'I'll let you know our plans in a couple of days.'

'You mean two days, no more?'

'Yes, all right, *two* days.' He smiled again.

14

THE LABORATORY hummed with the sounds of low, earnest conversations. On one wall a silent television monitor ran the latest newsreel footage. Oskar Frederik broke off from what he was doing and looked up at the screen.

'You are Nero fiddling while Rome burns,' he said angrily.

Claude watched the images on the screen dispassionately. She'd seen Third World villages go up in flames before. These people burned their neighbors' homes on a whim. These things happened. *C'est la guerre.*

She was far more concerned about Oskar Frederik. The man was no Lionel Rigby, that was for sure. Rigby, she had been able to bully and control. Oskar was as stubborn as Rigby had been malleable. For weeks the old man had refused to co-operate in any way and when, finally, he did begin to work, it was very much on his own terms.

The situation was becoming so combative that Claude grew anxious each time she needed to visit the laboratory. Frederik treated her with thinly veiled contempt and it wasn't helping morale in the place.

Claude would gladly have dealt with the troublemaker but, according to her superiors, the old man was not to be touched.

'If you people don't put a stop to all this very soon the consequences will be dire,' Oskar said with quiet intensity. 'I'm a scientist, not a magician.'

Claude gave a Gallic shrug. 'And I am the oily cloth, not the engineer.'

She left the lab and strode along the echoing corridor toward the elevator. The door was locked behind her. If all this was ever over she would make sure one of the primitives, *les primitives*, dealt with the old *connard* appropriately.

* * *

With nothing to do but stare at the back of your tray table and think, Liam told himself, a long black night at 30,000 feet should be delivering clarity. But instead, all it offered was more confusion. At every quarter he now confronted ambivalence. He worried deeply about leaving his mother to face her illness without him but, then, he needed desperately to discover who had murdered his father and why. He worried deeply about being responsible for leading Jia into danger, but, then, felt an unaccustomed exhilaration at the thought of being with her again. Calm logic told him the two disparate threads leading to Jiuquan were most likely coincidence, but, then, he was excited by the possibility that finding the mysterious Dyson might just provide the answers he was seeking.

Daylight and a perfect Queensland day brought no greater clarity.

'So you won't talk, eh?' Charlie said eventually, as the big SUV drummed along between ripening cane fields. 'Not a goddam word in half an hour.'

'Sorry,' Liam said, giving the big man a gentle punch on the arm. 'Worrying about my mother.'

Charlie looked concerned. 'Something happened?'

'No, I spoke to her yesterday, she seems fine. It's just guilt. Not being there, you know.'

'Yeah. I know.' Charlie nodded and bumped onto the unmade road. 'It's your call but I think we need to take that trip to Jiuquan. Maybe get some answers. Maybe just a week or two and then you can get back to your mom.'

'That's the other problem,' Liam said. 'I told Jia about Jiuquan. She insists on joining us if we go. Won't take no for an answer.'

'Her life, her call,' Charlie said after a brief pause. 'But I have to say amateurs always worry me. As long as she doesn't get in the way.'

They continued down the track in silence for several miles.

'How's your Mandarin?' Liam asked eventually, with just the slightest hint of defensiveness.

'Basic,' Charlie answered. 'Pretty basic.'

'Well, she may not get in the way then. Hers is perfect. So's her English.' Liam looked across to Charlie for a reaction.

He grinned, said nothing and nosed the SUV into a large, well-ordered equipment shed. He killed the ignition and led the way to the house.

'Way I see it is we have two possibilities,' he said over his shoulder. 'We try to get more information from the bank or we follow this possible Dyson thread of Cherry's. Neither one is a blue-chip option but we don't have anything else at the minute.'

Liam dropped his bag inside the front door and followed him into the computer room. 'Covert stuff in Nangarhar Province was tough enough, but I've been reading up on Jiuquan. The place is probably the paranoia capital of the universe; it's going to be a fucking nightmare.'

Charlie ignored the aberrant expletive, double-clicked the mouse and waited for the monitor to fire up. 'It would be a lot worse if the Chinese were still sending their official goddam shadows out with every foreign visitor. Now that was a fucking nightmare; used to drive me nuts.'

The screen flickered into life. It was cluttered with files, pages of numbers, codes and what to Liam's untrained eye looked like long lists of complex URLs.

'I've been trying to link that Rigby phone number to an address in Jiuquan. No luck so far. Somebody very competent is blocking it.'

'What about the bank?' Liam asked. 'Anything more there?'

'Nup,' Charlie shook his head. 'We may have to go over and shove a pistol into the manager's mouth.'

Liam checked Charlie's expression. He wasn't sure he was kidding.

'We have the Rigby phone number, we could just call it I guess. See who answers.'

'And if this character Dyson doesn't answer, we say what? "Can you put Mister Dyson on the line?" All we do that way is let them know someone's onto them.'

'What if a Chinese woman, say, a local woman calls, on a

163

local phone? If she gets Dyson she puts one of us on. If someone else answers. she apologizes... wrong number and rings off. Nothing strange about that.'

'You really want to involve Jia to this level.'

'She's already involved to this level. I have no say. She'll probably be in Jiuquan before we are. You can ask her what she thinks when we get there. It's her decision.'

'I'll need a few days,' Charlie said. 'Let me have your passport. I'll have to mock up an exit stamp. If you want to get back into China legally, it's better that you left legally.' He took Liam's proffered passport and dropped it on the desk then headed for the kitchen. 'Go get rid of that airline grime, I'll get you a *real* breakfast. A big Aussie breakfast.' He paused at the refrigerator door. 'We'll also need to come up with some way to get into that satellite facility.'

* * *

Candidates were, as usual, falling by the wayside, with every passing Caucus or Primary. With Wisconsin now out of the way, Arnott and Stone were still neck and neck, the two others remaining in the race a distant third and fourth.

The pundits, however, still had the incumbent President winning another term. They seemed keen to reiterate, as often as possible, that Stone and Arnott were birds of a feather, there was nothing to choose between them, and neither was cut out to be President of these United States of America.

Cherry checked their calculations. Normally she'd have been annoyed by the way they were being spun, but since Liam's visit the Presidential race had, gradually, seemed to be of less and less importance.

She'd been unnerved by the Jiuquan coincidence. Was it, in fact, a coincidence?, she asked herself during sleepless hours before dawn. And then the rational mind would take over once again and she'd move on to worrying about the practicalities. This was a story that had already involved several deaths and God knew how many others of which they simply weren't aware.

She knew the enormous risk Liam was taking in traveling to Jiuquan and worried about how much of an influence she might have had on his decision. She worried about the implications of the story Liam had told her, what it was actually all about and what its long-term repercussions might be. And she worried that she seemed helpless, stuck here as she was in Washington and unable to use any of her usual sources to try to get a lead, a sniff, the merest suggestion of what might be going on in those remote mountains.

* * *

The assassins, when they arrived, were remarkably low-key. The innocuous local charter yacht slid into the Gloucester Passage and nosed up into the gentle breeze. Three men in tropical shirts and shorts worked silently and methodically. One lowered the headsail, the second fed the anchor noiselessly into the still water, the third watched calmly from the helm.

A few hundred yards off the port beam they could just make out a scattering of low lights piercing the darkness along the shore. The tall blond man at the helm, the leader of the group, checked his screen. 'Montes cabins,' he said, pointing at the distant glow. 'Target's about five clicks along the beach.'

He fingered the button that illuminated the face of his watch. 'Departure from Hamilton Island at zero nine hundred. The pilot has been told not to wait.' He pointed into the darkness up ahead. 'Aerial surveillance tells us there are two subjects but we don't take that for granted. Check first. We'll have one hour to decide who we keep alive. There's only room for one in our gear.' He indicated a heavy-duty plastic case, used for transporting dive equipment. 'That means getting some very quick answers. We need to decide which of them calls the shots.' His two companions listened without responding. 'The isolation of the location is our friend: the odds are we'll be long gone before anyone notices anything. Either way, let's keep it quick, quiet and tidy.'

Around three, an hour or two before sunrise, the men, now in black skin-suits, slid silently into the tender and paddled parallel to the shoreline for several hundred yards, the feathered oars creating barely a ripple on the dark surface.

After five minutes of intense concentration on the dark landscape ahead, the leader of the group checked his GPS and then indicated for the paddlers to take the dinghy ashore.

He motioned them into the shelter of a clump of pandanus and pointed ahead. In the moonless darkness they could make out the outline of a large dwelling. They paused, slid thermal-imaging goggles over their heads and adjusted the lenses. Two of the men took machine pistols from their backpacks, the third removed a slim black metal case and opened it. Inside, cushioned against black velvet, were several steel syringes; they glistened in the starlight. He clicked the case shut and pointed to the house. They loped forward across the soundless sand.

Within minutes they'd located the generator room, disabled the power and disarmed the alarm system. The blond man worked the lock on the rear door while his companions stood to each side, machine pistols at the ready. The door clicked open and the three melted into the interior darkness in different directions. One by one they checked each room. Clear, clear, clear. Five minutes was all that was needed to establish the house was empty, deserted. Two beer bottles stood on the kitchen bench. The blond man checked them, a finger of liquid remained in one. Their targets were gone, but not long gone.

'Do we try to follow them? Find them?' It was the first time the dark-skinned man had opened his mouth in several hours. 'No, we're not equipped for that.' The blond man tried hard to conceal his irritation. 'We don't know when they left or where they went. We don't even know who they are yet. This is a fuck-up. We'll need to abort.' He pointed into the office. 'Get the computer and see if there are any others; we'll need to take everything with us.'

An hour later the charter yacht had cleared the Gloucester Passage and was on a heading for the airport at Hamilton Island. Charlie's computer was concealed amidst the dive equipment. But it was only one of his computers.

* * *

'Without Haste. Without Fear. We Conquer the World.'

The gigant ceremonial gate, though worn by time, was still the dominant feature on the roadside near the edge of the desert town. The vast scarlet characters in both Chinese and English proclaimed their message of indomitability to all who passed by. Most of the people wheeling their bicycles, riding three up on two-stroke motorcycles, or at the wheels of diesel-belching trucks, seemed to be totally impervious to the stirring proclamation.

Jiuquan appeared to be a mighty city built on sand. Empty apartment towers, in endless rows, marched towards the desert horizon in every direction, waiting anxiously, it seemed to Liam, for the future warmth and chatter of their yet-to-be-delivered human occupants.

'You scrub up very well,' Charlie said, eyeing the grey suit Liam produced from his luggage in the airport washroom. 'You could get a job as a bank manager.'

Liam managed a rueful smile but said nothing. It was the first time in his life he'd worn anything like it. He felt decidedly uncomfortable about meeting Jia again, dressed like a banker.

Charlie, too, sported a suit and carried a smart black leather attaché case. In it was a letter with a Washington address, printed crisply on a bogus US Media Satellite Inc letterhead. It was their ticket, if needed, to the commercial satellite launch facility.

A consortium of online publishers in the United States, it informed the reader, was interested in the feasibility of launching their own communications satellite. The two representatives in charge of the letter, it stated, had full authorization to act on behalf of the group.

A website had been created and a temporary office set up with a phone line and a receptionist to field any unwelcome enquiries from China. Cherry was to be the point of contact if the young telephonist struck any snags. 'I'll not only lose my freakin' job if this goes pear shaped,' Cherry said with some feeling when the idea was first floated. 'I'll probably end up in prison.'

Jia was waiting in her hotel room when the call came. She

167

hurried to the elevator and took it down two levels. Liam stood halfway into the corridor with his room door open. If she found the business suit strange she gave no indication it was so. Instead she produced a shy Chinese smile that made his soft Irish heart melt.

He could see Charlie warming to the young woman as soon as she entered the room and realized with surprise that he was actually relieved.

'Liam tells me you're determined to help us,' Charlie said, pouring three cups of green tea.

Jia nodded.

He slid the attaché case from the bed and took a package from the zipper section in the lid. 'I have a gift for you.'

She opened it and looked inside nervously.

'No deadly Australian spiders,' he said with a smile. 'Your new passport and PRC identity card. That's all. While you're in Jiuquan your new name is Meili. I don't want Zhang Jia to get into hot water on my watch.'

Jia opened the passport. 'But where did you get the photograph?'

'It was taken with a very fine vintage Nikon camera that a dear friend lost somewhere in the snow,' he said, raising an eyebrow in Liam's direction. 'I had to do a bit of doctoring. He's not the world's best photographer.'

Jia rewarded him with a hesitant little smile; she wasn't quite sure what to make of Charlie yet.

He returned to the open case and pulled out a wad of cash. 'The first thing we need to do is organize an apartment and a vehicle.' He paused. 'And a few other bits and pieces. Are you okay with using your local skills to fix that for us?'

'Of course,' she said. 'I need to find my father. I came here to help.'

'Once that's all organized,' he said. 'we'll go after the phone number again and the bank and if all else fails we'll keep the appointment we have out at the Satellite place. That's three days from now. It's a hundred-odd miles out into the desert, so if we can avoid the trip I'll be a happy camper.'

'Any results with weapons?' Liam asked.

'Still difficult this time,' Charlie said, shaking his head. 'If we meet people with guns we may just have to borrow them.'

Liam considered Jia in silence for a moment or two, then handed her a new cellphone and a folded piece of notepaper. 'This is the phone number Charlie's talking about. It may lead us to these people,' he said. 'Are you willing to try calling it?'

She looked from the phone to the slip of paper and nodded without speaking.

'If an American answers pass it across to me. If not, tell them you've called a wrong number, apologize and hang up.'

Jia called the number and waited for it to connect. A voice answered in Mandarin. She blurted out a quick apology and disconnected the cell with trembling fingers.

Charlie retrieved it gently from her hands, removed the battery and then took the sim-card from its slot and crushed it in his huge fist.

Liam stepped across and took her hand. 'Are you all right?'

'Yes, I'm fine,' she lied. But she continued to cling to his hand.

They sat silently hand in hand for several seconds. Charlie busied himself at the attaché case.

'I've been thinking.' Liam released her grip carefully, walked to the window and looked out at the strange city fanning out all around them. 'You said these may have been cash deposits.' He turned to face Charlie. 'Were they always made at the same time?'

'Within a few minutes either way I think,' Charlie answered. 'Why?'

'When was it paid?'

'Wednesdays, I'm pretty sure. Yeah, Wednesdays.'

'That's the day after tomorrow.'

Charlie nodded. The penny was starting to drop.

'Well,' Liam said. 'There's no reason to assume they're not still doing it. Why not simply wait at the bank around the time and watch for someone depositing a large amount of cash. If it happens then we follow. It's a long shot but it's worth a try.'

Charlie leapt up, stepped across to Liam and took his face in two big hands. 'You are a goddam genius, young Liam.' He gave him a big smacking kiss on the forehead.

Jia looked startled.

'Why didn't I think of that? I must be losing my sparkle.'

'Too simple an idea, probably.' Liam chuckled and tapped his forehead. 'Not intellectual enough.'

15

AN UNANNOUNCED helicopter was always a big event at Cape Zhelaniya. Normally the only contact with the outside world was the supply ship that came every few months, or the rare official flight from Arkhangelsk ferrying in new staff members and the occasional nosy bureaucrat.

The young woman, first to alight, strode across to Dashka, smiled a wide smile and shook her hand. 'Nataliya Petrova,' she said. 'Talia Pavelovna to my friends.'

Dashka warmed to her instantly. She introduced herself and then introduced Alexei, who seemed put out at being seen as of secondary importance.

'We're working with the UN,' Talia said. 'WHO. Checking the radiation levels across the islands. We're based at Russkaya Gavan down along the west coast there.' She pointed with a gloved hand. 'We thought we should start by taking readings here, given this is the only part of Severny Island that's inhabited. We'll try not to bother you too much.'

Her associates began to unload steel boxes from the helicopter.

'I doubt very much whether you will find any radiation here,' Alexei said tersely. 'We have a lot of work to do, if you'll excuse me.' He turned and walked quickly back to the laboratory building. At the door he paused and called out to Talia. 'We can't offer you accommodation here, we don't have the beds.'

'Don't mind him,' Dashka said, wrinkling her nose. 'A bit of submarine syndrome I think. He needs some bright lights.'

'I'm sure I'll be feeling the same after a few months of Russkaya Gavan. We'll be there through part of the winter unfortunately.'

'Too bad,' Dashka said. She introduced Ivor and pointed to the equipment building. 'We'll be up there if you need us. Please come in later and join us for lunch.'

Less than two hours later, Talia approached the building as Dashka was dismantling a generator. 'We'll be heading off now,' she said, seeming a little subdued. 'I came to say goodbye.'

'So soon?' Dashka stood up, handed her spanner to Ivor and wiped her hands. 'Finished already?'

'No,' Talia said. 'Your friend Alexei won't allow us into the laboratory complex to do our readings, not even the residential quarters. He says there is confidential stuff in there.'

'That's rubbish,' Dashka said spiritedly. 'They're just glorified clerks, that's all they are. Nothing confidential about that.'

She walked over to the doorway and looked down towards the complex. 'I thought it was just that they didn't like me, but now they're doing it to you.'

'It's a pity,' Talia said. 'If there's radiation there, that's where it will do the most damage. In there, where you spend most of your time.' She pointed across to the faded buildings with their dusting of snow.

'I'll talk to him,' Dashka said.

'No, don't bother. I don't want to cause problems between you. We've done a few readings around the exterior and it seems pretty low. Pretty safe. We'll just head off.'

She stepped over and gave Dashka a hug. 'I admire you for working out here like this. You must be a very strong woman.'

Dashka laughed. 'Sometimes I think I'm just a crazy woman.'

They watched from the doorway as Talia Pavelovna trudged down towards the waiting helicopter. She turned and waved and then the helicopter was gone.

'Strange,' Dashka said. 'We all know Alexei's a bit paranoid but making up some bullshit story to keep those people out of his precious lab. That's really weird.'

Ivor shrugged his shoulders but said nothing. The subject was of no interest.

* * *

The van edged carefully into a space on a side street close to Jiuquan's Drum Tower. The bank entrance was a dozen yards along and opposite. Charlie, a hat pulled low over his forehead, handed Jia a cellphone and without speaking she slid from the passenger seat and crossed the road. She glanced to her right, where a tall man sat astride a powerful motorcycle three car spaces down. A full helmet with dark visor in place made it impossible to see his face.

It seemed mid-morning was a quiet time for the branch and only two people were being served at the tellers' cages. Another man stood at a shelf against the nearest wall filling in a multi-page document.

Out in the van Charlie, slumped low in the driver's seat, punched the redial symbol on his cheap cell and lifted it to his ear.

Jia's ring tone echoed around the cavernous lobby. A teller glanced up briefly as she made for a quiet corner on the far side of the room and responded to the call.

'Remember, you're chatting to an old girlfriend, Jia.' He spoke very softly. 'Nice and light hearted, talk about anything, it doesn't matter but leave lots of pauses. Let your imaginary friend talk as well. If there hasn't been any action come ten minutes, finish the conversation and start making out an application for an account. Use your new identity. Take as long as you can without making them suspicious. I'll keep the line open but I won't speak unless I need to. Good luck.'

Five minutes passed and Charlie watched a half dozen people enter and exit the bank. One subject in a business suit carried a smart leather attaché case. Charlie lifted the cell and broke in on Jia's stilted monologue. 'Guy in striped business suit a possibility,' he whispered. He fired up the van's engine and waited. The man came out of the bank and walked back towards the Drum Tower. There was no sign of Jia.

Charlie was beginning to get anxious. Eventually, even a young woman chattering away quietly on a cellphone would start to attract attention in a bank. He was about to get her to move to phase two when a black Mercedes pulled up, facing into the traffic directly in front of the bank. A casually dressed man carrying a small backpack stepped briskly from the passenger side and jogged up the four or five steps to the entrance. Charlie spoke into the cell again. 'Okay, Jia. Another possible candidate on his way.'

She dropped the still-connected phone into her handbag and fished out a compact as the man approached a vacant teller window. She opened it and started applying make-up, watching the man in the small mirror at the same time.

He looked from side to side quickly, unzipped the pack and, as surreptitiously as possible, slid several bound stacks of banknotes across to the waiting teller. The teller scribbled something on a sheet of paper and passed it back to the man. He hoisted the pack onto a shoulder and strode across to the door, glancing once, with no great interest, at Jia as he went.

He skipped down the stairs, threw the pack onto the back seat and climbed back into the Mercedes. Jia stepped out onto the forecourt and nodded once in Charlie's direction as the car crossed the center line and accelerated away. Charlie pulled out onto the near-deserted roadway and fell in behind the receding black shape. The motorcycle which had been facing in the other direction performed a quick grit-spattering U-turn and roared off in pursuit.

Jia took the bank steps with shaky legs and set off in the direction of the recently rented apartment.

* * *

The font on the illuminated sign was almost identical to the one at the entrance to the far-off Altai Mountain site. It identified the single-story building as the administration office for the Future Prosperity Corporation. There was nothing to indicate the business that this arm of the corporation was engaged in. The black Mercedes stood on a narrow concrete strip in front of the door.

The tail had been incident free. The men in the car had clearly become careless over time and no attempt was made to take a circuitous route or to check for trailing vehicles.

Liam had suggested the motorcycle as a back-up in case the depositor had arrived on two wheels but it hadn't been necessary

174

and even Charlie's fairly ponderous van managed the pursuit with ease.

They sat now, behind the van's freshly tinted windows, a dozen vehicle lengths from the front entrance. Liam had the motorcycle standing in readiness, immediately beyond the rear doors. If anyone of seeming significance left the building he was primed to follow.

He was on the point of dozing off around mid-afternoon when a foreign-looking man they'd not seen before came out towards the car from the rear of the offices. Liam was alert and ready to go in an instant but the man simply removed something from the glove box and returned to the building.

Several hours passed and they'd established with reasonable certainty that there were three men inside the building with one woman. At around six the woman came out carrying a handbag and shopping bag and headed off towards a bus stop on the next corner. That left just the three men who, for the time being, didn't appear to be going anywhere.

'It should be dark in a little while,' Liam said, looking at his watch. He used a small set of binoculars to examine the two visible walls. 'Windows look straightforward enough, I'd say no alarms. If we don't find a rear door we can access one of those.'

An hour later, the street was in darkness. Two figures in black stole silently from the parked van and loped up to the unlit façade of the building. They slipped into the shadows on each side of the structure; one went clockwise, the other counter. They met at the rear. Liam held up two fingers. Two rooms lit. Two rooms to deal with.

Charlie fished a pair of small canisters from his flak jacket and handed one to Liam. The labels said 'Shaving Cream'. They pulled on lightweight oxygen masks and exchanged 'thumbs up' signs. Liam spent 20 silent seconds manipulating the lock before they eased their way into an unlit store room via a rear door.

They waited in the dark momentarily and then slid noiselessly into an adjoining corridor. It too was in darkness. Light spilled from rooms in each direction. Liam went right, Charlie went left. Simultaneously, with practiced expertise, the canister nozzles were activated and gas flooded silently into each room. They waited for several minutes and then entered.

'Sleeping like babes,' Charlie called down the corridor.

'Mine too,' Liam replied. 'Very peaceful.' The man they'd seen entering the bank had been watching television in a small reception room and was now comatose in an easy chair. The two men in the office sat slumped, heads down at their desks. Charlie took three near-empty bottles of Baijiu from his pack and dropped them onto the desk. He found three glasses in a washroom and dripped a little of the liquid into each. 'Chinese vodka,' he said with a chuckle. 'This'll take some explaining.' They lifted the heads of the unconscious men and poured the liquor into their drooping mouths.

A large mainframe computer filled one corner of the office. Charlie attached a portable drive and began unloading the data from the computer's hard drive. Each room contained a simple digital video camera, ceiling-mounted in a corner and facing into the center. Charlie dragged up a chair and removed the memory cards. He downloaded the data, deleted several minutes of recent recording and then returned them to their cameras.

Liam returned to the other room, rolled up the man's sleeve and slid a needle into a vein on his arm. He took a folded body bag from his pack, dragged it over the limp body and zipped it closed. A short search located the keys to the Mercedes parked outside. He produced two more syringes, one for each of the men in the office and then folded their sleeves carefully back into place.

Within 30 minutes the two intruders were back in the darkness at the front of the building. 'With a bit of luck they'll still be out of it when the woman arrives in the morning,' Liam said.

They checked the road. It was deserted in both directions. The area was one of small offices and workshops and at this late hour was silent and empty. They carried the anaesthetized man across to the van and tossed him into the back. Liam slid a ramp from the floor and wheeled the bike up next to the body-bag. He closed the door, headed back across to the Mercedes and started the engine.

Charlie fell in behind him and they drove away from town

until they found a lonely stretch of country road. Liam selected a small tree, accelerated and drove the passenger side fender into it. He dropped a vodka bottle onto the console, climbed out quickly, cut a small gash on the inside of the front offside tire, left the lights on, the door wide open and ran across to the waiting van.

He pointed at the Mercedes as they accelerated past. 'Our friend in the back should be a very unpopular boy when they find that.'

Within 20 minutes they were back with Jia in the near-deserted apartment building. The still-unconscious man was chained to a chair bolted to the concrete floor in a rear bedroom. Liam brewed a cup of tea and they got straight down to work.

'Anything on the hard drive yet?' Liam asked, after several hours of silent industry.

'Not so far,' Charlie said.

He was at one end of the small table, Liam the other. In the middle, next to an empty fruit bowl, were three appropriated handguns. While Charlie battled to decode the material from the office mainframe, Liam scrolled slowly through the security-camera footage on a slim laptop. Jia sat on a flimsy dining chair, knees to her chin, staring out at a leaden sky.

'This encryption is too fucking good,' Charlie said eventually. 'I'll need more time and probably more bandwidth. It may have to wait until we get back.'

Liam ignored him. He was looking hard at the small screen and scrolling slowly to and fro. 'Coincidence is a rare and wonderful thing,' he said with a hint of quiet triumph.

* * *

The nervous young Chinese man with a bad headache, was, not surprisingly, refusing to talk. His three captors sat in a semi-circle opposite, black balaclavas covering their faces. The two men sounded foreign, the woman was Chinese. The men were asking the questions, the woman was translating, he remained mute.

He looked around the room. There was no way of knowing

who these people were or where he was. Apart from the four chairs it was totally bare. A solitary incandescent bulb hung from the center of the ceiling and the single narrow window was covered with thick black fabric. It occurred to him that he may not even be in China any longer. The thought had a further impact on the level of his confidence.

'He's already been eight hours without food,' Charlie said. 'Tell him we can wait. We have all the time in the world. He'll starve to death before we lose patience.' Under the thick balaclava Jia's expression reflected concern but she conveyed the message.

Charlie stood and left the room. Liam and Jia followed. Liam paused at the door. 'We'll be back in a few days,' he said. 'Hope you don't die of thirst.'

The man spoke softly, almost imperceptibly.

Liam walked back into the room. 'What was that?'

'What do you want to know?' Jia translated.

He removed a folded sheet of paper from his pocket. It contained the *Dialog* photograph of Dyson. 'Ask him if he's seen this man.'

The captive shook his head and murmured something. 'He doesn't know him,' Jia said.

Liam left the room again and returned with his laptop. He opened it and began to run black-and-white footage from the security camera located in the lobby of the raided office.

The man now sitting opposite Liam was standing at the reception desk. A Caucasian walked in flanked by two others who were both very big men, black T-shirts straining at their biceps. They could have been Russian. The young Chinese man turned and greeted the white man off-handedly, ignoring the other two. The man was, clearly, Walter Dyson. The date on the screen indicated that the incident had taken place just days before.

'Does he want to reconsider his answer?' Jia was discomfited by the ice in Liam's voice. She translated.

'What do you want to know?' The man said again.

'We want to know where to find him, where he is. It's that simple.' Liam's voice had lost some of its icy edge.

The man shrugged.

'He says he doesn't know,' Jia offered. 'I don't think he's being truthful.'

The door banged open and Charlie stormed in carrying the man's own pistol. He shoved it against the firmly shut lips, forcing them apart, and slid it roughly into his mouth. 'Tell him I'm old, I have bad knees, I have gout and I get angry very easily. Tell him I'm tired of his nonsense and he has 30 seconds to answer before he meets his ancestors.'

The young man gagged on the gun barrel and tried to speak. The sound came out as a panicked gurgle. Charlie removed the gun and wiped spittle onto the man's expensive shirt.

Jia listened attentively while he spoke rapidly, glancing sideways at the large hooded figure of Charlie and the waving gun. 'He says the man is at the satellite launching place, it's a long way out of the city.'

Liam freed one of the man's hands, typed in the URL, found a satellite image of the site and held it in front of their now-quaking victim.

He pointed at the launch area. 'Here?'

The man shook his head 'no' and used his free hand to scroll across the landscape. A few miles further into the featureless desert stood another large rectangular building in a compound surrounded by smaller roofs. It was the color of the surrounding sand. The young Chinese man tapped the screen above one of the smaller buildings to the right of the central roof. He spoke excitedly.

'That's where they keep him,' Jia said. 'Not where they build the satellites, where they built the planes.'

16

THE EXECUTIVE read the formal letter from the President of US Media Satellite Inc a second time, smiled at the two Westerners in neat business suits and then turned to their pretty young female translator.

'We are honored to have these gentlemen here as our guests. Will you please inform them that I would like to offer some modest refreshments before we tour the facility. I have no doubt we can accommodate the need of their networks at a very competitive price.'

They spent the rest of the day eating, watching promotional videos, touring the facility, examining a variety of satellite options and eating. Liam was impressed with the apparently appropriate technical questions with which Charlie peppered his hosts. The external leg of the tour included a drive out to a launch site some distance from the main buildings. Liam could barely make out another facility across the desert in the shimmering heat and was fairly sure it was surrounded by high razor wire.

'Will you be returning to Jiuquan this evening?' their host asked.

'No,' Liam said. 'We have been granted permission to stay locally at the guest-house here in Dongfeng. We will speak with our colleagues overnight and if we need any further technical information tomorrow we will still be nearby if that is acceptable to you. We will contact you in the morning.'

'Very convenient,' their host said with a courteous smile. 'A wise decision.'

An hour after midnight the two Western men were back in head-to-toe black and flitting stealthily across the desert sand. Within a half mile of the floodlit facility beyond the satellite site, they slowed and dropped to their stomachs. Liam surveyed the fence line through his powerful binoculars. 'There are guards, towers and, if I'm not mistaken, dogs and, oh yeah, the razor wire.'

'Shame Dyson's not in Nevada. Area 51. It'd be a shitload easier to breach,' Charlie muttered.

'Why would they be building the aircraft out here?' Liam wondered out loud. 'This set-up is not exactly inconspicuous.'

'Langley would tell you there are literally dozens of secret military and nuclear facilities, of every description, scattered across these remote desert areas like confetti. Nobody probably gives it a second look.'

'Let's move in a little closer,' Liam whispered. 'Daylight's a way off... see if we can locate the specific building. It should be to the north of the main group up there.'

They crept around the perimeter, staying low to the ground. 'That's it,' Liam said eventually. 'The one smack between two guard towers.' He raised the binoculars again. 'I think I can see what might be runway lights on the far side. The main gate is over here on the western side. If we keep going we'll have to cross the access road.'

'I've seen enough,' Charlie said. 'If we're going in there we need some serious help. C'mon, let's get out of here.'

They jogged back across the featureless plain and slipped into the slumbering Dongfeng village without incident. The stairs to their first-floor rooms were on the outside of the building and the small reception area, near the stair-base, was in darkness and obviously unattended. Liam poured two glasses from a small bottle of rice wine and handed one to his companion.

'That's going to take some getting into,' he said.

'We'd need a dozen of my hard-assed special-ops buddies with automatic weapons and flash grenades, evac choppers nearby, the works,' Liam offered.

'Or a dozen of my hard-assed Uighur buddies. They're closer.' Charlie squinted through the pale liquid in his hand. 'Difficult but not impossible. But then we'd still have to get out of China with a billion people on the lookout for us.'

He studied the light refracting from the edge of the glass. 'You and me were given the label "covert" because that's how we

181

operated. Swift, silent and all the rest of it. A full-frontal attack on a heavily guarded compound in China would be, shall we say, imprudent and could not be referred to as covert.'

He walked across the room, kicked off his boots and dropped onto the narrow bed. 'Getting a big team up here would also mean a few days' wait and the longer we hang around Jiuquan, the greater the risk is going to get.' He tilted his head towards the desert satellite facility. 'How long before these folk make a connection between their Western buyers from Washington and the events back at Future Prosperity Inc?' He downed the last of the wine. 'We should try to get back to town early.' He closed his eyes. 'And now I need some sleep.'

* * *

They'd eased the young Chinese man's bonds and left him with enough food and water for their overnight absence. He was in reasonable health and seemed almost pleased to see what little of Jia's face peered from her mask when she entered the room ahead of the others.

'Did you find him?' He asked her with a smirk. 'The Gweilo?'

'Gweilo?' Jia said, returning the smirk with a hidden smile. She spoke in English. 'That's not a word we hear often in the north. They don't call white men Gweilo round here.'

'Ask him where he's from,' Liam said.

It required some careful diplomacy on Jia's part but after a circuitous exchange with the man she turned back to Liam. 'He's from Singapore. His family came originally from Guangzhou.'

Liam was momentarily thoughtful. 'Tell him he has two choices. We can get him safely back to Singapore or we can turn him over to his local friends who I'm sure won't be pleased to see him. Especially given he did a runner after he smashed up their Mercedes. If he helps us find Mr Dyson we'll get him out of here. If not...' He left the obvious unfinished. Charlie had been watching a local news broadcast in the other room. He joined them. 'You can also tell him that the remains of two of his local friends were found in a dumpster near the airport. They looked a lot like his buddies from the other night.'

The young man appeared visibly shaken.

'I'd like to ask him about my father too,' Jia whispered, a little hesitantly. 'I have a picture.' She patted the pocket against her heart to make sure it was still there.

Liam indicated they should leave the room. He sat her down on one of the dining chairs. 'He's from Singapore. That probably means he speaks English. We need to be extra careful now.'

He reached over and took her hand. 'I lost my father too. I understand what you're going through. My fear is if you show him your father's picture and somehow he then makes contact with his people, they will almost certainly work out who you are. At the moment nobody knows who any of us are and that's our great advantage. Our best chance of finding your father seems to be finding this Dyson. He seems to be up to his neck in all this.'

She nodded, but her eyes welled with tears.

Charlie called them back into the other room. 'He wants to talk with Jia.'

They had a quick exchange. Jia turned to her two companions. 'He says he knows when Mr Dyson will be coming to the city again. He comes to see a medical specialist, he makes regular visits. He will tell you where and when if you guarantee to get him to Singapore.'

'We'll give it to him in writing if he insists,' Liam said drily. 'And tell him he's welcome to speak English now.'

***

After a day of exhaustive discussion the decision to bring in 'a dozen of Charlie's hard-assed Uighur buddies' was taken anyhow; in spite of the extra time and risk involved. In reality there was no option. But the automatic weapons and flash grenades were to be left behind. It would have to be a small, covert operation.

Their Singaporean captive's name, they discovered, was Luo Chen. His English was excellent and the lure of a return to Singapore rather than facing his brutal local associates made him increasingly more co-operative.

Luo Chen, once he started talking, was hard to stop. His role, it seemed, had been fairly menial, as driver, courier and delivery man, and it became clear he genuinely knew nothing about the group's activities beyond the town boundaries. What he did seem to know was everything that happened within the town. Dyson, he revealed, had been having treatment for an unspecified illness. The procedure was weekly, around the middle of the day; performed at the Xincheng hospital, it took several hours. The patient was driven in from the 'plane place' as Luo Chen dismissively described it, by his two Romanian minders. Liam's interest pricked up when he heard that the round trip was done in a single day.

'They don't like to stay in the city overnight,' Luo Chen said. 'For security, I think.'

'What time do they normally head back to the Dongfeng base?'

'Around six in the afternoon, maybe. Sometimes a little later if they call into the office first,' Luo Chen said.

'That means it's dark before they get back? They travel in the dark?'

Luo Chen nodded. 'That's right.'

'Good,' Liam said. 'Very good.'

* * *

'There was nobody there, Mr Paul. Nobody in that godforsaken place.'

He removed a clean handkerchief from his suit coat and wiped the already clean table.

'We spent a lot of time, money and effort sending our people all the way to the wilds of north Queensland on a useless exercise. They didn't need a tropical holiday, Mr Paul.'

He made no attempt to disguise his distaste for his surroundings. 'And I didn't need another visit to Darwin so soon.'

Paul was getting very tired of the gratuitous sarcasm that had become a part of each meeting.

'I work as a signals analyst. I locate the source of transmissions.

184

I'm not in surveillance, my friend, I'm not a babysitter.' He tried a little sarcasm of his own. 'Perhaps you should have phoned first; made an appointment.'

'And I, Mr Paul, am not your friend.'

Nor I yours, you bastard, Paul thought, but left it unsaid.

'We've traced the ownership of the property to a Charles Casement,' Paul said. 'It took some doing, some very complex threads to unravel; complex analysis.'

He paused momentarily in the vain hope there might be some small compliment from the Singaporean. Nothing came back.

'The man is clearly an expert at hiding himself,' he continued sulkily. 'From what we can infer, he appears to be ex-CIA, NSA and seemingly every other dark and covert little operational group the Americans have ever put together. It seems he has a rogue streak. A bit of a maverick, an individualist, let's say. He left the States as soon as his service ended.'

'What a pity, then, that *he's* not working for us.'

Mr Paul was quite sure his associate had left the 'instead of you' intended but unsaid.

'And where is he now?'

'We're not sure. We can never be certain what name he might use on a passport. Our best guess, based on a possible recent sighting at Sydney's airport, is that he may be on his way to China.'

'Where in China?'

'It's a fairly big place. I'm afraid we don't have his street address just yet,' Paul said with a smug smile.

* * *

The Uighur group arrived in Jiuquan on the eve of Dyson's doctor's visit. The dozen had become six. It was adequate. After 15 minutes of backslapping and hugging Charlie, interspersed with loud roars of laughter, they settled down, cross-legged on the apartment floor, to take their instructions. Liam was relieved to discover the entire group understood English.

By midday, next day, Jia was positioned opposite the hospital car park in a small rental vehicle. Liam's binoculars were on her lap; two cellphones on the console alongside.

Liam, Charlie and the Uighurs were on their way to a roadside location halfway to the distant satellite facility. Luo Chen was with them, his wrists still loosely bound.

A 40-mile stretch of the sealed road cut an arrow-straight line across desolate, featureless ground on the western edge of the Gobi Desert. Nothing broke the monotony or isolation of the landscape. It was like being on the moon. The road, Luo Chen assured them, was little used, even during the day. At night it was all but deserted.

Jia watched Dyson and his two burly minders enter the hospital shortly after one. Luo Chen's information had been sound. The American looked frail. A tremor ran through Jia's hands, making the binoculars wobble, as she saw him in the flesh for the first time. This, after all, might finally be the person to lead her to her father. She started the motor and positioned her car closer to theirs; a driver sat dozing at the wheel. No matter how long the wait, she warned herself, you will not do the same.

By early evening Charlie's van was concealed behind a sun-hardened sand dune, just off the road, around 60 miles from town. Around 50 yards further along, an old truck, a panel shop's nightmare, waited behind a small barren outcrop of rock. Immediately behind it a battered sedan baked in the late-afternoon heat. The Xinjiang plates from both vehicles had been removed and stowed in the car's trunk.

The sun was low in the sky when Jia's perseverance was finally rewarded. The three men exited the hospital and walked briskly to the waiting car. Dyson appeared to be a little unsteady on his feet but neither of the two Romanians made any attempt to assist him. Jia eased the little rental out of its bay and followed from a distance. The car ahead made directly for the outskirts of the town and turned onto the road heading north to Dongfeng. She steered her car onto the verge and tapped in Liam's number.

'Yes,' he said brusquely.

'They're on their way. On the edge of the town. Driving a silver BMW.' She read out the registration details.

'Great work, thank you. Ditch the phones immediately and wait for us. We'll see you in a couple of hours.' He disconnected the line and checked his watch. 'We need to be in position in 55 minutes,' he called to Charlie, a hundred feet away chatting to his Urumqi friends.

As soon as it was dark, Liam had two of the younger Uighur men join him in the van. One was driven a few miles along the deserted road to the north and given a cellphone, a flashlight and infra-red goggles.

'Stop anything that comes down the road until you get our "all clear" call,' Liam told the man. 'If they're police or military, stay hidden and call us pronto.'

The second man was deployed to the south. Along with flashlight and cell he was given the BMW's description and registration number. He also carried an old set of night-vision equipment.

'Call me and let it ring three times when the BMW comes through,' Liam said.

The young Uighur walked to the edge of the pavement and concealed himself in a patch of sparse grey scrub, as Liam spun the van around and accelerated back to the others.

He positioned the van behind its dry dune and joined the men near the rock outcrop. At 45 minutes the old truck and its rattling companion were driven onto the road and a fake accident scene created, blocking both lanes. The hood on the rusting car was lifted and a small smoke bomb concealed below the radiator. Two men were positioned in the low dunes on each side of the road, 50 feet before the manufactured collision site, and given two of the three handguns. Liam held onto the third. Charlie had a small machine pistol donated by his big, bearded Uighur comrade. The final two men remained with the crash-scene vehicles that spread across the road. Luo Chen was left in the back of the van fastened to a seat frame.

At 55 minutes everyone was in position. Seven minutes and 35 seconds later, Liam's phone buzzed three times and stopped. Seconds later the BMW high beams flashed into view. They were traveling through the lonely landscape as fast as he'd estimated they would. The two men on the road stood in front of their vehicles and started arguing and gesticulating violently.

The BMW driver caught them in his speeding headlights, braked violently and slid to a gravel-spitting stop around 30 feet from the scene.

The two Romanians leapt from the BMW, automatic weapons in hand. One leaned against the rear window pillar and lifted his weapon into position. The other, weapon held loosely at his side, strode forward and uttered a string of Romanian expletives.

Seconds later the two men hidden in the dunes were walking onto the roadway a few feet behind the BMW, each handgun trained on a Romanian head as the van roared from its hiding place and shunted into the rear of the expensive German saloon. Liam and Charlie were on their feet, on the road, guns up before the van stopped moving. The Romanian at the rear door was sent flying, losing his weapon as he went. The other, closer to the collision scene, spun round and lit up the darkness with a short burst of automatic fire that disappeared into the desert darkness above Charlie's head. A split second later Liam put a single bullet into the man's bulky thigh. He went down, clutching his leg and wailing like a spoiled child. Throughout the action the BMW driver sat, pale of face, with his hands in the air.

Within 60 seconds all vehicles were off the road and hidden behind rock and dune. Charlie, busy getting the Uighur men to take charge of the Romanians and their driver, paused and looked across to Liam. He pointed to the back seat of the captured vehicle. Liam walked over and bent in to see a very pale, frightened passenger, still belted into his seat. He lifted his ski mask to reveal his face.

'Mr Dyson, I presume.'

It seemed to Liam that on hearing a seemingly friendly American voice the man's relief was almost palpable, even if a little restrained.

'We'll explain later,' Liam said and joined the others. Dyson was helped across to the van and the BMW was driven half a mile over stony ground and concealed in a shallow depression behind a low ridge. The wounded man was given rudimentary first aid and all three occupants were bound, gagged and locked into the car. Liam left a bottle of water on the console then took their cellphones, their guns and the car keys. He tossed the cellphones into the desert several miles down the road and the rest into the rear of the van.

Ten minutes later the six Uighurs were on their way home to Urumqi and the van was en route to collect Jia. Not a single vehicle had approached from either direction throughout the process. 'I love it on those rare occasions when things go right,' Charlie said.

'Who are you? What do you want?' Dyson spoke for the first time since his extrication.

'We're the US Cavalry. We're here to rescue you. I assume you wanted rescuing?' Charlie answered. 'Mr Rigby seemed to think so.'

Dyson turned his face to the darkened window. He said nothing, but in the reflection from the glass, Liam could see tears streaming down the older man's ashen cheeks.

Liam reached over and lay a comforting hand on his shoulder. He left it there for several seconds. 'It's okay, Walter. You're okay now.' He patted him gently on the arm.

They traveled for a dozen miles without any further exchange. Dyson was first to break the silence. 'So, what happens to me now?'

'You get out of China.' Liam said gently. 'We get out of China and we take you with us.'

* * *

A single 40-watt bulb illuminated the small apartment table. Charlie sat bent over a portable radio receiver. He switched from station to station and clicked through the various bands: short wave, AM, FM. A small television set stood in the corner of the room and Jia used the remote control to shift from channel to channel. Liam sat with a computer on his lap trawling silently through social media and internet news services. 'Nothing,' he said at length.

189

Jia shook her head without turning round.

Charlie looked up. 'If the Chinese government is involved in this, they sure don't want anybody to know about it. Normally the place would be going ballistic; soldiers on every street corner. So far, nothing. Not a peep on the radio either.'

'I'm not sure the government *is* involved.' Dyson sat quietly on a mattress next to the silent Luo Chen, whose manacles had finally been removed.

'What makes you say that?'

'I've been held there for nearly ten years.' He shrugged.

Charlie returned to his radio dial. 'Can you be sure they're *not* involved?' He spoke without looking up.

Dyson shook his head. 'No, I can't be sure.'

'We're all busting to know what you've been up to but at the moment we need to concentrate on what's directly in front of us,' Charlie said, not unkindly. 'Getting our minds around your ten years is going to take us more than ten minutes. We get you safely out of Jiuquan first and then we debrief you.'

The seemingly exhausted Walter Dyson appeared, suddenly, to find an inner strength. 'And how are you planning on getting me somewhere safe?' There was a hint of impatience. 'We're in the middle of China, surrounded by more than a billion submissive citizens. It's impossible.'

'*Almost* impossible,' Charlie corrected. 'Jia's not submissive. And those billion-plus people can also be a benefit. Think of us as five small needles among a billion stalks of hay.'

He shifted his attention from the radio receiver to Dyson. 'A business-class flight from Beijing would have been nice for all of us, but it's not going to happen. Traveling as a pair of Washington media executives with our Chinese PA, we'd probably be on our first champagnes by now. With you and Luo Chen along, the paradigm shifts.'

He returned to scanning the wavebands. 'We're still not sure who's going to be looking for us, how many of them there are and the lengths to which they're prepared to go to find us. If the air is still clear, come darkness tomorrow night, we'll take our chances.'

'And if not?' Dyson's face was still pale.

'Let's be optimistic, shall we?' Charlie's smile showed no trace of humor.

'So what is your optimistic plan?'

'We'll go out through Pakistan.'

Dyson's reaction was disbelief. 'But the border's thousands of miles away.'

'Just under 1200 miles, to be precise.' He clicked off the radio and stood to stretch his legs.

'The journey of a thousand miles begins with a single step,' Jia said softly without turning; her eyes still on the television screen.

Charlie looked at her back and smiled a genuine smile then turned again to Dyson. 'Our nearest border here is Mongolia. Around 300 miles north.' He pointed in the direction of the orange light filtering in from the street. 'We get there and we're still in Mongolia; effectively China. And, as far as we know, you're still a fugitive. Then there's Nepal, the Kazakh border or Pakistan, all roughly the same distance. If we choose Kazakhstan, we cross the border, we're still in Kazakhstan. Nepal is a possibility but then we have to cross Tibet first. Things are not going well there. The escalating situation has made them very jumpy. My money's on Pakistan. For all their problems, once we're over that border, all we have to contend with is the odd terrorist. And going that way gives us the advantage of a lot of wild, empty country. It means skirting the edge of the Taklamakan Desert and there's nothing I prefer to crossing empty sand when I'm fleeing, unless it's crossing empty sky. We can be there in around 24 hours if all goes well. With luck it may take them that long to find your Romanian buddies in the Gobi.'

'And we have friends in Pakistan,' Liam added quietly.

17

LUO CHEN was at the wheel. A baseball cap and dark glasses helped to conceal his intermittently illuminated identity. He guided the van with extreme care through the town's light traffic. Jia sat upright in the passenger seat while the three Western men in the rear lay in a tight space beneath a stack of crates labeled with the names of various automotive spare parts.

'Take us out of town to the east,' Liam directed. 'On the Beijing road.' He held a small GPS in his hand. 'There's a secondary road about 50 clicks along, it heads off to the south. We'll take that and double back. Pull off when you get there and we'll change the plates.'

Beyond the turn-off the three men sat up and Liam began to navigate a course through the mountains, on a web of narrow roads. They stayed well south of the main Silk Route highway and shared the night with very few other vehicles.

After an uneventful half-hour of relative silence, with all eyes staring anxiously along the dark road ahead, they began to relax a little.

'You said you'd been up there ten years.' Charlie tried, through the gloom, to study Dyson's pale face. 'Want to tell us how that came to be? What happened? What you were doing there and why? A man called Rigby told us you were a good guy but everything we've seen so far is worrying the shit out of us.'

'Lionel,' Walter Dyson said. '*Lionel* Rigby.' His sigh was audible in the darkness. He rubbed his tired eyes. 'In Arlington I was working for a small group within the Pentagon. A top-secret attempt to move forward from the B2 Spirit. An attempt to take an aircraft off the radar completely. One-hundred-per-cent signal neutral. Then one day I took a weekend off to walk in the Appalachians and I never came back. I was stopped on a quiet road in Pennsylvania by a group of men. NSA or something, I thought at the time.'

'American men?'

'Some of them. They offered me a small fortune to come to China voluntarily. I had no idea who they were. When I refused they took me anyway. I think they injected me with something, I'm not sure. The next thing I remember was waking up in Jiuquan. I've been there ever since.

'When I got there I discovered they had all the original blueprints for the B2 and some of the developmental material for the upgrade as well. Test aircraft were already some way into construction but they were having problems. I guess they brought me in to try to iron out the bugs.'

'Do you know where the plans came from?' Liam asked. 'Who would have access to them?'

'Just Northrop and the military,' Dyson said. 'Northrop run a tight ship, so not them. My money was on the military. Not long after my arrival in Dongfeng, I saw someone who looked a lot like a five-star man I'd seen at the Pentagon, but he was a way off and I couldn't be sure.'

Charlie moved unconsciously into interrogation mode. 'What are these bombers being built for? How are they being used?'

Dyson returned serve. His answers as curt as the questions.

'I don't know. I supervised their construction and occasionally their repair and maintenance, that's it. These people worked on a need-to-know basis.'

'Were you aware of one going down in Pakistan around seven or eight years ago?'

'Yes. On one of the early test flights of the bigger, upgraded version. A fuel issue. We solved it the following year.'

'What happened to the aircraft?'

'As I said, a fuel problem.'

'No, after the crash.'

'It was found, the wreckage was cleaned up and choppered out, brought back to Dongfeng. We worked on the recovered debris to locate the problem.'

'Was there a skirmish with Pakistani troops at the time?'

'I don't know. As I said, need to know only.'

'And, you really don't know how they may have accessed the original B2 plans?' Charlie leant into the darkness and gave Dyson's face a searching look.

'No, for Christ's sake. I didn't ask and they didn't say. All I wanted to do was stay alive. They made it quite clear that I had just two choices.'

He rubbed his eyes again, then rested his head against the cold metal shell of the van.

'I think my captors must have made a detailed study of the works of Kafka. They seem to take great delight in creating existential vacuums. I have no knowledge who they are, what they are doing or why they are doing it. My job is… was, to supervise the construction of the aircraft, to continue attempting to improve its invisibility and its payload and to iron out any problems that arose. I have no idea what goes on beyond Dongfeng. No idea where my aircraft are used or even based.'

'Altai Mountains, they're based in the Altai Mountains,' Charlie said.

'I'm vaguely aware of the Altai Mountains but I have no knowledge of the location you're talking about.'

'Why not just do whatever it is they're doing from Dongfeng, for Christ's sake?' Charlie was becoming increasingly frustrated. 'Why go to the trouble of moving them to the godforsaken site in Altai?'

'We've seen them flying out of there,' Liam said. 'Heading north we think.'

'Other than for secrecy, I can't imagine why they'd be there.' Dyson made a gesture of helplessness with his hand. 'I don't know. Perhaps they're based up there because of its proximity. It's what, a few hundred miles? Any occasional aircraft movement in or out of Dongfeng was carried out in the dead of night. A remote base less than an hour's flying away would help with concealment. What they did once they were there I can't say.'

Charlie's interrogation was interrupted by a startled exclamation from the hitherto-silent Luo Chen. He pointed up ahead. Lights flashed red and blue in the dark distance.

'Slow down a little,' Liam ordered as the three men in the back slid quickly into the space under the crates. Liam and Charlie lay on each side of Dyson, nursing the automatic weapons taken from the Romanians. 'Nice and cool, everyone. We all know what to do.'

Luo Chen pulled onto the verge and stopped just short of the two police vehicles. He and Jia both produced identity cards. Liam knew that Luo Chen's was as counterfeit as Jia's.

'Where are you going so late in the night, comrade?' the Chinese police officer asked, directing a weak flashlight beam around the interior of the vehicle.

Jia did the talking.

She indicated Luo Chen. 'This worthless bumpkin and I are taking these spare parts back to my husband's workshop in Ruoqiang. It's cheaper these days to collect them yourself than to pay the freight companies.'

'Cheating bastards, all of them.' He laughed briefly and nodded. 'Where did you buy these things?'

'Jiuquan,' she said in the most matter-of-fact tone she could manage. 'I spent my husband's money on some new shoes too.'

'Why didn't you go to Urumqi to buy this stuff? It's closer.' The police officer looked her in the eye.

Liam's index finger caressed the trigger gently.

'I don't much like the people in Urumqi,' she said. 'If you know what I mean.'

He laughed unpleasantly again. 'Show me your receipts,' he demanded with an impatient snap of his fingers.

Jia took the paperwork, created on Charlie's computer, from the glove compartment and held it into the beam of the man's light. 'It's all in order,' she said. Liam was certain he could feel the beating of her heart through the metal floor of the van. 'Do you want me to open the back so you can have a look?'

He handed the papers back. 'I've got better things to do with my time,' he boasted. He waved the vehicle away with a dismissive sweep of his light. Luo Chen pulled onto the road slowly, looked across to Jia and winked at her big, frightened brown eyes.

'Back so soon, Mr Paul?'

The Singaporean man gave the seat a wipe before he sat. 'I hope you have something more than speculation this time. We need to locate Mr Dyson urgently, Mr Paul. Mr Dyson can cause us trouble on an immeasurable scale.'

'The business at the Jiuquan office,' Paul said, determined to follow his own train of thought. 'It seems those men of yours were probably telling the truth about what happened.'

'How unfortunate for them,' was all he bothered to say.

'I've had people checking the state surveillance data from Jiuquan,' Paul continued. Two Caucasians posing as satellite buyers made a visit to Dongfeng a few days before Dyson was taken. We have the details of a van they were driving.'

'I'm not really a motoring enthusiast, Mr Paul. Perhaps you could tell me about the occupants.'

Paul refused to be provoked.

'We have them on camera at the satellite facility, in the lobby.'

He took two grainy photographs from a manila envelope and dropped them onto the table. 'Our face-recognition check tells us this is likely our friend Charles Casement.' He tapped the small likeness. 'The other, we think, is a guy named Doyle. Liam Doyle, Ex-US special forces.'

'So now we know what happened to Walter Dyson,' the Singaporean said. 'I wonder what game these two are playing and for whom.'

'Guess what Doyle's connection to all this is?'

'I'm not paid to guess.'

'The guy on K2, years back.'

'What about him?'

'This Doyle is his son.' Paul tapped the photograph. 'All grown up.'

'So why would he suddenly be giving us grief? What could he possibly know?'

'I couldn't say. Coincidence maybe? Or maybe he had more luck finding his father and the camera than your people ever did.'

'On top of K2? I think that's unlikely, don't you?'

'We've checked his background. He's a climber. Spent some time in Nepal.'

'Well, look into it. See if anyone out there knows anything. They're an incestuous little lot those climbing types.'

'I've already got people asking.'

'Does he have family? What about Casement?'

'Casement has nobody. Doyle has a mother somewhere but she's gone to ground. Was in Oklahoma we think, but not there now. The house is vacant, neighbors know nothing.'

'So where are they now, Doyle and Casement?'

'That's where I thought you might be able to help,' Paul said. 'We tracked a vehicle leaving Jiuquan on the Beijing road. Then we lost it. Not a sign of it anywhere further to the east. My guess is they turned off somewhere, possibly doubled back towards the airport.'

The man from Singapore shook his head. 'We have people there. They won't get Dyson out that way.'

'Well, we'll have to keep looking, see if the vehicle has been sighted anywhere else.'

'Find out what, if anything, Doyle knows about K2. Keep me informed.' He stood and left the table. Mr Paul gave his back a surreptitious two-fingered salute.

* * *

Liam removed the screwtop from a water bottle and handed it to Walter Dyson. He allowed the quaking man 15 minutes to settle down before speaking again.

'You said earlier you didn't think the Chinese government was involved. Why not?'

'The whole Dongfeng project is like one vast Russian Babushka doll; a facility within a facility, within a facility. A paradox within an enigma within a conundrum within a paradox.' He screwed the top back onto the bottle with hands now almost steady.

'From what I was able to piece together, the publicly evident satellite facility is now a joint venture with an international consortium. It may even be fully privately owned these days, I don't know. The Chinese military started a covert research set-up a few years back in the desert close to the launch sites. That was before I arrived. The rumor is they were attempting to build their own stealth bomber but that had no connection to what we've been doing.'

Dyson's nervous fingers fidgeted with the screw top for a while. He took another sip. 'On the surface, today, commercial and military satellites are being built. Behind all the security, in a separate, more remote facility, they're working on experimental aircraft for the Chinese Air Force. But in an underground area in another part of the complex, beyond a series of walls and doors, we were developing a more sophisticated aircraft. A very few VIP visitors, when they came, were aware of this inner sanctum or had access. Many others, sometimes even apparently high-ranking military officers, never got beyond the second level. Most of them seemed blissfully unaware of the project we foreign engineers and technicians worked on. And we were kept very much at arm's length.'

'How successful were you in taking these new aircraft off the radar?' Liam asked.

'Almost absolute. Virtually 100 per cent. But then, we had some help.' Dyson held his palms together and then moved them slowly apart. 'In normal circumstances, as soon as your weapons-bay doors are opened, you risk a significant radar return. In our model the weapons bay was reconfigured; sealed, never opened.'

'Why was that?'

Dyson shrugged. 'You'd have to ask Lionel Rigby.'

'Why Rigby?'

Dyson looked away, silent for a moment and then, deliberately it seemed to Liam, changed the subject. 'We even managed to address the significant issue of OTH radar.'

'OTH?' Liam queried.

'Over the horizon, OTH.' Charlie provided the answer, then persisted. 'What was your relationship with Lionel Rigby? Why would he risk revealing your location, do you think?'

'I don't know,' Dyson whispered. 'Perhaps he was trying to expose the whole insane process. Perhaps he was simply trying to save me.'

In the darkness none of the others noticed his fresh tears.

'In the initial construction stages we had regular dealings together. As I said, we needed to reconfigure the payload area. He wanted pressurized holding tanks on the aircraft rather than weapons bays. He knew the overall capacity he wanted, I had to work out the maximum available capacity of each aircraft and calculate how many I needed to build to deliver his payload.'

'What were they, extra long-range fuel tanks?'

'No. Not aviation fuel. Something else. They had some sort of discrete function.'

'Did it ever occur to you to ask what that function was?'

'Not my business...'

Charlie broke in angrily. 'What if these people were planning to use these things for some sort of global dissemination of chemical weapons, biological weapons? With the kind of capacity you're talking about they could kill every man, woman and child on the planet and they wouldn't even know they were breathing their last.'

'Look, don't take the moral high ground with me,' Dyson said angrily. His hands began to tremble again. 'I was their prisoner for years. You can have no concept of what that was like. I did what I was told. End of story.'

'Aha, the old Nuremberg defense rears its ugly head. You could have refused.'

'I could have, and I know full well what they'd have done to me. I'd have ended up in some isolated, unmarked grave somewhere on the edge of the Gobi Desert. I chose not to. I didn't have the courage. Okay? I'm not a soldier, a gung-ho goddam hero. I'm a scientist, an engineer.'

'And a potent symbol of why the world is in the sorry state it's in,' Charlie said softly. 'What the fuck did you think they'd do when they'd finished with you?'

'I planned to cross that bridge when I got there. Survival in Dongfeng was a day-to-day exercise.'

'Was Rigby a prisoner too?' Liam tried to remove a little heat from the conversation.

'No, I don't think so. Whatever he was doing had him deeply engaged. I think he was doing it willingly at first. "I wish I could talk to you about this," he'd say. "It's the most exciting challenge of my life."

'Then later, he changed: he was clearly worried when he visited. He muttered something about injector assemblies possibly being the problem, he wanted to see for himself. We brought back one of the aircraft and retooled the gear but it didn't help.'

Dyson broke off and sat, seemingly deep in thought, trying to recall a conversation.

'The last time we spoke he said something along the lines of things not going the way they should. He'd run the simulations, the models, over and over, reworked the algorithms a thousand times, he said. But the theory and the reality weren't co-operating.'

He looked up as the headlights of a passing truck illuminated Liam's face for a brief few moments. 'I haven't heard from him since.'

'That's because he was murdered,' Charlie said as the light receded.

They drove on in silence, Dyson with his face turned towards the window.

At length Jia's small voice filtered back from the darkness of the driver's cabin. 'Did you ever meet a Chinese man named Zhang Liu?'

Dyson failed to respond to the question for some time. 'No,' he answered, eventually, his voice quavering slightly. 'It's not a name I've ever heard.'

Liam wanted to comfort her, reach forward and put an arm around her, but he remained still and silent in the rear darkness.

Luo Chen leaned in close to her and whispered. 'I did. I heard that name once. They were talking about him.'

'What did they say?'

Jia sensed rather than saw his wordless shrug.

'Do you know?' her voice faltered. 'Did you know if he was alive... dead?'

'Alive, I think. Maybe. Dead maybe. Who knows?'

* * *

Alexei walked to the door and waited until Dashka looked up from the snowmobile. 'When you're finished with that, I need you to come in here,' he called across the melting snow.

An invitation into the lab – the first in months. She grabbed a rag, wiped her hands and headed towards the open door.

The chair opposite Alexei's was stacked with fat manila folders. He made no attempt to clear it or offer it to her. She stood with her hands clasped behind her back.

He indicated the computer; it had been unplugged and the back of the tower removed.

'You can fix these things,' he said. 'It won't boot up.'

He picked up the manila folders, locked them in a filing cabinet and then sat, folded his arms and stared at her.

'I'm not used to people watching me when I work,' she said, examining the computer's interior.

'Well, you'll have to get used to it.'

She spent the best part of an hour pulling the machine to pieces and putting it back together with Alexei's eyes never leaving her back. She hit the on button and the monitor glowed instantly.

'I'll just check to see if it's working properly,' she said.

'I can do that,' he said, moving in front of the screen. 'You can go back to your work. If I need you, I'll let you know.'

She was about to leave the room when he stopped her.

'One other thing. The supply ship will be arriving in a few months. Your services will not be required any longer I'm afraid. We have found a replacement. You will need to be on that ship when it leaves.'

Dashka's natural inclination was to reach across the desk and knock his teeth out, before demanding to know what the hell was going on, but she resisted the urge.

'Why?' she queried mildly.

'As I said a while ago, we think you need a break.' He looked down at his feet. 'We think the quality of your work is suffering.'

A late spring snowstorm howled and beat against the small window, protesting, Dashka imagined, at this unthinkable injustice. She knew a bare-faced lie when she heard one and this was up there with the best of them.

She remained poised. 'I'll be ready when the ship arrives,' she said before leaving the office.

'But not before I find out what in the name of God you two rodents are up to in there,' she whispered to herself out in the deserted corridor.

Ivor was waiting with the faulty snowmobile. 'I think the belt's too tight, it's rubbing against the spinning sheaves.'

Dashka ignored him and stalked off towards the workshop.

'What's wrong?' He jogged up to join her.

'Nothing,' Dashka answered angrily. Then added: 'The bastard is hiding something. They're up to something shady in there, for sure. You'd think his computer was the Kolyvan Vase, the way he protects it.'

'Maybe it's drugs,' Ivor said enthusiastically. 'Or maybe they're laundering money for the mafia?'

'On Severny Island?' she said scornfully. 'And who do you think they're selling the drugs to – the polar bears, the walruses?'

18

IN THE EARLY HOURS beyond midnight the van passed a few lonely lights that, according to the map, indicated a remote desert asbestos mine. There would be nothing now until they approached the outskirts of Ruoqiang, a few hours down a long, isolated and uninhabited stretch of road. It gave Luo Chen the chance to snatch a little sleep and he clambered over into the back while Liam took the wheel.

'How are we going to get across the border?' Dyson asked after a hundred miles of silent travel. 'I don't have a passport. Nor does Luo Chen.'

Charlie's answer boomed from the shadows. 'The border is at the high point of the Khunjerab Pass on the Karakoram Highway. It's usually crawling with tourists. The guards on both sides are fairly relaxed. Even with all the terrorist activity in the region these days the van should get through without an issue – we have fresh plates. He pointed at Luo Chen. 'The two of you will need to do a little mountain walking, though.' His laughter filled the van. 'But, don't worry, Liam will be there with you. He loves mountain walking.'

An hour down the track Liam pulled over onto the sandy verge. 'Five minutes to stretch legs and whatever else is needed,' he said discreetly. The men clambered from the rear and wandered off into the low sand scrub nearby. Jia stayed close to the van. Liam walked round from the driver's side and spoke softly.

'I hate to say this but I think maybe you need to prepare yourself for the fact that your father may not be coming back, Jia. These types don't keep people alive once they're done with them.'

Jia looked like she'd been struck a physical blow. 'How can you say that? Do you mean I should stop looking for him, give up?'

'I just think…'

Her eyes were bright with anger. 'You climbed a mountain to find your father. Right now, I am climbing a mountain. Every day I climb a mountain.'

He reached toward her. She pulled away. 'I see it in your eyes, Liam. You are the one with a problem, not me. You are a man without joy, without hope.' There were tears now. 'I won't become like that. I won't.' She took two steps and then turned. 'Perhaps you need to learn from Lao Tzu. "A man with outward courage dares to die…"' She paused, looking at him through her tears. '"A man with inner courage dares to live".' She turned, climbed back into the van and slammed the passenger door.

The others straggled back and a deeply unhappy Liam kicked the engine into life and drove off into the bleak desert darkness.

* * *

The first rays of early light fell across Jia's sleepy eyes. She yawned and stretched. 'Where are we?'

'Not far from Ruoqiang,' Liam answered. 'Luo Chen will need to take over again,' he said over his shoulder. 'And we'll need some gas.'

Jia turned and studied Dyson as sunlight revealed his haggard face. 'You look very unwell, Walter,' she said with genuine concern. Charlie opened his eyes. She was right – the man looked terrible.

'It's the kidney disease,' he said without drama. 'Ideally I'd be having the hemodialysis treatment three times a week but my esteemed employers weren't able to spare me that often. They believed they were being extremely generous allowing me to go once a week. I think they were afraid I'd blab to the doctors. A bit difficult with my Romanians breathing down my neck.'

'Do you need to take a break?' Liam asked.

'No, I'd rather push on. I've spent as much time in China as I ever need to. No offense to you intended, Jia.'

She smiled a little sadly but said nothing.

The seemingly endless dunes of the Taklamakan stretched 200 miles to their right as the dust-covered van hummed along the desert's southern edge. Ahead and behind, they spread over 700 miles, northeast to southwest; 140,000 square miles of uninhabited sand. The residents of the few fringing settlements they hurried through showed scant interest in their passing. In Qarqan, market day was in full swing and the locals were far more concerned with haggling over vegetables and consuming hot läghmän. By early afternoon they were rattling into the dusty town of Niya.

A traffic light in the center turned suddenly to red and Luo Chen was caught off guard. He was forced to pull up within a few feet of an elderly local police officer. The man strolled across slowly and peered into the back of the van.

'What's this?' He seemed more inquisitive than suspicious. Jia spoke rapidly. Luo Chen smiled broadly at the officer and nodded vigorously as her story unfolded.

'These eminent Western scientists are here to study and to learn from China's remarkably successful sandstorm mitigation program and to carry news back to their homes of our people's magnificently successful planting of a hundred billion trees.'

Charlie leaned forward and spoke a few words in the Uighur language.

The officer nodded appreciatively and waved them off with a wide smile and a gracious bow.

'What did you say?' Liam asked.

'I thanked him for treating us with such courtesy and allowing us to enjoy his beautiful country.'

'Smooth bastard.' Liam smiled; but momentarily.

'No sign anywhere of the People's Liberation Army,' Dyson said, almost to himself.

'They'll have relocated many of them to the trouble spots in the southeast, along the Yangtze and on the borders,' Liam said. 'The whole of the south of Asia is starting to resemble a powder keg.'

* * *

The aircraft lifted into a clear blue sky, banked right over

Indiana's grand State Capitol building, adjusted the trim slightly over Monument Circle, straightened and set a course for DC. Another Presidential Primary had come and gone with all the usual rumor and hoopla. For the President, it was looking like a clear freeway ride all the way to the August nomination.

Cherry wasn't too sure about the other side of the political fence: things weren't going so smoothly. The bulk of Indiana's delegates had gone Jason Arnott's way. At almost the halfway mark to the November poll, Californian candidate Donna Stone was in front of Arnott by only a handful of votes.

Meanwhile the search for information about the mysterious Lionel Rigby had hit a wall. None of the authorities in Moscow knew anything about him; or, if they did, they weren't saying. The official in charge of the case was already suggesting it had moved into the 'cold' file category. They'd located his Moscow address and the address of his mother in Maryland in the bloodstained breast pocket of his coat. His apartment, when it was checked, had been trashed and nothing of any significance had been found. The Russian authorities were not unwilling to provide the American media with the Maryland address but refused to go into detail regarding the nature of Rigby's death. Though Cherry got the distinct impression that the man was implying, against all the apparent evidence, that it might have been some sort of sex crime.

Cherry gave up a Sunday afternoon with a good book and drove out to Maryland, the address supplied by the Muscovite cop punched into her GPS. It was a modest apartment in a genteel neighborhood. The kind of place where people were inclined to keep the lace curtains drawn and mind their own business. The family in the apartment knew nothing of the previous tenant and inquiries among the neighbors revealed only the fact that old Mrs Rigby had died in a nearby institution a little while back. A quick, sad visit to the institution provided nothing extra.

With no more than three months to go to the first National Convention, each passing day saw Cherry more deeply immersed in the minutiae of domestic politics and for a while the Rigby story was forced to play second fiddle.

She handed the thin file to a junior research assistant. 'Do the database thing, criminal records, passports, credit cards, schools, colleges, all the usual stuff. See if you can get a whiff of this guy.'

A week later the search had gone nowhere. It seemed, at least in terms of the complex network of cross-referenced data held in the United States, that Lionel Rigby did not exist.

∗ ∗ ∗

'Well, we know where at least some of the Chinese military got to.'

Liam was spreadeagled atop a ridge high above the Karakoram border gate, a mile or so on the Chinese side. The van stood, concealed by the moonless night, a hundred yards off the road below him. He handed Charlie the binoculars.

'They're not PLA,' he said. 'They're not in official uniforms. I think that's somebody's private little army down there.'

At least 20 heavily armed men stood in the shadows of the great stone edifice straddling the road.

'Normally you'd expect no more than two or three.' He passed the heavy lenses back to Liam. 'They're not military choppers either.' Two black helicopters stood to one side of the road and were almost completely camouflaged against the dark mountain.

'Change of plan. We won't be going through there.'

Liam pointed at the formidable range immediately ahead. 'I'm pretty sure Dyson wouldn't cope with the walk across anyway. Even if you could talk the van through. We're looking at a ten-mile climb over tough terrain to get past that lot without being spotted.'

'Any bright ideas?'

They retreated below the ridgeline and Liam took a pencil flashlight from his shirt pocket. He directed the beam onto a folded map. 'We passed a road heading south near this place.' He tapped the small spot representing the town of Yecheng. 'But it would mean a back track of a couple of hundred miles. It doesn't cross into Pakistan. It looks like it eventually ends up thousands of miles away to the east, at Lhasa, but there's an isolated section

207

down here where it tracks within just a few short miles of the border.'

'There's a vast mountain wilderness south of there,' Charlie tapped the web of white veins representing glaciers and snow-covered peaks. 'Dyson would never make it on foot.'

'No, but Mahmood might just make it in a chopper.'

'What, violate sovereign Chinese airspace in a Pakistani military aircraft? Cause an international incident? You're crazier than I am!' Charlie said it with a hint of admiration in his voice.

'No harm in asking. I don't see any other option and Dyson is deteriorating fast. I can't see him lasting long without dialysis.'

'Be a shame to lose him now, given we went to so much trouble to get him,' Charlie said bluntly.

'I'll try to call Mahmood.' Liam indicated the van far below. 'Let's get back. There's no signal up here.'

'Something serious is on the go down there.' Charlie pointed in the direction of the border post beyond the ridge. 'Possibly it's us. Or maybe they're even more paranoid about each other these days, with the spread of all the so-called fundamentalism in this region. Either way, any voice traffic between Xinjiang and Islamabad is going to be heavily monitored. Possibly even blocked. So far they don't know we're here. It's a risk.'

They started their clamber down the rocky slope. Liam paused and checked the date on his watch. 'Do you think that would apply to traffic between China and the range country in southern Tibet?'

'No, not so much. No real reason. They're more worried about the river valleys in that part of the world. Why?'

'I'm pretty sure my dad's buddy Greg Carter is in Tibet. He was organizing a Shishapangma expedition round now. I borrowed his satellite phone when I was in Kathmandu. I have the number here somewhere. If he's not on the mountain right at this moment, he could be just a few miles from the Nepalese border. He may be willing to head back for us. A call from Nepal to Pakistan isn't going to make too many waves.'

'Worth a shot,' Charlie said. 'If you get through, lose the SIM and battery as soon as you ring off. Just to be on the safe side.'

* * *

The planned Shishapangma climb had been a debacle from start to finish. In spite of the written authorizations in triplicate, the authorities in Tibet were becoming more paranoid with each passing day and the group had been denied permission to go ahead. They were still cooling their heels in the trail-head town of Nyalam. Greg Carter had been negotiating on a daily basis without any resolution and was seriously considering pulling the plug. He would take a bath on the fees but climbing was like that. Liam's unexpected call helped him make his decision.

'I can be back in Nepal in a couple of hours. Give me those co-ordinates again. If I can actually talk a Pakistani bloke, who has no idea who I am, into visiting with you, on the off-chance that I'm not a lunatic, I want to make bloody sure I send him to the right spot.'

* * *

The stress of the past few days was beginning to take its toll on Walter Dyson. He was nauseous, dizzy and spent most of his time sleeping. He needed dialysis. The altitude wasn't helping either. They were over a hundred miles south of Yecheng, deep in the valleys of the towering Kunlun Range. The van was concealed in a shallow defile above the dry Yarkand riverbed, its headlights positioned ready to illuminate an area of wide gravel at the flick of a switch. Already 24 hours had passed since they'd placed all their hopes in the hands of two distant men, men who knew nothing of each other, and set off down the unmade mountain road. All they could do now was wait and hope. There was no way of knowing.

If Mahmood came he would almost certainly come in darkness.

* * *

The Singaporean's ill temper, it seemed, wasn't reserved for Mr Paul's exclusive benefit. He'd just endured yet another long journey from Singapore, this time via Beijing to Ruoqiang, and his small team of China-based fixers were experiencing some of his toxic heat.

'An old cop down in Niya talked to them and was smart enough to record their details,' a thickset tattooed man was saying. 'The vehicle registration was different but everything else fitted. They went into the police system and that set off our warning signal. We have the border crossing locked down tight and so we...'

'I really don't need the narrative. Tell me where they are and what your plan is to stop them. That's all the information I need.'

'We've had reported sightings in the south and one reliable eye witness,' the man responded hurriedly. 'We think they're on the Kunlun road. Heading for Lhasa is my guess.'

'Lhasa, why would they head for Lhasa?' The irritated Singaporean looked down at the map.

The man ran a stubby finger along the route. 'That's where the road goes. It's the only logical destination along that road.'

'Yes, 2,000 kilometers along that road. Why would you travel 2,000 kilometers to the west of Xinjiang if your intended destination is another 2,000 to the east? That's not a red herring, that's a great white whale.' He attacked the map with an insistent index finger. 'No, look. This point here, just a few kilometers from the Pakistani border. That's where they'd be heading.'

'But that's in the middle of nowhere, they'd have to walk through Pakistan for days, weeks. The man Dyson, he's not capable of that. He's ill.'

'Then I guess they're not walking.' His finger thudded onto the map again.

'Get somebody out there, quickly.'

'Our choppers have gone north. We got a call saying they were needed in the Altai.'

'Well then, send someone on the fucking ground. Buy them fucking bicycles if you have to. Just do it.'

* * *

Some time after midnight Liam held his hand up to silence

the muted riverbank conversation. As he listened, he became increasingly certain it was not his imagination. He could hear the sound of a motor. It seemed to be coming from the valley to the south across the river. Or was it coming from the cutting to the northwest, somewhere up the road they'd traveled the previous day? No, it was coming from the south and it sounded like the unmistakable thud of a helicopter. But moments later it seemed to be a different sound coming from a different direction.

'Two engines, fuck it,' Charlie said urgently. 'There's a chopper but I think something's coming up the road.'

'We'll have to risk the headlights,' Liam yelled, racing back to the van. 'It's our only chance.'

The river valley took a sharp turn just ahead and a steep ridge on the far side concealed the entrance to the deep ravine from which the insistent thudding came. As Liam's headlights flickered on they were answered by the bright beam of a spotlight bursting round the rocky rim. A military chopper clattered into view an instant later and came racing towards them.

Somewhere back along the road, the sound of other powerful engines reverberated like thunder off the walls of the narrow valley that still concealed them.

The chopper hovered for a moment in the dim headlights and then eased expertly to within six inches of the surface.

Off to the west, two sets of dazzling high beams and fogs split the night as two big SUVs came roaring out of the gorge, fishtailed around the tight bend and accelerated towards them. They were now just a few hundred yards away and closing fast. Liam heard the sound of gunfire.

He lifted his weapon and sent a stream of bullets into the leading headlights. The heavy vehicle skidded across the loose surface and slewed to a stop. The other kept coming.

Jia and Luo Chen manhandled the groggy Dyson onto the metal floor and then clambered in themselves. In the eerie console glow, Charlie caught a glimpse of Mahmood's grim face. He and Liam rode the skids, as the chopper powered up and dipped to the south. Two bursts of fire penetrated the darkness and Liam heard the whine of a round displacing air nearby. He held on with one hand and fired again at the vehicle, which was now no more than a hundred yards away.

A returning round ricocheted off a skid and a small piece of shrapnel embedded itself in Charlie's left buttock.

'Goddam,' he yelled, as Liam shoved him into the chaotic, vibrating space. He fired off one last burst as they disappeared behind the sharp spur.

'We'll have to stop meeting like this,' Mahmood said without smiling, as Liam swung his long legs up onto the metal floor.

19

'SOMEONE'S been in there.'

Charlie stood hunched over a small tablet. Liam broke off from shaving and walked into the room.

The screen image was monochrome and revealed a group of shadowy figures moving around in a space that looked a lot like Charlie's Queensland living room.

'How'd you get that?' Liam asked, wiping soap from his chin.

'The cameras are hidden. So is the computer. It's under the floor. I've got it programmed to send me a clip in an email if anyone breaches the place when it's in lockdown; even if they take out the power. According to the date, this happened the night after we left.'

'So I guess now we won't be going back. Jia doesn't get a chance to relax poolside.'

'No, goddam it, not wise for a while.' He touched his bandaged buttock gingerly. 'This little adventure of yours is turning into a pain in the ass.'

'It may explain the little party south of Yecheng last night. If they know who you are they probably know who I am too. That puts everyone in danger. We'll need to be super careful now.'

They heard the doorbell chime from the other room. The door was opened and they heard Jia greeting Mahmood.

'I'll just finish shaving,' Liam said and walked back into the bathroom.

He dried his face, pulled on freshly laundered clothes and moved to the doorway into the adjoining room. He stood with his back to the curtained window and watched his two good friends as they talked easily; Mahmood sitting comfortably, Charlie standing leaning on a stick.

The Islamabad hotel was beginning to feel like a second home and his debt to both of them was growing exponentially.

'What's happening about your illegal cross border incursion?' Charlie was asking.

Mahmood's smile was a little thin. 'The story my superiors have agreed to is engine trouble and navigation problems. I was only in Chinese airspace for a few minutes and, technically speaking, I was never on the ground. I thought your van might complicate things. You can be sure the Chinese authorities will go over it with microscopic precision. But so far they are being remarkably sanguine.'

He ran a finger over his neat military moustache. 'The impression I'm getting is that, given the current situation in both countries, the last thing that either government wants to do is make more waves.'

He waved the subject away airily. 'I'm not too concerned about it, really.'

Liam strolled across and joined them.

'What I am very much concerned about is your Mr Dyson.' Mahmood looked up at Liam without smiling. 'The people at the hospital are very nervous,' he said. 'It's a private facility. They don't want to lose their license. We have to get him out of there soon.'

Charlie nodded, then shrugged. 'Yep, that's right. But where?'

'Why not just hand him over to the US Embassy here?' Mahmood suggested. 'Make him their problem.'

Liam looked harassed.

'We still don't know exactly who's involved. What we do know is they kill people without a second thought. The site may be in China, but the aircraft are basically American and so is the man who was responsible for building them. He claims some of the people who recruited him were Americans.

'We can't be sure US agencies aren't involved. If we turn over Dyson and it's their show then he's a dead man. I think we have to stay off the grid. Finish what we started; find out what's going on and who's behind it and then try to get Cherry or somebody else to tell the world.'

Charlie pointed at the computer standing surrounded by a tangle of wires on the hotel-room desk. 'Meanwhile I need time to break into that hard drive of theirs.'

'Then you'll need to get out of Islamabad,' Mahmood said with some finality. 'I can't keep you safe here. I don't have the resources. Peshawar, Islamabad, Pindi; they are all going berserk. If these China people want to get rid of you they have a thousand easy options. Nobody would even notice you among the stacks of other corpses.'

He looked across to Jia and gave her an apologetic half-smile.

'I can organize a small apartment for you in Karachi. It's not DC, Liam, but it's the best I can do. You should be relatively safe there for a while if you're careful – it's not quite as tumultuous as the north. There are enough Westerners that you won't stand out if you have to move about. But there's still Dyson...'

Jia had been listening from the sidelines. 'If we can get the right equipment, I can do Walter's dialysis for him in the apartment. I know people do it. I'm willing to try. I studied first aid in Beijing.'

* * *

They were like two powerful and malevolent monarchs, their snarling hounds at their sides waiting to tear each other to pieces the moment a royal finger gave a twitch of permission.

This was a private meeting. Too sensitive to share with all but the few in the inner sanctum. Just four gleaming helicopters straddled the residual patches of snow beside the gabled building.

The ski lodge, high in the Spanish Picos, was closed for the summer. The nearest town was an hour's drive away and the track in, perilous at the best of times, had been rendered impassable by heavy spring rains.

Polson had never liked his pretentious British associate and he knew the feeling was mutual. Theirs was a business arrangement, a partnership based on reciprocal advantage, a marriage of convenience, devoid of affection but held together by a grudging and wary respect.

If the liaison between the two superiors was civilly pragmatic, that between their two attack dogs could be described as nothing less than poisonous. It was a relationship beyond redemption.

'These assholes, Casement and Doyle, they seem to be pissing all over your security guys.' Polson took great delight in offending the pompous Brit with his crude language. 'What the fuck is going on?'

He turned his attention to the seething Singaporean. 'How many times now is it that your crack commandos have come up short? Three, four?' He glanced back at the Englishman opposite. 'And now this prick Dyson is gone. Lifted from under your noses.'

The scarred flesh on Cassidy Millston's face stretched a little with his grin. He was loving this.

Polson rounded on him. 'What have you got to smile about, you little shit? You haven't exactly bathed yourself in fucking glory either.'

'This isn't helping, Edward,' the aristocratic man said, feigning calm. 'Dyson is a game changer. To date all these people have, as far as we know, are a few vague suspicions. God knows where they originated.'

'Don't fucking look at me,' Polson said. 'The problems are in the fucking east.' He pointed in the direction of what he imagined was China. 'That's got nothing to fucking do with me.'

'And, if Dyson isn't located, they'll be all over the north, the south and the west very shortly. We are just a few months away from achieving all our objectives. It would be extremely regrettable if everything were to fall apart now.'

The half-dozen expensively dressed people in the room nodded their agreement and turned to face the Singaporean with expectant expressions.

'Well, what do you intend to do about it?' a heavily overweight Russian asked in a Sobranie-ravaged voice.

'We believe these people, including Dyson, are still in Pakistan,' the Singaporean said. 'It's a difficult place to monitor; extremely chaotic currently. I have all the people I can spare looking for them, but it won't be easy. Even if they're using their phones we'd need to monitor hundreds of millions of calls a day. Filtering on that scale is nearly impossible. Dyson will need dialysis, that may be a way in; we've already started checking with the hospitals and clinics.'

'Well, just get the fuck on with it. I'll send Millston over to give you a hand,' Polson said. 'He might as well do something to earn the king's fucking ransom he's paid.'

A fly on the wall would have noticed the fleeting expressions of mutual horror that crossed the faces of both subordinates.

'That won't be necessary,' the Singaporean said hurriedly. 'I'm taking control of this one personally.'

* * *

They stepped from the taxi into an exotic world of multicolored chaos. The waterfront smelled of old fish. Very old fish. A smell of fish that had lingered, secreted somewhere in thick sisal rope, canvas sail or rush baskets, perhaps for centuries. Liam wrinkled his nose until his olfactory system began to adjust. The apprehensive Luo Chen didn't seem to notice.

Small, ancient boats jostled for space along the length of the piers on both sides of the oil-slicked channel; in places a dozen or more deep. They walked slowly, careful not to lose their footing on the thin gel of oleaginous fish waste coating the slippery stone.

Liam located the boat, greeted the weathered skipper and then handed Luo Chen an envelope.

'I'm glad we didn't shoot you,' he said, smiling. 'You're not that bad a guy.' They shook hands. 'They should have you in Singapore in a few days. Try to stay out of trouble.'

Luo Chen stuffed the envelope into his newly acquired backpack without checking the contents. 'Thank you.' He took Liam's hand and shook it again. 'Thank you.' He paused, not quite sure what to say next. 'My brother, he makes the best chili crab in Serangoon. You must try next time you come to Singapore. I will pay.'

Liam watched as the small crew cast off and maneuvered out into the busy waterway. They exchanged brief waves and then the young man motored slowly out of his life.

He walked back to the apartment through the steaming, teeming Karachi streets. Sometimes the longing for the cold solitude of the Kerry mountains felt almost like a physical pain.

Charlie was still hard at work on the pilfered data.

'Any luck yet?'

He shook his head in response. 'Not much. Some strange entries here. The cash deposited in the bank in Jiuquan appears to be withdrawn from another local bank. That money is a transfer from a cash deposit into a busy central bank in Moscow. No way of knowing where those funds originate.'

Liam gave him an encouraging thump on the shoulder and stepped softly into the nearby bedroom. Walter Dyson was awake and looking much better.

'Jia's a fine nurse,' he said in answer to Liam's comment on his improvement.

'You had no idea what Lionel Rigby did?' Liam sat on a stool next to the silent machine. 'Never had an inkling? Never even hazarded a guess?'

'I had my own dramas,' Dyson gestured helplessly, taking care not to dislodge the dialysis tubes. 'Our best was never enough. We built a functioning fleet to a deadline that would have destroyed your average workforce. But a few months later we were onto a second fleet and, of course, it had to be more efficient, bigger, quicker. It was never-ending.'

'That first aircraft that crashed, do you know where it went in?'

'Yes, as we discussed, Pakistan.'

'No, I mean specifically.'

Dyson shook his head. 'I wasn't told.'

'The plane crashed near K2, Mount Godwin Austen, in the Karakoram Ranges. I was a boy at the time. My dad was on that mountain. He saw it. And for that they blew a hole in his chest this big.' He held up a clenched fist and allowed it to drift a little toward Dyson's startled eyes. 'We passed within just a few short miles of his body in Mahmood's helicopter the other night.'

The freshly cleansed blood being pumped through Dyson's circulatory system wasn't enough to prevent his face from turning a shade paler.

'I'm sorry. I don't know what to say.'

'There are victims,' Liam said quietly. 'There are always victims. Real flesh-and-blood victims with families, loved ones. I know you believed you had no choice, I know you were in a sterilized world, a scientific world; of machines, mechanics, mathematics... I understand your fear.' Liam paused for moments, hoping his words would sink in. 'But your actions had consequences. Real, live, human consequences. They're still having consequences.'

He stood and walked to the foot of the bed then turned and faced the prostrate man.

'And so I ask you once again. Humor me. Use your imagination. If you had to take a wild guess at what Rigby might have been involved in, what would it be?'

Dyson lay silent for several minutes. The only sound in the room was the quiet humming of the pump.

'If I was to hazard a guess, I would say that the biological-weapon scenario is unlikely. If I was pushed, I'd say perhaps...'

'Sulfur,' Charlie said, walking into the room. 'Were you about to say sulfur?'

'Sulfur dioxide?' Liam gave him a questioning look. Dyson said nothing.

'Yeah, SO_2. Made from burning coal. When coal is burned, the sulfur combines with oxygen in the combustion air to produce SO_2.'

'Yes,' Liam said. 'So?'

'So, Xinjiang,' Charlie said. 'Coal. A simple way to get SO_2 in large quantities is from scrubbing coal, coal mines. Xinjiang is rich in coal resources, they have estimated reserves of over two trillion tons, mainly in the north. The place is littered with unregulated, illegally operated mines.' He returned to the other room and brought back a sheaf of freshly printed pages. 'Look at this, from a few years back.' He read aloud from the top page. 'Explosion at illegally operated Xinjiang coal mine kills 21.' He skimmed further down the page with the help of a big squat finger. 'This one was at Baiyanggou. That's around 60 miles west of Urumqi.' He looked up at Dyson. 'Area ring any bells?' He went back to reading from the page. 'Listen to this. "Lax

219

enforcement of regulations and safety standards…" The place is littered with these illicit mines and nobody bothers to monitor them.'

He shuffled through the pages, found another and held it up triumphantly. 'It's all here in their paperwork. Our friends were buying sulfur dioxide from every dodgy coal-burning setup in northwestern Xinjiang. Buying it by the truckload.'

He dropped the papers onto the foot of Dyson's bed.

'Are you saying what I think you're saying?' If Liam was still uncertain, Dyson clearly wasn't. He was paler than ever.

'Yeah, what I'm saying is there's one potentially very unpleasant explanation… I'll get back to you.' Charlie left the room and returned to his computer.

* * *

The big, perennially gregarious man had spent nearly 24 uninterrupted hours hunched over his glowing monitor and Liam had never seen him so shattered.

He slammed a huge fist onto the table, making the used tea cups rattle nervously.

'Goddam.' He pointed at his screen. 'Nothing.'

Liam gave him an enquiring look.

'I sensed there was something not quite right months ago but I couldn't put my finger on it,' Charlie said. He pushed back from the table and stood, indicating the monitor again.

'The billionaire geo-engineering mob. They've gone silent. Not a murmur out of them for months and months. They'd been talking up the benefits, no, the necessity, of intervening with some kind of technofix to counteract climate change for years. Learned articles in science journals, international seminars and symposiums and then suddenly not a peep out of them.'

He dismissed the material on the screen with an impatient gesture. 'The odd well-meaning scientist is still doing the research, getting a paper published now and then, but the big push from the serious end of town?' He shook his head. 'Nothing there. Disappeared. Suddenly gone all secretive.'

'So what you're suggesting is that they're using the SO_2 to...' Liam began.

Charlie finished his sentence for him. 'Mess with the climate. Aerosol sulfate formation happens when sulfur dioxide is released into the atmosphere and combines with water vapor to form aqueous sulfuric acid. It condenses onto particles of solid matter, things like dust blown up into the stratosphere.'

Liam nodded. 'I know, I know. The aerosol particles also create larger particles or droplets. It's a process they call coagulation. They spread up there across the stratosphere for a while and stop sunlight, heat, from getting through to the surface.' He paused and shook his head. 'Holy shit. They're trying to geo-engineer the planet's climate.'

Charlie nodded. 'Secret bombers. Sulfur. It's all starting to add up.'

'But that's crazy. There are so many questions about the knock-on effects of this sort of stuff that haven't been answered yet.'

'That's not necessarily going to stop sociopaths.'

'Well, we need to find out – quickly. We can't wait, we need to do something now.'

'Until we know who's behind all this, I'm not sure what we can do.' Charlie said. 'If it's being run by a government, or even a number of governments, including our very own, then we are in deep shit.'

'If it is a government, then why not just come out and say "Hey, look, we're doing this"?'

'Because it would cause a riot. And because that's not what governments do. They prefer to keep things secret from the great unwashed. "We the people" are a pain in the ass to them; they see us as a great big chaotic, unstructured obstacle that always gets in their way. The people just bitch and protest.'

'Not a lot of the people I know. Most of them couldn't give a damn until something affects them personally.'

Charlie looked like he was on the verge of total capitulation. 'Yeah, perhaps you're right.' He ran tired hands through his hair, stood and walked to the window and looked down at the chaos that was Karachi. 'Perhaps we should just walk away. Leave them to it.'

Liam ignored him. 'It still sounds to me like the media is our best option. Our *only* option,' he said. 'There's no point going to the police, the FBI, CIA, NSA, MI5, MI6, the Sûreté or Mossad, if half of them could be up to their necks in it.'

'No, probably not.'

'But we don't have enough to take to the media yet, to Cherry.'

'No, probably not.'

'What about Walter?' he indicated the other room. 'Living, breathing evidence.'

Charlie shook his head.

'He says he knows nothing about the sulfur and all I have is stuff from a hacked hard drive and a hunch. Their first question would be: why did he really disappear? Was he working on some secret project for the Chinese? They'd either try to create doubt around his story, discredit him completely... or just kill him.'

He returned to the table and stared down at the computer.

'We've had this conversation before,' Charlie said. 'We still need to know who they are.'

'Well then, there's only one answer,' Liam said. 'We keep digging.'

'Yes.'

'I'll get onto Cherry and ask her to run the Rigby search again, get her to add atmospheric sciences, geo-engineering and that stuff to the mix, see if she can come up with anything more.'

Charlie's sapping emotional energy seemed to kick back in. 'Meantime we need a quiet, safe, isolated place to base ourselves while we try to sort this out. Karachi's not it. You know the rules. Once they're onto you, you keep moving. Besides, if our covert friends don't get us, a terrorist car bomber probably will.'

'There's always Ireland,' Liam said. 'My dad's old cousin lives in Dublin now but he has a little place on the Beara, in the Caha Mountains. It's in the west. Miles from anywhere. You don't get much quieter than that. And maybe that way I could spend a little time with my mom.'

'Can I get online there?'

'There's accessible signal, I'm pretty sure.'

Liam indicated the other room with a raised thumb. Jia was busy with Dyson's dialysis. 'Jia has her own passport; no reason why it wouldn't still be legit as far as I can tell, there's no reason they'd know who she is. What about Dyson? We'll need to keep him with us for the time being.'

'I've never done an Irish passport,' Charlie smiled and winked. 'What color are they?'

'Not green.'

Liam picked up his phone. 'I'll see if Mahmood can suggest any way of getting us out of the country. It might be best if we didn't fly out of a Pakistani airport.'

'There's always Kabul,' Charlie said with a grin. 'They've probably missed us.' His brief period of despondency seemed to be behind him.

20

CALIFORNIA, as expected, had gone Donna Stone's way in convincing fashion. Cherry was back in her Washington office briefly before a quick drive up the freeway to New Jersey and another hectic round of Primary wheeling and dealing.

She located the prepaid phone in the bottom of her cluttered bag, attached the battery, inserted the SIM card and punched in the international code for Ireland.

'We've had another look for Rigby, did what you suggested,' she said, when Liam answered. 'We found a Leonie Rigby. She went to school in Washington but did her postgraduate work in Atmospheric and Oceanic Sciences at UCLA.

'Her college yearbook lists her main research interests as "Stratospheric and tropospheric chemistry, and their role in the biogeochemical cycles and climate". She was also one of a very few women chess grandmasters.'

'Impressive,' was all Liam said.

'After UCLA, she went on to the National Center for Atmospheric Research in Colorado. Nothing out of the ordinary, nothing too radical. Only one thing the least bit unusual. There seems to be some evidence of an interest in gender reassignment surgery. She had dealings with a clinic in Boulder. There's evidence that, a few weeks later, she took off into Eastern Europe, Ukraine, somewhere like that. Then the trail goes cold. We checked with passports. The next of kin listed was a woman with the same Christian name as Lionel's mother. Same Maryland address.'

'Did he have a sister, Lionel? Have you found her?' Liam's mellifluous words flowed down the line from across the Atlantic. She could hear new traces of the old Irish already.

'No, we've been through births, deaths, marriages, adoptions, every filing system possible. Nothing. Leonie was an only child. No siblings, biological or otherwise.'

'So then maybe Lionel was…?'

'Yes, Leonie. Lionel was Leonie. One and the same. That's the only conclusion we can come to. We're looking into gender-changing surgical facilities in eastern Europe as we speak.'

'Explains the total lack of any Lionel footprints.'

'Yes. Anyhow. Gotta go. New Jersey awaits.'

* * *

Midday had been and gone before the fog finally tore itself to ribbons on the jagged ridges and revealed the horseshoe of peaks surrounding the farmhouse.

Liam's black dog was loitering again as the days drifted by without any clear direction. Inactivity had always been anathema and he could feel the darkness starting to mess with his mind.

He wandered around the farmhouse from room to room. Jia was working on the much-improved Dyson's dialysis. Charlie was tinkering with a series of computer towers, in pieces on the kitchen table.

'The only lead we have now is Rigby and Moscow. We should get ourselves to Moscow.'

Charlie looked up, his attention still directed to the maze of equipment in front of him. 'No point unless we know exactly where in Moscow,' he said absently. 'It's a big place.'

'Yeah,' Liam said with a grudging nod. 'I know. I know.'

He pulled on a pair of sturdy boots. 'I'll see you later.'

The farm was at the very end of the narrow valley; four miles of additional isolation beyond the already-isolated Glanmore Lough.

Directly above, to the north, Lackabane towered to around 2,000 feet. Behind it, Eskatarriff was less than ten feet lower. To the south loomed Derryclancy and the Caha's highest, Hungry Hill; 250 feet taller than its fellow across the valley. Lackawee and Knocknagree completed the natural enclosure to the west.

It was a perfect place for anyone not wishing to be taken by surprise. Unless they knew the landscape intimately, nobody was likely to attempt an approach over the mountains, and the only other way in was long, narrow and winding. A sheer rock buttress jutting into the track, 400 yards before the house, created a sharp dogleg, and one of Charlie's alarmed cameras, placed in a crevasse and wired back to the dwelling, would give them ample warning of any clandestine approach from the east.

Liam surveyed the soaring ramparts with satisfaction and decided on a quick stride up the steep southern flank of Lackabane.

A soft mist was rolling over the high western col as he bounded down the last few hundred feet less than two hours later and, even in the midst of a fine summer, a chill crept silently up the valley floor.

Smoke already curled from the chimney as he covered the last few yards at a trot and kicked off his boots in the wet room.

Jia walked in as he was hanging up his parka.

'Did you have a nice walk?' she asked coolly. He nodded.

'I'd like to come with you next time you go.'

He looked at her delicate frame dubiously. 'It's pretty steep and rough up there and even at this time of year, if the weather turns it can get very cold very quickly.'

'I managed to cope all right when we were in the Altai,' she said. 'I didn't slow you down. I'm a lot stronger than I look. I still have my boots.'

'Okay,' he smiled. Their relationship had been a little strained and formal since he'd upset her in China and he hoped her request indicated a thaw was on the way. 'Maybe I can take you on an "introductory ramble". There's a reasonably easy route up to Derryclancy. We'll take a picnic if the weather's good. There's a fine lough nearby.'

'Thank you,' she said without smiling and walked back into the house.

* * *

The billboards along the freeway now carried only two Photoshopped faces. New Jersey, it seemed, would decide whether the Party's Presidential candidate was to be a man or a woman.

226

Stone and Arnott had ebbed and flowed with every state event held. One set of Primaries saw him looking the likely choice. Just a few weeks later, another state, another poll and it looked like she would take the prize.

With only New Jersey to go it was anybody's guess.

'The decision now is all yours, good people of New Jersey,' Donna Stone cried out to the sea of red, white and blue.

'Your decisions today will decide which of us two, the last two standing, will represent our great party in November's Presidential contest.'

Her voice rang out, loud, clear and confident.

'The fact that at the end of this long, long journey, after all the miles we have traveled, all the many Primaries we have contested, there are two candidates still on their feet, speaks, I think, volumes for the unity of the party's beliefs, our ideals and our policies.

'I believe the issues facing us today in South Asia, all the complex problems of the various regions, the various conflicts, need to be addressed in a new, a wiser way; with more grains and fewer guns.'

She paused to allow the roaring of the assembly to subside.

'So too does Congressman Arnott.' This was followed by more cheering.

'I believe, in spite of recent events in the Arctic, that it is essential we sign the Fossil Fuel Phase Out agreement in Lyon early next year. So does Jason Arnott.

'I believe that we must take this great manufacturing nation into the future and lead the way, with sunrise technology, to a modern and innovative world and so, I know, does Jason Arnott.

'But. I believe, too, that, here, now, on this day; no, at this *moment* of reckoning, I, Donna Stone, am your best choice and only I should be given the privilege of your nomination as our party's Presidential candidate.' She smiled. 'At this point Congressman Arnott and I part company.'

The laughter and applause of the faithful echoed around the vast space.

'While some of these beliefs may not make me the most

popular candidate ever to visit your fine state I know, in my heart, that I must take the hard road. I will not shirk from that responsibility and that, I believe, makes me the nation's right choice for President.'

Donna Stone lifted her arms high above her head, clenched her fists and gave them a mighty shake. The crowd roared its approval.

'Thank you people of the great state of New Jersey. The decision is now yours.'

A deafening thunder of approval followed her from the stage, buoyed her along a series of cold corridors and accompanied her out of the building.

* * *

'Where are you two off to?' Charlie came out of the house and watched them pulling on their boots.

'Picnic on Derryclancy,' Liam said, grinning like a schoolboy. 'I'm introducing Jia to the wonders of Irish mountain walking. Once you've been bitten you're hooked for life. You should try it yourself, you'd love it.'

'Yeah,' Charlie said with feigned uninterest. 'I'll take your word for it.'

Jia finished her laces and walked 50 feet across the grass to test her footwear.

'It's great to see you two communicating again,' Charlie said very softly. 'But just remember, you need to stay focused.' He waved to Jia and walked back into the house.

'This is the first time we have been alone together since we were in the Altai,' Jia said after they'd climbed in silence for a while. If she was breathless she wasn't showing it.

'And that wasn't exactly fun,' Liam said without smiling. He looked across at her; she seemed a little crestfallen.

'I had fun,' she said. 'A sort of fun.'

The day was windless and warm, with just the odd puffy cloud riding the higher mountains to the north. Even at the relaxed pace Liam allowed for Jia, they were on the edge of the Coomadayallig

Lough within a couple of hours.

'This is so beautiful, so wonderful after all that anxious time in China, in Pakistan and all that horrible shooting.' Jia sighed. 'It's so lovely to be able to relax.'

Liam gazed out over the Lough towards Bere Island without responding.

'You never talk much,' Jia said as they sat and ate their sandwiches. 'Not about yourself, your feelings. Not to me at least.'

Liam shrugged. 'Maybe it's a military thing, I don't know – I spent a lot of time alone. I had some…' he changed his tack. 'Or maybe it's just an Irish thing.'

'My mother always said that same thing about me. "You're so quiet, Jia. You say so little."'

She hoped Liam would ask her about her mother but he remained silent. They finished their lunches and lay side by side on the rug, staring up at the remarkably cloudless Caha sky.

'What do you think of me?' she asked at length.

He sat up and turned his head. 'What do you mean?'

She fiddled with a wilting wildflower. 'I mean how do you feel about me? Do you like me, do you have any feelings for me?'

Liam colored up. 'Yes, of course I like you.'

Charlie's words of caution hung like a mist between them. 'Stay focused.' This was a bad time for this to happen. As deeply as he felt for her, as hungry as he felt for a greater intimacy, his instinct for discipline, his need to keep his mind on the job had kept him silent and distant.

He looked into her trusting brown eyes and sensed the hurt an evasive answer, a lie, might cause. 'I like you very, very much,' he said, then turned his head and surveyed the ragged rocky strata that funneled up to the nearby summit.

'Like?' She asked. 'Like a sister?'

'No, not like a sister.' He shook his head. 'But I'm not somebody to get involved with, Jia. I have… issues. My time in the military, I get these very dark…' He trailed off.

Jia ignored him: she sat up, knelt on the rug, then leaned over and kissed him lightly on the lips.

'Is it *that* kind of liking?' she asked with a smile.

229

He nodded, resisted for just a heartbeat and then kissed her in return, a little more fervently. She parted her lips slightly and allowed her tongue to explore the beginnings of his mouth. He responded and a few moments later she was grasping at the buttons on his shirt, undoing them eagerly. Liam's hand slid gently to a place just above her breasts, she closed her eyes and then, without warning, a sad-faced image of the missing Zhang Liu filled her head and she tore herself away.

'No, no. I can't. Not yet.' She stood up, rearranging her clothes.

'What's wrong?' Liam asked, bewildered. 'Did I do something?'

'No, it's me,' she said. 'It's me.'

She searched for a way to explain it, to comfort Liam, who was clearly wounded. 'You've heard of Lao Tzu?'

Liam nodded.

'Lao Tzu said that new beginnings are often disguised as painful endings.' She looked out over the Lough. 'He was very wise.'

She scooped up her small backpack and started off up the slope towards the ridge. Liam folded the rug, stuffed it into his pack and jogged off after her.

By the time they reached the cottage a bank of cloud had moved in from the northwest and a light rain was falling.

* * *

Liam rinsed the four boots, leaned them against the wet-room stones and scuffed into the house. He could feel the warmth coming from the hearth two rooms away. He walked into the living area, slumped beside Charlie on the big sofa and propped the damp socks on his large feet across the top of a log in front of the flames. They sat in silence for some time, mesmerized by the infernal patterns deep beneath the glowing timbers.

Jia was the first one to break the spell. 'There is something I have been thinking about,' she said. The soft firelight created fleeting shadows across her graceful features as she turned to face them.

'When my father disappeared, they had a new person to replace him in just a few days.' She looked from one to the other uncertainly. 'When Lionel Rigby was killed there maybe was nobody to do his very special work. Perhaps we should try to check to see if someone with the similar special skills has left their work suddenly or disappeared from their home.' She hesitated, unsure of the viability of her idea.

'That's brilliant, Jia. That's fu... that's absolutely brilliant.' Charlie lifted himself stiffly from the sagging springs of the easy chair, took one step across the face of the fire with his tree-trunk legs and planted a kiss on her head.

Jia's golden skin flushed a little and her expression fluttered uncertainly, from nonplussed, to pleased, to nonplussed again.

Three hours later she was dozing alone, curled up in front of a grate filled with glowing embers. Charlie was back at his electronic jigsaw.

'Found something,' Liam called out. 'In the *Oxford Mail*.'

Jia stirred and stretched herself. With the unconscious elegance of a beautiful Burmese cat, Liam observed silently, glowing with a secret pleasure that quickly turned to confusion.

He returned his attention to the computer.

'Not all that long after Lionel Rigby was murdered this guy went missing from Oxford. Seems he went for a walk one morning and didn't return. No sign of him anywhere. He has a sister. Says he would never just leave. His health was fine, physical and mental. His passport was still tucked away safely in a drawer at his home.'

Charlie walked in and peered over his shoulder.

Liam tapped the image on his screen. 'Oskar Frederik. Senior Professor in the Department of Atmospheric, Oceanic and Planetary Physics. This guy's got a resumé made in heaven. He's a scientist, inventor, chemist, physicist and specialist in stratosphere and climate. He's published a list of academic papers as long as your arm.'

Liam clicked across to a new link. 'The department he headed up has been modeling different geo-engineering possibilities for years.'

He looked from one to the other. 'Oh, and he's from Latvia originally, fluent in Russian. That would probably be quite handy in Moscow.'

'They did it to Walter,' Jia said softly. 'They kidnapped him. Why not Mr Oskar?'

'So there has to be a fair chance he's in Moscow now,' Liam added.

Charlie nodded. 'If they have grabbed him to replace poor old Rigby he should have a fair idea of what they're up to by now,' he said. 'I'm a betting man, I'm willing to act on those odds.' He smiled ruefully. 'Now all we have to do is pick him out from the other 12 million souls.'

* * *

Dashka had decided to confront Alexei Denisovich. To demand to know what they were doing, what was going on. Otherwise, she would tell them, she planned to contact the authorities in Arkhangelsk and let them know something at Cape Zhelaniya seemed very wrong.

She procrastinated for several weeks, finding reason after reason to postpone the event. It was not fear that stopped her but the uneasy feeling that perhaps it was nothing and she was overreacting; becoming paranoid perhaps because of too many years on the island.

The arrival of the ship and her planned departure grew closer by the day. Summer had arrived and brought with it warmth and distraction and an increasing sense that maybe she should leave things be.

In a place like Cape Zhelaniya anything over 60 degrees Fahrenheit was considered a heatwave. In the insulated generator room the temperature was high enough to have them sweating. Dashka was crouched beside a back-up machine with Ivor very close by. She had stripped down to a light singlet in the heat and Ivor was bare chested. As she worked she could feel the warmth of his body, hear his breathing close to her ear.

'Pass me that spanner,' she said, extending a hand, without

looking. Instead of a spanner being slapped into her waiting palm, she felt the soft caress of a finger. She looked up, a little startled. He smiled and asked an unspoken question with a tilt of his handsome young head.

The charm was there still, but so too, the devious side, the doubt. When the vodka disappeared from the storage room, for example, everybody immediately assumed it was Ivor. But no proof was found and, while the subject was dropped, the suspicions remained.

Dashka ran her eyes over the young man's lean body. It had been years since she'd felt the intimate touch of a man's skin and the arousal that accompanied it.

She considered her options quickly and chose the charm, the arousal.

She suspected, even as she shuddered with an ecstasy so long forgone, that it was a mistake. But, as her cries grew more frequent, more urgent, she simply didn't care.

They lay without speaking for several minutes, on a jumbled bed of discarded clothes, tarpaulins and oil rags. For Dashka it had been no more than a sexual encounter; scratching an itch. Ivor, on the other hand, was quite sure he was in love.

She stood and pulled on her clothes.

'That was a first and a last time. It doesn't happen again,' she said as she left the overheated room. She'd been flattered by his desire for her, but was not interested in turning a single indiscretion into a relationship; apart from the fact she was nearly ten years older than he was, he wasn't to be trusted.

Ivor stared at the door that had just been slammed. He knew that she still thought of him as immature, as a kid. Well, he would give her a reason to take him seriously. She'd see.

21

A DAY AFTER the New Jersey Primaries Cherry finally had a moment or two to catch her breath. Stone had the numbers: it was all over. All that was now required was that the nomination be officially ratified at the National Convention in Philadelphia, the following month. Jason Arnott had agreed to join her team in the contest for Vice President. Cherry could not have been happier with the result. What still bothered her was that the President continued to poll significantly better than anyone else, on either side of politics.

As the plane reached cruising altitude and broke through a scrim of high cloud, she used her hand to block the cabin lights and gazed out into the darkness of the northern sky. 'I wonder,' she whispered to herself. 'I wonder.'

Almost 24 hours had passed before the backlog was cleared from her neglected city desk and she had a few spare minutes to make a quick international call.

'Hi there,' Liam sounded as warm as ever.

She could never quite get over the quality of ingenuousness she sensed whenever she heard his voice. 'Hi Liam, how're things in West Cork?' She attempted an Irish accent.

'South Kerry… by a whisker,' he said. 'Grand,' he laughed with pleasure. 'Just grand.'

'I was right,' she said. 'You are reverting to type. It didn't take long.'

He laughed again. It was a delightful, unrestrained sound and 3,000 miles away she smiled in return.

'I've been thinking about all this. Rigby, the planes, the sulfur. You know, of course, that, against all odds, for a couple of winters now the Arctic ice has been coming back?'

'Yep,' he said. 'I've heard that.'

'I'm probably being paranoid but I'm wondering if our friends

234

have anything to do with that?'

'Holy shit. Of course.' He was silent for a long moment. 'Holy shit. We really need to find these people, don't we?'

'I think we do, Liam. I really think we do.'

Liam said goodnight, went into the other room and unloaded Cherry's theory onto Jia and Charlie.

'Not impossible.' Charlie, as usual, was the first to comment.

'And that would explain their choice of the Altai Mountain site. The Arctic, a straight short flight due north, largely over Siberian wilderness,' Liam offered.

'Yes, it probably would,' Charlie said.

'But if you want to spread sulfur over the Arctic it's around 3,000 kilometers from there over possibly hostile Russian territory,' Jia said. 'Why give yourself such a long journey? Why take such a risk?'

'The original B2 has a range and speed that could cope, so I suspect this pilfered variation would do even better.' Charlie paused, considering Jia's question. 'Even if you located yourself in northern Siberia, you would likely come under more scrutiny than you would in Xinjiang.

'Xinjiang is a long, long way from Beijing, Shanghai, Guangzhou, even Chongqing and prying eyes. It's an autonomous territory full of troublesome Uighurs. It's a bit of your wild west. Miners die in illegal mines on a regular basis and nobody takes much notice. It's barren and relatively empty. In China, with a population well over a billion, Xinjiang has around 20 million and most of those live in a scattering of small cities. It has massive mountain ranges and deserts. You could fit Britain into the Taklamakan twice and still have room left over for Ireland; and it's damn near empty. The province as a whole is bigger than France, Spain and Germany put together. Not a bad place to hide out and fly off to the Arctic under the radar.'

'Or right through it,' Liam added.

Charlie shrugged wide shoulders.

'Frankly I wouldn't be surprised if the plan was to *start* with the Arctic and, if it proved to be successful, move to lower latitudes and eventually possibly even into the southern hemisphere. In that context Xinjiang makes perfect sense. You have all that access to coal and are unlikely to be bothered by the Beijing bureaucrats 2,000 miles away.'

'I still can't get over the audacity of the whole thing.' Liam shook his head.

'Billionaire moguls and their scientist subordinates have been exploring the possibility of all sorts of high-flying theories to slow atmospheric warming for years. Using sulfur dioxide to filter out the sun's rays is just one of them. Makes sense that if the sun doesn't radiate as much heat down into the polar atmosphere then the ice comes back... Talking of ice.'

He went to the fridge and found himself a cold beer.

'But what else happens, meantime? What these people seem to have conveniently overlooked is the odd problem. If their geo-engineering gives humanity an excuse to keep pumping out carbon then we keep adding it to the atmosphere. If at some stage, for any of countless reasons, they needed to stop suddenly, stop the effects of the atmospheric sulfur distribution, then the increased CO_2 in the air combined with a return to our normal dose of sunlight would be catastrophic. And that's before we even factor in all the possible side-effects the process might have – like the effect on the ozone layer for one.'

'But why would they do this?' Jia asked. Even as a woman in her mid-twenties she was still having trouble accepting that human beings had the capacity for such hubris.

'Their reasons are very simple, I suspect. If the process ends up a success, so the spin goes, global temperature stops rising and we can go back to all the dirty business as usual. The planet's fossil-fuel people are paid to continue digging the stuff out of the ground and paid to try to cool the stratosphere at the same time. It's a bit like short selling. They make billions creating the problem on the way up and then they make billions claiming to solve the problem they've created on the way down. Win win.'

Liam laughed, but there was no humor in it. He shook his head. 'For decades the world's best medical scientists have been trying to find a cure for cancer, Parkinson's, MS, you name it, and so far, they're all still killing us. As a species we've been spectacularly unsuccessful at controlling the complex health of our own bodies, let alone...'

Charlie interrupted, creating a wide arc with a sweep of his bottle.

'Let alone the infinitely more complex goddam planet. What kind of runaway arrogance makes these people think they can use their nascent technological fixes to solve the immense goddam problems we're having with the climate?'

He paused for breath and shook his head. His smile suggested a grudging admiration.

'Mind you, whoever they are, I have to say, they're good, these people – very good. If your buddy Cherry is right about the Arctic, then they're very good.'

'Or just very powerful,' Liam added.

'To carry out something of this magnitude without leaving any footprints, that's quality. No chatter, no rumors, no hint of anything going on. I've been trawling for days. Usually there's a leak, something on Facebook, Twitter, Tumblr, Instagram, Pinterest, Wikileaks, somewhere! Some disgruntled minion, some blog somewhere, someone who's heard something from someone else who heard it from a third party. Something.'

Liam wasn't buying into the admiration, grudging or otherwise. 'But do they truly think they can get away with it indefinitely, without the world finding out? Building stealth bombers, flying all over the planet, bombing the stratosphere at will, changing the climate. It's science-fiction stuff.'

'These people are sociopaths, young Liam,' Charlie said, quieter now. 'You've seen how the extremist think tanks and lobbyists, the media, have been used to continue to deny there are major problems, in the face of all the physical evidence; almost universal agreement from every relevant scientist; every peer-reviewed journal; every reputable organization. Their greed and arrogance have made them blind, made them unhinged. Doing something like this is just another step, a small escalation.

'They know all they need to do is create a tiny chink, a tiny bit of doubt. "Look," they say, "the Arctic is cooling again, the ice is back, it's just another natural cycle," and the average Joe will sigh with relief and yell business as usual. Nobody wants to have less of anything, that's what everyone's afraid of and that's what they prey on.'

He made a dismissive gesture with his free hand. 'Anyhow. Enough of my soap box already.'

'Still. It's crazy stuff.' Liam shook his head. Jia looked troubled.

'Yeah, and I'm about to go crazy trying to find out where Rigby was performing his dastardly deeds in Moscow, before they topped him.' Charlie tapped his screen. 'I have his home, I have his church, I have the post office. Logic tells me they'll be operating somewhere within that triangle or very nearby. These people would want to keep him within easy reach. But there's nothing that shows any promise. Nowhere really suitable to run a major program like this. If I knew more of his habits, where he shopped, his bank, his chess club, it might help. I don't have enough to go on.'

'Pity.' Liam shook his head. 'There's a fair chance that if they've grabbed Oskar Frederik that's where he'll be.'

Charlie yawned and stretched long, muscular arms towards smoke-darkened rafters. 'I think I'll sleep on it.'

* * *

A cotton white tablecloth of cloud enveloped Hungry Hill as Liam sprinted over the last rise before the summit. He checked his watch. He could be back at the farmhouse in time for a late breakfast if he took the steep way down across the Knocknagree ridge.

As he jogged along comfortably, something occurred to him. It came, it seemed, from out of the Beara blue and he suddenly remembered Charlie's words from months before.

'You can't keep something this big a complete secret... someone will make a mistake, there will be leaks.'

He lifted his pace, leaping down the precipitous slope with the grace and agility of a Bilberry goat.

He banged into the farmhouse. Charlie looked up, startled.

'What? Visitors?'

'No,' Liam slowed down. 'Just an idea.' He started rifling through a sideboard drawer. 'Where's the article on Dyson? The thing from the *Dialog* that Rigby sent?'

Charlie reached patiently into a folder lying alongside the computer and thumbed methodically through the contents until he located the photocopied page.

Liam examined it closely. 'Is this a copy of a hard copy, an actual newspaper, or a copy of an online page?'

Charlie shook his head. 'What do you mean?'

'The *Dialog* has an online service that's free but its content is different from the news-stand version, not as comprehensive. You can download an electronic version of the actual newspaper content, the entire content, but you have to subscribe, you have to pay.'

'Yes..?' Charlie was starting to go with him.

Liam studied the page through a magnifying glass. 'This looks like a copy of the electronic newspaper to me – look at the edge of the page.' He passed it back to Charlie.

'Remember what you said to me in Queensland, "eventually someone will make a mistake".'

Charlie nodded. 'Basic rule of espionage.'

'This is not taken from a hard copy of a Washington paper. I'm thinking maybe Rigby was paying for an online subscription and I'm wondering if that's the mistake.'

'There are international newsagents in Moscow,' Charlie said. His expression suggested doubt. 'It *might* be from a hard copy.'

'No, look at the page, this faint code here at the bottom.' He handed Charlie the magnifying glass. 'Rigby was gone for nigh-on ten years. He'd have been hungry for news from home. Why would you go trudging out into the snow if you could get it right there on your computer, as it happened?'

He retrieved the page and looked again at Dyson's fading image. 'If it was a subscription, could you find the location the payments were coming from?'

'Theoretically, yes.' Charlie indicated his monitor. 'If you can access the newspaper's banking data. You find the computer that's making the payment, you locate their server and the server provides the location; the address of the user terminal's location...'

'But?' Liam said, anticipating the inevitable downside.

'But, he may have simply used an internet café, or a 4G burner SIM. Avoided their network completely.'

'No,' Liam persisted. 'An outfit as controlling as this lot would never let him have a cell that wasn't monitored. He'd be supervised day and night. Look at Dyson. The first sign of him heading anywhere near an unsecured cell or computer, they'd come down on him like a ton of bricks. It may even be why he was murdered.' He pointed at Charlie's big screen. 'I say he'd have been at his safest when he was using the organization's network. When he was working would be the only time he wasn't being watched – possibly the only time they relaxed a little.'

Charlie shook his head. 'If he'd tried to use their network he would have been stopped. Not much chance he'd get away with that kind of security breach. An outfit like this would have its own encrypted and anonymized dark servers and routers. They'd monitor everything coming in and going out; they'd have filters inbound and outbound; they'd use transparent proxying; the latest traffic-monitoring software; identity authentication, you name it. Fort Knox in digital form.'

Liam dismissed Charlie's concerns with an impatient gesture. 'But is hacking *out* of a network any harder than hacking in?'

'Getting out is a little easier,' Charlie still looked doubtful. 'But he'd need to be very careful. And he'd need to be very goddam skillful.'

'And yet, I suspect,' Liam said with a grin, 'that in spite of the greater degree of difficulty and all the multiple levels of security, that you would feel reasonably confident that *you* could get in?'

'Well, it's virtually impossible,' Charlie said with mock bravado. 'But someone with my extraordinary skills might be able to do it.'

'Hey, if even *you* could get *in* without being pinged, why couldn't Rigby get *out* without being pinged? He was a *real* genius.'

Charlie tossed a thick book at his head. Liam ducked quickly and it thudded harmlessly into the wall.

'C'mon Charlie, we don't have anything else at the moment. What have we got to lose?'

Charlie looked up as Jia came into the room, then turned back to Liam. 'I guess I don't have any better suggestions,' he said quietly.

* * *

'Global'nyy issledovaniya infektsionnykh zabolevaniy.'

The Russian accent wasn't bad, Liam thought, but there was room for improvement.

'According to Jia, it translates as Global Research into Infectious Diseases. Makes sense, the acronym on their English language website is GRID.' Charlie indicated the company name and address on his screen, using the half-eaten sandwich in his hand.

'I was wrong,' he admitted. 'This place isn't inside Rigby's triangulation, it's around ten miles west of his stamping ground. They must have placed a lot of trust in him initially to give him so much latitude. This set-up is right out on the edge of the city, in the middle of a goddam forest.'

He swung the remains of the sandwich around and pointed it at Liam.

'You, on the other hand, were right. Brilliant lateral thinking, young Liam. Seems Rigby spent his days too far from the local supply of US newsprint for his own personal comfort and so he subscribed to this thing online.'

Charlie tapped the old *Dialog* page with his middle finger. Mayonnaise dripped onto the surface, next to the ring left by his coffee cup. 'I still don't know how he got around their security software. Maybe he *was* even smarter than I am.'

'Infectious diseases. Interesting.' Liam wiped away the mayo with an index finger. 'I guess that's enough motivation to keep rubberneckers and inquisitive journalists at a distance. Nothing like the threat of a little Ebola or Marburg Hemorrhagic fever to make sightseers lose interest. I wonder how legitimate that side of their business is.'

'It seems Rigby was more or less free to come and go. If Professor Frederik is there, given what we've heard, it's likely he's there against his will; a prisoner.' Charlie shook his head. 'I can't imagine we'll be lucky enough to get two guys that need to pop out to get dialysis on a regular basis. If we want to talk to Oskar Frederik I think *we'll* have to go to *him* this time, try to extract him ourselves.'

'From a secure facility in Moscow? I hope you have a cunning plan,' Liam said.

'We'll need to get over to Oxford first and find out from his sister whether there's any chance he's there by choice. Talk her into giving us his passport at the same time. Your Irish blarney should come in handy for that.'

* * *

'This site of theirs is a new build, glass and steel. Not much more than ten years old. The plans are easily accessible; they're in the public domain. It seems it may have been purpose built as a genuine infectious-diseases facility.' Charlie tapped the computer screen. 'But these deep basements are unusual in a building of this vintage. They don't appear to have an infrastructure function. Lighting, heating, power, fiber all handled up here.' He tapped the screen again.

'What does this indicate?' Liam asked, pointing to the area around the perimeter.

'That's a very high wall topped with razor wire.'

'Okay. And beyond that?'

'Some lovely dark, dense and mysterious woods. Privacy for them, a surveillance paradise for us.'

Liam nodded. 'Good. But *if* he's there and *if* we get him out of the building, how do we get him out of the country? I don't fancy another drive through Xinjiang, or Kazakhstan, or one of your many other exciting global hotspot tours.'

'Two choices,' Charlie said. 'Aeroflot economy or I hire a hang glider and try to fly him out.'

'My vote's the hang glider,' Liam said.

Jia looked perturbed.

'It's his idea of a joke,' Liam said, touching her gently on the arm.

Charlie turned serious. 'The first thing we need to establish is whether he's there,' he said. 'The second is a way to get him out.'

'What we'll really need if we're going to try to pull him out is a diversion of some sort.' Liam pointed at the glowing monitor. 'That place will be crawling with security.'

'Any bright ideas?'

'Perhaps a bomb,' Jia said. As always, she spoke softly. Regardless, she now had their undivided attention.

'I like the way this young woman thinks,' Charlie said, turning to the silent Walter Dyson.

'These people must be hiding their real activities behind their apparent research into deadly viruses,' Jia continued. 'So they can manipulate the climate without fear of any disturbance because everyone is terrified that if they go near the place they'll be contaminated by Ebola or something equally terrible.'

She stood, walked over to Liam and sat very close to him.

'Perhaps that fact could be turned against them?' She cocked her head. 'If people are already frightened, it should be possible to push them over the edge by manipulating the fear they already feel. Even if there is no real bomb, just the thought of a bomb might be all you need.'

'Sounds rather Confucian to me,' Dyson said.

Jia nodded. 'When it is obvious that your goals cannot be reached, don't adjust your goals, adjust your actions.'

'It might just be a good idea,' Liam said thoughtfully. 'The fear of all those killer viruses being blasted through the air would be enough to send most people bolting off in every direction. It could cause absolute chaos.'

'I'm impressed,' Charlie said, looking across at Dyson.

'Jia is a very impressive young woman,' he answered. 'I hope you appreciate her.'

'It looks like we need to take a little walk in the woods.' Liam

243

took Jia's hand, interlacing their fingers, then covered it with both of his. 'I don't suppose I can persuade you to stay here in Ireland with Walter?'

Jia turned her head and looked him in the eye. Her reply was a frosty silence.

'No, I didn't think so,' he said quietly.

'You'll need someone on the ground with you that speaks Russian anyhow,' Charlie said. 'And if I'm providing the taxi ride it can't be me.'

'Which is probably just as well,' Liam said.

Charlie allowed himself the briefest of smiles. He looked from one to the other, turned to Dyson and then turned back and focused on the young couple. 'How comfortable are you about doing this on your own? Degree of difficulty ten,' he said. 'Do we need to bring some others on board?'

'I've done solo extractions before,' Liam replied quietly. 'From more dangerous locations than Moscow.'

'Are you sure?' Charlie studied them both.

'And this won't be solo,' Jia added softly

22

THEY SAT in cool darkness on the woodland's edge. To their east the sky was radiant with reflected fire; the lights of the great city.

Jia slipped a new SIM card into a cheap cellphone and called the number for Moscow's major news agency.

'Da?' The call was answered in seconds.

'Listen carefully. We are the Crimean People's Liberation Front. We will no longer be subjected to the tyranny of Moscow's oligarchs and KGB criminals. There is a bomb located within the complex of the Institute for Global Research into Infectious Diseases. It will be detonated in 20 minutes and Moscow will learn to suffer in the way our beloved Crimea has suffered.' She paused.

'Long live the Crimean People's Republic.'

She hit disconnect, removed the SIM and handed it to Liam, who crushed it between powerful fingers. She tossed the phone and battery into the woodland and they drove away.

Liam had spent most of the past week concealed among the sturdy limbs of various trees in the forest skirting the Institute's perimeter. Jia, having recced the route to the airfield, waited patiently in her hotel room and collected the relevant telephone numbers. On the fourth evening, with lights still indicating activity in several areas of the complex, the ground-level window in a large basement room was suddenly illuminated and an older man turned, walked across and closed the drapes. Liam spent several hours the following day observing the room through a powerful telephoto lens. A number of people, most in lab coats, sat at monitors or worked at various bench tops using laboratory equipment. There was no certainty any of them were the older man. Liam waited with trained patience as, towards evening, the room gradually emptied. At nightfall he was still straddling branches, his numb extremities something he'd learned to accept as part of the job. The lens was focused on the same window when the older man reappeared. He was clearly a creature of habit. Liam fired off several shots then enlarged the image on the screen. Unmistakable. Oskar Frederik in the flesh. He studied the routines of the armed guards, checked the locations and timings of the security cameras, estimated the room's co-ordinates and then scrambled down from the tree. He slipped across to the wall, found a foothold and made cuts in the razor wire a few feet apart.

'Okay,' he said to Jia as he walked back into the hotel room. 'He's there. We go tomorrow night. Are you sure you're up for this?'

She nodded but said nothing.

'We'll need to get there with the first lot of emergency people. We don't want him evacuated by somebody else before we arrive.'

Within minutes of Jia's threatening phone call, the external plaza in front of the building was pandemonium. Emergency vehicles with flashing lights were scattered all over the rain-sprinkled marble pavement. A police tape ran from the street along both sides of the plaza and ended at the portico. A hundred yards down the road, another line of barriers kept those locals and media, more inquisitive than prudent, at bay.

In the ensuing panic, nobody took any notice of two more anonymous figures wearing regulation personal protective equipment, as they slid from an innocuous grey vehicle, flashed a quick ID at a harassed police officer and joined the emergency crews entering the building.

They made directly for the basement, using the empty stairwell and avoiding the chaotic foyer and its deactivated elevators.

At the foot of the stairs they encountered a locked door. Liam stood back, flexed his large body and aimed a kick just below the lock. He hit it with all his force and, on the third attempt, the timber splintered and the door sprung open.

He used his small IPS device to guide them through the maze of corridors towards what he hoped was Oskar's location. They turned a corner. Directly ahead, two men stood guarding a doorway, hands poised above the handguns on their hips.

The corridor rang with the near-deafening shriek of sirens. Red and blue lights flashed alternately, turning the claustrophobic space into a Dantesque nightmare. The two men looked up nervously as the suited figures approached; one was trying to get a signal from a walkie-talkie while the other seemed on the edge of panic.

'You need to evacuate, quickly,' Jia ordered in loud, authoritative Russian. She reached out to him with a gloved hand. 'Give me the key. We'll bring the scientists.'

The terrified man all but threw the key at her before he and his partner sprinted off along the corridor toward the stairwell.

Jia unlocked the door. The room, it seemed, had once been merely a laboratory but now performed the added role of prison cell. A door at the far end led into a smaller room. A bed in the corner stood next to a washstand and portable latrine.

Oskar Frederik was sitting alone in front of a blank computer screen, trying to write on a pad using the intermittent lighting. He looked up as they entered. 'What in God's name is going on? What's all the racket about? Who the hell are you?'

They lifted their visors. 'We only have a very few minutes, Professor Frederik. We're here to take you home but you'll need to move quickly.'

'What are you talking about?' Oskar didn't budge. 'Who are you, what are you up to?' He was confused, angry and perhaps even a little frightened.

'We don't have time,' Jia said. 'Please trust us.'

He looked into her pleading eyes and softened a little. 'Why? Why should I?'

She reached into the pocket of her coveralls and produced a folded A4 sheet. 'This is from your sister. Please read it *quickly*.' She produced a slim penlight and held it out to him.

Oskar took the light, found his reading glasses and started to scan the page; more deliberately than either of his would-be rescuers might have preferred.

As Liam listened for the sound of thudding footfalls in the corridor, he scanned the room with his own flashlight beam. He noticed a glass crystal box on a high shelf. Even from a distance it looked expensive.

'What is that?' He pointed. 'Is that a chess set?'

Oskar looked up momentarily, then dismissed it with a wave of his hand. 'Yes, a chess set. It belonged to someone who was here before. I've had no time for chess.'

Liam reached up and lifted the object down carefully. It was heavy. He brushed a layer of dust from the surface and lifted the gold-hinged lid. The strobing lights reflected and refracted from a thousand facets of intricately carved, crystal chess pieces. Some were clear, some as black as obsidian. A small gold plaque attached to the underside of the top, with tiny solid gold screws, contained a simple message.

LR
Success! Well done!
Stay cool
EP

There was no date. Liam clicked the top shut and checked the bottom of the glowing box. The name of an expensive Fifth Avenue jeweler was engraved discreetly into the glass.

'A second mistake, maybe,' Jia said quietly to Liam.

He nodded. 'I don't imagine they've sold too many of these.' He handed her the box.

'LR. Lionel or Leonie Rigby,' he said. 'EP? Well, we have ways of finding you, my friend.'

Oskar stuffed his sister's letter into a pocket and reached for his glasses case. 'All right, I have no choice but to trust you. I have no great desire to stay here.'

He glanced up and Liam wasn't sure that the man hadn't actually smiled. 'I won't bother to pack a bag.'

They hurried him into the corridor, checked to make certain the way was clear and then continued along under the flashing lights, away from the stairwell.

'I don't know how you imagine you'll get me out of Russia.' Oskar panted. 'I don't have a passport.'

'Yes you do,' Liam said.

A large steel-framed door with a formidable stainless steel

locking bolt barred their way. Liam took a soft package from his bag, molded it to the lock, inserted a detonator and then moved his companions behind a bulkhead. The sound of the small explosion was all but drowned by the incessant wailings of the alarms.

The panicked and manic activity was still centered at the front of the building and on the upper levels. The maintenance area at the rear had been brightly floodlit but was, for the moment, deserted. Rain fell softly as they made their way across the narrow space, avoiding the pivoting cameras and staying in the shadows of two verdant chestnut trees. Liam removed the section of razor wire he'd severed the previous night, they helped Oskar over the high wall and doubled back through the darkness of the woods.

* * *

The entire extraction process had taken less than 20 minutes and within a half hour they were well on their way to their rendezvous with Charlie.

Liam spied the Cessna Skylane standing on the apron, lights on, engine ticking over, as he pulled into the parking area in front of the small rural terminal.

The neglected building was badly lit by a row of sickly green fluorescent tubes.

A solitary, drowsy official had been dragged from his slumber and sat at a table near the door leading out to the airstrip. A well-used AK47 stood propped against the wall behind him.

'I've cleared our flight path with the Russian authorities,' Charlie said. 'You'll need to show this gentleman your passports.'

The man perused each document at a deliberately unhurried pace. He flipped through Oskar's British passport until he found his photograph. The page listed his birthplace as Riga. The man looked up from the page, looked Oskar in the eye and spat slowly and deliberately at his feet. 'Latvian.' He used it as a term of contempt. Oskar stepped forward, and was about to assault the man. Liam took him firmly by the upper arm and led him out onto the airfield.

'Thank Christ you made it in time,' Charlie yelled as the plane gathered speed and lifted into a swirling summer sleet.

'I didn't know you cared,' Liam shouted back.

'I don't.' Charlie kept his eyes trained on the darkness ahead. 'I'm leasing these things by the hour. If you'd been any later I'd have needed to sell my house. I'm taking her to a small strip northwest of Kiev. My flight plan says Riga, Latvia, but we'll ignore that. It should take them some time to notice anything's wrong. With luck we can be out of Russian airspace in under three hours. Once we cross the border, that area of eastern Ukraine is so volatile one small aircraft will go virtually unnoticed. Unless, of course, some trigger-happy rebel shoots us down by mistake. I'll stay relatively low. By then it should be daylight, so we should be fine.'

'Unless it's a short-sighted, trigger-happy rebel,' Liam said, softly enough to go unheard in the rear seats.

Charlie ignored the comment.

'We'll switch aircraft other side of Kiev. The owner will collect it in a day or two. If these people are as big as we think they are they could soon enough be looking for this one's call sign all over Europe.'

* * *

The official at the Moscow airstrip stood out in the cold and watched the blinking wingtip lights of the Cessna until they had been swallowed up by distance.

He returned to the relative warmth of the terminal and sat staring at his phone for many minutes. Getting one's superior out of bed on an unseasonally cold Moscow night was never a good career move; especially if there was no good reason. Eventually he made a decision and punched in a number.

'I thought you should know. A Latvian has flown out of here with two Americans and a woman,' he said. 'They had all the papers but I have a feeling something was not right about the whole business.'

'Did you get their names?' The man's superior reached for pen

250

and paper. 'The Latvian?'

'Yes, I memorized them,' the man said, pleased with his presence of mind. 'The Latvian bastard's name was Oskar Frederik.'

'You need to give me the call sign and flight-plan details,' his boss said, still sounding sleepy, and less than impressed by the disturbance.

'I have those too,' the man said, reaching for a slip of paper on the desk near the Kalashnikov in the corner.

Within minutes the message had been sent off along the twisted limbs of an intricate electronic grapevine. It continued until it finally reached somebody who understood its significance.

Cassidy Millston punched in the international code and waited while the far-away number connected. 'That useless French bitch Claude has screwed up yet again. This terrorist bomb thing was bullshit. There was no fucking bomb. It was a cover to get Frederik out of here. I finally talked my way in past the emergency people. The stupid bastards made me wear a fucking clown suit. He's gone. Frederik's gone.'

'Fuck.' The venom in the expletive lost none of its potency as it raced across continents.

'They're in a light aircraft. Heading for Riga.'

'We're all getting very tired of your fucking mistakes, Millston. You'd better make sure you can persuade some of your military friends over there to intercept them.'

'Or just shoot the fuckers down,' Millston said angrily.

The voice was silent for a second or two. 'The same people I presume. Doyle and Casement?'

'We don't know. The security cameras were all deactivated during the shutdown. Not the names on the passports but the airfield guy's description fits.'

'I'd put fucking money on it.' There was another silence. Even from 4,000 miles away, Millston could feel the malevolence. 'They're playing us for fools. Sort them out before this gets out of hand or I'll find some less useless fucker to do it.'

* * *

251

Jia slept, her head on Oskar's slim shoulders. He didn't seem to mind and made no attempt to move her as he spoke suddenly. 'These people have tampered with natural forces they don't fully understand: forces none of us fully understand. What they have done is inexcusable, culpable. They're answerable for one of the most irresponsible acts of wanton destruction the planet has ever seen.'

He leaned forward, making sure not to disturb the sleeping head and lowered his voice.

'Every major technological change comes with major sociological implications. This has always been so. Rampant free-marketeers either don't comprehend this or simply refuse to accept it.

'They have gone out there and attempted, without really knowing what they were doing, to engineer the planet's climate. They have spent God knows how many billions and will be responsible for the deaths of God knows how many billions.'

Jia shifted and murmured something in her sleep.

Charlie was half listening with a single headphone covering one ear. Liam could only just hear the intermittent crackling of the military frequency he was tapped into.

'They've clocked us,' he said. His face was suddenly grave. 'That was quick.' He took the Cessna down to a few hundred feet and increased his airspeed to maximum. 'It sounds like we have a couple of Sukhoi fighters scrambling from the east.' He checked the console clock. 'Those things can manage over a thousand miles an hour. We're around 15 minutes from the Ukrainian border. Given the situation between them, the ceasefire, we can only hope they're not willing to violate Ukrainian airspace. It's going to be close.'

They sat in silence, willing the vibrating Skylane forward.

'Two minutes to go, but these fucking guys are closing fast,' Charlie said. He dropped the small aircraft until it was skimming along between the treetops. Liam was certain he could hear the approaching fighters.

'That's it,' Charlie whooped a moment later. 'Goddam Ukraine. Keep praying.' Thirty seconds passed and then, with an ear-splitting snarl, two sinister fighters tore apart the darkness at either end of the Cessna's wingtips, climbed almost vertically and turned for home.

'Holy shit!'

Liam had never seen Charlie's hands shaking before.

* * *

'It's dark down there,' Liam said. 'I hope you've been eating your carrots.'

Less than two hours had passed since the border crossing and the lights of Kiev were already well astern on their port side.

'The airfield uses PAC. Pilot-activated lighting. I'll leave the approach lights off as long as possible. It's an isolated little strip but you never know who may be snooping around out there.'

Several minutes passed. The soft illumination from the console lights revealed the deep concentration on Charlie's face, his eyes intent on the gauges. He reached up suddenly and keyed the microphone five times in quick succession. Directly ahead and no more than a few hundred feet away two rows of lights blinked on. Charlie put the plane down gently and taxied up to a second Cessna standing at the far end of the deserted airfield. He retrieved a bag from the back, tossed it to Liam and hurried his companions from one plane to the other. Within minutes, as dawn began to announce itself over the now far-off Moscow, they were airborne again.

'This one is fitted with long-range tanks.' Charlie indicated the glowing fuel gauges. 'We should be in Ireland by nightfall.'

'I was hoping to get back to Oxford,' Oskar said quietly from the passenger seat.

'Oxford's not safe at the moment, Professor.' Liam leaned forward in his seat and touched the man on his shoulder. 'It's best you spend some time with us somewhere a little more secure.'

'Do you plan to take me through Irish customs, immigration?'

'I don't,' Charlie said. He waited until he had the aircraft leveled off before he spoke again. 'There's a small private strip on the edge of Bantry Bay. I'll take her in over the Celtic Sea then bring her about and approach from the west over the water. This'll be almost a touch-and-go landing; as little time as possible on the ground. The car is on the track outside the perimeter. The keys are in the bag.'

Liam pulled open the bag at his feet. It contained water bottles, a set of car keys, a machine pistol and a handgun with silencer. He said nothing.

'I'll need to get off the tarmac as quickly as possible and get this thing back to Dublin. Hope I won't have to answer too many flight-path questions when I get there.'

It was somewhere over the Erzgebirge Range that Liam decided he would ask Jia to marry him when all this was over.

She'd been silent for most of the journey, waiting patiently while the exhausted Oskar Frederik slept, now in the front seat. She allowed him several minutes more to become fully awake once he stirred and then leaned across and placed a tentative hand on his shoulder.

'Have you seen or possibly heard of a Chinese man with the name of Zhang Liu? He's about 50 years old.'

Oskar didn't answer immediately. When he did it was with a shake of his head. 'No, that name doesn't sound familiar.'

She passed him a small photograph. He took it and held it under the console light. 'No. I've not seen him.' He handed the picture back. 'Is he important to you?'

'Yes. Thank you,' she said simply. She rested her head on Liam's shoulder and allowed the sadness to run silently down her cheeks.

'Will you marry me?' he whispered into her sweet-smelling hair.

She glanced up, momentarily stunned and, after a long silence, brushed away a tear. 'When I have found my father.'

Then she smiled. 'Perhaps.'

'Do you have any idea who the people who snatched you were, the people behind all this sulfur business?' Charlie lifted a headphone from one ear but kept his eyes on the hazy skyline directly ahead.

'No, not really, no specific individual. A French woman, a few Russians, some Americans. There were never any names, but I can hazard a guess...'

Oskar turned his body so he was facing the three of them.

'There is a power struggle under way in Russia, ex-KGB criminals and their oligarch accomplices trying to cling to power against the more democratically inclined members of the Duma. But it's not just Russia. In China it's the old corrupt guard of the Communist Party versus the newer younger wave who see the need to democratize. In the West it's the arrogant, entitled old billionaires and their globalized corporations. In the Middle East it's the crooked sheikhs and their ruling cronies. But in almost every case, if you dig deep enough, you'll find fossil fuels at work. Coal, oil, coal-seam gas, oil shale, tar sands – they're hanging on for grim death.'

He pointed over his shoulder with a thumb. 'These people in Moscow, they thought for a while that they were very brilliant. They'd developed a new technique that allowed them to inject far less sulfur than was originally envisaged. The data showed they were cooling the Arctic. It only took a little longer for the data to show what else they were doing.'

Charlie held up a hand as the headset crackled into life. 'I'd better concentrate on this radio traffic, Professor. Don't want any nasty surprises.' He lifted the earpiece back into place, then lightened up a little. 'All being well, you should all be home in time for tea and soda-bread and I'll see you some time tomorrow.'

The airstrip at the edge of the dark bay was silent and deserted. The Bantry town lights radiated a soft yellow glow around two miles to the east.

The Cessna was back in the air within two minutes of touchdown and Liam watched it disappearing into the faint beginnings of a sunrise over Gougane Barra, as he led the way through the darkness and over the low fence to the waiting car.

He was happier than he could remember. Happier, perhaps, than he'd been since the day he'd come down the mountain to the news about his father all those years before.

'I'd like my mother to meet you,' he said to Jia as the car

255

wound its way towards the fog-shrouded Caha Pass. 'It'll only take a few minutes.'

'It's the middle of the night,' Jia said.

'No, the sun will be up in under half an hour. She'll be in her kitchen making tea. She's always up with the first light. Old farming habit.'

Jia frowned. 'Perhaps another time.' She indicated Oskar with a small movement of her head. 'I think it would be safer to get back to the cottage.'

'But we'll virtually be driving right past her front door. She'll be so happy. I promise, no more than five minutes.'

23

THE DECISION to break into the laboratory was made on a day glowing with the last hours of the year's precious sunshine. If Dashka Anasovna wanted to find out what the bastards were up to in there, then he, Ivor Petrovich, was the man to find out for her. He would simply wait for a night with falling snow.

Security in a place as remote as Cape Zhelaniya had never been as strictly enforced as it might have been in Moscow or even Arkhangelsk. Perhaps, in addition, the men at the base were a little too contemptuous of the young Ivor Petrovich and his criminal skills for their own good.

Either way, accessing the laboratory was a lot easier than he had imagined. Alexei's office was always locked, but, Ivor guessed, for a guy with his skills it would require very little effort to breach. He'd kept a close eye on Alexei recently and had noticed that the lab keys were locked away in the hostile old bastard's desk drawer. Ivor was reasonably certain he could crack it with a little old-fashioned dexterity and the aid of a couple of small tools brought with him from Arkhangelsk.

He waited until midnight, made sure all the lights were out, rugged himself up in his darkest clothes and, flashlight at the ready, flitted across the poorly lit square of fresh snow between the living quarters and the office buildings.

The keys were where they had always been, along with a bottle of single malt whisky. He pocketed the whisky and within minutes was slipping silently into the laboratory complex. He booted Alexei's desktop machine, attached a small external drive and began to transfer the computer's data. While it was loading, he ran his thin beam around the room.

Apart from a surveillance camera in one corner it seemed depressingly ordinary, boring – not the slightest indication of conspiracy here, certainly no drugs. He opened drawers and cupboards and peered up at shelves but there was nothing even worth stealing. It was quite possible, Ivor decided, that she'd imagined the whole business but, for him, the important thing was to show her how much he cared, just what he was prepared to risk on her behalf and, not least, to demonstrate his considerable skills.

He disabled the camera, made sure nothing in the room had been disturbed, closed and locked the door and crept down the corridor and out under the cascading snowflakes. The base was in darkness.

From the stillness of the living quarters someone watched him exit the office.

The only good thing about a shithole like this, Ivor thought, was the absence of barking dogs. Nobody would subject a dog to these conditions and yet, he reflected bitterly, his father had been willing to send him here.

He made his way to the machine shed, knowing that his tracks would be covered within the hour, sprung the lock and walked inside warily. It too was deserted.

Across in the living quarters a thin shaft of light appeared from Sergei's doorway.

Ivor completed his business in the shed, took a swig from the whisky bottle, and turned to leave. He stepped out into the biting cold, bent into the falling snow and began to plod back to his room.

He all but collided with Sergei who was standing, still and silent, five feet away.

'Christ,' Ivor said. 'You scared the shit out of me.'

'What are you doing?' Sergei asked with ice-cold hostility. 'It's after midnight.'

'I couldn't sleep,' he said breezily. 'I often take a short walk in the snow when I have insomnia.' He paused, brushed off a few flakes. 'Have you not heard me before? You must be a heavy sleeper.'

Sergei said nothing.

* * *

'This place is beginning to feel like a refuge for fugitive scientists,' Dyson said, shaking Oskar's hand. 'I've heard of your work, Professor. Read some of your papers. Very impressive.'

'Thank you,' Oskar sighed, slumping into a chair. Too tired, Liam noticed, even to summon up a smile.

'How are you, Walter?' Jia reached up and gave the man a spontaneous hug.

'I'm fine, dear girl, just fine. If I'd known self-administering was so straightforward I'd have started years ago.'

'That's excellent,' she said, hugging him again.

He turned to Liam. 'I have to say I'm very pleased to see you. Sitting around in darkness for nights on end with a shotgun on my lap is not my idea of recreation.'

'Did you get out at all?'

'Yes, I went for a short walk up the hill behind the house one morning. Cabin fever. Mind you, I never let the place out of my sight. Anyhow, an uneventful few days. Just me and the sheep.'

'Good,' Liam said, then turned to Oskar. 'On the plane you said something about the data revealing what else they were doing?'

Oskar rubbed his eyes. His exhaustion was obvious but he put it to one side and stood.

'You've heard the term "The Third Pole?"' It was a rhetorical question.

'It is a description gifted to the Himalaya because the ice fields contain the largest reserve of fresh water outside the polar regions. Virtually every one of Asia's great rivers has its source in either the Himalayan ranges or on the Tibetan Plateau. A vast catchment of snow and ice. It's the source of the ten great river systems that provide life-giving irrigation, power and drinking water for over 20 per cent of the global population.'

He crossed to the world map that Liam's elderly cousin had fastened to the wall and started punching it with a closed fist. In the soft light from the standing lamp, Liam could see dust lifting off the surface.

'The Indus, Ganges, Brahmaputra, Irrawaddy, Mekong, Yangtze, even the Huang He, the Yellow River. Most of Asia...

poor, struggling Asia, relies on them for their subsistence, *existence*. Snow and ice.' He thumped again. 'Glaciers.'

'The data makes it quite clear now that this attempt at solar radiation management, the sulfur distribution in the Arctic, has had feedback consequences that have effectively stopped the Indian monsoon in its tracks.

'Even before this criminal scheme started, things were going wrong. This has made it accelerate exponentially, made it infinitely worse.'

He ran his fingers from left to right across the laminated surface.

'Initially, given the extra heating caused by the additional CO_2 in the atmosphere, the snow and ice melted more quickly. Consequently all those countries, north and south have had severe floods. People drowned, crops were destroyed, topsoils that had taken thousands of years to collect and store their nutrients were washed away in a few months.

'After the floods came yet more heat in winter and precious little precipitation. There have now been several consecutive years of chronic drought. No rainfall, no snowfall. Without the snowfall, there's no ice, no water, the glaciers are in rapid retreat, and the once-great rivers have been reduced to a trickle. Nearly a quarter of the globe's population, almost two billion, are on the brink of going hungry and so they're fighting, fighting over their pathetically wretched resources.'

He held a helpless hand up in front of the splash of white across the map.

'The greatest irony of all is that Himalaya is a Sanskrit word. The literal meaning is "abode of the snow".

'The Western media continue to provoke controversy about an Islamist State planned for the whole of South Asia, a Pan-Asian Caliphate. These lunatic Islamic fundamentalists, they insist, want sharia law from the Mediterranean to the South China Sea. It simply isn't true. While it is true of some in the Middle East, Syria, North Africa, Iraq… this is not simply extremist Islam fighting the rest. Cambodia and Thailand aren't about Islam – nor Laos, nor Burma. The Yangtze is not about Islam. This is about food and water, about survival. This is about land.'

His fist thudded against the wall map again.

'This changes the whole geo-strategic nature of things. If your choice is between starving or fighting, what do you do?' It was, again, rhetorical. He knew the answer already.

'And this has all been provoked by our friends in New York and Moscow.'

'And China,' Dyson said softly, looking at the floor in front of his feet.

'I was dragged away from my home in Oxford and told to find a way to fix it,' Oskar continued angrily. 'Just like that. Such arrogance. "Fix it".'

'But how have they been getting away with something this big? Why haven't the rest of the world's scientists noticed the sulfur in the stratosphere?' Liam asked. 'Why hasn't there been an outcry? The bombers, the changing skies, everything…?'

Oskar shrugged. 'These people seem to have limitless power. They have taken control of dozens of monitoring stations circling the globe, here, here, here.' He jabbed at the map again. 'They continually corrupt the data, put out false information. I suspect anyone who has seen anything that bothers them and opens their mouth to protest is dealt with the same way as my predecessor. Aerosol sulfate levels in the Arctic stratosphere have been much higher than they're admitting and they're filtering south: the northern skies are whiter than normal, but so much of northern-hemisphere air has been so fouled by photochemical smog for so long that nobody seems to notice any more.' He shook his head. 'But the truly chilling aspect of all this, the terrifying thing, is that if anyone starts to question what's happening, to make waves, I believe they simply locate them and get rid of them. The world is awash with unexplained deaths, so-called suicides, disappearances. It happened to one of my colleagues in Cambridge.'

He moved, a little unsteadily. 'I need a bed. I can give you a more detailed explanation later on if you care to hear it.'

* * *

A thousand yards from a windswept beach, on the lonely west coast of Skye, another meeting was under way. A little distance to the southeast, the Black Cuillins clawed at the sky with their jagged basalt fingers.

Inside the isolated Georgian mansion, at a long table that spoke of age and privilege, a group of well-groomed and well-fed men had gathered. On the stone wall behind them a tapestry the size of a small cinema screen displayed a prominent British coat of arms.

A handsome man in his late fifties was speaking. The elegant German industrialist wore a fresh San Tropez tan and a perfectly tailored silk suit.

'When I became a part of this group, when I signed up, I signed up to a business deal.' He examined the clear varnish on his freshly manicured fingernails as he spoke. 'I believed we had found a way to overcome the fear-mongering of the radical Left and the Green terrorists, a way to ensure that we kept the wheels of industry turning efficiently and made a modest return at the same time.'

He looked up and surveyed the assembled group, then indicated a small document on the table in front of him.

'I did not sign up to this. I will not be a party to this. There are clearly people in this room who are comfortable with genocide. There are others, like me, who are not.' He made a point of shifting his gaze to the English aristocrat. 'I believe it is time that everyone had a chance to air their views. I believe it is necessary that we take a vote.'

The gathering sat in silence waiting for the response and what they assumed was its inevitable nature. When it came it was as expected.

'Whatever, Mein Herr, gave you the impression that you were dealing with a democracy here?' the Englishman asked. He didn't wait for an answer. 'We are here today to review the ongoing financing of this project and to discuss the most effective way to move forward, given our changed circumstances. Nothing more. It's really just a little bit late to be getting cold feet.'

He turned and studied the men at the table.

'I am a realist, gentlemen.'

He lifted a hand towards the tapestry on the wall behind him; a ruby on his ring finger sparkled momentarily as it passed in front of a narrow leadlight window.

'The wealthy, the privileged – the elite, if you like – have always resisted change. Change has never been in their interest. Kings and emperors have always resisted altruism, when it came to the suffrage of the common man; the egalitarian urge; their belief in the right to equity, to a voice.

'For half a century or more, wealthy merchants and traders resisted the emancipation, the ending of slavery. It was not in their financial interests. Mine owners too fought tooth and nail against the removal of small, pale children from their deep, black hells. Again, not in their commercial interest.

'For a hundred years industrialists resisted the growth of trade unions. A fair day's pay for a fair day's work may have been in the workers' interest, but it was not in theirs.

'And today, we extractive-fuel people resist the inexorable progression towards renewable energy. Why? Not for the good of the people, not for the benefit of the worker, but simply because it is in our financial, our economic interest to do so.'

He returned his attention to the German man and held his gaze; the man eventually looked away.

'If we postpone the inevitable for just ten more years. If we ensure that world governments procrastinate for another decade or so, well then, put crudely, that's a further ten trillion pounds sterling in our pockets.'

He turned away from the discomfited German, pale now in spite of his tan, and addressed the gathering again.

'We all committed to this program, gentlemen. We all agreed that if we could make these aerosol sulfates work in the atmosphere, bring back the Arctic ice, that only then would we go public. We would be forgiven our slight duplicity, celebrated as visionaries and could continue to make money from fossil fuels while making a very healthy return on our ongoing geo-engineering investments. What we face now is a minor setback. I am quite confident that with a little time and money it can be addressed.'

The German returned to his fingernails and said no more.

Cass Millston sat diagonally opposite his Singaporean rival. They were two perfectly honed fighting cocks, mentally strutting round the small rings of their minds. Millston's territory included Europe, the States and South America, the Singaporean looked after Asia and the rest and fumed, constantly, at the fact that his region was seen as somehow secondary. He thought of Millston as an incompetent fool, Millston saw him as an arrogant incompetent.

As the meeting broke up and the limousines and helicopters warmed their engines outside, Ed Polson signaled for Millston and the Singaporean to remain behind. He conferred briefly with the tall aristocrat and then walked across to them.

'You.' He stuck his index finger close to Millston's nose. 'Get your useless butt into gear and get back out there and sort out those two assholes. And don't fuck up again.' He turned to the Singaporean. 'And you, take a detour via fucking Munich and put a little bit of steel into that German's fucking spine and if that doesn't work, put a bit of steel in his spine.' He handed the man a folded slip of paper. 'This is where you'll find him.'

The Singaporean smiled to himself as he walked away. It was clear even Polson knew Millston was an idiot.

* * *

A mist-filtered moonlight reflected pale blue off a wall of wet rock, below high ramparts to the south of the cottage. Dawn was several hours away. A black Land Rover, traveling without lights, slid silently to the edge of the track, a little to the north.

Liam sat dozing next to the big monitor in a time-worn but still comfortable chair. Charlie had rigged a series of infra-red cameras around the perimeter of the house on the day they arrived and the various monochrome images now shared a single screen. Liam heard a soft sound and opened his eyes, reaching automatically for the pistol.

Backlit by the bright embers of the fire, Jia stood looking at him without moving. She wore a long thin singlet and, it seemed to Liam, nothing else beneath. One sleeve had dropped from her shoulder, revealing the smooth contour of a breast.

'I couldn't sleep,' she whispered. 'I keep thinking of what Oskar said.'

She tiptoed over to him, bent and kissed him with parted lips, then let her singlet drop to the carpet. She led him across to the fire and undressed him silently, then urged his naked body down on top of hers. They lay in the glow of the firelight exploring each other tenderly without speaking. Liam was about to enter her when the soft sound of a buzzer came from the monitor across the room.

'Fuck!'

He leapt to his feet, pulling on his trousers as he made for the screen. Three figures in head-to-toe black were passing silently beneath the camera secreted near the bend in the track. Each carried an automatic weapon. They had around 400 yards to cover.

'Quick. Hide those two in the priest hole like I showed you and then hide yourself.' He handed Jia the Uzi. 'Don't come out.'

He grabbed his shirt and a handgun and sprinted for the back door of the house while Jia retrieved her singlet and went to rouse the two men.

By the time the shadowy figures had slackened their pace and were slowly approaching the front entrance, he was concealed behind a rock 50 feet from the north wall of the house.

The leading figure signaled for the others to head left and right round the house. Liam waited until the one closest was out of sight of the front door and then lifted the silenced pistol and put a bullet into the man's head. In one fluid motion he was pointing the gun back towards the front door as he headed around to the rear. He turned the corner and saw the second man disappearing into the cottage through a window. A moment later the interior was illuminated by a short burst of fire. He recognized the sound of the small Uzi instantly, and then, almost immediately, heard the sound of the front door splintering. He was about to follow the man in through the window when a voice came from around the front of the house.

'I have your friend in a very compromising position.' The accent sounded American. 'Come around with your arms in the air and, when I say so, drop your weapons.'

Liam considered his options momentarily, then walked silently to the corner and looked round. The man was standing just inside the front door. He had an arm around Jia's neck and a handgun pressed against her temple.

Liam walked into the now-illuminated space before the entrance, held his pistol aloft and tossed it away when told to.

'We meet at last, Mr Doyle. May I call you Liam? My apologies for dropping in on you at such a late hour. My associates would have been here earlier but I wanted to be a part of the festivities myself. Where's that fuck Casement?'

'He's not here,' Liam said. 'Feel free to search the place.'

'Oh, I do. I do,' the man said expansively.

Liam could see the body of the second man lying on the floor behind Jia's bare feet.

'I need the scientist too, Liam. Who knows, you may even be able to throw some light on the whereabouts of Mr Dyson.'

Liam shrugged. 'I have no idea what you're talking about.'

'Then why did you kill my team?' He pushed the gun barrel hard against Jia's head. Her eyes widened slightly but she gave no indication of fear.

The man began to move slowly into the now brightly lit room, keeping the wall at his back. Liam followed at the same pace, his arms still in the air. 'I tell you what, Liam. I'll count to five and then, if I don't see you making any effort to produce some answers, your little friend will join my friends.'

The man had reached a count of three before Liam spoke again. 'I'll have to get past you to get to him. He's hidden.'

The man swiveled slightly to allow Liam into the room but increased the tightness of his grip on Jia and shoved the gun hard into her bruised temple again.

'You have just a few...' His final words were interrupted by a small section of his head exploding outward towards Liam as Jia was sprayed with blood, bone, brain and black wool.

Charlie's pale face appeared in the dark space of the side

window, smoke still curling from his gun. 'Timing, as they say, is everything. Just as well I don't like Dublin.'

Liam grabbed Jia and held her close, supporting her weight. She appeared to be about to collapse on top of the dead man.

Charlie walked around to the shattered front door. 'I saw their SUV on the side of the track as I was coming in.'

Liam reached down and dragged away the dead man's bloodied ski mask.

'Looks like somebody got to his head before we did,' Charlie said dispassionately.

Apart from the bullet hole, the face carried another wound. The old scars of a severe burn running down one entire side.

'This character looks familiar. I've seen that face, the scars, before somewhere, I'm sure.' He dredged through his memory, trying to find a place for the face in his past.

'Well, well,' he said eventually. 'Cassidy Millston. I'm pretty sure this bastard's an ex-black ops guy.'

'You know him?' Liam tightened his protective arm around the now chalky-faced and trembling Jia.

'No. I know *of* him. He went rogue in Afghanistan, years back. Shot up a wedding celebration, I seem to recall. All innocent people. Got the bride, the groom, kids, the works. Went AWOL and just disappeared. Wanted posters plastered all over the base for months. Rumor was, a few years later, that the Taliban got him.'

'I killed a man,' Jia whispered. Her legs appeared to be on the verge of folding under her again. She was staring horrified at the two bodies.

Liam needed to get her out of the room, quickly. 'Could you let them out of the priest hole?' he asked her gently. 'I'll be there in a minute or two.'

She seemed to gather what strength she had left, nodded tearfully and backed out of the room.

'If we know who he is, maybe we can use him to track down his employers?' Liam whispered.

Charlie shook his head. 'I doubt it. He'd work for anyone who was prepared to buy him a gun. This guy's a paid liquidation agent, a pro. He wouldn't leave any traces.'

Liam bent and started to search through the man's pockets. He found a cellphone and checked it. 'The phone's clean. No numbers, no calls.'

While Jia was out of the room, he took a couple of quick close-ups of the man's shattered face with the phone and then dropped it into his own pocket.

'We can't take this to the police, we're too close now. They'd trample all over it. We'll need to keep it quiet for the time being.'

Charlie nodded.

'I'll go see how Jia is getting on and then I'll bury these guys.'

'Don't worry. I'll do it.' Charlie went outside to find a shovel.

Liam checked his watch. Dawn would be another hour or two. He called his mother's number.

24

'WE CAN'T stay here.'

Charlie was grilling bacon. 'We're blown. I don't know how they found us but this place is blown. Shame really, I was getting to feel quite at home with our little family of Irish misfits.'

'Most likely my fault,' Liam said. 'I called in to see my mother on the way back. Five minutes at most; regular back-door precautions; in and out in the dark; but someone observant was obviously watching the place. They must have followed me. I missed them completely, I should have seen them.' He closed his eyes and rubbed them with thumb and forefinger. 'They could have tortured her to get to me; killed her.'

'Is she okay?' Charlie looked up from his pan, spatula poised mid-air. 'Have you checked?'

Liam nodded. 'While you were outside earlier. She's fine. Bit annoyed at being woken.'

He went to the hallway and peered towards Jia's bedroom at the end of the darkened corridor. 'Still sleeping. Shock, I guess. She's pissed off too, badly shaken, won't talk to me.' He returned to the kitchen. 'I nearly got her killed,' he whispered. 'If it hadn't been for you...'

'It happens,' was Charlie's only response. 'It'll be a lot easier for all of us now if we can find somewhere else. Preferably still in Ireland.'

Liam shook his head. 'I'm all out of contacts and ideas. Besides we've just killed three men and buried them in a field without telling anyone, the Garda, their families...'

'That bothers you?'

'Yes,' Liam said hotly. 'It bothers me. I don't like killing. Never have.'

He stepped outside and breathed the cleansing morning air deeply for some time before returning to the kitchen. 'There's another issue, too. If our friends decide to go public about their missing ninjas and let the police know about this place, their dogs will find the bodies in five minutes and our faces will be plastered all over the country.'

'I don't think they'd take the risk. They don't know what's happened to their people yet. Might be in a pub celebrating our demise as far as they're concerned.'

Charlie rearranged a slice of bacon on his toast. 'Too many questions to answer if they did go public anyhow.'

'I wish I could be that sure.'

Walter walked in from the next room and poured coffee into two cups. 'Why are you doing all this?' He was clearly angry.

'Doing what?' Liam looked up.

'Risking our lives, your lives, breaking the law, kidnapping people, killing people? What do you hope to achieve? Do you believe you have a moral right to take the law into your own hands like this? Why are you doing it?'

Liam was silent for a moment. 'They murdered my father.' He shrugged. 'They'd have killed Jia without a second thought. And you.'

Walter made to return to the other room then paused as Charlie joined in.

'Why are *we* doing this?' He took a tub of butter to the fridge.

Jia entered the room, looking haggard and still half asleep, and sat at the far end of the table. She listened to the conversation but made no attempt to contribute. Liam poured her a cup of tea but her only response was silence.

'Do you believe that global governments, the world's military, transnational corporations... do you believe they have a moral, an ethical right to do the things that *they* do?' Charlie asked angrily. 'Every fucking day.'

He slammed the fridge door closed.

'I tell you what, Walter, I'll start obeying the laws when the lawmakers who make them start obeying them themselves. Ask yourself this. Who broke them first? Who breaks them every day of the year in every town and city, every office tower, every goddam great marble banking hall and every grand

270

government fucking edifice?'

Charlie stabbed the air near Walter's head with an accusatory butter knife.

'You've been breaking the laws of your country, your sacred undertaking, for fucking years.'

'I was given no choice,' Walter said, leaving the room.

'There's always a choice.'

'I have access to a place in Greece,' Oskar called from the other room. He took the cup offered by Walter, stood it on the table and joined them in the kitchen. 'An old friend was married to a Greek seaman years ago. He left her a country house on an island called Othonoi. It's in the Ionian Sea in the middle of nowhere. Not many tourists and the house is far more isolated than this place. The road is hell.'

'Online?' Charlie asked.

'Satellite,' Oskar answered.

'How would you get them there?' Liam asked Charlie.

'Them?' Charlie looked quizzical.

Liam was silent for a little while. Charlie watched him expectantly. Jia looked up.

'It's time I took the whole sordid story public I think. Before I get you all killed. I need to get back to DC. There should be enough there. We don't know *who* but we know *what*. I'll detail the story, put all the photos together, get Oskar on camera and see what comes out of the woodwork. Should be enough to blow the thing wide open. If it's not being orchestrated by the government, just a bunch of mad assholes, then we can maybe let everybody go home.'

'But we still don't know who's behind it.' Charlie was angry and frustrated. 'And if it is being orchestrated by government? If our esteemed President is in it up to his crooked neck, then what?'

'Then I'm the only one that ends up being skewered. You'll all be in a nice warm place somewhere, eating souvlakis.'

'Perhaps you should have someone come with you to Washington?' Jia spoke softly, but was unable to keep the anxiety from her tone. She had not slept and looked pale and distressed.

271

Her hand trembled slightly as she lifted her cup.

'No. I don't think so.' Liam smiled and shook his head. 'I think I need to do this one alone.' He walked to the window and looked out into the all-obscuring mist. 'James was *my* dad. Besides, I've caused more than enough trouble already.' He turned back and punched Charlie's arm gently. 'And you still have to find a way to get this lot of escapees out of the country and onto a Greek Island. I'm not sure which is worse.'

Charlie watched Jia as she left the room in silence and then turned back to Liam. 'You handled that well. Very sensitive,' he said. 'Okay, you get all your shit together and take it to the States. Let me worry about getting to...' he turned to Oskar. 'What's that goddam island's name?'

* * *

'Congratulations on winning your party's nomination once again, Mr President.' Cherry spoke into the portable microphone, her voice cascading around the room.

'Thank you, Cherry,' he said without enthusiasm. 'What can I do for you?'

The auditorium in Atlanta was bright with the stars and stripes and red, white and blue bunting. Balloons jostled into every square inch of the high ceiling and the crowd, it was obvious, was as partisan as they came.

She summoned up her courage, yet again.

'You recently claimed that the return of the Arctic sea ice, these past winters, once again raises questions about the veracity of the scientific community's consensus on the changing climate and the wisdom of Candidate Stone's promise to sign the international treaty on the phasing out of fossil fuels. Do you stand by those claims?'

A group at the back of the room booed loudly and something she couldn't decipher was yelled. It seemed likely it wasn't a compliment.

'As I have shared with you before, Cherry,' the President said with contrived tolerance. 'What we need for our economy, for our investors, from our scientists, our academics, is certainty. I accept there are parts of our planet that are having major issues with their weather. I accept that many of our scientists believe there is a major global problem. There are, of course, others who don't. Whether we are the cause, well, weather has been changing for millions of years and with all that lovely fresh cold Arctic ice in mind, I think we, once again, have reason to say that the science is not yet settled.'

He gave her his kindly uncle smile for two seconds and then turned to another, less confronting, questioner. She raised her voice, refusing to be ignored.

'If you are re-elected, elected to a second term, will you or will you not sign the Lyon Agreement to phase out the use of fossil fuels within ten years? While the Arctic may again be cooling, climate issues in other parts of the world become daily more catastrophic.'

'Well, Cherry, let me put it to you this way, these recent events in the northern latitudes do seem to contradict the popular wisdom and it is my belief and the belief of some very fine, very informed people, that we need to be very certain before we take these kinds of radical and irreparable actions. Actions that will, no doubt, have profound, long-term consequences for the economic future and prosperity of this great country.'

'So you do not agree with the vast majority of scientists, military strategists and economists who say that all the consequences will be significantly more dire without the FFPO treaty?'

'We can't be sure, Cherry. We can't be sure. That's the problem.'

'Next question,' an aide said – a Clark Kent clone who pointed quickly to the other side of the room.

'Like the slimiest of slippery, slithery eels,' Cherry said to a nearby camera operator.

'Yeah, but he's still in front,' the man responded, without taking his eye from the viewfinder.

She hurried from the auditorium and hailed a cab for the airport.

Back at the office she punched in Liam's cell number.

'So?' she said when he answered. 'You called.'

'Yes. We've had some serious issues, I'll fill you in later, but we have him here with us. Oskar Frederik. I think we finally have our story.'

'That's good.' She sounded less than ecstatic.

'You don't sound too sure.'

'I'm not. If anything I'm terrified. The consequences...'

He interrupted. 'I'm coming over. We've just got a couple of things to do first. Did you have any luck with my chess set?'

'Yes, your chess set.' She double-clicked her mouse and brought up a file. 'This little beauty cost thousands. They've sold 11 in the past five years. None were paid for by a person with the initials EP.'

'Bugger,' Liam said.

'Hold your horses. One of them was bought, a few years back, paid for by a transnational conglomerate with offices off Wall Street. Turner, Polson, Galloway.' She paused for dramatic effect.

'Yep. Go on.'

'The company's CEO is a guy named Ed Polson. EP. An absolute shit of a man by all accounts.'

'Wonderful. Great work. Fits the mold perfectly,' Liam said. 'I may have to pay him a visit.'

He lifted the dead Millston's cellphone from the table and brought up the screen, illuminating a short, newly arrived text. 'Where the fuck are you?' it said. He clicked up the sender's number.

'I have what looks like a New York number here.' Liam read out the digits. 'Can you run a name and address search for me?'

Cherry double-checked the number. 'I can do better than that. It's here on my screen. That's the delightful Mr Polson's home number. A penthouse on Park Avenue.'

'Excellent. See you very soon.' The line went dead.

* * *

'I will try to keep this simple so you can communicate it to the person in the street.'

274

'Right,' Liam said. Walter's short piece to camera had been recorded before the Moscow trip and now it was Oskar's turn.

Liam hit the record button and Oskar's gentle, serious face filled the small LCD screen.

'Recording,' Liam said.

Oskar cleared his throat. 'Geo-engineering by injection of sulfur dioxide into the stratosphere has long been proposed as a way to counteract the warming effect of greenhouse gases. The sulfur dioxide injected reacts with the hydroxyl radicals present in the atmosphere and aerosol sulfates are formed. Simply put, it reduces the intensity of solar radiation reaching the planet's surface.'

He spread his fingers above his head to filter imaginary sunlight.

'We all knew modeling showed that stratospheric aerosols could potentially reduce the surface temperature. However, there has also been a body of science concerned about the possibility of other unwanted effects for some years.'

He shook his head sadly.

'But these criminals in their arrogance and haste have chosen to ignore these things and, instead, sow their wind. And they, or rather the peoples of Asia, are now reaping the whirlwind.

'What we have now unequivocally established is that tropical rainfall is extremely sensitive to change. Using geo-engineering to counterbalance surface warming from excess carbon dioxide has other consequences, including a reduction in precipitation, rainfall, what we call the hydrological cycle. What we are now facing is a critical disruption to this cycle.'

It was clear Oskar had spoken to camera before.

'Because of this covert aerosol sulfate distribution across the Arctic, there has been a precipitation change, a weaker summer monsoon over India and the Himalayan plateau, as well as a reduction in rainfall over the Sahel in northern Africa.'

Oskar paused, closed his eyes briefly and then continued to camera.

'To put it in the simplest terms, the key driver of a monsoon is a wind system dependent on the thermal contrast between land and ocean. This differential in relative heating and cooling leads to seasonal changes in wind speed and direction and is responsible for large changes in precipitation.

'When a low-pressure area is created over a hot landmass, the heated air rises and cooler air from over the ocean is drawn in to replace it. The faster heating on land is something we are familiar with and is partly a product of the large thermal inertia of the ocean. The ocean, however, not only warms more slowly but, because it is a vast body of water, more of the incoming energy is taken up by evaporation of surface moisture than by increasing surface temperature. This moisture-laden air is drawn as wind toward the area of low pressure on land. Once over the landmass, it rises, cools in the higher atmosphere, condensation takes place and we get tropical rain. Life-giving monsoon.

'But the success or otherwise of this monsoon is influenced by the complex dynamics of a significant number of other climatic phenomena: the overturning circulations, that is the Hadley and Walker circulations, the Inter-Tropical Convergence Zone, ENSO, the Indian Ocean Dipole, The Mascarene High...'

He looked at the map for a moment, tapped it in the vicinity of Mauritius and then slid his finger up towards Tibet.

'Even the particular climate of the Qinghai-Tibet plateau. These and many others.'

He adjusted the glasses on his nose and, for a moment, the small Irish cottage became his far-off lecture theater.

'But essentially, for our current purposes, I will deal with the shift in the Inter-Tropical Convergence Zone.'

Liam was about to ask, but thought better of it and remained silent. Oskar returned to the map and ran a finger from left to right near the equator.

'This area is known as the Inter-Tropical Convergence Zone, the ITCZ we call it.'

He turned back to the camera.

'Sailors, on the other hand, call it the doldrums. This, of course, is because it is essentially a low-pressure area with very little wind. It is, in effect, the band of ascending air, cloud and heavy tropical rainfall that tracks the ascending branch of the

Hadley circulation. It is formed by the convergence of the north and south easterly tradewinds in the region of the equator.'

Once again he put his hands to work, creating the north and south winds and then bringing them together in the center.

'In a northern summer, under normal conditions, it moves across the equator to the north and creates a region of low pressure over the Indian subcontinent. The moisture it carries from the waters of the oceans to the south is driven over the hotter landmass, falls as rain and produces the South Asian monsoon.'

Oskar paused and held up an open palm.

'But all this has changed. Our fears of a global atmospheric teleconnection mechanism and its possible consequences have proven to be valid.

'We have now established the existence of a teleconnection bringing extratropical cooling to the tropical monsoon climate by way of the development of an interhemispheric thermal gradient.

'A teleconnection, put simply, is the capacity of the large-scale atmosphere to transfer its influence to other, sometimes very distant locations, by the use of atmospheric planetary waves. One well-known example of a teleconnection is the El Niño Southern Oscillation. However, unlike El Niño, whereby shifts in the tropical convection alter circulation in the extratropics, this teleconnection, even though it originates in the high latitudes, significantly modifies the large-scale patterns of tropical convection.'

He paused again and gave the camera an angry look.

'What has happened is this. The introduction of sulfur to the top of the atmosphere, the stratosphere in the high northern latitudes above the Arctic Circle, has reinstated the Arctic ice but at the same time as there has been enhanced cooling in the proximity of the high latitudes, we have also seen a general hemisphere-wide cooling.

'These people have created a hemispheric assymetry in energy terms. This Arctic cooling means energy is drawn north from the lower latitudes, both the tropics and extratropics, and this, in turn leads to an interhemispheric thermal gradient. In other words a cooler northern and a warmer southern hemisphere. The effect of this is to drag the Inter-Tropical Convergence Zone towards the warmer hemisphere. To relocate it from its normal summer location in the north down into the southern, if you like, the "unperturbed" hemisphere.'

He created quotation marks around the word with his fingers.

'The ITCZ, as I say, is largely responsible for the South Asian monsoon. Its relocation further to the south means the monsoon has been severely affected. It has, to all intents and purposes, been stopped in its tracks.'

Oskar stopped, rubbed his eyes, then sighed softly and continued; his voice suggestive of a profound fatigue. Liam watched the older man carefully as he shifted his weight unsteadily from one foot to the other.

'As I said, initial modeling that explored the efficacy of stratospheric aerosol sulfates in reducing global temperature warned of this possibility.

'Normally moisture drawn from the tropical ocean surface rises.' Oskar struggled on, using a hand on the dining table to support himself.

'It is then relocated via the combined engines of the overturning circulations, expands and cools in the colder air of the upper troposphere and becomes precipitation: it falls as monsoon rain. This process has been stalled, all but shut down completely, we have established, by the aerosol sulfates being released in the stratosphere to the north.'

He made a sign for Liam to stop recording.

'I'm very tired now. Why don't we finish this off a little later?'

* * *

The President was enjoying a soft interview on a morning chat show.

'The latest polling continues to give you a significant lead over Candidate Stone, Mr President,' the interviewer said with a supportive smile. 'Why do you think this is the case?'

'Well, Britney,' the President flashed his teeth. 'I think there

278

are several reasons. Candidate Stone and her bleeding-heart predecessors had us pull our forces from the Middle East. As a consequence we now have ISSA, this self-styled Islamic State of South Asia, advocating and killing for a Caliphate from Syria to Saigon. So, I ask again, why did we withdraw from the Middle East?'

The pretty blond interviewer smiled ingratiatingly and allowed him to continue.

'Candidate Stone tells us she wants to rebuild our nation's manufacturing base without coal or gas. Well, I respectfully ask the Candidate: where's the power coming from to run all this new-found manufacturing?'

'Tell the fucking dinosaur about the huge revolution in renewables, the breakthroughs in storage,' Cherry yelled at the screen, but in response the woman smiled back out at her then turned, admiringly, again to the President.

'Donna Stone tells us the science is settled,' he continued. 'And yet this winter the Arctic has had its biggest freeze in several years. So, I ask again, how can the science be settled? How can we say there is no doubt? If you vote this woman in as our President, in November, then America as the powerhouse of global industry will be gone, finished, dead.'

Cherry lifted the remote control, pointed it at the President's head and fired. The screen went dead.

She carried her breakfast dishes into the kitchen, called Richie and had him drive her to the office. Today there was no time for the usual long walk. Liam had called from the airport. He had claimed he was carrying something that would blow the thing wide open. It was music to her journalist's ears, even if she still felt deeply skeptical and not a little anxious.

25

SAXON MELVILLE poured himself another coffee and walked back to his seat at the head of the boardroom table. 'We need to get our science people onto this, Cherry. If this stuff is true, it is beyond outrageous.'

Oskar Frederik's face was frozen in pause mode.

Melville signaled for Liam to resume running the video. Liam tapped the pause button and Oskar re-animated.

'Lionel Rigby kept telling them but they wouldn't listen. After they took me captive, I kept telling them but I too was ignored.

'While these processes are riddled with infinite complexities, we have analyzed and re-analyzed. Rigby believed, and I believe, that this criminal enterprise is having consequences well beyond the Arctic Circle.'

Oskar turned to the map and swept his hand from the top of Asia down to the Indian Ocean.

'I have mentioned that the interhemispheric thermal gradient causes a southward shift in the Inter-Tropical Convergence Zone. I will now briefly address how thermal forcing, that is the difference between sunlight absorbed by the planet and energy radiated back into space from the extratropics, can drive this hemispheric assymetry.

'Rigby and I have created a definitive energy-flux framework that has allowed us to interpret the response in the tropics to extratropical cooling. This has given us a quantifiable link between energy transports and the extent of the change in tropical rainfall.

'We have confirmed past observations that cooling of the extratropics requires an increase in energy transport to the northern extratropics, toward the Pole. The southward shifting of the ITCZ facilitates this by permitting a greater transport of energy across the equator.

'The key to this is, of course, how the Hadley cell transports this energy across the equator but I will not trouble you with too much detail.'

Oskar removed his glasses and wiped his eyes.

'It is perhaps a little too technical, too complex to go into here in any depth, but, in essence it is what we refer to as an anomalous cross-hemispheric atmospheric heat transport.'

He smiled a tired smile, took a sip from a glass of water and continued.

'Given certain known criteria, we have been able to quantify the change in the extent of the transport of tropical lower tropospheric mass. This has allowed us also to quantify the level of tropical precipitation response.

'Put simply, what I am saying is that what we refer to as mid-latitude eddies are instrumental in driving this circulation.'

He created counter rotating circles with his long slim index fingers.

'These eddies are simply the rotating highs and lows that you see on the daily pressure chart on your television weather and the winter storms that affect the mid-latitudes. They are associated with what we call the mid-latitude storm tracks and transmit the energy changes from the high latitudes to the tropics.'

Oskar looked off camera for a moment and spoke to Liam directly.

'This is all based on a complex set of many interconnected processes but if your people in Washington are interested in the detail I have a small drive containing some 10,000 pages of data I can provide them with.'

He turned again, thumped the map and then looked back at the lens.

'As I have said, the greed of these people has had devastating consequences in regions vulnerable to droughts and famine. But they don't appear to care, they appear to be incapable of empathy.'

He shrugged tired shoulders helplessly.

'This Himalayan glacier melt and the lack of replenishment is having a vast impact on food security. It's causing catastrophic events. Cross-border conflicts are flaring up over water short-ages and forced migration and much of this in countries that are desperately poor and whose populations are ill equipped to adapt. The Indian monsoon is, arguably, the most important weather cycle on the planet and for good reason: half the region's billion plus people are dependent on agricultural work and 70 per cent of their yearly rains fall between June and September. While irrigation has expanded, most farmers still need the rains for a successful harvest. There's not a larger group of people anywhere on earth that has a greater dependence on a single climate phenomenon. And it is now failing them annually.'

He thumped the map again somewhere near the source of the Yangtze.

'In China they have been suffering from a nationwide shortage of water resources for many years. Water security for China is crucial. If the Yangtze and the Huang He continue to lose flow from their Tibetan sources, the nation will be thrown into existential chaos.'

He made a despairing gesture with upturned palms.

'What we can now say, with great certainty, is that the accelerating and catastrophic failure of the monsoon and the resultant intensification of the South Asian drought follow directly from the introduction of sulfates to the Arctic stratosphere. They follow almost seamlessly. The relevant data, readings, models, observations, the comparable meteorological charts and graphs, all of them, factoring in a response interval, unfold as parallel as a pair of railway tracks.'

Oskar removed his glasses again and began to clean them with a tissue. He glanced back to camera.

'Tragically, this coalescence of symbiotic processes is having a devastating effect on the lives of over a billion people.'

Liam pointed the remote at the screen and Oskar disappeared. 'So that's the story in a nutshell.'

'It's going to be fun getting all that into a sub-head,' Cherry said drily.

She walked to the window and drew back the curtains, allowing daylight to flood in. Saxon Melville sat as still as a stone Buddha, his hands together against his lips, as if praying silently.

'Holy fuck.'

It didn't sound like a prayer.

'These are unbelievably serious allegations,' he said eventually. 'This is the most incredible thing I've seen in 40 years of publishing. If it's true, it has the potential to send the whole financial system into meltdown.' He shook his head. 'This will have cataclysmic consequences.'

'So, then. Are we prepared to publish?' Cherry walked back to the polished table and sat directly opposite the *Dialog*'s proprietor; her body language radiated challenge.

He adjusted his designer glasses on his well-proportioned nose and looked across to Liam. 'You are 100-per-cent certain this is all kosher? The stealth aircraft, the sulfur thing, your sources, everything?'

Liam nodded. 'Yes. I have a dead father on top of K2 to prove it.'

'Have you considered all the consequences if we lift the lid on this? Forget Pandora's Box, we could be opening her whole goddamned cabin trunk. This could create global panic, send the world's markets into freefall.'

He ran a hand through his silvering hair.

'This is not John Grisham, where good triumphs over evil in the end and the heroic young lawyer walks down the corridor with a wry, satisfied grin on his face. There is no win here. Clearly, if the process continues, Christ knows what the outcomes will be. On the other hand, expose them and what do you achieve?'

He indicated the blank screen, so recently filled with Oskar's anger. 'What, according to Mr Frederik, happens if they stop spreading the sulfates? How long's it been going on? If it's suddenly stopped, the global temperature, with all the added CO_2 in the atmosphere, could spike quickly. Again with potentially catastrophic consequences. It could make things worse. So, where's the victory? Where's the vindication? Have you considered that?'

'We've considered all of that and more,' Liam said softly. 'According to Oskar, it will make things significantly worse if they *don't* stop. *Right now*. They're interfering with forces they know virtually nothing about. For me, I'm just terrified by people who believe they're more fucking powerful than the planet.'

Melville stood, walked across to the wall and tapped the monitor. 'Unfortunately there's no hard proof. All you have are these two. Their accusations, affirmations.' He pointed to the window. 'Those people out there, whoever they are... they have to know they're about to be exposed and they'll be covering their tracks as we speak. Shutting down their sites. Destroying evidence. Rewriting the narrative.'

'We have three lots of hard proof buried in an Irish field,' Liam said softly.

'All that proves is that you killed three men.'

Liam tried to keep the frustration from his voice. 'There's my father. The cannon shell from the fighter plane that blew him apart would have left traces of metal. Forensics could almost certainly identify those.'

'Perhaps.' Melville shrugged. 'But right now he's on top of K2 with winter on its way.'

Liam let the exasperation explode. 'There's Polson. I'll talk to fucking Polson. A guy that heavy must be up to his fucking neck in it.'

'I'm totally with him on this, Saxon,' Cherry said.

Melville walked to the window and stared out at the Capitol, partially obscured by a misty rain.

'Why should *we* do this? I accept the truth of it all but that's not the point. Why us? Why the *Dialog*? This is a story that has the potential to destroy a media organization my grandfather started a hundred years ago. It's a story, in fact, that has the potential to see us all in early graves. I'm having trouble coming to terms with why *we* should run it. Why is that?'

'To quote the great John Lewis,' Cherry spoke very quietly, '"If not us, then who? If not now, then when?"'

He threw his hands up. 'Well, I guess that's my answer then. Let's publish and be damned.'

'How do you want to play it?' Cherry asked. There was no triumphant smile.

'Lockdown immediately. Front page, first edition in the morning. As many internal spreads as you need, maps, diagrams, expert opinion. Online release as the papers hit the sidewalk. Then call a conference for the electronic media around mid-morning. Make sure it happens here. In these offices. It's our story. We own it for as long as we can. We control the sources.'

'Lawyers. I'll need to get the legal guys involved.'

'You bet your sweet life.'

He walked around the table and looked down at the still-seated Liam. 'Are your sources somewhere safe? Do they need protection? Do they need money?'

'No, they're safe for the moment.' He looked across to Cherry then back to Melville. 'I'd like one more day. This thing points to this guy Polson. I'm sure if we tapped his phone for long enough we'd get something of real value, but we're running out of time. I think I may get something more if I... if I speak to him. We still don't really know how wide this thing is spread.'

'We probably do, to a point,' Cherry said. 'But specifically...' She shrugged. 'You've heard of the separation of powers, you know, government, judiciary and bureaucracy acting independently? Checks and balances?' She reached across the table and poured herself a glass of water from a silver jug. 'Well, it's a load of steaming horseshit. In reality they're one big writhing cesspit of intertwined serpents.

'There's a lot more to Washington than just the White House, Congress and the Pentagon. Add in the globalized corporations, the international investment banks and organized crime and you have one massive amorphous organization: a six-sided beast. Once you accept that, you'll find most things fall into place.'

'Don't forget the church,' Melville said sardonically.

Liam laughed. 'Bugger, and I thought I had a bit of a challenge on my hands.'

'The point of a global conspiracy, as clichéd as it sounds, is that it's global,' Cherry said without smiling. 'That means it has tentacles that reach into every corrupt and stinking rat hole on the planet. It becomes impossible to know who is ultimately behind it. Your closest friend may be involved. The more you dig, the more paranoid you become. And in the end, even if you expose the whole insane business to the light, you may never actually know how high up the thing went, how wide was its reach and who you are actually exposing.'

'In any event, be careful,' Melville warned. 'I know Polson. The guy is an animal. His people are trying to make moderate, sane, conservatives obsolete. These guys make the Tea Party look like... a tea party.'

'Everything I've read about him makes him come across like a caricature,' Cherry said.

'People like Polson don't just exist in bad fiction.' Melville pointed to the wet window pane. 'They're out there, every bit as extreme, as extravagant, as you've heard. I've met them, lunched with them. They're terrifyingly real.'

He turned to Cherry. 'This thing could have momentous ramifications, Cherry. Are you prepared for the fallout?'

'It could get us all killed,' Liam said simply, before Cherry had time to respond.

'You ran the original Dyson story, Cherry.' Melville frowned. 'You're in this up to your neck. Perhaps you should be in hiding with these people too.'

Cherry shook her head. 'Once we publish, the whole paper will be in it up to their necks. I have a Presidential election to cover. I'm sure I'll be fine. We don't murder journalists in Washington.'

'Well, I'll feel better if you have a couple of security people with you at all times. Make sure you arrange it.'

She acquiesced with a small nod of her head.

'This is the biggest story this paper is ever likely to tackle. It may be the last story we ever tackle. What are we planning to run it under?' Melville asked.

'Liam has an idea.' She inclined her head towards him.

'What is it?' Melville asked.

'The Killing Sky,' he said.

'The Killing Sky Conspiracy,' Melville replied.

* * *

Liam sat on the hotel bed and tapped a text message into the dead Millston's cellphone. 'In NY now. Meeting?'

Two hours later he had Polson's response. '18.30. Pk Av.'

He arrived at the Park Avenue address an hour early and cracked the lock on the service entrance. He waited until the concierge had been coaxed out onto the sidewalk by Cherry's assistant spilling an armful of parcels onto the red carpet, then slid into the elevator lobby and buzzed the penthouse intercom. No answer. He approached the elevators. A mechanic was about to begin some work on the first so he waited for the second to arrive. He selected a floor a few levels below the penthouse, stepped out and climbed the stairs the rest of the way. In the stairwell he pulled a ski mask over his head. The front door was relatively easy and he slipped silently into the apartment with 15 minutes to spare. The place looked like someone had knocked off a French chateau and dumped it in Manhattan.

He located an office and disabled the video surveillance system, then found a safe and a series of reinforced filing cabinets in a walk-in closet. Whoever had installed them was better at keeping things locked than Liam was at unlocking them. He checked his watch and returned to the living room. By six he was sitting comfortably on a dining chair, hands resting on the table in front of him.

Polson's limo dropped him at the front door five minutes later. He tossed a cigar onto the sidewalk, ignored the concierge's greeting and strode across to the elevators.

'This one's going to be out of service for a while,' the mechanic said. Polson looked up at the indicator; the other elevator was stationary a few levels up.

'Tell you what, buddy, I'll ride it to the penthouse. Then it can be out of service for a while.' He pushed past the mechanic and skewered the penthouse button with a blunt index finger.

Liam heard the front door open then click shut and a moment later Polson walked in from the polished marble vestibule.

'What the fuck are you doing here?' If he was afraid, there was no sign of it.

Liam sized him up without speaking. He looked physically strong, mentally tough and very aggressive. He carried a little extra weight around the middle but it didn't look all that soft.

'Get the fuck out of here now. You have one minute and then I fucking blow your brains out.' Polson reached into his coat pocket and pulled out a slim little silver handgun. It looked tiny and almost absurd in the man's beefy hand but Liam had no doubt a single shot would effectively carry out Polson's threat.

He made a point of ignoring the weapon and the ultimatum. He stood, instead, and walked calmly to the end of the table. Polson followed him with the gun's snout.

'I was interested in meeting the man who murdered my father,' he said, testing the water.

'What the fuck are you talking about?'

Liam reached up slowly and dragged the ski mask from his face.

'My name is Liam Doyle. My father was James Doyle.'

'Ah, Doyle. So not just a common fucking junkie. What a buzz.'

'A buzz? But possibly not for long,' Liam said.

Polson walked over and stood opposite him. Liam had the bright light from the vast windows behind him, Polson was looking directly into it. A small advantage, but an advantage nonetheless.

'You and your buddy, what's his name, Casement? You really are starting to piss us off. How much do you want?'

'From you, nothing,' Liam said. 'By this time tomorrow your whole lunatic scheme is going to be blown sky high. You're being exposed, Eddie. The whole sorry saga will be screaming from the world's media for all to see.' He could tell the 'Eddie' was an irritant and he decided to leverage it further.

'You think you can link any of it to me? You're fucking kidding yourself.'

Liam shrugged. 'But maybe not after we've been through your safe, Eddie, your filing cabinets. You don't make them that secure unless you have something to hide.'

'So now you're planning to go through my fucking safe, are you, my files? You fucking muppet. Maybe you didn't notice but I'm the one holding the fucking gun.'

'I don't think even you are dumb enough to kill me in your own penthouse, Eddie, when I've just spent the day unloading to the media, the government. With you and your story plastered all over the front page tomorrow. It wouldn't be sensible.'

Polson was getting angry, his face flushed. The strategy was working. Anger, Liam had been taught very early, was a wonderfully effective thing to manipulate.

'You think the fucking media will do anything? Ride in on a white fucking horse?' Polson was shouting now. 'The fucking law? The government? Print your fucking headlines, be my guest. Who do you think is going to give a shit? In a few weeks there'll be another story and we'll all be back to business as usual.'

He banged his fist on the table. The butt of the gun left a small indentation in the varnished timber.

'Do you know anything about the real fucking world? Do you know how it really works? If it wasn't for people like me, you'd all still be starving, living in fucking caves.'

Liam nodded. 'I'm willing to bet I've spent more time in the real world than you have, Eddie.' He looked around the sumptuous Baroque interior. 'If you want a dose of the real world I suggest you try the mountains of Afghanistan some time. I lived in caves there. And people are still starving. I've yet to see any proof that your concept of the real world has anything to do with reality.'

'Well then. Let me give you a lesson in *geo-strategic* fucking reality.'

He paused, breathing heavily, trying to take back control.

'The engines of globalized financial capital and commerce are what keep the world turning. They're too fucking important to be driven by the whims of the planet's fucking bleeding-heart liberals, the law, the moral media. If we left things to the politicians nothing would ever get done. Even the leaders of the most repressive fucking regimes on earth aren't immune to

289

this shit; even *those* patsies ultimately allow themselves to be pressured by the *people.'*

He assigned a particular level of contempt to the term 'people'.

'We, on the other hand, suffer from no such vulnerability.' He created an imaginary sphere with a sweep of his outstretched hands and continued in a voice toxic with sarcasm. 'We *global corporate villains*, we *masters of the universe,* in the end, are answerable to no one, that's why we get things done. Today, it's not only our stealth aircraft that fly under the radar.' He tapped his chest with the gun butt. '*We* also fly under the radar. We are the *human* fucking stealth bombers, the B2 Spirits of the fucking species.

'If we need politicians, we buy them; if we need five-star generals or admirals of the fleet we buy them. We own them. Without our bankrolls, our influence, they wouldn't have a fucking snowball's hope of being appointed, elected. Governments don't run things, politicians and bureaucrats are there to do what they're fucking well told. If anybody gets in the way...' He shrugged, knowing the statement needed no further clarification.

He backed across to a drinks cabinet and poured himself a large double bourbon. He returned to the table and drank quickly. The gun stayed pointed at Liam's head at all times. Polson's hand, he observed, revealed the slightest of tremors.

'What are you, Doyle, 25, 26?'

Liam ignored the question.

'Me, I'm 50. I've been around the block once or twice.' He glanced at his watch. 'I have a little time up my sleeve so let me give you a little history lesson. A few years back it was clear we were going to end up with a bleeding-heart, fucking environmentalist in the White House for at least four years; possibly even eight; with a majority of his fellow travelers in both houses. We could see where they were going. They were taking their cues from the soft middle-class socialism of Europe.' He drained the dregs of the bourbon. 'Climate change is *so* middle class.'

He rattled the ice in his glass.

'The world's industrialists were under massive threat. And so we decided we needed to expand our activities. We needed to get the 'people' questioning the corrupt scientific establishment, the mad socialist nihilism of the left, the latte liberals. We stole the show and created the fear that if the "people" returned a pussy to the White House yet again then they would destroy American industry and all the global jobs that go with it. For no good fucking reason.' He paused and then added, almost as an afterthought, 'The smartest of us also started to plan ahead.'

He shrugged and swallowed the ice melt in his glass.

'We got our guy back but, even so, after a while our shtick wasn't working any more, everyone was whining about the planet warming, the Arctic was starting to resemble fucking Florida. The IPCC, the UN, the fucking scientists, the Europeans, the Chinese, every fucker was on our backs. Denial was good in the short term but we needed a longer-term strategy. We had to do something; something that shifted the narrative: we had to create another tranche of doubt.'

He produced a strange little bleating laugh.

'Fortunately it was already well under way. The quickest, cheapest solution – in reality the only fucking solution – was to do a bit of selective geo-engineering, a little sulfur spraying, cool the upper latitudes, bring back the Arctic ice.' He laughed again abruptly. 'What a fucking symbol. What a show! What a blast!'

For the first time since Polson's arrival, serious seeds of doubt about the man's sanity were beginning to take root in Liam's mind.

'We figured if we picked up the pace a little, we could have it sorted before this coming election. And we have. The ice is back to stay and the doubt is back to stay. We've recreated uncertainty and while ever there's a grain of uncertainty, nobody is going to vote for anyone who challenges their comfortable fucking indifference. We have geo-engineered things so that another term for a sensible, pro-business president is just weeks away.'

'Who's we?' Liam asked.

'Everybody whose anybody, son, everyone who's anyone.' He laughed again. 'Nah. Just a small group of philanthropists, really, setting out to save the world.'

'Like you're saving the Himalayan rivers? A billion people starving, dying, largely because of you and your "philanthropists".'

'Listen to me, you fucking moron.' He used the gun as a pointer. 'The moment a newly born infant clamps his gums around his mother's teat he has become a consumer. Life is consumption. We measure success by consumption. The very rich consume more, ergo, they are successful. The planet has eight billion of us all trying to consume as much as we can. Something's gotta give and you can be sure it won't be the very rich.'

He tapped his chest with the gun in his fist. 'At the risk of appearing self-interested, we'll be okay. We'll get by.'

'But what if you don't, what if New York is flooded, inundated, destroyed?'

'Think of it as a development opportunity. I do. I'm in property, in steel, in construction, in armaments, in oil and gas and coal. Think how much money I can make rebuilding New York from the ground up. Magnificent challenge.'

He walked to the window and looked down on what, to him, were clearly the tiny, irrelevant, termite people below. 'We have contingencies in place. You can't make an omelet without breaking heads. So the weather changes? It gets a little warmer, there is the odd storm, flood, famine, water-war. People die sooner or later anyway. I'm okay with that.'

He turned back to Liam and waved the gun from side to side.

'I'm not subject to the stultifying inertia created by the absurd ethical struggle you liberals subject yourselves to, trying to decide what's right and what's wrong every time you drop your pants. If it's good for me, it's right. End of story. If that makes me a sociopath, well, so be it, I'm a rich, contented sociopath.'

Polson produced an expression of mock sympathy.

'You worry about killing, about violence, it bothers you, you think about the person you hurt or kill, you care about them or their families and so you try to avoid it. We, on the other hand, don't much care. In fact it can be a positive experience for us. Killing can be stimulating. It reinforces our sense of control.'

Liam's gaze was steady. 'I guess you've never climbed a mountain then.'

Polson had no idea what he was talking about. 'I'm also a sociopath with a short attention span and now I'm bored.' He moved closer and waved the gun, indicating Liam should sit. Liam ignored him.

'So, that's it, you're done with me, time to indulge in a little stimulating killing?'

Polson let the hand holding the gun drop slightly.

'And get blood on my Safavid silk?' He indicated the carpet with the gun's snout. 'That's 16th-century Persian, buddy, priceless. No, I get a minion to handle the distasteful things.'

He checked his $50,000 gold watch. 'In fact he should be here to escort you away any time now.'

Liam shook his head. 'Cassidy Millston won't be coming, I blew his brains out a couple of days ago.' He made it sound matter of fact. 'There's a picture of his miserable corpse on his phone.' He reached carefully into his pocket and dropped the cellphone onto the table.

Polson's arrogant certainty wavered for a split second and he glanced down at the gruesome image. It was all the time Liam needed. His right foot cut a hard arc through the air, broke Polson's thumb and sent the gun flying. Polson tried to make a fist of the injured hand and took a swipe at Liam's head. He might have been a boxer in his day but he knew precious little about hand-to-hand combat. Liam easily avoided the blow, grabbed the swinging wrist and used Polson's own momentum to spin him face down onto the floor with a bone-crunching thud. Polson lay stunned. Liam retrieved the gun from the carpet, but didn't bother to point it at the man.

Polson staggered to his feet, clutching at his swelling thumb, and glanced again at the picture of Millston's shattered head. He was much paler now.

'We may have to come to some sort of arrangement.' He backed towards the window and steadied himself on the sill with his good hand. 'Your people are clearly very resourceful.'

There was a splintering sound and a neat hole appeared in the thick glass followed instantly by a far more untidy cavity in Polson's temple.

Liam was already horizontal as the second shot penetrated the glass a hair's breadth above his head. He hit the deck just inches from Polson and watched as the life and the blood drained from the billionaire's body onto the priceless rug.

'So are your people, Ed, so are yours.'

He checked Polson's pockets. There was nothing that looked like it would get him access to the secured information in the office and he had very little time. 'Pity Charlie's not here with his Semtex,' he said to the lifeless figure. He stood and, crouching below window level, moved quickly toward the door, then paused and looked back at the dead man. 'What a shame you never climbed a mountain.'

26

OSKAR FREDERIK sat with his back to the surveillance camera; he had a hat pulled low over his forehead. Walter sat two seats away staring into space.

'You were more involved than you have ever admitted, Walter,' Oskar said without looking up.

It was a statement not a question and it hit Dyson like a sledgehammer. He turned to Oskar. 'What on earth do you mean?'

'Don't bother, Walter. That poor, sad Rigby left some personal notes behind in Moscow. I know.'

Walter looked frightened. He checked to see if the other two were listening but they were standing facing the glass wall, watching an aircraft lift off.

'Why haven't you mentioned this to them?' he indicated Charlie with a tilt of his head. 'You've had plenty of time.'

Oskar gave a tiny nod. 'I suppose I was hoping you would make a clean breast of it eventually. I saw the guilt on your face when I spoke of the droughts. But you said nothing and so I thought about it for a while and decided I could watch you more effectively if you didn't know I was watching.'

'You don't understand,' Walter said bitterly. 'Aeronautical architects, engineers, electronics people, IT people, designers, scientists, meteorologists, climate scientists: they promised us money we could never have dreamed of, couldn't have made in ten lifetimes doing anything else. At first we were told it was a little aerosol injection experiment to see what the atmospheric temperature effect would be, a public service. They kept repeating and repeating that global carbon mitigation was never going to work, talked endlessly about world leaders squabbling like kids in the schoolyard.

'But the thing went on and on and got bigger and bigger and

by then it was too late, we were in, they kept us in line with greed and fear. If we behaved we got small bonuses, if we made trouble we were threatened, or the people with wives, sons, daughters, had their families threatened. And it just got worse and worse. Occasionally people simply disappeared, but there were always eager new faces with dollar signs in their eyes, ready to replace them. It became a case of every man for himself. Even so, when I left, when I was "rescued", I left without a cent. Nothing to show for all those years of hard graft and fear.'

'As a child,' Oskar said softly, 'I lived in Latvia, under the Soviet bullies. I learned very early how important it is that the strong take care of the weak, the healthy take care of the sick, the young take care of the old. Otherwise we are no different from the lowest forms of life.'

Walter looked around again. 'So what will you do now?'

'Nothing,' Oskar said. 'You are the one who has a decision to make.'

They sat in silence until the Athens flight was called. 'I need to use the toilet,' Walter said. 'I'll see you at the gate.'

Oskar smiled and nodded. 'Of course.'

* * *

The *Dialog*'s meeting room was a whole lot messier than the journalists' desks beyond the glass panels. Whiteboards created an obstacle course round the scattered chairs; computers, heaped documents and used coffee cups filled every square inch of the large table. Liam and Cherry sat at opposite laptops, tapping away furiously.

Liam paused and looked up. 'How well do you trust Saxon Melville?'

'Pretty well, why?' She gave him a strange look. 'I've known him for over ten years.'

'Only three people knew I was seeing Polson. Me, you and Saxon. I trust me, I trust you – that leaves Saxon.'

'Perhaps someone followed you. Maybe the bullet wasn't meant for Polson. Maybe they were after you.'

'That, I suspect, will be the inevitable spin. But no.' Liam shook his head with certainty. 'Professional snipers who shoot that well don't make those mistakes. If I was the primary target I wouldn't be here now.'

'Yes,' Cherry said thoughtfully. 'And I guess his safe and filing cabinets wouldn't have been cleaned out within minutes of your exit. I'm told the police were there no more than a half hour after the shots were fired and the cupboard was bare.' She shrugged. 'Anyways, I can't believe Saxon is anything but dead straight. Never had any reason to think otherwise. Guys like Polson make lots of enemies along the way, they get it in the end. That's *karma*. Probably just coincidence.' She returned to her typing.

The story hit the stands exactly 24 hours later. Under Liam's byline.

'KILLING SKY CONSPIRACY.'

The *Washington Dialog*'s headline sprawled across the full width and almost the entire depth of the broadsheet front page in big, bold, Gill Sans capitals.

Polson's death and his alleged involvement in the scheme were heavily covered. Within minutes of its online release, the story went viral. Social media flamed into immediate meltdown and the midday briefing to the electronic media overflowed from the small *Dialog* auditorium out onto the street, with camera operators and reporters fighting for space and, once or twice, coming to blows. Headlines from Santiago to Mumbai shrieked 'Killing Sky!' – always in page-dominating sans-serif type.

By late afternoon almost every major government and agency in the world had released a response of some sort.

'The reactions seem to run the gamut from mild but righteous indignation to absolute moral outrage,' Cherry said to Liam over the top of her tortoiseshells. 'There's also a whiff of polite skepticism in the subtext.'

Liam looked up from his cellphone. 'And Russia is rejecting it outright as just another Western fabrication. This one claims it's an outrageous slur.'

The evening bulletins were wall-to-wall 'Killing Sky' with

experts of every conceivable scientific and strategic persuasion rolled out and interviewed by earnest anchormen and women.

Notable by its absence was any meaningful response from the White House. 'The President is examining the issues very carefully and will provide a response at an appropriate time,' was the only statement released.

Liam and Cherry shared her sofa, sipped red wine and watched the various nightly news bulletins. No matter which network she selected, there they were being interviewed, again and again. Eventually it became too much and she clicked the sound to mute.

'So what happens now?'

'I've no idea,' she said. 'Let's wait and see who comes out of the woodwork. Hopefully we haven't started a world war.'

'With the possible exception of North Korea, I can't see anyone taking credit for this and going the belligerent route. I think the most likely option is frantic track covering followed by stony-faced denial. The Chinese are doing it already.'

He found something amongst the pile of papers on Cherry's floor and started to read.

'Reports coming in from Xinhua, the official Chinese news agency, are quoting an authorized statement from the Chinese Government claiming that they have investigated the outrageous Western media accusations made regarding the Dongfeng facility by the American government agent Dyson and have found them to be without substance. Furthermore, investigations in the Altai Mountains have shown no trace of foreign aircraft. The facility there is, as stated in the Chinese media, a Global Seed Vault.'

'A comprehensive investigation in less than 24 hours. That's efficient,' Cherry said.

'But then they would say that, wouldn't they?' Liam returned the paper to the stack. 'Whether they were involved or not. Face is a powerful force.'

* * *

If he were not covered in a fine dusting of fresh snow you might have imagined that young Ivor had simply sat down against the shed to rest for a while. He didn't really look dead. But the color of his skin left little doubt, even before Dashka took the superfluous step of checking his pulse.

She ploughed towards the office as fast as the deep snow would allow, yelling for help. Alexei came out, followed by Sergei, and they returned to the waxen corpse.

Sergei lifted Ivor's sleeve to reveal several needle marks on the soft flesh at the crook of his arm. 'Drug overdose,' he diagnosed, without a hint of emotion. 'Stupid kid killed himself.'

'Where would he get drugs on Severny?' Dashka wasn't sure whether what she felt was shock or grief. Either way she was angry. 'And he did it out here in the cold? In the snow? That's crazy.'

Sergei stood, shrugged and started back to the lab. 'He probably brought them with him,' he called over his shoulder.

Alexei moved to follow and then turned to Dashka. 'Get someone to put him in the store room. We'll have to send him back when the ship arrives. I'll have to inform his imbecile father now. He should never have sent him here in the first place.'

The next few weeks for Dashka were a surreal rollercoaster of confusion and fear. She searched Ivor's room and found nothing. She went through the pockets of his small cache of clothes and found only a short, poorly written love poem addressed to her. The lack of skill shown did nothing to stop her tears. But there were no drugs. It didn't make any sense. There was no sign that Ivor had brought a stash with him from the city and was just biding his time before suddenly, months afterwards and for no apparent reason, injecting himself with a fatal overdose.

It was only several days later that the possibility he had been murdered started to take shape in her mind. She was working on a snowmobile with a skid-frame that was overdue for greasing. She located the tub of thick lubricant and carried it over to the upturned vehicle. As she drove her hand into the gel she felt something solid at its center and scooped it out. It was the size of a small cellphone, a slim flat object wrapped in plastic. She wiped her hands and shook the object from the grease-covered wrap, recognizing it immediately as a powerful miniature solid-state drive. She concealed it in the pocket of her parka and kept working as if nothing had happened. Returning to her room at the usual time, shortly after dinner, she plugged it into her computer.

She lay staring at the unseen ceiling. Apart from the commonplace daily contents of what looked like Alexei's computer, his hard drive, she was certain, contained figures detailing readings of the various gases and particulates present in the atmosphere. It had been a nervous, stealthy look, with Dashka half expecting a knock on the door at any moment. But she was certain there were two different sets of figures for the same period. That, in itself, seemed odd, but she decided it was prudent that her light was switched off at the usual hour and her networked computer shut down. There hadn't been enough time to tell whether the two sets of figures might mean anything sinister. She spent the rest of the sleepless night trying to figure out what it all meant and by morning's twilight was more confused than ever.

She tried to remain calm and insouciant at breakfast but her head was in overdrive and it was clear that Sergei sensed something was not quite right.

Was it Ivor who'd hidden the hard drive in the grease? It had to be. Is that what got him killed? Did they know Ivor had downloaded the files? Was he aware of their contents? Could they possibly suspect she had it, that Ivor had given it to her or she had found it? And what did it all mean, anyhow?

Sergei and Alexei sat across the breakfast room deep in earnest conversation. From time to time, one or other would glance up and give her a hostile look. She wasn't quite sure what to do next but, given the men couldn't be sure what she did or didn't know, there was possibly a little breathing space.

A very little.

The ship's arrival was still some time away and, with the way they were glowering at her, she didn't rate very highly her chances of surviving long enough to be wished a *bon voyage*.

* * *

A tabloid headline shrieked at Cherry from the news-stand in an attempt to get the story off the front pages.

'IT'S NOT THE KILLING SKY, STUPID. IT'S THE ECONOMY.'

It was a faint hope. In media across the country, the presidential race, the economy, social security, illegal immigration, even Pan-Islamic ambitions were all being forced to take a back seat to the much more titillating story of atmospheric geo-engineering and worldwide conspiracies. The resultant effects of the catastrophic Asian drought often appeared on the second or third page of the report.

Candidate Stone brought the presidential race and the Killing Sky issue together, a day later, with dramatic effect, when she addressed it in prime time with a response that was as forceful as the President's had been restrained.

'Since these allegations relating to criminal acts of geo-engineering have surfaced, there have been vehement denials from many international sources. In spite of this, I am, as of today, announcing that if, in November, I am trusted by the people of this great nation to lead them, then as my first act as President I will institute the widest-ranging of investigations, at all levels, to get to the bottom of this so-called conspiracy. No stone will be left unturned. If it is, indeed, a conspiracy, global or otherwise, the conspirators will be left with no place to hide.

'In order to indicate that I assign the highest possible priority to this investigation, I will, if elected, appoint my Vice President, Jason Arnott, to oversee it and to report directly to me.'

Arnott, standing to her right and slightly behind, nodded without his customary wide smile.

'This will be a multi-party, multi-agency, inquiry,' she continued. 'You have our word that we will stop at nothing to get to the source of these activities and, if necessary, to root out the alleged conspirators. Once that is done, if any individual or group is found to have been guilty of these heinous acts, mark my words, the perpetrators will face the harshest penalties it is

301

within my presidential powers and the powers of international law to impose upon them.'

Jason Arnott stepped forward holding a few sheets of notepaper. The hint of a smile was back. He removed his glasses, placed them carefully on the podium, scratched his nose and read from his prepared statement. 'It is a great honor to be entrusted with this extremely important task and the people of this great nation have my personal promise that I will move heaven and earth to make sure this investigation is carried through with the greatest possible integrity and diligence. If this investigation reveals there is even the smallest shred of substance to these allegations then, for the guilty parties, as Candidate Stone has said, there will be no place to hide.'

* * *

A small, elite group of the planet's more Machiavellian individuals sat together in a large drawing room. Among them were the senior representatives of arcane and powerful non-profit foundations and globally influential think tanks. Using the seemingly endless resources provided by their un-named corporate masters, some had been manipulating public and political opinion since the early days of the tobacco wars.

Beyond the bay windows, a stone's throw from the house, a cluster of helicopters waited idly on the lawn at the edge of the Western Isles loch. This late in the stalking season, the estate on the Hebridean island's southwest shore was as remote a location as one could possibly desire.

The British aristocrat stepped out onto a small podium erected at the front of the room and held up a hand for silence.

'Houston,' he looked around unhurriedly. 'Or perhaps I should say "Harris"… we have a problem.'

He waited for the mutterings to die away.

'This is not a battle, my friends. It's a war. In wars, from time to time, we face the odd setback, we lose the occasional skirmish. That is all. Think of the present situation as no more than a skirmish.'

As he spoke he operated a small handset. A series of large dissolving electronic images on the wall at his back displayed one sensational headline after another.

'We are currently all over the front pages of virtually every major publication on earth. Social media is having an attack of the vapors and the world's networks are contemplating hour-long exposure specials as we meet. If you listen carefully you will hear the saliva dripping from the tongues of every investigative reporter on the planet. To top it all off, we've suffered two unfortunate losses. You know of whom I speak.'

He allowed five seconds of respectful silence and then continued.

'Professors Dyson and Oskar Frederik are at liberty and, it seems, will continue, until persuaded otherwise, to create significant problems for us. I won't pollute the island's pure air with my opinions of Casement and Doyle.

'What we have here is an unnecessary distraction and eventually we will deal with those responsible. For the present we will be dispatching our fleets to many different and well isolated locations and deactivating our various sites until all the excitement dies down – and die down it will.'

He paused, his hands together against his lips, and remained silent until he sensed the group's growing unease.

'Which, of course, is where you come in. You, the masters, nay, the *creators* of the modern disintermediation.' He delivered each syllable of the final word with a slow relish then threw his arms wide to embrace the roomful of listeners. 'Your job is to nip this thing in the bud. Do what you've always done. Dig up whatever dirt you can on these people: Doyle, Davitt and her newspaper, Casement and the scientists.'

He hit the pause button as Oskar Frederik's image appeared on the screen.

'Discredit the man and you discredit his message.'

He prowled the podium from edge to edge, turning like a large caged predator.

'Bombard every medium from every side. Question the morality, the sanity of the leakers and the eyesight, the motives of the witnesses, question the veracity of any images provided. Say they've been doctored by Photoshop experts; that still works. Dispute the science, question the evidence, the proof. We'll get our scientific teams to write articles; swamp them with data. Make sure they get published. Put pressure on the science journals, dispute their findings. In other words, people, as you've managed to do so effectively in the past, create *doubt!'*

He studied the gathering. 'I see a couple of new faces here today. Welcome. I'll keep this brief but I do want to remind you all and particularly our new associates what we, here, are all about.'

He smiled a Cheshire Cat smile and, by rotating his head slowly from left to right, managed to share his smugness with everyone in the room.

'Denial is a wonderfully efficient tool – so simple to use, but a tool of incandescent brilliance, along with that other humble masterpiece, "repetition". All that's required to succeed is denial repeated over and over and over again.

'The story must, of course, be consistent. When one owns many of the means of dissemination and many of the people doing the disseminating, getting the gullible to believe is a process of exquisite simplicity: we simply deny and keep on denying. We've been doing it effectively for centuries. If we wish to convince the great unwashed that black is in fact white, we simply say it over and over again in a sincere and assertive way and fairly soon you have them dreaming of a black Christmas.

'The marvelous thing about denial is that it sows that tiny, but breathtakingly fertile, seed called doubt and, once that seed is sown, simple humanity's own natural inertia, their disinclination to embrace difficult decisions, to choose change, means they nurture and develop that seed themselves, without any further help from us.'

His oratory began to take on an evangelical fervor. He raised his pitch just slightly.

'The job of each and every one of you, our job, is to say over and over again, there is No Killing Sky. There simply is No Killing Sky. Where is the proof, where are the aircraft? There

304

aren't any. It's the climate alarmists again, it's no more than a crude socialist plot, it's the commercial self-interest of corrupt scientists, it's the lunatic far-left fringe, a green conspiracy, eco-terrorists, an attack on democracy, on free enterprise.'

He paused for rhetorical effect.

'Any inventive excuse will do. Remember, all you need do is deny, deny, deny. There is *no* killing sky. There is no chance of defeat if you repeat, repeat, repeat.'

A couple of the younger audience members made covert eye contact and raised quick eyebrows, but nobody challenged. Nobody spoke.

'All right, get out there and go to work.'

The man from Singapore remained seated in the front row. The Englishman turned and motioned to a couple of very large bullet-headed men, in dark suits. They loitered, relaxed but alert, at the edge of the podium; one revealed the edge of a tattoo just visible above a tight collar. They sauntered across.

'Get the helicopter organized and make it snappy.' He waved them away with a dismissive flick of the wrist.

If the Singaporean at times seemed arrogant, he had more than met his match in his British superior. He was summoned by a slim, aristocratic finger.

'It seems that our so-called security teams, you people paid good money to take care of our interests, are proving yourselves to be less than competent.'

The Singaporean bristled slightly but said nothing.

'This whole sorry business is getting well out of hand. If these issues had been addressed when they should have been, we would not be in this predicament now. Two men and a pair of women have brought us to our knees. Why is that?'

'That is because Mr Millston was simply not up to the job he was given.' The Singaporean took a silk handkerchief from a pocket and wiped his hands. 'In future I will handle these issues personally.'

'Mr Millston wasn't responsible for the Xinjiang fiasco, or Jiuquan.' The Englishman walked to the end of the podium and swung round. The room was now empty. 'Do you have any idea what's at stake here?' He was shouting now.

The Singaporean spoke softly. 'I don't need to be reminded what's at stake, *sir*.' There was insolence in his tone. 'I have lived with poverty, extreme poverty, and I have lived with wealth and I know which I prefer. I also know that wealth and weakness are incompatible. Soft men don't become rich men. So, be assured, there is no softness, no lack of resolve here. I am not Millston.'

'Well, find those fucking people then!'

It was the first time he'd ever seen the icy blood of the born-to-rule aristocrat come to the boil.

'And there's one more thing we need to do,' the Englishman said, working to calm himself. 'It's important that those elements of the media who are keen to keep milking this story are given reason to reconsider.'

* * *

Liam used a callbox at Manchester Airport to punch in Charlie's latest cell number.

'Okay, I'll be in Athens in a few hours. What's the best way to get over to that island?'

'I don't know,' Charlie said. 'I've never been there. Where are you?'

'Airport. Why?'

'Good. Go to the news-stand inside the departure gate: the woman there is holding a map book for you under the name on your new passport. You'll find a small asterisk against one of the islands. I'll explain when you get here. You can get a connection from the main Athens airport. Pay cash, they won't bother with your passport or ID.'

'Okay, see you in a few hours.'

Charlie paused. 'This whole Killing Sky thing is going ballistic,' he said. 'Even way out here. You'll need to keep dyeing your hair, change your look, keep a low profile.'

Liam spent both flights trying to figure out why Othonoi in the Ionian Sea to the west had suddenly been replaced by an Aegean island with an asterisk in a book. He was no closer to an answer when the small Dash Eight thumped onto the rutted runway on the barren island of Astypalaia.

Charlie was waiting with a more-than-compact Korean car at the tiny whitewashed terminal. 'This was the best I could get,' he said, as he squeezed Liam's pack into the trunk.

'These roads are murder on the suspension. Make the Paris to Dakar look like a Sunday picnic.' They drove along a small section of sealed road towards the Chora, a tightly packed cascade of sugar-cube houses tumbling down a steep hillside to the sea, crowned by what looked like a crumbling stone fortress all but concealing two church towers.

'Great little island,' Charlie boomed, pointing to the picturesque town. 'Fantastic food and not a tourist in sight at this time of year. In fact half the island population seems to be off trying to find work on Rhodes or in Athens.'

He passed a hillside windmill, then skirted around the town and headed north along a truly dreadful road paved with razor-sharp stones and loose dust.

'How's Jia? How's everybody?'

'Dyson's gone,' Charlie said casually.

Liam wasn't sure whether the careless tone was there to hide Charlie's embarrassment.

'He went missing at Manchester. We gave him two minutes to go to the toilet on his own and he never came back. I couldn't find him, our flight was leaving, you had his taped confession in your hot little hand, so I just figured fuck him. And here we are.'

The front wheels hit a huge rock embedded in the middle of the track and the car left the ground for a moment. A scattering of goats took off in fright, the bells at their necks jangled chaotically.

'Jia confessed to me that she'd left a cellphone in the cottage when you two took off for Moscow,' Charlie said. Less matter of fact now. 'I checked the memory after we lost Walter. Someone in the house called a Westminster number twice while we were away. He was the only one there. She took the phone back when you came in from Bantry that night.'

Charlie approached another deep hump without bothering to brake and once again the tiny car became airborne.

'You've been driving in bloody Queensland too long,' Liam said in a reasonable attempt at an Australian accent. 'So I guess that explains why we're on Astypalaia and not that other place.'

'Oskar was smarter than Walter.' Charlie took his eyes from the road momentarily and glanced across at him. 'He gave us the name of the other island to see how Dyson would react; told me about Astypalaia in private later. He didn't trust Dyson, he'd heard stuff in Moscow and he sensed something none of us noticed. You and me were too busy and it seems Jia only ever sees the good in people.'

'Everyone but me,' Liam said ruefully.

'She's just not used to your odd ways. She's not used to people who have dead and bleeding bodies lying around the house. She's never killed before, it takes time. She'll come round.'

Liam frowned. 'That's my fault too.'

'Anyhow, Oskar got his answer, seems he was right about Dyson. I'd say you can stop beating yourself up over visiting your mom that night. I'd bet good money Dyson was responsible for Millston and his thugs arriving. Inadvertently or otherwise.'

Charlie laughed. 'And if it was deliberate, the next lot he calls in will head for an island way off over on the other side of Greece. So much for his credibility.'

'But why would he do that? Surely he'd realize they'd get rid of him sooner or later too?'

'You'll have to ask *him* that. If you can find him.'

Charlie turned in through a tumbledown timber gate and pulled up outside a group of ancient farm buildings. They sat high on a saw-toothed saddle between two bare mountains. The exterior was a shambles of sharp stones and rusting farm implements half buried in the weeds; the interior had been converted into a spacious, comfortable home.

27

'WHERE IS Charles Casement, Mr Paul? Where is Liam Doyle?' They sat at their inevitable table. 'I have enough frequent-flyer points to circle the globe a dozen times. First class. I don't need to be flying to Darwin every other week.'

'The man Dyson. His intelligence turned out to be unreliable then?'

'Beware of geeks bearing gifts,' the man from Singapore said. His upper lip gave a supercilious little twitch. 'Mr Dyson is like Cassidy Millston, a loose cannon. They both made mistakes. I don't make mistakes, Mr Paul.'

Paul attempted a relaxed shrug. 'The simple answer is we still don't know.' He refused to allow himself to become flustered by the man's contempt.

'We're reasonably certain Casement left Ireland for Greece but after that...' he shrugged. 'What you have to understand is this man is a professional through and through.' In an attempt to conceal the admiration he clearly felt, Paul turned and watched an aircraft taxiing across the wet tarmac.

'I suspect he carries more passports than all of ASIO put together,' he said. 'They change their clothes constantly, they wear hats, coats, sunglasses, colored contacts, wigs, they dye their hair, grow beards, shave them, they know where all the cameras are and never face them and they rarely go where you expect them to. Seems they've even worked out a way to fool biometric scanners. We followed one young woman in a hijab, thought she was a possibility. Turned out she was working with Mossad.'

'Keep looking, Mr Paul. If you don't locate him soon, I will have trouble convincing my superiors that you are of any further use to us.'

Paul frowned. 'Is that a threat?'

'No, it's a timely word of advice.'

'Strictly speaking, these people are no longer in my quadrant, my region of responsibility. Have you tried anyone else?'

'Have we tried anyone else?' The man from Singapore almost smiled. 'Why would we need anyone else's help with you in control of things, Mr Paul?' He reached over and gave Paul's knee a patronizing squeeze. 'You're the only one on the entire planet that we rely on for this important work.'

He managed to convey sarcasm and menace simultaneously.

'Keep looking, Mr Paul.'

He stood and left the table without farewell, checked in for the Singapore flight and made for the small first-class lounge. All the technology in the world seemed not to be getting them very far. It was time to use a very old technique. Time to use a technique they had used on game birds during his brief years at Cambridge. Time to flush them out.

* * *

The polling was looking fairly consistent. The President was in trouble. In spite of the best efforts of a slew of viciously effective Super PACs operating well beyond campaign finance laws, Donna Stone was way out in front by every calculation, with the election just days away. The release of the 'Killing Sky' story had seen the President's status take a nosedive, while Stone's had gone through the roof.

Cherry perused the detailed numbers on her screen. It seemed Stone's choice of Jason Arnott had paid dividends. Her tough pragmatism and his relaxed populism created an effective symbiosis. She was good with policy, he was good with people.

The intercom on Cherry's desk buzzed. 'There's a guy called Dixon on the phone. Won't say what it's about. Sounds serious,' the secretary said.

'Okay, put him through.'

'Cherry, Mark Dixon. May I call you Cherry?'

'What can I do for you, Mr Dixon?'

'I wanted to speak to you about this Killing Sky story your paper has been circulating.'

'Who are you?'

'I'm with one of the federal agencies. That's all you really need to know.'

'Which agency, Mr Dixon?'

'As I said...' He paused then continued, his voice revealing an edge that hadn't been there initially. 'We are interested in speaking to the individuals involved. There are significant national-security issues raised by these allegations of yours. We need to know where they are and I was wondering if you might be able to tell us.'

'I've no idea,' Cherry said. 'And, if I did know, I'd need to find out a lot more about you before I handed over the information. If you want to speak to me further I suggest you make an appointment with my assistant to see me...'

She was about to hang up but the man cut across her. 'If you are involved with their disappearance in any way, or if you know where they are, you are potentially contributing to the harboring of fugitives. You could be charged as an accessory. The charge has the potential to lead to a long jail term. On the other hand, help us and you could find it very rewarding, financially and otherwise.' Threats, implied or actual, always made Cherry angry. They were part of a journalist's lot and you had to get used to them but this one sounded colder, more chilling than most.

'I find it interesting that not one of you people, not a single agency we spoke to, in fact, had ever heard of Mr Dyson when he vanished ten years ago, you knew nothing about him. Now suddenly he and his friends are the most popular kids on the block. How come?' Cherry made no attempt to hide her anger.

'The allegations your paper and all the others have made about American-designed aircraft operating out of Gansu are very disturbing.' Dixon was a little more conciliatory now. 'We are eager to know what Mr Dyson's involvement may have been, Cherry.'

'You mean the facility in Dongfeng that, according to your friends in the Chinese government, is non-existent?' Cherry asked with delicious sarcasm. 'I have no idea where Mr Dyson is, but if I did know I would advise him to remain there until he can be guaranteed his safety. There is clearly something very disturbing going on and why should he believe that you and your associates are not up to your necks in it; not involved?'

'Take my word for it, Ms Davitt. We… I, am not involved.' He rang off.

* * *

Another monsoon had come and gone, leaving scarcely a thimble's worth of rain. In the valleys suckled by the Ganges, the Irrawaddy and the Brahmaputra, the meager stalks struggling for life turned to withered dust on the ground.

People were hungry and hunger soon turned to anger. In weeks the anger became violence and the immediacy of globalized television news and social media meant the shocked tourists, safe in their comfortable homes, continued to stay away. It meant, too, that the world's climbers stayed away.

And Sherpa families across Nepal went, yet again, without food.

Lakpa Sange trudged along the dusty track linking his village to Kathmandu. He had been walking since just before dawn and was nearing the city's outskirts. The chances of getting any paid work were almost non-existent, but what else was a man with a family to do? There was no point sitting at home waiting for the climbers to come. The season was at its end. They weren't coming.

A new and expensive-looking SUV pulled in alongside him, covering him in fine particles of dust. The driver's tinted window slid open silently. Two Westerners looked out at him from behind aviator shades.

'Can you read?' The man in the passenger seat leaned across.

'Read? A little,' the wary Sherpa said.

'English?'

'A little,' he repeated.

The driver reached down toward the console, came up with what looked like a brand new cellphone and handed it to him with a folded slip of paper.

'You know this person?'

Lakpa unfolded the note and perused it quickly then nodded. 'I know him.'

'Call the number, read what is written there. Make it sound convincing, like it's not being read and I'll give you enough to keep your entire family in caviar for a year.'

He held up a small roll of banknotes.

The young Sherpa looked back at the cash. To people like him, a small fortune. He'd met some crazy Western climbers in his time but these two, even though they clearly weren't mountain people, were the craziest yet.

He pointed at the money. 'The money first, so you don't cheat me.'

'You think I'm going to drive off while you've got my phone?' The man laughed and passed the banknotes across.

Lakpa punched in the number and delivered the message with a little extra embellishment of his own before disconnecting.

'You should be in the movies,' the man chortled.

Lakpa pointed to the contents of the note in his hand. 'I will come on your climb if you need people for this. Very experience. Very good rates.' He made to hand back the note.

'We don't need you.' The man reached out and grabbed the cellphone and the vehicle accelerated away in a cloud of dust, leaving the bemused and enriched Lakpa still holding the puzzling note.

* * *

Jia's greeting had been as cool as he'd expected and much cooler than he'd hoped.

Liam stowed his bag in the room that had been made up for him and joined the others on the rudimentary stone terrace. The view was as spectacular as it was rugged. Roiling cloud filled the crags on the nearby mountain top and sparse, straw-colored vegetation clung to the pulverized rock faces that plunged down to a distant, ink-blue Aegean.

'What a magnificent planet,' Oskar was saying, gazing down

the valley. 'How sad that we value it so little.'

He turned, welcomed Liam far more warmly than had Jia and then continued.

'As a species we have now become powerful enough to preside over our own extinction. But, it seems, not altruistic enough, not selfless enough, to prevent it. We appear to be infected by a pandemic of narcissism; the product, I suspect, of a chronic nihilism. We are lemmings charging headlong towards the edge of a cliff that we know full well is there. Perhaps this is simply a part of nature's inexorable process. Each species has its time under the sun and then simply sows the seeds of its own destruction and disappears. Sometimes other species come along in their place, sometimes not.'

'I think the average person just wants to be left alone to raise a family, put food on the table and live a normal life.' Liam said, drinking in the tranquility of the scene.

Oskar was silent for a while, contemplating the world around him. 'I don't think the average person has that luxury any longer, my boy. We've used up all the planet's credit. We need to start paying back the loan, otherwise we all face biological bankruptcy. If we want to survive, we have to change and it seems increasingly clear that the change won't come from the top. Your average person will have to step up to the plate, as you Americans say.'

He paused again, studying the distant horizon. 'We are, quite, quite possibly, the only beings in the entire Cosmos who have been gifted with this exquisite, profound and terrible burden of realization. The awareness of the remarkable actuality of our own existence and the consciousness of our own likely annihilation. And we are not using our gift.'

For several minutes nobody spoke, unwilling to appear to have taken Oskar's passionate oratory lightly.

Jia, unusually, was the one to break the spell.

'Did you manage to ask the man Polson about Zhang Liu, about my father, before he died?'

'No, I didn't have the chance,' Liam lied. 'I, uh, wasn't with him for very long before he was shot.'

In truth it hadn't occurred to him to ask and now, with Jia's earnest question, her hope-filled eyes, there was yet another reason for him to feel guilt. It was immediately obvious that she had seen through his poor attempt at deception and it did nothing to improve the state of their relationship.

For several days, he hiked aimlessly along the island's network of rough mountain tracks, a distraction that would normally make him joyful but, for the moment, simply added to his misery and made him feel very alone.

He was seriously contemplating actually trying to communicate with Jia when, once again, they were overtaken by events and his emotional life was driven back into its dark hole.

* * *

The phone in the study started jangling. Cherry dropped a handful of thin spaghetti into boiling water, wiped her hands and hurried down the dark corridor.

'Cherry Davitt.'

'Hi, Ms Davitt, Cherry. I need to speak to Liam Doyle. Urgently.'

The accent sounded Australian.

'How did you get this number?'

'A young bloke in your office gave it to me.'

She made a mental note to find and fire.

'Why call me?'

'He, Liam, spoke about you a fair bit.' He paused.

'So who are you and what do you want? I'm in the middle of cooking my dinner.'

'Sorry but, look, I'm a friend. Tell him Kathmandu. Shishapangma. He'll know.' He spelt it for her. 'Please get him to call me. He has the number.'

As the line went dead she heard an unfamiliar crackling sound. It seemed to come from somewhere in the vicinity of the front entrance. She dimmed the table lamp and drew back the curtain. The two security men who'd been on the building's front step were gone. She checked across the narrow road. The police cruiser that had been there all day was nowhere to be seen.

She dropped the curtain and raced to the kitchen, without bothering to turn on the light, she bent over the sink and looked down to the pool of light outside the rear entrance. Nobody there. Her last defender, gone.

She dragged a carving knife from its rack and did a quick nervous sweep of the apartment. All as it should be. But for how long? The missing security men could only mean one thing.

Cherry clicked off the gas under the pasta, grabbed her purse and tablet, retrieved a passport, a Charlie special, and a small bundle of cash from a wall safe, gulped down the dregs of her wine and slipped out into the corridor.

She opted to avoid the elevator and had descended no more than a half dozen stairs when she heard footsteps from below. She froze and listened. They were coming toward her and the footfalls were soft and careful. They were not police-issue soles.

She removed her shoes, tiptoed silently past her front door and up to the rooftop. The area was in darkness and she stood in the shadows listening for a moment before groping her way across to the edge. The gap between her building and the next was no more than a foot or two wide and she crossed it with ease. The next building along was butted up against its neighbor but the fourth building was a good six feet away and long jump had never been her sport of choice. She looked around, heart thudding against her ribcage. The external staircase on the old building ended more than a level below. She checked the other side of the dark machinery room. There had to be some way out. Her eyes fell on something gleaming in the light that spilled from a tall building across the street. An extension ladder lay beside a neat collection of paint cans. She dragged it across to the unlit concrete chasm between the buildings and managed to lift it into an upright position near the edge. She let its own weight carry it across the gap and it fell with a metallic clang, bounced twice and came to rest straddling the space and creating a precarious but functional bridge. Cherry slung her purse across her chest and crawled across the narrow metal rungs without looking down; badly bruising her knees and shins as she went.

She dragged the heavy ladder toward her and then let it fall clattering loudly all the way to the floor of the alley below. She leapt to her feet and jogged around the perimeter, searching until she located a fire escape. This one was fine. She leapt down onto the first metal flight and as her head was about to disappear below the parapet she heard a shout. She peeked back in the direction she'd come. On the roof of her building, a long stone's throw away, two men stood in silhouette against the soft glow of the Washington night sky. She didn't wait around to find out if they'd seen her, taking the grime-encrusted stairs four at a time. In the alley she turned west and headed for Pennsylvania Avenue. Her plan, if it could be called that, was to put ten blocks between her and the apartment before concealing herself somewhere safe, calling Richie in his cab and asking him to get her the hell out of there. She'd gone just two city blocks when she heard a crash from behind her. A man running toward her had sent a trash can flying. Cherry kicked off her shoes again, scooped them up and sprinted away; oblivious to the astonished looks of passers-by. She dodged across a busy intersection and then glanced back. He was still there, too close, but no longer gaining. She sped toward the next crossroad and dashed across against the lights. A tourist coach braked with a shriek of big tires and the driver pulled hard on the steering, swerving to the left as Cherry grazed past the wing mirror on the right. Her pursuer was less nimble and smacked into the stationary coach, bouncing off and falling hard onto the pavement. It was the break Cherry needed: she sprinted across two more intersections, weaving expertly though the stunned crowds and made it to Pennsylvania. She spotted a vacant cab, whistled shrilly for him to stop and threw herself into the rear seat. 'Drive,' she yelled at the startled driver. 'Just fucking drive.'

For the first time since bolting from home she had time to think… time to think. Who to trust in Washington? Friends? The few she had would be way out of their depth. Saxon Melville? She was no longer certain about him. There was Donna Stone, possibly, but it seemed she had more than enough problems of her own. The answer, sadly, was nobody. The only people she truly trusted were on the other side of the globe.

'Dulles International,' She said to the driver. If he noticed her disheveled state in his rear-view mirror he was wise enough not to comment.

Half a mile short of the terminal she shocked him again, as he came down the exit ramp, by getting him to pull over to the verge. She paid the fare with cash and sent him on his way. She crossed the road and approached the brightly lit terminal in the dark cover of a row of fall-drab trees. She paused at the edge of the soaring glass wall and surveyed the exterior concourse with great care. Everybody seemed to have a purpose, they moved to and fro. There were no sinister men standing, waiting, watching. She entered the building cautiously and followed the same procedure. Clear. As far as she could tell. She slipped into a restroom, cleaned up as well as possible, then headed for the ticketing desk. The next Athens flight was six hours away.

'Anywhere to the east,' Cherry told the woman behind the counter. 'Anywhere that's not fucking Washington.' A Paris flight was departing in a little under an hour. 'That's just fine,' she told the bemused woman. She paid for her ticket, located the lounge and found the darkest corner she could.

She'd been sitting for half an hour, had polished off two strong bourbons and was considering a third when a uniformed security guard noticed her in her quiet refuge.

He sized her up for a few seconds then walked over slowly. Oh, Christ, Cherry thought. Surely he wouldn't shoot me here. If he tries to arrest me, I'll scream blue murder.

'Are you Cherry Davitt?' he asked, with the polite restraint so typical of modern police procedure. Iron fist, velvet glove; she remembered from her college days.

'Why, what's wrong?' she stalled.

'No, nothing wrong.' He held out his right hand and she flinched.

'I just wanted to shake your hand and say thanks. The Killing Sky thing, your story in the *Dialog*. That's as bad as it gets.' He helped himself to her limp right hand and gave it a friendly squeeze. 'Good to see there's still a little journalistic integrity left.'

Cherry surprised them both by bursting into tears.

In a rush she blurted out the saga of her past few hours, ending it with a plaintive request. 'I don't suppose you could walk me to the gate?' she asked.

'I can do better than that, ma'am.' He dropped a relaxed palm onto the butt of the gun at his waist and looked around casually. 'I'll escort you to the plane.'

What seemed like an eternity later she found herself standing alone in a tiny Greek waiting room, on an island so remote, so rugged, after the bustling slickness of DC, that she was certain she'd died in the Washington encounter and was about to cross the River Styx.

She walked out into the dusty sunshine in a state of near trauma and was instantly assaulted by the wild Meltemi blowing hard from the north. Grit filled her eyes but out here, at least, she had a faint signal. She called Liam's number.

'Where are you?'

'Here at the airstrip, Asty... whatever.'

'You're here, on the island? Christ, why didn't you call, let me know you were coming.'

'I've had other things on my mind,' she said drily.

In truth she'd been too afraid to use her phone in DC, Paris or Athens. Looking around now, she couldn't imagine using it anywhere safer.

'Wait there – I'll come and get you,' he said. 'Half an hour. I'll be coming from the west.'

She looked around. The aircraft she'd arrived on had already departed and the entire place was deserted, save for a solitary elderly man who was locking the terminal's front door with a hefty bunch of brass keys.

She decided to walk.

She'd managed to hobble around two miles along the stony verge, when a small dusty car pulled up alongside. She kept walking without making eye contact.

'Where are you going, Madam? Chora?' She glanced across

quickly. He was large and swarthy and the other bookend sat next to him on the passenger side.

'I can give you lift if you like. Ees a ver big walk.'

She was deciding whether she should decline politely or just panic, when she recognized the large driver in the miniature car coming towards them. She broke into a run.

'They were trying to pick me up,' she spluttered as Liam pulled over and the laughing men accelerated away with a blurt of foul-smelling smoke.

He laughed. 'Probably they were just being courteous, hospitable. It still happens in some places.'

'I don't know how to play this game,' she wailed.

He helped her into the passenger seat and watched in amazement as his editor – forever so cool and on top of things – burst into tears. 'I've ruined my bloody shoes.' She laughed and cried simultaneously. 'And they're Prada!'

Later, after a sleep and a shower, Cherry joined them on the small terrace with a glass of wine. Far below, clinging to the rim of the parched valley, a minute whitewashed chapel glowed in the last rays, as the sun slid into the burnished western Aegean. A small party of placid goats, their bells melodic in the distance, created a tinkling counterpoint to the conversation.

'Oh Liam, I almost forgot. There was a call from a man looking for you, just before I got out of Washington.' She reached into the pocket of her chinos. 'He was calling from Kathmandu, he said.' She handed him a piece of paper with a single word scrawled across it.

'Shishapangma,' Liam read. He looked up. 'Greg Carter. What did he want?'

'He didn't say. Just for you to call him. He was in a hurry, sounded stressed.'

She took a sip from her glass. 'Said you had his number.'

'It'll be the middle of the night there now. I'll call him in the morning.'

28

WALTER DYSON stood at the window and gazed out over the Palace of Westminster, admiring the graceful gothic spires. His nerves were ever so slightly on edge but his resolve was as firm as it had ever been. He wanted something for all those wasted years. He deserved something. This was, for instance, the first opportunity he'd had in his 60 odd summers to visit London.

'He'll see you now.'

He was led into a vast dark-paneled boardroom by a man who, judging by his dress, might have materialized from of one of the 19th-century engravings on the corridor wall.

A tall, slim and aristocratic-looking man sat at the head of the table, his face as much concealed as illuminated by a desk lamp at his side. He didn't bother with a greeting, indicating, instead, that Dyson sit, several seats away.

'How did you find us? Who gave you this address?'

It was a hostile beginning.

'Lionel Rigby shared it with me some time ago.' He paused, trying to moderate his voice. 'As an enthusiastic volunteer, initially, he had privileges I clearly didn't.'

'And why have you come to us at this late stage, Mr Dyson? The damage is done. You've had many weeks to change your mind, choose your sides. You have no idea how much costly trouble you've caused for us.'

'I believe I proved my *bona fides* by contacting the organization and offering to come in,' Dyson said defensively. 'I suspect it was my call that alerted you to our location in Ireland.' He paused and then continued in a petulant voice. 'It wasn't my fault your people weren't up to their appointed task.'

'Why wait until Ireland? Why not contact us while you were still in China, or from Pakistan? You'd have saved us a significant amount of time, trouble and expense. And now look where your irresponsible actions, your loose tongue, have landed us.'

'I had no opportunity in China. I was very ill, frightened, confused. You'd had me locked up for years. I'd simply exchanged one set of jailers for another.'

'Jailers who paid you a small fortune... And always treated you with utmost respect.'

'Not a penny of which I've seen.' Dyson failed to point out that his recent minders had, if anything, shown even greater respect. 'Those aircraft are mine, my sweat and tears, my creation,' he continued angrily. 'Without them... me, you would never have been able to pull any of this off.'

'Be careful, Mr Dyson – you are not in the strongest of positions.' The man moved his head slightly and it was consumed by shadow. 'So what is it that you want?'

Dyson hesitated. He reached for a glass and helped himself to a splash of water from a cut-crystal jug. 'I will, for a price, go public and say my confessions were made under duress; I'll tell the world's media that I was pressured to say those things about Dongfeng. It has a grain of truth to it anyhow.'

The man responded with an amused chuckle. 'Why would we not simply dispose of you? Has it not occurred to you that you have caused us more than enough grief already?'

Dyson, his hands concealed below the polished timber of the table top, clenched his fists. 'I'm working on the carefully considered assumption that you won't do that. I've seen what you are attempting in the international media already, discrediting the whole process, sowing your seeds of doubt. If I go public and claim I know nothing about these imaginary Chinese aircraft, it will add a great deal of credibility to your story; help enormously to fuel the doubt.'

'Perhaps,' the Englishman said, with a degree of skepticism.

Dyson ignored the tone. 'If I don't recant, my confession remains on record, continuing to damn you, to make life difficult.'

'How much?' The man asked coldly.

'An amount that will be very insignificant to people of your means.' Dyson slid a small square of paper toward the center of the table. 'Just so there can be no misunderstandings about the sum.'

He stood and started to move to the door. 'And, of course, as we see so often in movie clichés, if anything were to happen to me in the future, another, even more damning video and witnessed legal document would swiftly find their way to the law, the international news networks etcetera, etcetera, etcetera.'

'I'll consider your proposal and get back to you within 24 hours,' the man said, dismissively. 'Where will I find you?'

'I'll find you,' Dyson said. 'Twenty-four hours.' He left the building, made sure he wasn't being followed, then rode the tube to Knightsbridge and checked into a private clinic.

* * *

'Kathmandu is a small town when it comes to climbing,' Carter said. 'The Sherpa rumor mill has been running hot. Some very ugly people were apparently here some time back asking questions about you. Seems somehow the story of your finding James might have leaked out. Now the same crowd seem to be sniffing around again. But they're staying away from the usual outfits. Trying to freelance a team it seems.'

'For what?' Liam was instantly very alert. He took the phone off speaker and held it close to his ear.

'Word is they're wanting to put together a team of Sherpas to locate a body on K2. No takers to date, I'm told. Wrong season. Besides, it's too dangerous. The whole area is a war zone.'

Liam's heart beat a little faster. 'My dad?'

'I think so, mate. That's what I'm hearing. Makes sense. I'd say they're trying to tie up loose ends given all this shit has hit the fan.'

'You think they want to bring him down?'

'No, I reckon they'd probably just destroy him. Evidence, you know.'

'They've already destroyed him.'

'Yeah, mate. I know.'

'Well damn them all to hell. It's not going to happen. I'll not let them violate him again. I'll bring him down myself.'

'Or die trying,' Carter said softly.

'Or die fucking trying.'

Liam was silent for several seconds and when he spoke again his tone had softened. 'I also made a promise to my mother. I don't know how much longer she can wait.'

'It's a big ask, mate, a big task,' Carter said. 'You'll need help. When do you reckon you'd plan to go?'

'As soon as possible.'

'Winter? Midwinter? Not on. Can't be done. It's never been done.'

'I wouldn't be attempting the summit. Dad's barely on the edge of the death zone. Small team, people all used to high altitude, lightweight folding rescue sled. Lots of line. We'll strap him in and belay him ahead of us as we descend. Up and down, light and fast.'

'But winter?'

'I know, but if these people are going after his body they're possibly even crazy enough to try a chopper retrieval, they'd have the resources. I guess it's not impossible they've found out the co-ordinates.'

'Not from me,' Carter said. 'But people talk.'

'I'll check out the Northeast Route the Americans climbed in '78. A German team has recently summited that way.'

'Yeah, I heard,' Carter muttered. 'And terrorists took out two of them on the return journey.'

'Could just as easily have happened on the mountain,' Liam said, dismissively. 'Given Dad's location, the Northeast Ridge should allow me to avoid that massive ice wall. I'd say we'd also get more of what little sun there is and it's more protected from the prevailing winds.'

'Possibly,' Carter said – but he didn't sound convinced.

'Plus one upside of the drought is that it hasn't just screwed up the monsoon, it seems to have affected the winter storms as well. Last winter on K2 was fairly mild.'

'But still, do you really reckon you'll find a team willing to go with you at this time of year?'

Liam considered the question. 'I'm pretty sure I can get Hassan Baig again, but I'll need a couple of others; perhaps his brothers. Not too many been climbing this year with things the way they are, not since the murders at Nanga Parbat really. The guys will be anxious for the income.'

'Well, you've got one other. I loved your old man. I'll probably regret it but, if you want me, I'm in.'

'Thanks Greg, I appreciate that. I'll be in touch.' Liam disconnected as Jia walked in from the lean-to kitchen.

'So you are going off to find your father, bring him home. In the middle of winter.' They were the first words she'd said to him in a week. 'You are not right in your head.'

'I have to,' he replied in a small voice. 'I don't have a choice.'

'Me neither,' she said and started to weep.

Liam reached out his hand but she brushed it away.

'What have I done?' he asked. 'I don't know what I've done wrong.'

'Nothing,' she said. 'You have done nothing. That's the problem.' Her tears were falling freely now. 'You do nothing. Nothing!'

She clenched her small fists and held them against her chest. 'I have lost my father too. I have a heart too. My heart is hurting, breaking, but you and your friend go on with your stupid boys' adventure like I don't exist. Jia the translator. Jia the messenger. Jia the killer.'

She turned her back on him and stood at the window listening to the bells tinkling in the distance.

'I love you,' she said quietly. 'I worry about you and think of you every hour I am awake and you, you are so preoccupied, so busy with playing soldiers you never give me, my grief, my sadness, my love, a second thought.'

Liam stood silent and wretched, not knowing how to respond, what to say.

'You see,' she cried. 'You say nothing. Nothing. Just more silence. You are locked away, all locked up like a stupid big cupboard and you've lost the key.'

She looked at him and then, unexpectedly, started to chortle at the absurdity of her statement. Tears, mingling with laughter from the beautiful young woman, were more than Liam could bear and he pulled her into his arms and held her hard against his chest.

* * *

'Jia's right, buddy. It's a crazy idea.' Charlie sat against the terrace wall trying to avoid the wind and capture the final weak rays of late-season sunshine. 'Wait until spring. He'll be safe up there until then. Nobody's gonna go after him in winter.'

Liam walked to the edge of the stones and held his phone aloft, checking for signal. 'Sorry, Charlie. I can't rely on that. These people have already started to crucify us; Oskar, Walter. The media is tearing our story to pieces.' He rotated his body, slowly examining the small screen. 'The only solid evidence we have right now is a flight recorder, but apparently that's untraceable. My dad, on the other hand, has a hole in his chest from an aircraft-mounted gun. There will be traces of the shell. So far they haven't covered those tracks. I'll not have them destroy him completely just to protect their own miserable fucking butts.'

Charlie capitulated with raised hands. 'If your mind's made up, I can't stop you but you know where I stand.'

Liam nodded silently. The wind tried to pluck him from his feet as he stood attempting to get three bars by pointing his phone at the telecom tower standing on top of a distant hill.

The signal was poor but after a couple of attempts he managed a connection and conveyed his plans to the distant Mahmood.

'If I try to use a military helicopter on your behalf again I will be in serious trouble,' Mahmood yelled down the dodgy line in response. 'I am already on a warning for our last two escapades. It would be the end of my military career and there's every chance I would end up in a Pakistani prison and that is not something I would want.' He laughed, a deep, rich sound.

'I could get my hands on a commercial chopper for you if you were prepared to pay.'

'How much would it be?'

'I can get a special price. I can check.'

'Don't worry,' Liam laughed. 'I'll sell Polson's chess set.'

'Fine,' Mahmood answered. 'I'll organize it. When will you be here?'

'In around a week or two,' Liam said. 'I'll need to arrange supplies, move my equipment up from Islamabad.'

The signal dropped out for a few seconds, he repositioned the aerial and it crackled back to life.

'I'm willing to fly it for you,' Mahmood was saying. 'But it will only be to bring your father from base camp to Pindi. There is no way they will let me attempt to take one of their machines to 8,000 meters on the face of K2; especially in the middle of winter. The altitude is beyond their capacity. Their insurance wouldn't touch it.'

He paused momentarily.

'If we crashed, of course, neither of us would be around to pay the owner but it is not something I would do to the man. He is an old friend.'

'I understand. I wouldn't do it either. We'll just have to walk up. At least it will be nice and cool at this time of year.'

Mahmood ignored Liam's flippancy. 'Do you have any idea how much of a risk you are taking? Fifty degrees below freezing, terrorists, hurricane winds, winter avalanches: nobody has ever done it before. Your chances of coming back are very poor. Virtually non-existent.'

'Better to die on your feet than live on your knees,' Liam said glibly.

'A young man's statement,' Mahmood replied with quiet frustration.

* * *

By a deserted Aegean beach, on a fine late autumn day, the passion, inflamed in front of an Irish fireplace all those weeks before and so rudely interrupted by Cassidy Millston's nocturnal visit, had finally been assuaged.

Liam lay gazing up at the cirrus scudding across an eggshell sky, Jia's head rested on his naked chest. How strange, he thought, that this beautiful, clear and innocent void above them could be the source of so much conflict and despair.

Jia sat up suddenly and wrapped her arms around her bent knees. She stared silently out to a hazy island on the dust-colored horizon.

Liam was spent but not beyond coveting, still, the soft, curving gold of her naked back.

'You are leaving again,' she said, without turning her head. 'You go off to find your father and bring him home, bring his spirit some peace. I sit here doing nothing.'

She indicated her nakedness with an open palm held against her breasts. 'Doing this.' She pointed into the haze. 'I should be out there trying to find my father too.'

Liam sat up and wrapped the picnic blanket round her shoulders.

'The difference is we don't know where your father is. If we did, we would move heaven and earth to bring him home to you.'

She pulled away and shook the sand from her clothes.

'You are choosing to go to one of the most dangerous places on earth, to do something no one has ever done, I will probably never see you again.' She dragged a sweater over her head. 'I think we are both being eaten up by our obsessions. Those two old men are becoming more important to us than our own lives. Than us.' She indicated him with a graceful arc of her hand and then swept it back toward herself. 'You and me.'

She sat back next to him and laced up her shoes. 'Maybe it's time for us both to accept our fathers are gone, say our goodbyes and start living like normal people.'

She turned and took his hand, holding it to her breast. 'Please don't go. Please. You won't come back, I know.'

'I have to go, my… I've come too far. My starting this has created such a massive problem for everyone, for all the people I care about.' He kept hold of her hand, pulled it across and clasped it against his chest. 'If I'd known all this was going to be the result, I'd never have climbed the blessed mountain, never have gone looking for my dad in the first place. But I did and I can't leave it unfinished now.'

'Well, at least take Charlie with you then,' she said, tears filling her eyes. 'Perhaps he'll keep you safe.'

'But I couldn't keep *him* safe. Charlie's not a climber and his wound hasn't fully healed yet. He would be in far more danger than me. This is one thing I must do without him.'

'I know,' she said leaning in and hiding her face in the nape of his neck. 'I know.'

'I'll come back in one piece, I promise.'

29

ACCORDING TO Amin Baig, the weather gods of the high Karakoram were smiling on them. Amin was Hassan Baig's younger brother by a year and, according to Hassan, an even better climber than himself. An older brother, Gohar – just as skilled, he claimed – would climb with them too.

To save time and distance, Liam had opted to move the base up to Camp One at the head of the Godwin Austen Glacier. One of the porters knew of the site from a previous expedition. Near the foot of the Northeast Ridge, it was a location free from the risk of avalanche or rockfall from the ragged pinnacles high above.

The first week had seen merciless weather envelop them and the fragile group of brightly colored tents had struggled for days on end, cracking and whipping in a violent southerly wind.

The decision to take the Northeastern Route had required many hours of intense analysis. At 23,000 feet they'd face a knife-edge ridge with a vast drop on each side. A wind of any intensity up there, depending on its direction, would see their lives ending in either China or Pakistan. The narrow ridges were also crowned with dangerous snow cornices; overhangs that could fail and take a string of climbers with them at any second.

Initially Greg Carter had argued in favor of taking the Abruzzi route again.

'It's a far more direct line to the site and there are none of those endless traverses.'

His argument was punctuated by yet another avalanche calving off an ice cliff just beneath the summit. It thundered down through the upper levels of his preferred route, obliterating it in a chaos of boiling white powder.

'Then again, perhaps not,' he said with a grim smile.

'Apart from the unstable slopes, there's that massive ice

wall, with all those unstable seracs above it, separating the site of Dad's body from the Abruzzi,' Liam said. 'Getting a loaded rescue sled across that would be nigh-on impossible. And even if we somehow managed that we'd still need to maneuver it down the Black Pyramid and then House's Chimney. An impossibility in winter, I'd say.'

'Yeah, you're probably right,' Carter said. 'But at this time of year every approach will have its own set of problems and the Northeast is much longer.'

Hassan, who'd been listening silently, nodded in agreement.

'I still think the Northeast is our best shot, in spite of the traverses.' Liam shifted his gaze to the right again. He pointed to the looping ridges just visible through swirling clouds. 'The German team left fixed ropes all the way along those traverses between three and four, no more than a couple of months back. If we can drag them out of the fresh powder I'd say we could use them pretty much as they are. That's a big time and effort saver.'

He looked from Carter to Hassan and his brothers and then back to the now-shrouded route. 'In spite of all its difficulties, it seems to make the most sense.'

Carter nodded. 'It's arguably the least suicidal, I guess.'

Amin stepped from the tent early on the morning of the eighth day, tugged his Gilgit cap a little closer to his ears, looked up at the cold, still, blue sky and made his pronouncement. It was time to go. The plan was to limit the number of further camps to four, travel light and fast, get the sites in place and lightly stocked as fast as possible, use fixed ropes left by previous teams wherever feasible and climb Alpine-style wherever and whenever the weather and conditions allowed.

The ascent as far as Camp Three was uneventful. The slopes, although long and steep in places, were climbed without fixed ropes. They worked as two teams. Carter roped up with Amin, Liam with Hassan and Gohar. Less snow had fallen on the lower part of the ridge than they'd predicted and the extreme cold had converted it from powder to a compacted base fairly swiftly.

As they gained altitude, they tried, wherever possible, to avoid planting heavy boots on dark rock, preferring to struggle, at times knee deep, through the crackling whiteness. The bands of granite gneiss were loose and frost shattered in places. The ever-present danger was that the lead climber could inadvertently dislodge a wayward boulder and send it hurling down to brain the person below.

Within a few days they were pitching their tents on a sloping, pocket-handkerchief, platform at the start of the razor-sharp traverse. Immediately above and a little to the left, a round-topped mass of packed snow and ice reared above them like a giant albino whale, forever frozen.

The Germans, efficient as always, Liam and Hassan discovered the following morning, had left expertly fixed eight-millimeter ropes in place all the way across the traverse. The breathtaking steepness of the slope they crossed meant that much of the snow, fallen since their visit, had cascaded on down the mountain and shaking out the lines from beneath the snow was necessary in only a few places. By day's end they were clear and ready to use.

Night-time temperatures stopped falling at around 30 below and the sky remained bright-star clear but the benign weather held for just two more days. Their luck ran out just shy of the 26,000 mark, as they completed the setting up of Camp Four. Liam looked back, shaking his head in wonder as they retreated quickly down the mountain. Two tiny tents were perched precariously atop a minute platform hewn from snow and ice at the end of the serrated ridge. A single careless step from either entrance, in either direction, would send the climber tumbling, unstoppable for thousands of feet, to be shattered on the rocks and ice way below.

Snow was falling heavily as they struggled back, tired and wet, into Camp One; feet and hands frozen and icicles hanging from beard and brow. There, once again, to wait out the capricious weather.

A week later, having had another period of respite from the storms, they'd reached Camp Five and were huddled in their tents high on the eastern edge of the shoulder, surrounded by the gear needed for the final push. James, by Liam's reckoning, was less than a thousand feet above them. The plan was an early-morning start, in the bone-numbing cold, a fast retrieval and then the beginning of the long struggle down the mountain with their unwieldy human cargo.

Amin's weather gods called a halt to their well-laid plans some time around midnight and for three days the relentless snow-starved wind howled and mocked at their hubris.

The three Baltistani men were little troubled by the extended time at high altitude and Liam seemed to cope reasonably well but Greg Carter, it appeared, was starting to suffer. He said nothing, but as the days wore on Liam watched him with increasing concern as he supported his head with his hands.

On the fourth night, an hour after midnight, Hassan peered from his tent at a calm, star-filled sky. 'We go today,' he called to the tent nestled against his own. 'One hour.'

'Okay,' Liam's sleepy voice filtered through the cold fabric. He reached for his insulated but still frozen boots and started to drag them on. 'We're on our way.' Within seconds his fingers and toes were numb.

For long hours they trudged heavenwards, towards their appointed rendezvous; a meeting between the living and the dead. Five tiny snails, seen from an eagle's eye view, leaving a silver trail across the newly whitewashed walls of a Balti giant.

A few feet higher, a stop to catch breath and then a few agonizing feet more. On a summer climb they would be wading waist deep in this snow but the winter freeze was so intense they sank just a few inches before the compacted ice took their weight.

An outcrop of rock loomed up above and the vast wall of vertical ice beckoned, contemptuous and taunting, close by on their left. 'Cross me if you dare,' it seemed to be saying to Greg Carter. He thanked the mountain gods that it wasn't something required of him.

James was precisely where Liam had left him all those months before.

A bank of snow blown hard against his windward side had half-buried him, while the rest of his body, still exposed, was covered in a rime of blue-white ice. Hassan knelt on the impervious crust and began to chant an ancient ritual prayer for the dead.

Liam's plan was to strap the body to the folding carbon-fiber sled and then belay as the weighty burden was lowered, fastened to a series of ropes. Two climbers would go ahead, to anchor the sled at the end of each pitch, while the three above secured themselves to whatever was available and guided the load down. A series of small pulleys were rigged between the sled and the belaying point to help with the weight.

For the first few hours all went well – the system, although slow, difficult and exhausting, seemed to be working.

And then Greg Carter sat down.

'I'm feeling pretty weird, mate,' he said to Liam, cradling his head in his hands. 'I'd put money on a bout of AMS coming on. I've been fighting it for a few days. I had it once long ago on Kanchenjunga.'

'Oh shit,' Liam panted. 'We'll need to get you down as soon as possible.' He beckoned to the three Balti men. They unslung their packs, used their picks to anchor them alongside the sled and plodded across. 'Altitude sickness,' he said, indicating the sitting Carter. 'We'll need to leave my dad here and get Greg down pronto.'

'No way,' Carter said. 'We came to get James, we're not going without him.'

'Listen, Greg, if you stay here you die. A day from now it could be full-on cerebral edema. I don't want that on my conscience. The living are more important than the dead.' He pointed at the lonely sled. 'Even him. He's been up here alone for years, a little longer won't make any difference.'

'I'll take him down,' Amin said quietly, nodding toward Carter. 'You, Hassan… Gohar, you can bring the…' He wasn't quite sure how to say it.

'No, not alone. Gohar must go with you. Getting Greg down safely is number-one priority now.'

He patted Amin on his padded shoulder.

'Maybe we can try to bring the sled down. See how we go.' He turned to Hassan. 'I don't know if we can manage that, just the two of us, Hassan?' He looked dubious. 'I don't want to kill *anybody.*'

Hassan shrugged his strong shoulders and spat on the snow. 'We can.' He gave a tiny nod. 'We can.'

Amin helped Carter to his feet, splitting most of the contents of his pack between Gohar's and his own. They roped up together and, with Amin taking the lead, started trudging slowly down the steep slope.

Lowering the sled had been difficult with five people working; with just two, it was almost impossible and their progress was excruciatingly slow. It was well after dark by the time they reached Camp Five and the other three had already been and gone.

The next day and half the night passed in a blur of mind-blunting pain and repetition. Belay, secure, lower slowly, secure, descend, belay... and then the whole process would begin again.

As the weak sun, far off to the south, created anemic shadows on the peaks below, they reached the beginning of the insanely steep traverse that would take them to Camp Four. Liam was sure he could see a single bright tent still clinging to the postage-stamp space at the other end of the blade-like saddle and glowing faintly in the fading light.

They used the fixed ropes left by the earlier climbers and, with infinite care, with one gathering in and one paying out, guided the dead weight across the hazardous space. Liam imagined that at any moment the sled would sever the line and go plunging into the void, already deep in afternoon shade.

A lacerating winter nightfall closed in around them early and they struggled on into darkness, their frail, lonely pinpoints of light, lurching convulsively with every involuntary movement of a head, briefly illuminating a pitifully inadequate swathe of surface snow and achieving almost nothing against the dark enormity of the homicidal mountain.

At Camp Four they were overtaken by the weather again and Liam spent two frozen and sleepless days and nights listening to the screaming rage of the wind and lying just inches from the body of his much-loved father, lashed to the ice outside the tent.

On the second morning, in spite of the still-howling gale Liam was finally able to raise someone on the radio.

'Is that you, Amin?'

'Yes… Amin…' The voice was faint and intermittent.

'Where are you?'

'Base camp… we are… base camp.'

'Thank Christ,' Liam said, trying to refrain from shedding tears. 'How's Greg, is he okay?'

'Okay… sleeping… he… okay, I think…'

'That's fantastic, Amin. Thank you so much and thank Gohar too.'

Liam looked across to Hassan. The Balti man had been unable to suppress his emotion as effectively as Liam had and he wiped away two big tears as they rolled down each cheek.

'Amin,' Liam shouted into the mouthpiece. 'Can you ask Tahir to see if he can raise Mahmood on the radio down there and get him to fly up and take Greg Carter down.'

'Amin? Amin?'

The signal was gone.

30

LIKE ALL headline stories, even stories as potentially earth shattering as this had been, the media soon tired of it. The audience followed and within a few weeks it was on page three. A week later it had been relegated to just two columns on page seven.

And then Walter Dyson went public for a second time.

He stood, gripping a lectern for support, in front of a sea of news cameras and bright lights filling a vast Washington auditorium. His hands trembled slightly as he held up the prepared statement and started to read.

'Many of you would be aware that I was recorded recently making a number of controversial allegations. These claims included statements regarding an illegal attempt to geo-engineer the climate using aircraft, the construction of which I had allegedly supervised.

'At the time I made those statements I was being held captive by what I now know to be a radical environmental group.' He looked up over the top of his glasses. 'You now know their names... and the statements were made under duress. They were and *are* not true.'

The previously well-behaved crowd was transformed instantly into a noisy, unruly mob, filling the air with shocked and outraged exclamations. Walter looked up, blinked at the bright lights and then continued reading.

'Since that time I have managed to remove myself from their custody and I am now under the protection of the Washington Police Department. I am here today to put my rejection of all previous statements relating to this event on the record. Nothing I said in those statements was true. They were words put into my mouth. I have not, at any time, been involved in this so-called operation your associates have chosen to call "Killing Sky".'

Walter let the paper in his hands drop to the lectern and looked up.

'Are you, in fact, Mr Dyson, now retracting *those* statements under duress?' a reporter called from the rear of the room. 'Are you doing this under pressure?'

'No, I am doing this of my own volition; there has been no pressure.'

'You would understand, Mr Dyson, why the public might be a little skeptical about your sudden about-face?'

'Perhaps. As I said, my original comments were made under duress. They are, I repeat, untrue. You would need to talk to Doyle and Casement to find out why I was pressured into making them.'

'If the original claims weren't true,' another reporter asked, 'how do you explain your sudden disappearance nearly ten years ago?'

'There's nothing remarkable or sinister about that.' He ran a hand across his eyes. 'I was going through deeply troubled emotional times. Personal things I don't intend to discuss. I left the country by choice. I lived alone, in fact I had always been a loner and simply didn't bother to tell anyone I was going. The media, as it does, came to its own conclusions and it was assumed I had met with foul play...'

A third questioner broke in. 'Or perhaps they had already started to lay the groundwork for their later implausible scheme, Mr Dyson? The *Dialog*'s Cherry Davitt has been embroiled on both occasions.'

'Perhaps. I don't know anything about that.'

'What were you doing in China for all those years, sir?' asked a grey-haired journalist squeezed into a space below the lectern.

'It was no secret. I worked developing satellite technology for a private corporation based in Dongfeng. My employment record is available for anyone who is interested.'

A young woman standing to Dyson's right stepped forward and presented the gathering with a mouthful of expensive, gleaming teeth. 'Mr Dyson is not a well man, he is in need of dialysis fairly shortly so I think we will end this there. If you have any further questions for Walter, please submit them via his agent and they will be addressed promptly. Thank you.'

She turned and, with a gracious professional smile, took Walter's elbow and ushered him from the room.

'Unbefuckinglievable,' Charlie roared in a room 5,000 miles away, thumping a big fist onto the coffee table.

'Shit,' Cherry said. 'Well, that's not going to help things one little bit. I wonder what it's going to do to Donna Stone's chances.'

✳ ✳ ✳

The last time Dashka had placed any trust in the state-run Russian media, she'd been seven years old. Since then, with the benefit of an online world, she'd been able to stay in intermittent touch with the news from the rest of the planet without needing to rely on the officially sanctioned version. Her favorite sources of trustworthy information and a good way to practice her English were London's *Guardian* newspaper, the *Sydney Morning Herald* and the *Washington Dialog*.

She had been dimly aware of a recent commotion over some affair the *Dialog* was calling the Killing Sky but hadn't really taken much notice. The crazy Americans always seemed to be going on about the Russians and the Chinese and their endless conspiracies and she tended, generally, to ignore them. It was only a more comprehensive examination of Ivor's small external drive that persuaded her to look at the stories again.

A failed primary generator had kept her working round the clock for the best part of a week and, despite her anxiety, it was several days before she found a second opportunity to safely attach the device to her computer.

Her introduction, by Dmitri, to the Periodic Tables, so long ago now, had piqued her interest in elements and chemicals and their derivatives, and the presence of large amounts of sulfur dioxide in one set of readings bothered her. Her sleepless nights had not been without justification.

As little as she understood these things, she knew from being shown Dmitri's readings in the past that this much sulfur in the heavens directly overhead seemed very wrong.

Shreds of the Killing Sky story started to filter back to her and she recalled with a rush that they had been accusing somebody in Moscow of dumping sulfur into the stratosphere.

The work on the generator was still incomplete and she had no choice but to leave things as they were for a couple of days. As soon as she was able to get a little private time without arousing suspicion she was online, clicking furiously from one media source to the next. It didn't take long to discover that the Killing Sky, although it had originated with the *Washington Dialog*, had been on almost every front page. In many of the publications it was being ridiculed as a leftwing hoax. No mysterious sites had been located, no aircraft had been found. Dashka knew nothing of sites or aircraft, but proof of excessive aerosol sulfates in the atmosphere she was now convinced she had seen with her own eyes. Alexei had, she concluded, been feeding the world misleading data. Suddenly all the secrecy, the paranoia, made sense.

She had the evidence. It was essential that she get it out to them. But any attempt to make online contact from the base could, quite possibly, trigger a reaction and set all sorts of alarm bells ringing.

Her thoughts were interrupted by a loud knocking. She hid the laptop under her mattress and opened the door a crack. A grave-faced Alexei stood inches from the jamb.

'What is it, Alexei Denisovitch?' she queried, trying to sound indifferent.

'Have you been into the lab recently, alone?'

'No, as you know better than anyone, I'm not allowed in there these days.'

He nodded.

'We have a security camera in there, these days,' he said, then paused. 'But the disk drive was damaged.'

Too bad,' Dashka said, trying to sound sincere. 'Still, I haven't been in there.'

Alexei shook his head. 'Sergei sent it off to Arkhangelsk. The data has been retrieved.'

'Well then, you know I haven't been there,' she said, her

heart pounding. She knew for certain it had been Ivor. They apparently didn't. Perhaps in the darkness it wasn't clear who he was. Perhaps that meant they weren't aware of the download. Perhaps...

Alexei looked directly into her eyes. Her gaze didn't waver. He shook his head. 'Well then, if it wasn't you, it must have been Ivor. But then, if it was him, why? Who might have put him up to it, do you think?'

Dashka remained silent but shrugged and shook her head.

He turned, took a few steps along the corridor then swung back to her. 'Be careful, Dashka Anasovna, Sergei is a dangerous man. You don't know what you're dealing with here.'

She was more convinced now than ever that she did not have the luxury of remaining at the base until the ship arrived.

* * *

Waiting for something completely beyond their control to happen thousands of miles away was playing on everyone's nerves. Liam had left for K2 some time before and for days Jia had been miserable.

Oskar had finally persuaded her to drive him into the Chora to pick up supplies from the tiny hillside shop, while Cherry and Charlie killed time playing endless games of chess, using Lionel Rigby's expensive set.

'And that, my friend, is checkmate.' He picked up his king and tossed it into the air. 'Goddam, at last, someone I can beat at this crazy game,' he yelled. 'Where have you been all my life, you gorgeous woman?'

'I've been in Washington nearly 40 years, in the directory for most of that time; easily found. You're the itinerant.'

She set up the pieces again.

'How long since you've had sex with a woman?' she said, shifting a pawn.

If Charlie was surprised at the sudden question, he didn't show it. 'Sex with a woman as opposed to sex with what?' he asked, hand poised above his bishop.

'C'mon,' she laughed. 'Quit stalling.'

'Much, much, longer than is good for me,' he said, moving the bishop.

'Yeah, me too,' she said. She shifted another piece with a painted fingernail.

'So what are you saying?' Charlie looked down at the board, contemplating his next move.

'What do you think I'm saying?'

'Nope, you started. You tell me.' He shook his head.

Cherry looked at her watch. 'Well, they don't start counting votes for a couple of hours yet, you probably wouldn't need that long.'

'Don't count on it,' he said, standing and reaching for her hand.

'I'm talking casual sex here, you understand,' she said as they headed for Charlie's bedroom. 'I'm not interested in a long-term relationship.'

'No, no, me neither. Casual sex only, very definitely.'

Muffled and intermittent laughter was still filtering through the heavy wooden door when Jia and Oskar returned, carrying their shopping into the kitchen.

* * *

Late at night, on their far-flung Greek island, the news eventually filtered through. The United States had a new leader.

Donna Stone's ticket had won the popular vote in a landslide. Endorsement from the Electoral College in a few weeks' time would be a mere formality.

One of the reasons for the decisive vote, according to the always-wise-after-the-event analysts, had been her uncompromising response to the Killing Sky issue. The now departing 'Lame Duck' President, they argued, had shown himself to be surprisingly ambivalent on this. The general conclusion was that this had created widespread anger on both sides of the political spectrum and had cost him dearly.

It seemed that either the bulk of voters had not been inclined to believe Walter Dyson's recanting or it had simply arrived too late to gain any traction.

Within hours of the result, Donna Stone had gone public, once again, with her promise to get to the roots of the illegal and treaty-breaking geo-engineering activities.

Cherry sat close to the small screen and watched the nation's next President speak.

'Your Vice President Elect will, as promised, conduct the most rigorous investigation it is within our capacity to conduct. Meanwhile, good people of the United States of America, I will say once again that I will not let this investigation get in the way of a most pressing commitment. As you all know, the foremost global powers have had what they hope to be a binding agreement on the table now for four years, the FFPO. And that agreement is to phase out the use of all coal within the next decade. The UN agrees, the World Bank agrees, the IMF agrees, the G20, the OECD and ASEAN agree. All the planet's major polluting nations agree.

'The only stumbling block to sealing this landmark global agreement has been *our* recalcitrant President and his deeply dysfunctional colleagues. Driven by greed and fear, they still cling desperately... frantically, to their tired old ways.

'Recent questionable events in the Arctic have not swayed us from our course and I will today, once again, confirm that, having been given the great privilege of becoming your new President, I will sign off on this internationally binding document in Lyon early next year and within ten years this small, vulnerable blue sphere in space, on which we all depend for our existence, will be on its way, finally, to a renewable future.

'This will not be an easy time. It will be a time of adjustment, a time of sacrifice, but the sacrifices we make today will be celebrated, honored for a thousand years to come by our children, our grandchildren and countless generations that follow.'

Cherry tapped at the screen searching for early media reaction.

'STONE UNTURNED.' Was one tabloid's take on the speech.

'I think we should head back to Washington,' Cherry said an hour later. 'Even though it didn't seem to affect the results

343

you can bet they'll continue to milk Dyson's reinvention for all they're worth. He's done a major hatchet job on our integrity and our credibility. I think we need to go public and confront him. The character assassinations are already coming out of the woodwork. Listen to this.'

She tapped on her tablet. '"Oskar Frederik a Soviet communist",' she read from her screen. 'And this. "Why are these people hiding?" Here's another one. "Hit and run".'

She put the tablet to one side. 'I think we need to respond to this shit in person.'

'I still say it would be very dangerous for us over there,' Charlie said. 'With Liam away, I have far more chance of keeping you guys safe out here than I would in the middle of DC or Manhattan.'

'With Stone as President Elect now, I think she would have the resources to keep us safe.'

Charlie's answer was a skeptical look. 'She also has the resources to arrest us.'

Cherry shook her head. 'No, I trust her. She wouldn't do that. She'll wait for the results of Arnott's inquiry now. I can contact her directly and ask her for a personal guarantee if that would make you feel any better,' Cherry said.

'Not much better, but if you're determined to go, it might help a little.'

'Lend me your phone,' she said. 'I ditched my last one a week ago.'

31

LIAM HAD LOST count of the days. All he knew was that their nightmare journey through a frozen white hell was still far from over. The weather had eventually cleared but before they could attempt to move James along the ridge from Four, it was essential to travel the route first, to drag the fixed lines from beneath the new snow and, wherever possible, to kick down the fresh accumulation in the hope of preventing the sled starting an avalanche as it was maneuvered across the void next day.

Toward the far end, the traverse from Camp Four to Camp Three involved an uphill section across another near-vertical wall. Ahead of them they could now see the fixed lines of the German team looping into the distance like fine, pale hairs on a freshly laundered bedsheet. Liam surveyed the suicidal slope and wondered, not for the first time, whether he'd selected the wisest route down.

The Germans had placed the ropes close to the ridge line, hoping to minimize the risk of breakaway snow and ice from above, but the sharp edges, always overhead, held accumulated cornices that could come crashing down at any time.

They inched the heavy sled diagonally upward across the unforgiving face, taking it in turns to lead or follow. The weather remained calm but even so, from time to time the weight of gravity would cause a snow boulder to dislodge itself from above to go careering past, annihilating itself eventually and producing the sound of rolling thunder from somewhere far below.

The lead climber steadied himself at the forward anchors and then, hand over hand, slowly coaxed the sled along the fixed line. The following climber stayed with the sled and, with the added clumsiness of mittens essential because of the intolerable cold, was forced again and again to clip and unclip, detach and secure the sled's harness each time they reached another protection point holding to the wall. At each belay point, the already exhausted man would be forced, for a second or two, to take some of the weight of the sled until the carabiner was once again clicked into place. The short transit completed, they would head off again on the seemingly endless journey.

As the day wore on, a windless snow started to drift down steadily. Their goggles froze over constantly and they were forced to lift them onto their foreheads again and again, in order to assess the best way to travel the sled across the ropes. Within minutes the glare became unbearable and the icy air filled their eyes with stinging tears.

While the climber's weight was distributed between ice ax, harness and crampons, the entire weight of the sled was being taken by the fixed line. With no more than a hundred feet to go to safer ground, Liam looked ahead, through ice-slicked goggles, toward Hassan and spied the beginnings of what he had hoped and prayed would never happen. As the weight of the sled shifted gradually from the previous to the next fixing, the leading edge of an anchor appeared from beneath the snow. It shifted slightly and then tilted. As Liam watched helplessly, the still-gleaming steel pulled away from its ice housing and he and the sled began to slide. The radio transceiver at his hip was torn away and went tumbling towards the glacier, disintegrating against unyielding granite a hundred feet below.

Instinctively, he plunged his ax deep into the frozen snow. It slowed his fall but he was still descending, cutting a deep groove as he went. The weight of the sled was pulling them both down.

The fixed points behind and ahead took up the strain with a sudden jerk and managed somehow to take the weight of both man and sled without failing, saving Liam the horror of yet another zipper, this one almost certainly fatal.

The elasticized rope, held at both ends like a bow string, vibrated to a stop, leaving them bobbing up and down gently, some 20 feet below. Hassan, up ahead, had been jolted by the fall and had lost his footing, slipping a body length before bringing himself to a halt with a plunge of his ice ax.

Liam checked the fastenings on the sled, made sure his father's body was still tightly held and then, with ax and crampons, climbed painfully back up again, fixing the line a little along from where it had come adrift. Within the half hour, and with a greater sense of relief than he'd ever thought possible, they completed the final few yards of the uphill traverse. Hassan had already collapsed, breathing heavily, onto a small patch of near horizontal snow and Liam dropped down almost on top of him as his legs all but gave way. The sanctuary of Camp Three was now just a hundred diagonal yards below.

A day later they had clawed their way below the 23,000-foot mark, with Camp Two still an hour's slog away, when the weather gods finally tired of the human folly unfolding at their feet and sent a blasting gale of icy blizzard at the puny humans attempting to defy the mountain's might.

They huddled, frozen through, against the sled and clung to a narrow snow ledge, ice axes deeply imbedded, as the near hurricane-force winds funneling down on them tried to pluck them from their precarious perch and send them spiraling through the driving snow to their deaths.

High above their heads, unheard, unseen, the sound and fury of the tempest drowning out all with its own unrelenting roar, a serac the size of a small cathedral fractured, cracked and then broke from its mooring and started to plummet toward them, gaining momentum with every passing second.

* * *

The *Washington Dialog* was first with the news yet again.

The front page featured a photograph of the reclusive foursome, recently arrived from Astypalaia, under the banner headline: 'OUT OF HIDING.'

The story, written by Cherry, was a first-person account. It described where they had been and why, explained their reasons for returning and the risks they believed they were taking. Their integrity was being questioned, Walter Dyson was fabricating a story and making accusations about them that were manifestly untrue and the media seemed to be falling for it.

Two days later, Saxon Melville finally succumbed to the reality that he could own the story no longer and allowed an afternoon media conference in the newspaper's compact auditorium.

The crowd of competing media, as was expected, overflowed out onto the street. The aggressive questioning had been under way for some time when Melville managed to extricate himself from a meeting and slip into the rear of the space to watch and listen.

'Walter Dyson has gone public and said on the record that none of this is true,' a grizzled old tabloid scribe was saying loudly to Oskar. 'He claims he was coerced by your small group of radicals to fabricate the story in order to create confusion, to pressure the President into signing the international treaty on fossil-fuel phase-out against his will.'

'Mr Dyson is lying.'

'Why would he lie?'

'You would have to ask him that.'

'You say you were held captive in Moscow. Is that any more plausible than Mr Dyson's retraction?'

'Read the report,' Oskar said. 'It goes into great detail, provides a comprehensive analysis of all that has happened, where and why. You can decide for yourself whether it's plausible or not.'

Another man attracted Oskar's attention. 'What is your problem with geo-engineering? The science community is well and truly divided on this issue, there is no certainty regarding what the long-term effects might be. It may, ultimately, be our saving grace.'

'I have many problems with geo-engineering generally,' Oskar said in carefully measured tones. 'But my current issue is with this specific instance.'

The questioner persisted. 'So, let me get this straight, Mr Frederik. Are you saying any climate engineering, all climate engineering is out of the question? No matter what the consequences? You're willing to let the planet fry?'

'What I'm saying is that attempting to engineer, to interfere with the climate with the level of knowledge we currently have, that these people currently have, should be out of the question. This planet is an infinitely complex organism. It seems they have enough intelligence to be dangerous, but not enough to be wise.

'Any attempt to engineer the climate without knowing the full spectrum of unintended consequences is nothing short of criminally irresponsible. And for these global agglomerations to use climate engineering as an excuse to avoid the costs of mitigation, and as a potential commercial enterprise, is the height of human arrogance, human folly.'

It was becoming clear to the gathered journalists that they weren't going to get a headline-generating gaffe from Oskar, so they switched their attention to Charlie.

'Where is Liam Doyle, Mr Casement?'

'He had family business to attend to.'

'Why is he not here?'

'Because I'm big and ugly enough to answer for both of us.'

'Does he not think that this is more important than his family?'

'No.'

A woman at the back broke through the scrum of men. 'Ms Zhang, er, Jia?' She wasn't sure.

'Jia is fine.'

The woman smiled, relieved. 'Can you give us the female, the woman's perspective? What is your role in all of this?'

'I am looking for my father, Zhang Liu. He was taken by these people many months ago and I don't know where he is or even if he's still alive.'

The sensitive young questioner left it at that, which didn't stop a male colleague closer to the front pursuing the angle. 'How can you be sure it was "these people"? Do you even know who "these people" are?'

Jia considered him with her large brown eyes for a moment and then looked down at her clasped hands. 'No, I don't know who is behind my father's disappearance.'

Oskar's voice cut angrily through the resultant clamor.

'You.' He pointed an accusatory finger into the auditorium. 'The world's media, have vilified and demonized our small group on every day that has passed since we had the temerity to expose a great wrong. We have been sent to Coventry, abused and threatened with our lives. You have pursued us without reason, like a baying pack of semi-human hounds.'

He thumped the lectern with a closed fist.

'It's way past time you people turned your lenses on yourselves. Time to examine what you have allowed yourselves to become with your incessant search for sensationalism, your cheap provocative headlines and your deliberately misleading narratives. How many of you have taken this easy option, this cowardly road? How many of you have crossed over; crossed that fine line between ethical analysis and agenda-based propaganda? What have you allowed yourselves to become? Servants of what master?' He shook his head sadly. 'I think we all know the answer.'

Oskar touched his chest with an open palm.

'What is our great sin? We are trying, simply, to save lives… lives of millions of men, women, children, of *your* children and grandchildren. We have risked *our* lives to bring you the truth and for this we are crucified… and you, the world's media, are driving in the nails.'

Oskar's final few ringing syllables echoed off the rafters and splintered into microscopic fragments of sound before dissolving into a profound silence.

Saxon Melville pushed through to the front of the room and raised a hand. 'That'll do, ladies and gentlemen. These folk have not long flown in from Europe, they have had a series of interviews with government and security committees all morning, and I think it's time you gave them a break. We'll be distributing a full report shortly.'

* * *

Dashka had been on Severny Island longer than anyone else at the base. She believed she knew it as well as she knew the motors of the snowmobiles or the particular whims of the various generators.

Around two in the morning, she bundled herself up in her

warmest clothes, packed extra layers, some food, a flashlight, cellphone and her computer, and stole silently from her room.

'Where are you going?' The voice seemed to come from nowhere. She spun round. Alexei's door was open a crack and he stood in the darkness watching her. She paused and looked at him but said nothing. He opened the door and stepped out into the corridor.

'I said: where are you going?'

Without thinking, Dashka curled her hand into a tight ball and drove it into his face at short range. Ten years of manhandling heavy motors had given her muscles she didn't know she had and he went down like a stunned heifer.

She hammered a big solid boot into the side of his head below his ear and then, for good measure, stomped on his already-bloodied nose. She ran to the end of the corridor and lumbered, panting and weeping, through thick snow, toward the vehicle shed.

The door creaked loudly as she forced it open. She checked the extra fuel already strapped to the fastest of the three snowmobiles and congratulated herself for having had the foresight to disable the other machines earlier in the day. She had covered just 50 meters, headlights blazing a trail into the darkness, when a group of fast-moving flashlights arrived at the shed.

Dashka was relying on her belief that there was nobody at the base who would have the will or the ability to follow her on foot into what most people perceived as a frozen hell. What she failed to realize, in her haste, was that one of the other vehicles was not as disabled as she'd hoped.

Severny was the northernmost of the two islands that made up the archipelago of Novaya Zemlya –'New Earth', to its discoverers. Yuzhny Island was to the south. From the 1950s the Soviet Union had used both islands to test atmospheric and underground nuclear weapons. The Tsar Bomba, the most powerful nuclear device ever detonated on earth, was exploded in 1961 near Severny's southern end.

She knew she was taking a risk. Rumors about the level of radiation deep in the interior of the islands had been circulating for years. But she was certain that she had no option: this was her only chance. The irony was that the radiation might ultimately be her salvation. Some 200 kilometers to the south, she knew, Talia and her group of scientists were at work taking readings, attempting to assess just how bad things might be. Although Dashka had met her just once, and briefly, she felt like the woman was a kindred spirit and was certain that if she could reach their group she'd be safe. The past few years had seen the island's west-coast waters ice-free in places, even throughout winter, and so the scientists had stayed, battened down and enduring the long darkness.

She ploughed on cautiously through the Arctic night, knowing that even at midday the light in the sky would be no more than a faint reflection. Glacial chasms and insomniac polar bears were just two of the possible obstacles ahead. If all went well she could be at the small settlement on the barren shores of Russkaya Gavan within six or seven hours.

The first inkling that she was not alone in this vast wilderness was a flash of light reflected from a nearby snow embankment. It was off to the right and clearly not from her headlights. She stole a quick look over her shoulder. A few hundred meters back and closing fast, another snowmobile bounced across the uneven ground, throwing great billows of powder into the dark sky. A few seconds later the thud of gunfire was close enough to hear over the roar of the engine.

Dashka opened the throttle and increased her speed way past what was safe for the terrain. Ignorance of the treacherous landscape had the pilot of the other vehicle throwing caution to the wind and he was traveling much too fast.

Dashka, on the other hand, knew the landscape intimately. She knew that no more than 500 meters ahead a deep ravine crossed their path and just one narrow snow bridge gave access to the far side. She pushed the snowmobile forward at full throttle. Her pursuer was still gaining. She steered well to the right of the access point and at the last moment veered left and, on one skid, bounced across the straddling finger of packed snow. The following rider had no time to react and was airborne before he knew the ravine existed. His bright headlights cut an arc through the air for just seconds before beginning their slow-motion tumble into the icy abyss. Dashka, swerving to correct her travel on the far side, caught a quick glimpse of the man's terror-stricken face. It was Sergei, she was sure. She slowed, spun round, returned slowly to the edge of the chasm and craned forward. No light and no sound. Just enveloping silence and darkness. She sat quietly for many moments, lonely and empty, and then, when her hands had stopped shaking, threw the machine into gear and slid slowly away.

Three hours into her journey a wind from the north ran her down. It began as a trifle but within minutes had exploded into a gale, before making things significantly worse, by starting to pelt her with increasingly heavy snow. The high beams on the flying vehicle reflected back off the big flakes and made visibility virtually non-existent. Snowflakes whipped into her exposed cheeks and lips and quickly formed an ice coating.

She slowed and checked her GPS. Cape Sakharova was somewhere beyond the maelstrom to her right, beyond the ghostly and seemingly endless undulations. The Soviets, she knew from her research, had long ago constructed a facility, isolated way out here on the edge of the central plateau. It was built to service the atomic testing program and had stood lonely and deserted, unused for years. It would be, she estimated, no more than a dozen kilometers to the south-west.

The buildings might, of course, be radioactive and most likely in a sorry state of repair, but it was better than coming to grief in a crevasse or freezing to death in the middle of this confronting nothingness. She turned the vehicle to a new compass bearing and skimmed along, much more slowly now, keeping a watchful eye on the glowing needle. Twenty minutes later she came over a powder-covered knoll and dropped down hard onto an unnaturally flat surface. She turned the vehicle to the right and moved the light along the edge of what she surmised was a runway. A hundred meters further along, a small group of rudimentary timber buildings materialized gradually from within a vortex of ice crystals. They were in surprisingly good condition. Dashka stowed the machine under a low overhang and pushed her way through the howling wind into the largest of the buildings. She played the beam of her flashlight around the icy interior. Something caught the edge of her eye and she redirected the beam into the far corner. Two men sat quietly, wrapped in blankets and staring with wide eyes back into her light.

32

THE MONOCHROME IMAGE revealed a man in a dark suit firing two shots through the open rear window of a black limousine in an underground car park. A person sitting in the car appeared to be hit and slumped to the seat. The shooter was then quickly brought down by two others crouched close by, with weapons drawn. Moments later the automobile, with tires squealing, sped away, disappeared from the frame and reappeared on a second camera as it vaulted from the exit at high speed.

A replay of a digitally enlarged version of the first few seconds revealed, quite clearly, who the victim was.

Donna Lynn Stone had just achieved the undesirable distinction of being the first US President to be assassinated since John Fitzgerald Kennedy.

The announcement of her killing was chillingly similar to that of his, all those years before.

A television newsreader, less famous than Walter Cronkite, but no less emotional, broke the news to the nation.

'We have breaking news from San Francisco, California. We're hearing, and we believe it is official, that President-Elect Stone has been shot dead. I repeat, the President has been shot dead. Reports say that President Stone died at midday Pacific Standard time, three o'clock Eastern Standard Time.'

He paused to wipe his eyes. 'Just repeating, the President is dead.'

Within the hour, news services around the world were replaying, over and over again, the grainy images from a parking garage in downtown San Francisco and the leaders of a dozen countries were beginning to convey their heartfelt condolences to the nation.

Several hours after the first announcement, confirmation

was received, in Washington, that the shooter was one of the President's own trusted security detail. He, in turn had been killed by two others. Reports were already coming in that the man had links to an Islamic terrorist organization. His body was being kept in a secure facility at an undisclosed location until an autopsy could be performed.

Charlie sat in darkness with Oskar and Jia, watching stunned as the drama unfolded on the small television set in their safe house. The President's personal physician was providing details to a packed media gathering at the marble-lined entrance to the hospital in which she lay.

From time to time they'd catch a glimpse of Cherry as the cameras roamed across the crowded vestibule. Her need to be where the story was happening, where her friend lay dead, had proved stronger than her sense of self-preservation and she had been on a flight to California within half an hour of the first announcement. Charlie had not been happy.

'President Stone suffered massive trauma from a number of bullet wounds and as a result of her injuries, cardiac arrest and subsequent severe ischemic injury, global brain ischemia.'

The surgeon allowed the shocking news to sink in.

'The President's body will remain in our ICU until her family can be here. Her husband, as you know, is serving with the diplomatic corps in the Middle East and will be returning, we hope, within the next several hours. We are awaiting his visit and his permission to turn off the machines.'

'Are you saying, therefore, that the President is not clinically dead?'

'No, the President is dead. There is massive brain damage. There is no brain activity, she is brain dead. We are simply waiting for her husband to return to say his farewells.'

* * *

The vast bulk of the falling cliff of ice and snow had dashed itself to pieces on a series of crags above them and, as its residue thundered past, had swept them off their feet, deposited them at the base of the narrow couloir and showered them with several tons of cascading chunks and powder.

Hassan Baig had been partially buried almost upside down in several feet of soft snow. He cleared a small breathing space with his ice ax held close to his aching body and then used hands and ax to dig his way slowly up and out. He clambered from the mound, cleaned his ice-caked goggles and checked his ribs. At least one broken, probably. He looked around the wilderness of fresh white. Eventually he located Liam, almost totally buried a hundred nearly vertical feet above him and 50 feet below the protruding sled. Liam watched helplessly as Hassan checked his ribs again, paused for a moment, shrugged snow from his coat with slow painful movements, shook his head just once and then turned and disappeared down the mountainside.

Liam dragged himself from the tumbled morass, struggled back up to the sled and began digging it out. Pain and fatigue made it a heartbreakingly slow process. The storm tore at his clothes and supped on the meager remains of his body's warmth. An hour passed and then another and another.

No one. No sound. Nothing returned from below but the howl of the wind and the incessant, swirling slivers of stinging flake-ice.

'Just you and me now, Da.' Tears of physical and emotional exhaustion were freezing on Liam's cheeks. 'Like the old days.'

He struggled on, pay out, secure sled, follow down, secure self, pay out. Liam had long taken a secret pride in his great physical strength. But the heavy sled appeared to have a mind of its own and it was all he could do to stop it tearing the rope from his tiring grip and sending them both hurtling into oblivion. Within 30 minutes he was done in. His hands and feet were numb, his arms powerless, his legs like jelly. He secured the unstable stretcher to a rocky outcrop, dragged a bivouac sack around his shivering body and sat, then lay, next to his dead father. The bright orange bag was soon concealed by a dusting of soft flakes.

For Winston Churchill the 'black dog' had always been a metaphor; a way of describing his deep depressions. For Liam, since his year of captivity in the Spin Ghar mountains, his black dog had been a living, breathing reality. To the medicos, it was no more than a product of his damaged unconscious. 'A post-traumatic pooch,' one flippant psychiatrist had called it, but to Liam, always real enough as an omen: a presentiment of the onset of a suicidal depression.

And now the mongrel was back, over there, deep charcoal against the blinding white; burning ember eyes. Liam rolled towards his dead father, still secured to the stretcher, and closed his eyes.

He had no concept of how long he'd been unconscious when something made him start awake. The animal was there. Still. Lurking on the edge of his vision. As he watched, mildly interested but somehow detached, it pricked up its ears momentarily, turned its head and then skulked off into the blinding snow.

What had the beast seen? Heard? With a huge effort, Liam sat up and looked round. There was nothing but the storm raging on and on. Nothing but forsaken slopes of rock and snow. But there was... a sound. There it was again. A voice on the wind perhaps. Someone was coming.

Below, almost obscured by driving flakes, a figure began to take shape, then another and another and another. Their upward progress was excruciatingly slow and by the time they were within 50 yards Liam had staggered to his feet, not willing to take a bullet lying down.

But there was no gun, no flesh-tearing missile. Hassan Baig was back, exhausted, in great pain, but smiling. Behind him stood Amin, Gohar, the ageing Shamim Ibrahim and his grinning sons. Shamim lifted a gloved hand in a restrained greeting and then, without a word, they took charge of the snow-covered sled and started with casual, instinctive skill to lower it down the steep slope.

'I knew Allah would keep you safe.' An emotional Hassan Baig put a supportive arm around Liam's shoulder.

'Tahir has been on radio to Mahmood Khan.' Amin too, appeared to be struggling with his feelings but hid them better than Hassan. 'He will be at base camp when we get down.'

* * *

Cherry gazed out at the flag flying above the White House. It fluttered wistfully at half-mast.

'So what happens to this whole thing now? What do we do?'

Charlie sat opposite, grim-faced. He followed her gaze. 'Circle the wagons again, I guess,' he said. 'Wait for the outcome of the investigation.' He turned and eyed the two armed guards on the other side of the glass partition. 'Or the next attempt to get rid of us.' He looked back to Cherry. 'Hopefully, it'll be the former and we'll finally see the whole goddam thing ended; get back some sort of normality.'

'So you trust Arnott then?' She looked quizzical. 'I'm not sure *I* do.' She tapped at the screen of her tablet. 'They're saying he might bring the announcement forward.'

'What's your problem with Arnott?' Charlie looked puzzled. 'He's always seemed okay to me. He was Donna Stone's chosen VP for Christ's sake.'

'Call it a woman's intuition,' Cherry said.

Charlie's puzzlement turned quickly to concern. 'Look, if you think there is even the slightest chance there's a fit-up on its way then it's not smart to wait until he comes for us. We should grab Jia and Oskar and get the hell out of here now.' He reached for his cellphone.

'What about those two?' She indicated the armed men.

'I can handle them if I need to, if you're sure.'

She sat watching the billowing stars and stripes in the distance, making no attempt to respond.

'That bastard Dyson has a lot to answer for,' Cherry said with feeling. 'This thing could be over now if he hadn't changed his story. I don't understand the man.'

Charlie stood and walked to the window. 'Stockholm Syndrome, perhaps.' He was talking to himself as much as to her.

'What do you mean?' she asked.

'Stockholm Syndrome, the Patti Hearst thing. Y'know, when captives eventually start to develop sympathy, empathy with their captors, perhaps even start to support them.'

359

'I know what it is,' Cherry said angrily. 'I just don't think it applies to Dyson. You're being too generous. As far as I'm concerned, the man is just a lying bastard.'

'It's hard to…'

Charlie's continued defense of Dyson was cut short by the desk telephone ringing.

'Excuse me,' she said, lifting the receiver. She listened for a while, looking increasingly perplexed.

'I think it's Russian,' she said handing the phone to Charlie. 'A bit of English, maybe – I'm not sure.'

Charlie said something in heavily accented Russian and then listened carefully.

'Da,' he said. 'Da, da, yes, da…'

He spoke again while Cherry watched, mystified. He grabbed a pad and pen from her desk and began to jot down a series of numbers, then listened to what was clearly another long explanation. 'Da, da…' he said at length. 'Spasibo, spasibo. Thank you.'

He returned the phone to its cradle. Cherry gave him a questioning look.

'Very strange call that, a patch in from a radio transmitter. Somewhere in Russia.'

'What was it all about?'

'I'm not sure yet. A smoking gun, maybe.' He sat looking perplexed.

* * *

White-hot needles of pain stabbed at his toes and fingertips as they struggled their way through the last of the icefall maze towards the edge of the glacier.

Two helicopters, Liam thought, trying to make sense of it through his mind-numbing fatigue. He looked across: a pilot sat at the controls of the closest machine, staring directly ahead. Why two helicopters, one with its blades still rotating?

The answer became clear as they staggered closer to the small forward base camp. Gathered together into a tight group near the scattering of tents were Mahmood and all the porters, save one, sitting cross legged on the moraine with hands on heads.

Two men holding automatic weapons stood a little apart and forward, facing the returning group. The remaining porter stood with them but was not holding a weapon.

'Congratulations and thank you, Mr Doyle. You have saved us a lot of trouble.' The accent was either German or Austrian, Liam wasn't sure. 'You have shown remarkable tenacity. None of us ever expected you to come down alive.'

'What do you want?' Liam asked as calmly as possible. He knew the answer already.

The man indicated the sled with the snout of his gun. 'Your evidence.'

'And then, of course, you'll wipe us all out. Do you think we're all going to stand around while you do that?'

The man shifted the gun towards the sitting group. 'Let us see.' Nobody made any attempt to move or speak.

'And do you really think you'll get away with the mass execution of all these people?'

The man indicated the gun in his hand with a jerk of his head. 'The weapon you see here is the kind much beloved of Taliban terror groups. Who do you think will be held responsible? This will be shrugged off as merely another attack by Islamists.'

In one of the tents, buried in a jumble of down bags, the still mildly delirious Greg Carter stirred and opened his eyes. The snippets of conversation filtering in over the clattering chopper sounded tense, discordant. He dragged himself up and peered through a gap in the flyleaf.

The man outside with his back to the tent was pointing to two of the watching porters. 'You and you, take the stretcher and load it into the helicopter.'

The men made no attempt to move. He turned his gun on them: 'Raus! Raus!'

They shambled across slowly towards the swaddled corpse. Liam held up a hand. 'Over my dead body.'

The porters shuffled to a halt. Uncertain. Afraid.

'I can arrange that immediately, Mr Doyle.' The gun swung

back to him; pointed now at his head.

Even through his delirium, Carter could grasp the gravity of what was happening. He turned and rifled around among the discarded oxygen bottles, the climbing gear, sleeping bags and a now deflated Gamow bag.

The man giving the orders beyond the tent flap summoned the porters with two curled fingers.

'If Mr Doyle tries to stop you, I will shoot him through the head,' he said with absolute conviction.

'Leave it, my friend,' Mahmood called to Liam. 'They won't get far. The Air Force will take them down. They won't make it past Concordia.'

'Air Force?' The man turned to Mahmood and laughed. 'But who will call them when you are dead?'

Liam was sizing up the distance between them and assessing his chances when Carter staggered from his tent, an ice ax in each hand. The noise from the helicopter camouflaged the sound of his stone-crunching approach. He struck with all his failing strength.

The first ax buried itself deeply into one man's back, separating two vertebrae at the disc and severing his spinal cord. The other man had time to turn and send out a quick burst of fire before the remaining ax smashed between two of his ribs and entered his heart. The complicit porter tried to run across the broken ground but was rugby-tackled to the stones by Gohar before he'd covered ten yards.

Carter had taken at least one bullet and went down quickly, bleeding profusely.

'Fuck,' Liam yelled, grabbing a fallen weapon.

He sent it spiraling away across the moraine and then dropped to his knees next to Greg Carter. Mahmood was there a second later. He took Carter's hand and held it tightly.

Amin had dragged the other weapon from the second man's now-useless hand and was sprinting, firing wildly, towards the chopper, its engines now screaming as the rotating blades picked up speed. Amin reached the machine as it lifted toward the high peaks. He leapt into the air, clung to a skid with one hand as the chopper rose and fired into the cockpit with the other. At 30 feet he dropped into a patch of wet slush, landing like a cat. Smoke billowed from the engine as the stricken machine banked away towards the west before sliding into a low spur on the mountain's flank and transforming into a ball of orange flame.

Liam gently unzipped Carter's bloodied thermal. 'Oh Christ,' he whispered.

'Don't worry, mate.' Carter coughed up a wad of blood. It congealed as it hit the cold air. His face was losing color fast, his breathing shallower with every struggling intake. Liam bent in close.

'It's okay.' He coughed again. 'It's okay.' It was no more than a whisper now. 'I couldn't think of a better place to die.' He fluttered a hand toward the stretcher; toward James. 'Or a better bloke to...'

His life ended with a soft sigh, inaudible against the exploding avgas. Liam stood, the tears becoming icy as they rolled down his cheeks. The small, shattered gathering watched Greg Carter's blood create a bright red shape against a small patch of unsullied snow atop the indifferent harshness of the glacial rocks.

A day later, Liam had said his farewells to the peerless people, all the quiet men who had risked their lives to save his, and Mahmood's chopper was ferrying two bodies and the injured Hassan Baig down the valley towards Askole.

* * *

A low-category cyclone off the Northern Territory coast meant the flight from Singapore had been delayed for 24 hours. It meant that Mr Paul had been required to spend a fretful, sleepless night in a cheap Darwin motel listening to the palm fronds slapping about in the tempest outside his window.

The flight was, at last, on final approach through the steaming rain.

'Have you been to this stinkhole before?' The Singapore man's sneering question took the dark-skinned man alongside him by surprise.

'I live here,' the man said. 'Born and bred here, matey. My family comes from here. Been here around 60,000 years.' He grinned.

His fellow passenger chose not to share his humor and turned to watch the wheels scudding across the waterway the airstrip had become. He was in a foul mood. Once again he'd been let down. First the incompetent Millston and now these clowns in the Karakoram. One exhausted man and a couple of useless porters to sort out and they'd managed to lose a helicopter and get themselves killed instead. And now the endless questions from the Pakistani authorities. At least they'd *buried* that bastard Millston when they'd finished with him.

It was clear: if you wanted something cleaned up efficiently, you did it yourself. This one he would do himself. He smiled a grim smile. And actually enjoy doing it.

He walked into the airport cafeteria, chose the seat opposite the one he'd used on every previous visit. He failed to wipe the table. The security camera was pointed at the back of his head.

The meeting, as usual, commenced without a greeting. 'What is it that you want, Mr Paul?' The man from Singapore was clearly very unhappy. 'I hope this time you actually have something worthwhile. You have no idea how tired of these meetings I am.'

Mr Paul ignored both question and statement, summoning up an expression of deep concern instead.

'There's been some bad news from Pakistan, I hear. You lost some people and a helicopter in the Karakoram?' Mr Paul was enjoying the Singaporean's discomfort.

His associate said nothing.

'Well, I have some *good* news for you,' Paul continued expansively. 'We believe we have managed to locate the missing hardware. A message originating from somewhere on Novaya Zemlya was picked up just a few hours ago.'

'Novaya what? Can you be a little more specific, Mr Paul? Perhaps a location, within, say, a thousand miles.'

'It's an archipelago in the Arctic Circle, north of Siberia. We don't have the exact location, I think the transmitter may be faulty, or it may be the effects of polar magnetic sub-storms or even the Aurora Borealis. But it's definitely somewhere to the north of Severny Island.'

'Who was the message sent to?'

'This is the interesting bit,' Mr Paul said, not bothering to hide his excitement. 'Our friends in Washington. The *Dialog* office. Whoever it is that's transmitting chose to contact the media.'

'Then Casement would know about this, no doubt. How interesting. Good work, Mr Paul. Congratulations.' It was the first time in nearly ten years Paul had seen him smile.

He reached across to shake Paul's hand. 'Thank you.' He took the hand in his then reached for Paul's elbow with his free hand. Paul felt something sharp enter the fleshy inner crook of his arm.

'What the fuck are you doing?' Paul pulled his hand away and grabbed his arm.

'Putting out the trash, my friend. Putting out the trash.'

As Paul, clutching his arm, slumped backward, the man from Singapore stood and started yelling in feigned panic. 'Heart attack. This man's having a heart attack, we need a doctor.'

An alarmed crowd gathered quickly and two well-meaning young tourists, in tropical shirts and rubber flip flops, dragged the dying man onto the cold tiles and attempted to resuscitate him. In the confusion, the Singaporean man, like the true professional he was, slipped quietly away.

Within the hour he was high in the air over Bali. 'Yes, Severny. We have assets there,' he said into his cellphone. 'Casement. There's a reasonable chance he'll be on his way as we speak. There's always a chance we'll find Doyle with him too. This one I'll handle in person. I have one quick detail to sort out on my way through Singapore and then I'll get it organized.'

* * *

'I have more bad news,' Mahmood said to Liam, raising his voice over the engine clatter rather than using the intercom. 'Your American President, Stone. She is dead. Killed. Assassinated.'

365

For the second time in less than an hour, Liam felt like he'd received a physical blow to his heart.

'Holy fuck, you're kidding me…?'

Mahmood said nothing, just shook his head.

'How? How did it happen? Do they know who…?'

Mahmood nodded. 'They're saying it was a member of her own security detail,' he shouted. 'He was shot dead by the others himself.'

Mahmood kept his eyes on the peaks to each side and shook his head again.

'His grandmother was born in Brooklyn but his grandfather was born in Pakistan so, needless to say, the Western media have already branded him an Islamist terrorist.' He spoke with undisguised bitterness. 'The crazy people are already out of their holes urging a nuclear attack on Pakistan, the world is in meltdown. Some are even suggesting that a group of radical misogynists are responsible.'

'I think we know who's responsible,' Liam yelled. 'If they wanted to create a distraction, deflect public attention, deflect the heat, redirect it somewhere else, they couldn't have found a better way. Assassinating the President sweeps everything from the headlines, even the Killing Sky.'

He looked out at the swiftly passing panorama and shook his head.

'There's always the risk that the world will link the assassination to the conspiracy, to the plot, and escalate their problems, but I guess when the stakes are this high it's probably a risk worth taking. After all, there's always the slight doubt, "maybe it was a Muslim terrorist after all".'

He shook his head again.

'The whole fucking country should be taking to the streets.'

'I get the sense, from what I have seen, that they are in a state of shock. More shock than anger or even grief.'

'It is shocking. Shocking, terrible news,' Liam said, still trying to take it all in, still reeling. 'I really liked the woman, thought she could make a difference. Have they appointed anyone to take her place yet?'

Mahmood adjusted the chopper's course slightly as they flew over the foot of the Baltoro. 'The Vice President, Jason Arnott, was sworn in a few days ago. Automatic succession, I think.'

'When was the funeral? I'm sure Cherry would want to have been there. That's a huge risk.'

Mahmood shrugged and the helicopter responded with a slight dip.

'I don't know, I've been too busy trying to organize this chopper and get permissions and what have you.'

'So Arnott's the new President? Well… he seems okay. I guess he'll stick to the narrative. Unless these bastards go after him as well.'

'Nothing's impossible,' Mahmood said.

Liam looked out at another mighty peak close by on his right; if he reached out, he felt as though he could touch it.

'Have you heard from Charlie? Jia? Cherry? They must be devastated.'

'Charlie sent a text for you last night.' He passed Liam his phone.

'Meet me in Arkhangelsk ASAP,' was all it said.

'Arkhangelsk?' Liam looked blankly across to Mahmood.

'Don't ask me,' Mahmood said. 'He wants me there too. The more I see, the less I understand.'

They flew without speaking for some time, the thud of the engine reverberating back at them from the massifs on each side. 'We will need to leave immediately,' Mahmood said eventually. 'I will make sure their bodies are kept safe until we can return.'

33

JASON ARNOTT wasn't enjoying his first weeks as President. He scanned the weighty document while his two associates waited expectantly at the other end of a secure line.

At length he leaned forward and spoke. 'You must have paid off a lot of influential fucking people.'

'We are able to find very deep pockets when it is in our interest to do so.' The Englishman sounded like he was making an announcement for the BBC.

'For Christ's sake, the President's body isn't even cold yet. How do you think this will look? Have you ever heard the term "indecent haste"?'

'Let us worry about that.' The precise vowels vibrated off the small speaker.

'Listen, my friend, even *you* are not influential enough to carry *this* off,' Arnott said into the phone. He smacked the document with the back of his hand.

'And *I* don't have to.' The English voice was maddeningly calm. 'There are people more powerful than me. As you more than most would know, Mr President, there's always someone else out there, someone a little higher up the food chain.'

Arnott thumped the thick document onto his desk. 'It's too soon. The media will be yelling cover-up from every rooftop.'

'Some media,' the aristocratic man said. He paused. 'Some media. The rest, as always, will do our bidding. In a few weeks it will all have blown over, all be forgotten.'

'But the people on the street? Even the most gullible won't buy this – they'll see it for what it is. They'll holler conspiracy.'

'Fuck the people on the street. The *market* will buy it.' The third man on the line spoke with a mid-Atlantic accent. There was possibly a trace of Antipodean in his past. 'Look, Mr Arnott, global markets are in chaos. Stocks, particularly *our* stocks, are in freefall. Commodities have gone to hell. Our derivatives are in a diabolical state. CDOs, forwards, futures, options: everything's been going down the toilet since this shit went viral. Selling short isn't saving us this time.'

He appeared to have made his point and then remembered an additional grievance. 'That bitch's assassination hasn't helped either. The media are giving us hell.'

'Ironic really,' the Englishman said. 'But, an ill wind...'

'There are more important things to consider than the market,' Arnott said quietly, but his tone, even across so great a distance, betrayed his acquiescence.

'And what would those be?' the third man said, making no attempt to conceal the contempt he felt for the new US President. The line went dead.

Jason Arnott replaced the receiver, moved over to a mirror, ran fingers through his thinning sandy hair and straightened his tie. He collected the weighty document from his desk, opened the office door, joined the loitering security detail and headed towards the waiting world media.

He stepped up to the podium. 'Today I can announce that the investigation into the media-styled Killing Sky conspiracy has been completed.'

He paused, adjusted his glasses, and continued.

'It is with some relief that I can tell you that, after the most comprehensive, the most exhaustive, series of forensic investigations arguably ever undertaken by the United States authorities, we have established that there is no substance to these claims.'

He waited until the incredulous response from the waiting media scrum had died down, then turned and, with a flourish of his right hand, indicated Walter Dyson standing nearby, with a large man on each side of him. Walter smiled nervously.

'The highly respected aircraft designer and American patriot Mr Walter Dyson has now sworn under oath that he was compelled by these people to provide false evidence on camera. He has now revealed that the wild, improbable stories regarding the fleet of stealth aircraft are a total fabrication.

'Our friends in China and Russia have comprehensively investigated the accusations made regarding the criminal use of specific locations in their countries and have found them to be without substance.

'Professor Oskar Frederik, we know, has communist links that go back all the way to his youth spent within the Soviet Union and has proven to be a hostile and unreliable witness. Irishman Liam Doyle is a man discharged from the US Military in controversial circumstances after spending a year with the Taliban and we are currently investigating possible IRA connections. Charles Casement has been known, by his ex-intelligence community masters, to have had extreme and radical ideas for some years. The journalist, Cherry Davitt, spent several of her college years involved with anarchist, feminist and environmental groups and has a long history of consorting with radicals.

'It has become clear that this, at its roots, has been a cleverly orchestrated campaign by a number of deeply radicalized socialist and environmental groups to sow doubt regarding the leaders of our community and to demonize the American free-market system.

'Now we know a small number of arguably reputable scientists has expressed concern regarding the droughts afflicting the poor folk in the South Asian region and the increased levels of sulfur dioxide in the upper quadrant of the stratosphere to our north. Let me deal first with the drought. Our investigation has come down strongly on the side of natural, cyclical weather phenomena. While humanity may be playing a role, it is a small role. The United States, of course, will be contributing generously to a fund for helping these people out.

'As to the slightly enhanced atmospheric sulfur, our detailed investigations have revealed this is most likely due to exceptional underlying activity from Icelandic volcanoes and may have been exacerbated somewhat as the result of a significant industrial accident in a remote area of Siberia.'

He removed his glasses, placed them carefully on the podium and scratched the right side of his nose.

'Having conducted an exhaustive scientific, forensic and

security investigation and weighed up all the evidence, I believe I can now say, with absolute confidence, that there is no conspiracy other than theirs, there is no Killing Sky conspiracy. There is "No Killing Sky".'

He raised the thick document above his head. 'The report will be made available to members of the media and the public later today.'

'No questions,' an aide said as the President turned quickly and disappeared into the White House.

* * *

The Singaporean man cleared customs at Changi and headed for the taxi rank. He was back in his perennially steamy home town. Today it seemed to be drier but hotter than ever.

This next 'loose end' was a rank amateur. No effort would be required and he would be back on Holland Road enjoying a shower, a dry martini and efficient air-conditioning within the half-hour. Then Arkhangelsk and, with luck, the last little piece of housekeeping.

He rode a cab across to Serangoon, found the street number and checked the name, painted on a warped sheet of plywood next to two inexpertly rendered red crabs. Three or four diners sat scattered around the outdoor space and a single waiter poured frothy Tigers in the far corner.

He moved quickly into a narrow laneway, scrutinized the passport-size photograph in his palm, then entered the small shack silently by a rear door. The cramped lean-to kitchen smelled of garlic, hot oil and stale sweat. A man stood bent over a large wok with flames licking up from the gas hob beneath. The intruder stepped across to a stack of metal bowls and sent them deliberately crashing to the concrete floor. The man at the wok spun round. He matched the photograph perfectly.

The fastidious assassin, who had disposed of Mr Paul without a second thought, was about to claim another victim. He took a starched, folded handkerchief from his pocket, unwrapped a gleaming hypodermic and removed the plastic cap covering the needle. He advanced on the frightened-looking cook without bothering to conceal the syringe. The hot wok clattered to the floor, scattering crab shells and red chili sauce in every direction.

At that precise moment, Luo Chen entered the kitchen carrying a stack of heavy cast-iron dishes and saw the man preparing to end the life of his twin brother.

He gave an almighty heave and several of the heavy plates struck the man on the side of his head. The sight of two near-identical faces unsettled the trained killer for just a few precious heartbeats. It was a mistake. It was sufficient. Luo Chen lunged for a large cleaver and plunged the razor-sharp blade deep into the man's exposed throat, severing his carotid artery. The man dropped to his knees, brought down by his own arrogant insouciance. He fell against a rusting steel cabinet, splashing it with bright red blood.

Luo Chen's brother found a plastic chair and staggered onto it as his legs went from under him. 'What the...? Who was he, lah? Why was the Seow Kow trying to stab me?'

'He wasn't. He'd come for me.' Luo Chen stepped over the dying man and touched his trembling brother's shoulder. 'Sorry. It's the price you pay for having a bastard twin. I've been expecting him.'

'Who was he?'

'He was me.'

'What the fuck are you talking about?'

'It doesn't matter.' Luo Chen shook his head.

'I've been there.' He indicated the corpse with a thrust of his chin. 'He was just another nameless *hùndán*. A nobody.' Luo Chen's face had drained of blood and his voice quavered slightly. 'They do the shit work for the *real* bastards. They think they're indestructible, but sooner or later, they all die like lonely dogs and nobody gives a shit; least of all their paymasters.'

He reached for the grimy handset on the wall with a trembling hand and punched in the three-digit number for Singapore emergencies.

* * *

372

Alexei Denisovich was surprised and perhaps a little afraid. The helicopter had appeared out of the Cape Zhelaniya darkness and produced four very dangerous-looking men and their equipment. Within minutes it was headed back to collect their leader, who was flying in, they said, from somewhere further afield later in the evening.

A man with what, to Alexei's still-bruised ear, was a strong foreign accent, approached him. 'Where are your snowmobiles?' the newcomer asked.

Alexei pointed to the shed. 'The woman, Azarova, wrecked them before she took off. One of my men went after her on the only one left working, but he hasn't come back.'

'I'll have a look at them while we're waiting.' The man took a dark metal case from the stack they'd unloaded and headed for the shed. 'We won't all fit in the chopper.'

The deadline for the helicopter's return came and went and, eventually, one of the waiting men used Alexei's satellite phone to locate the pilot, cooling his heels at a military airfield near Arkangelsk.

'Your man was not on the Moscow flight,' the pilot told him. 'There is another due in an hour. I am still waiting.'

A day went by.

The foreign man had managed to repair just one of the snowmobiles. 'She did a fucking good job on those things, that bitch,' he spat. 'The other one is totally shit. I had to use it for spare parts.'

* * *

'What's Jia doing here?' Liam's joy at seeing her was immediately tempered by his concern for her safety.

'I needed a translator,' Charlie said, giving Mahmood an expansive hug. 'If there was anyone else I could trust at such short notice, she wouldn't be here.'

'I've just been responsible for the death of one good friend,' Liam said, turning to Jia. 'I don't want to get you killed as well.' He seemed emotionally exhausted and close to collapse.

Jia took his hands in hers.

'It was my decision,' she said gently. 'Some day you will begin to understand that I make my own decisions.' She kissed him on the lips, embraced him for a few seconds and then turned to Mahmood, gave a tiny bow and shook his hand.

Charlie walked across and wrapped his big arms around Liam. 'I'm sorry about your buddy Carter,' he whispered. 'We're going to make these assholes pay.'

'What's happened to Cherry, Oskar? Are they safe?'

'As safe as I could make them,' Charlie answered.

'So what's this all about?' Liam asked tiredly as they exited Arkhangelsk's Soviet-era Talagi terminal and walked to a waiting van.

'I'll tell you when we get airborne. The chopper's just over the other side of the main runway,' Charlie answered.

He turned to Mahmood. 'I'm glad you can fly one of these. I get very uncomfortable without a pair of real wings.'

'As long as it has one rotor overhead and another on the tail then, don't worry, I can fly it.'

'Well get Jia to sit up front with you so she can translate the Cyrillic on the dashboard,' Charlie said. He heaved a large sports bag into the back of the big machine as Mahmood started to explore the controls. 'Liam can get some much-needed shut-eye on the way.'

Half an hour later they were airborne and heading northeast into the winter darkness.

Liam leaned forward and unzipped the sports bag. It held three automatic weapons and a number of spare clips.

'Are you imagining we may have to use these?' Liam asked, looking up at the back of Jia's head.

'We can't be one-hundred-per-cent sure it's not a trap. The call sounded genuine and we've done a little checking but, given who we're dealing with, we can't afford to take any chances.'

Liam nudged the bag with his foot. 'Where did you get these?'

'Don't ask,' Charlie said. He took a phone from a zipper pocket and tapped up a map on the screen. 'The strip is here, we think, a ways in from the coast. The buildings appear to be

374

clustered up here at the northern end. Fortunately it's going to be virtually dark the entire time.'

He pulled on a set of headphones and spoke loudly to Mahmood. 'You've got the co-ordinates punched in, haven't you?'

Mahmood nodded, reached back and gave them a silent thumbs up.

'This thing is fitted with long-distance tanks, should get us there with plenty to spare.'

'I hope so,' Mahmood's voice crackled from the intercom.

'If my source is reliable, you'll be able to refuel there. If not, we're in the shit,' Charlie yelled over the din of the rotors. 'When we get there, give us a careful circuit at 500. I've had the most powerful searchlight I could find fitted up front. If everything seems kosher I'll get you to put her down a couple of hundred yards from the buildings to the west of the strip. Keep your revs up and be ready to go at a moment's notice. There's a weapon in the bag for you.'

The night was clear and Liam leaned against the perspex looking up at the brilliant stars. It was hard to imagine that an invisible screen of aerosol sulfates was performing its stealthy task somewhere up there above their heads. It was the last thought he had before falling into a deep sleep.

The clock on the console indicated the arrival of early morning as the chopper came in low over Severny's desolate west coast; even if the horizon did not.

Mahmood located the strip and flew a couple of tight circuits. It appeared deserted apart from the small group of buildings at one end and something bulky covered by what looked to be a wide spread of camouflage netting.

He put the craft gently into a drift of hard snow and Liam leapt out, weapon at the ready, followed by Charlie. They loped along in the cover of the heaped snow on the runway's edge. Up ahead all was still, silent. They stole swiftly from building to building, checking each interior quickly and thoroughly.

The third building they entered was bigger and better maintained than the others. Liam probed the darkness with his flashlight; the room looked deserted.

'Hello,' Charlie said. 'Anyone there? You called us. In Washington.'

The soft sigh of shifting fabric made Liam spin the beam into the left-hand corner. Charlie's finger tightened on his trigger. A woman stood with one hand in the air and another shielding her eyes from the light.

'I am Dashka Anasovna Azarova. I called. The men are there.' She pointed to a stack of packing crates at the rear.

* * *

Mahmood sat at the controls with the searchlight trained on the buildings, rotors spinning, a gun on his lap. He watched and waited, not knowing whether he would ever see his friends alive again. A door in the large building opened slowly. Liam stood in the shadowed darkness of the doorway and identified himself with his own light-beam, before stepping out onto the snow and waving the chopper in. Mahmood took it the remaining few hundred feet between them and put it down a couple of chopper lengths from the door.

Charlie came out into the dazzling white light followed by a tall, fair-haired woman and a grey-haired Chinese man.

Jia disconnected herself from the helicopter seat, seemingly in slow motion. She looked at the man, took two tentative steps forward and then stopped, unable, it seemed, to trust her eyes. The man took a step towards her and held out his arms. Tears began to stream down her face. She stepped slowly across the brightly illuminated tableau and swayed slightly. Liam was concerned that her buckling legs might not carry her all the way and moved to support her but she reached the man on her own and embraced him tightly.

'This is my father,' she whimpered to Liam. 'This is my father, Zhang Liu.'

The man said something to Jia. She turned and spoke through her tears. 'There is a young pilot in there who is wounded – he needs help.'

'We need to get things moving,' Charlie said gently. 'The sooner we're out of here the better. There's a first-aid kit in the chopper, Mahmood.'

* * *

Twenty-four hours later, the group of edgy men at Cape Zhelaniya were still awaiting the return of the helicopter and the arrival of their missing team leader. The foreigner, who seemed to have a little more initiative than the rest, commandeered Alexei's phone again and made another call.

'It looks like he didn't even board the flight out of fucking Singapore yet,' he said, tossing the satellite phone back to Alexei with a dismissive gesture.

Without a leader, the men seemed unsure what to do next and were becoming hostile and uneasy. They sat in the small canteen drinking Alexei's precious supply of vodka and playing a noisy and aggressive game of poker. By what would have been sunrise a thousand miles to the south, Alexei had finally had enough. He decided someone needed to take control and, in the absence of anyone better, it might as well be him.

'I think you must make the decision to go without him,' Alexei said, addressing the entire group. 'Call the helicopter back. Meanwhile two of us will head off with the snowmobile; we have the co-ordinates. The longer we leave it, the more chance there is of them finding some means of escape.'

Alexei was a little taken aback and not a little relieved when none of the men objected to his giving them orders. 'With luck we can all arrive there at around the same time.'

* * *

'NO KILLING SKY!'

The three-word headline, it seemed, had circled the globe at the speed of light and was now being seen and heard in a hundred languages in several billion homes.

In major cities worldwide, leading politicians and corporate heads were going public, praising the new President for his timely report. The consensus they attempted to build was a simple one. The enquiry, they insisted in media of every shape and color, had been efficient, thorough, honest and forthright.

Saxon Melville sat in the darkness of the newspaper's boardroom. The midnight offices of the *Dialog* survived, still, but were silent now and deserted. He trawled the glowing screen from one site to another, one international daily to the next.

It would be reasonably clear, he thought, to any informed observer who might be honestly assessing the authenticity of the Killing Sky phenomenon, that the overlords of free-market fundamentalism, the sleek elite, those who had been winning for decades, had won yet again.

Melville hit 'sleep' in the corner of the screen and the reflected computer glow disappeared from his troubled face.

Half of the bastards he knew personally. In the darkness he slowly shook his patrician head.

The oil barons, the coal moguls, the bankers and the moribund elders of the media, he knew, would uncoil with smug satisfaction, this night, in the salons of their villas and on the decks of their super yachts. They'd sip at chilled vintage Krug and nibble on critically endangered Beluga roe, flown in fresh this very morning from the Caspian. They'd lounge, in a fog of insouciance, on hand-sewn calfskin leather, or exquisite silk; gossamer threads woven into extravagance by small children with empty bellies and faltering eyesight.

This, after all, was a victory worth savoring. One more link in the long chain of evidence that proved they were now so powerful as to be unassailable.

* * *

They worked methodically through the night.

Mahmood gave the injured young pilot as much first-aid attention as the limited kit allowed. It was clear he wouldn't be flying anything any time soon. He cleaned and bandaged the wound and administered pain killers, making sure not to put the man to sleep.

Dashka led the others out onto the airstrip and they began to remove the cargo netting from the bulky machine standing silent in the darkness.

It was, as they already suspected, an aircraft with a remarkable similarity to the B2 Stealth bomber, the Spirit that Charlie had flown several times as a young pilot; but, as he had guessed the first time he saw the images James had captured, it was considerably larger.

The camouflage paint job featured a cloudy, blue-grey sky belly and a tundra, ice and rock upper fuselage.

'How come the runway is clear?' Charlie asked, looking along the all but snow-free strip.

'I found an old snow-plough in one of the other buildings,' Dashka answered. 'I worked on the motor a little and managed to get it going. I cleared the strip yesterday and luckily we've had no snow since then.' She paused and smiled at Charlie, who was clearly impressed. 'I also refueled the aircraft. It's not a full tank. I knew I would need to keep some for a helicopter.' She smiled again. 'There is also a working generator over there next to the plane if you need it for power.'

Mahmood left them to begin refueling the chopper while the others went back to the relative warmth of the building. Charlie and Jia joined the Chinese pilot and, with her doing the trans-lating, began to get the lowdown on the aircraft's controls. From time to time, Jia cast wistful glances in Zhang Liu's direction. It was clear with whom she'd prefer to be spending her time.

Liam found a perch on a packing crate opposite Dashka and between them, using a patois of English, Russian and Chinese, with a little sign language thrown in, Zhang Liu's story unfolded.

'When I discovered the problems with the fuel supply in Pavlodar, I challenged my supervisor. A man named Yuri. The next thing I knew I was in a fuel tanker being taken to the east – to my death, I thought. I knew they were interested in the development of synthetic fuels and so I told them I could help to create a more efficient, less expensive aviation fuel. I think it is the only reason I'm still alive.'

Dashka shook her head sympathetically. She understood how similar their stories were and how similar their fate could have been; could still be.

'They took me to a place deep in the mountains,' Zhang Liu created a peak with his fingers. 'A long narrow valley. I still don't know where it was.'

'Altai,' Liam said. 'The Altai Mountains in China.'

Zhang Liu nodded and continued his story. 'Some years ago a company called Syntroleum started to develop synthetic fuels, converting gas or coal to liquids. Back in 2006 the US Air Force flew a B52 powered solely by synthetics for the first time. I have spent the time since I was taken developing and refining our own synthetics using the CTL, the coal to liquid, approach. Its success has kept me alive.'

He looked across to Jia. She looked up and they exchanged a tender smile. Liam found it disconcerting, suddenly having to share her with somebody else but, at the same time, was deeply relieved she'd found her father alive.

'And then, I don't know how long, how many months,' Zhang Liu continued, 'they came and started shredding files, moving computers, destroying my laboratory equipment. Then the aircraft started leaving. The airstrip became chaos as the ploughs moved to and fro, keeping the runway in service.' He moved his hands vigorously from side to side. 'One after another, the bombers lifted and turned towards a dozen different compass points.'

Zhang realized, suddenly, that he was becoming overly loquacious and made an attempt to regain his composure.

'The pilots, we heard, were all being directed to take their planes to different places. To hide them. We didn't know why. Someone started a rumor that they were being given cyanide capsules, but I could never confirm that.'

He pointed across to the young pilot, now sitting up, talking earnestly to Charlie.

'I had befriended Gao Jin over the time we were both there. He seemed a decent boy. Different from the rest. I knew that, when all the aircraft were gone, they would kill me and the

380

others who were no longer of any use, so I pleaded with him to take me when he flew away. At first he was too afraid, but after a little while his good heart won the battle with his fear. He smuggled me onto the aircraft in the dark and we got as far as the runway before one of the others noticed me and raised the alarm.'

He paused, reflecting on the awful memory. 'And then they started shooting. As we lifted off, a bullet came through the cockpit canopy and Gao Jin was hit.'

'Through the canopy,' Liam said sharply. 'So the aircraft has no pressurization?'

Zhang shook his head. 'We flew all the way here at low altitude, no pressurized cabin, but Dashka has repaired that somehow.' He smiled at her. 'She is a hero.'

'Why come here?' Liam asked.

He pointed out into the darkness where the big machine stood.

'Gao Jin was very ill. He was worried he would pass out and crash. He knew of this airstrip from his earlier flights to the Arctic. It was one of their back-up strips, in case of mechanical failure. They have many scattered around the Arctic Circle in remote locations.'

Zhang Liu looked over to Gao Jin again. His expression seemed almost fatherly. 'He is a remarkable young man. Losing blood, on the edge of passing out and yet he flew that aircraft all the way up here and landed us safely. I hope he will be all right. Another hero.'

'Why not go somewhere closer, less isolated? Somewhere he could get help?'

'We talked about it but we were terrified. We knew of nowhere we would be safe from these people. He knew there were supplies here and a radio that wouldn't locate us immediately in the way the one on the aircraft would. We thought we could...'

'Time to go,' Charlie called.

As they lifted the pilot gently into the helicopter, Liam felt the twinge of an emotion he'd not experienced before. The young Chinese man, he'd noticed, was exceedingly handsome and Jia seemed exceedingly solicitous of his welfare. She held his hand and gave a gentle squeeze as he winced with pain at each movement. Liam, for the first time in his life, confronted jealousy and Jia noticed it in an instant. She smiled surreptitiously and held the man's hand a little tighter.

*** * ***

By Alexei's estimation they were no more than half an hour from their target. He sat, holding on tight and clutching his weapon to his chest, as the snowmobile careered across the hard ice surface.

As they became airborne over yet another small ridge he heard a different sound. A second engine. Moments later, the helicopter, lights blazing a trail across the barren landscape, clattered in from the north, low above their heads, before disappearing into the darkness ahead.

Liam and Charlie stood next to the silent, ominous warplane and watched as Mahmood lifted off with his four precious passengers. Then they, too, heard the sound of the incoming chopper. It thundered low overhead and streaked towards Mahmood's machine. Short bursts of automatic fire lit up the sky.

Mahmood, with the skills and instinct of a fighter pilot, dropped instantly to the right and almost stalled as the speeding pursuer overshot. Mahmood's engine screamed again as he hit full throttle and with an impossibly steep turn, locked onto the tail of the other machine.

Realizing his peril, the other pilot banked tightly to his left, but it was too late. Liam saw a figure, Dashka he thought, step out onto the skids and fire forward. The aggressor had, in an instant, become the victim. Flame blossomed from the helicopter's tail and for the second time in just a few days, Liam and Mahmood were forced to watch human beings plunging to their fiery deaths in the snow.

Mahmood turned the chopper toward the two men on the ground, flew in close enough for them to see his thumbs up and then banked off towards the southwest.

34

ON THE COLD, dark, desolate airstrip surrounded by snow to the horizon, Liam and Charlie pored over a map. With the chaotic few days they'd just endured, they had overlooked making one very significant decision: where they would actually take the aircraft.

'We'll need to put this thing on the ground somewhere that's as open and democratic as possible. Somewhere they won't be able to shut the media down entirely,' Charlie said.

'What about Stockholm?' Liam tapped the map. 'That's less than 1500 miles as the crow flies.'

Charlie did a quick mental calculation. 'There should be enough fuel for that. As long as the engines hold out. Our friend Gao Jin was less than optimistic.'

He readied the machine for take-off, went through his checklist quickly and then eased it out onto the snow-slick concrete.

'You sure you can fly this thing solo?' Liam asked.

'Listen, son,' Charlie said. 'If necessary, I could fly the goddam Space Shuttle solo.'

They had begun to gather momentum when a snowmobile's powerful light cut a swathe through the night sky as it burst over a powder mound at the end of the strip.

The aircraft continued to lumber forward but the snowmobile was closing the distance at high speed. Liam looked back along the strip and saw the flash of automatic fire coming at them from the figure on the rear seat. He waited for the impact but it never came: the erratic shuddering of the small machine as it hammered across the packed snow sent Alexei's volley spraying into the sky.

The vast bomber's acceleration was taking valuable seconds to build and for an agonizing few moments it seemed the machine would run them down. Alexei fired again.

'That illuminated switch to your left,' Charlie yelled. 'Hit it.'

The Chinese characters meant nothing to Liam so, with a leap of faith, he used a gloved hand to lunge at the control.

Deep in the digital bowels of the aircraft a series of high-capacity jets exploded into action and pressurized tanks began to spew liquid sulfur from the payload bay. Within seconds, as the liberated liquid turned instantly to gas, the snowmobile and its riders were enveloped in a burning, suffocating cloud of deadly fumes.

The aircraft accelerated away and, with a great roar, leapt into the sky. Below them, the snowmobile rocked and plunged then hurtled out of control into deep snow at the edge of the strip, rolling and sending its writhing, gasping passengers tumbling though the air.

Liam looked down as Charlie banked steeply to port and saw two deeply distressed men flailing about in the snow.

'Poor bastards,' he said softly.

'Them or us, young Liam. Them or us.'

Charlie straightened the plane up, checked his gauges and set a course for Sweden.

'Okay now, let's see if this goddam thing is as invisible as our friend Dyson claims it is.'

They flew in silence for an hour and, as the first natural light they'd seen in days made a tenuous promise from far off on the eastern horizon, Charlie spoke into the intercom.

'Send a message out to the world, young Liam. "Operation Killing Sky. Stop. The Smoking Gun. Stop. On its way to Stockholm. Stop."' He laughed loud and long.

Liam decided, for prudence sake, not to use the radio and instead sent Cherry a text.

CHERRY. SMOKING GUN. ALERT WORLD MEDIA. ABBA'S HOME TOWN. EST 0800 GMT.

Ten minutes later, Charlie broke silence again, his tone this time very different. 'I think we have a problem. We may be losing fuel. The tanks are reading near empty.'

'We maybe took a bullet back there,' Liam said. 'I didn't feel anything.'

'She's flying fine,' Charlie answered. 'Maybe something, shrapnel perhaps, nicked a fuel line. I don't know the beast well enough.' He grinned into the darkness. 'Be a bit of a fuck-up if we got this far and then ran out of gas.' He eased off the throttle just a little. 'I know you're not a religious boy, young Liam, but I suggest you start praying.'

* * *

Dyson's claims had not been idle boasts.

The tanks were now reading empty but they were well within Swedish airspace, with the outlying suburbs of Stockholm glittering in the low morning sunlight, when the first Swedish fighter jets swooped in alongside. They radioed, politely, for Charlie to fall into formation and follow them in. Immediately ahead and not far from the gleaming city, he spied a long straight freeway. The lanes heading toward the city were jammed with traffic, those heading out carried relatively few vehicles.

'They won't shoot,' he said into the intercom.

He descended obediently between his air-force escorts but, at the last moment, peeled away swiftly, slotted the aircraft into a line with the wide roads, located a section between the free flowing traffic and dropped her expertly onto the slick concrete. The Swedish jets pulled out, the pilots making no secret of their frustration.

'Nice folk, the Swedes.' Charlie gave a triumphant chuckle. 'There's no way they'd risk blowing their own people off the road.'

A taxi driver heard the aircraft's roar, took one look into his rear-view mirror and careened off onto the ice verge. Charlie hit the brakes and threw the machine into reverse thrust; the trailing edge flaps leapt into action with a loud protesting whine.

A few hundred yards up ahead an 18-wheeler cruised along in the slow lane, the Norwegian driver blissfully unaware of the machine bearing down on him. Smoke billowed from the plane's tires as Charlie fought to keep it traveling in a straight line. The driver of the truck suddenly became aware of his plight and plunged the accelerator hard against the floor. The heavy vehicle gathered speed with maddening sluggishness as the bomber closed the gap. Charlie brought the aircraft to a grinding, shuddering halt no more than a dozen feet behind the truck trailer and its terrified driver. The truck slewed off the road, its heavy wheels ploughing a long furrow in the muddy snow, and stopped, buried to its axles, a hundred or so yards ahead. The driver leapt from his cabin and galloped back toward them shaking his fist in the air and yelling something incomprehensible.

Within minutes, military helicopters hovered overhead and police cars, fire trucks and emergency vehicles of every description were screaming in from all directions. A thousand vehicles in the oncoming lanes had slammed to a stop suddenly as the plane landed and a mile-long traffic blockage had already formed. Moments after they had been ordered from the cockpit by a phalanx of SOG special forces, assault rifles trained on their heads, the world's media arrived.

'It's going to be difficult for our friends to explain this one away,' Liam said to Charlie. They were both grinning widely as they walked, hands in the air, towards the twitchy Swedish military. Liam studied the body language of the men around them carefully. 'I don't think they're arresting us. I think they're protecting us.'

* * *

The sinister-looking aircraft was being lifted from the Swedish freeway onto a huge low loader. News cameras still surrounded it, beaming every possible angle and detail of the prosaic activity to every corner of the globe.

Charlie and Liam sat sipping beers and watching the footage, not for the first time, on an airport television monitor. 'I still can't believe we haven't been charged with anything. We must have broken a dozen Swedish laws.'

'We?' Liam said. 'You were the pilot.'

'Navigator's just as culpable.'

'They're obviously not *too* happy with us. There are a couple of guys over there watching to make sure we take our flight.'

'Fine by me. They were happy to pay the fare; I was happy to leave.'

'It'll be interesting to see what kind of reception we get in DC, all the same. We've made Jason Arnott look pretty silly.'

An intercom voice, calling their Washington flight in a lyrical Swedish accent, interrupted the conversation.

Nine hours later they were walking towards the exit at Dulles International.

'The President would like to see you.' A man in the mandatory outfit – dark suit and shades – approached them. Another two provided low-key back-up nearby.

'The new President?' Charlie looked suddenly worried.

'Yes, we have a car waiting.'

'This'll be interesting.'

They were taken to the White House basement and made to wait for an hour, then led along a confusion of corridors and ushered into the Oval Office.

Cherry sat facing the door ensconced in a big soft sofa. The President was opposite her, one bandaged foot resting on a pillow perched on a heavy coffee table. Cherry caught Charlie's eye and smiled awkwardly.

The President turned and looked up at them.

'Good morning, gentlemen.'

'Ah, President… Stone, we were told…' It was the first time Liam had ever seen Charlie lost for words.

Donna Stone turned to Cherry and held out an upturned hand. 'Your meeting.'

Cherry uncrossed her legs and leaned forward awkwardly, her elbows on her knees.

'I have a confession and an apology to make. It wasn't Saxon that leaked the information about your visit to Ed Polson, Liam. It was me. I told somebody you were seeing Polson.'

'Who?' Liam looked from one woman to the other, trying to stay composed.

'I told President Stone. I felt I owed her a heads-up on the

387

Killing Sky story before we went public.'

Both men remained silent, neutral for the moment.

'No, the President wasn't a party to Polson's killing.' Cherry leaned back into the soft cushions, reading their minds. 'Once Polson was murdered we both knew there had to have been a leak. The only other person *you* told was Saxon Melville. Donna, the President, had told the Vice President and two or three others about your planned visit. That's all.

'The others are people the President trusts with her life. For a while she didn't even trust me. She set an agent called Dixon onto me to try me out. Apparently I passed the test. We talked then and figured it had to be either Saxon or Arnott.

'I've known Saxon for years. I trust him. My money was on Arnott, I believed he must have had some kind of involvement in Polson being hit. We… the President, needed to know whether she could trust her VP, whether or not he was up to his neck in arguably the worst crime of the century.'

Donna Stone took over the story.

'Arnott was obviously planted a long time ago. A parachute job into Congress. Big end of town people, we believe. It's called covering your bets. Making sure you have powerful lackeys on both sides of the aisle.'

She beckoned them a little closer.

'If they were willing and able to kill someone as powerful as Polson, once he was blown, why not the President? Polson was one of their own, for God's sake. I was certain that I'd be next. Things we were hearing on the DC grapevine only reinforced that view. The old administration still had Washington by the throat. Apart from a handful of long-time loyal people, I had nobody I could trust completely.'

Liam shook his head. 'Things are pretty grim when the most powerful person on the planet can't even trust her own people.'

'Most powerful person "elect",' the President corrected. 'And you're right. Things have never been so grim. There's a war going on just below the surface, the civilized veneer of the Western world, and it's just as bloody and brutal as any other war. The privileged few that have always controlled things are gradually losing their grip and they don't like it one little bit.'

She looked from one to the other. 'As you two have seen... in fact, nobody knows this better than you... these people will stop at nothing, they have no ethical ceiling.'

She adjusted her foot on the cushion with a slight grimace.

'I was hearing stirrings and I was certain it was only a matter of time until they came for me. We figured they'd wait until the Senate confirmed the Electoral College numbers and strike when the Presidency was 100-per-cent secure.'

She pointed in the general direction of the Capitol. 'These people see this as a defining battle, perhaps the final battle in a protracted war. In that context getting rid of an enemy, who just happens to be the President, is simply another military tactic.'

'The heartland of darkness,' Liam murmured.

'Unfortunately, yes,' she continued. 'My advice said Section Three of the Twentieth Amendment meant that the transfer of the Presidency to the VP elect was legitimate as soon as the Electoral College votes had been cast, even before the Senate count was completed, so we decided to get in first. Basically assassinate me before they did.'

She let the complexity of the detail sink in before going on.

'We were sure it was coming, but there was nothing we could sheet home to Arnott. He was the perfect sleeper: lovely guy, squeaky-clean; on the surface, 100-per-cent onside with every policy. The key was to see how he'd handle the findings, the investigation, the Killing Sky issue, when I wasn't calling the shots; if I wasn't there applying the pressure, breathing down his neck.'

She tapped her foot carefully with a slim ebony cane.

'The broken ankle is genuine. I took a tumble, that's all. The rest of the story clearly wasn't. My secret-service guys got all efficient and started yelling about calling an ambulance. That's when the crazy idea occurred. If they were planning to kill me, why not beat them to it? Control the narrative. Less than a dozen people on the planet knew what was really happening.

'With me gone and Jason in the Presidency, I was pretty sure all that fresh rope meant he'd hang himself sooner than later.

He confirmed my suspicions with indecent haste. Your Swedish "smoking gun" has provided the final piece of the jigsaw; it's been the *coup de grâce*.'

'I'm starting to understand why organizing the chopper in Arkhangelsk was so easy,' Charlie said with a chuckle. 'It was something that puzzled me.'

'Nice little touch, the security cameras,' Liam said. 'The whole world sees you being shot, live, well dead, on camera. Simple.'

'Simple being the operative word.' She smiled thinly. 'I did a little theater in my college days. It's a sobering experience to realize how easily a major policy-shattering deception can be imposed on the American people.' She laughed. 'For a while there, after I saw how simple it was, I was even having doubts about Apollo Eleven.'

'Seems like a huge gamble to me,' Liam said. 'What if he, Arnott, had gone the other way? Found against the conspirators, condemned the whole thing?'

'Then I'd have a truckload of free-range eggs on my face and the nation would likely be facing a constitutional crisis. As it is, the Washington rumor mill is already cranking up; there are whisperings of impeachment from some of the more rabid folk on Capitol Hill.'

She shook her head. 'I was very sure of my suspicions and it was a gamble I felt I had no choice but to take. You don't get to be President of the United States if you're not prepared to gamble.'

She smiled and looked at the three of them. 'But then you three know all about taking gambles.'

Liam failed to return the smile. 'I have a friend in Pakistan who wasn't too happy about your people using the Islamic extremist story yet again.'

'I'm deeply sorry about that.' She sounded genuinely concerned. 'We had to make it look like the kind of bu... the kind of xenophobic cover-up the other side invariably tries to use.'

'So what happens to Arnott now?' Charlie asked.

'For the moment he's being held in a secure facility. My people are in the process of persuading him to share the contact details of his friends with us. It appears he's dropping names like a Hamptons socialite. I hear they make for very interesting reading.' She tapped the gold Presidential seal embossed into the face of a folder on her lap. 'China and Russia are coming on board – in fact the whole Security Council. We're going to get these people.'

'You knew about all this?' Charlie turned back to Cherry.

'Some of it.' She nodded. 'Some. Sorry, sworn to secrecy.'

'Let's hope it's for the last time. I'm getting real tired of secrets.'

The President checked her watch. 'Anyhow, I'm out of time, I'm afraid. I'm flying out to Paris in a couple of hours. We have an emergency G20 meeting to discuss ways of addressing this South Asian crisis.'

'I hope you do more than just talk this time,' Liam said.

'I'll do my best,' she answered. She used the cane to help her stand, then reached out and shook his hand firmly.

'My real reason for calling you was to say thank you and to suggest that you try to get a little help next time before you take on the world,' she said. Formal now. 'There are still a few people you can trust.'

'No doubt,' Charlie said. 'I'm sure there are. Finding them, as you said yourself, is the problem.'

'I managed to find a few,' Liam said quietly.

* * *

Walter Dyson walked over to the television set, lifted the remote and clicked it off. He moved to the window, looked just once at the large white cruiser tied off in front of his Caribbean waterfront, then lowered the electric hurricane shutters. He eased himself onto a Queen Anne chair, took a wallet from his hip pocket and located a small photograph. Two fresh-faced teenagers, pressed close together in bathing suits smiled back out at him. He flipped the picture. On the back, in faded blue ink, were a half-dozen words. 'Walter and Leonie, summer, Long Beach.' He turned off the table lamp, sat in the darkness and waited for the inevitable.

* * *

Zhang Liu and Jia stood side by side next to the young pilot's hospital bed. His wound had been attended to by the Arkhangelsk doctor and he was sleeping peacefully. They could hear the Stockholm saga, now days old, continuing still through the static from a small television set three beds along. Everyone in the ward still seemed to be mesmerized by the story and several nurses, who should have been going about their duties, loitered in the doorway near the security guards.

* * *

Mahmood Khan lay spreadeagled on a wide hotel-room bed in Moscow. He had the remains of a limp room-service salad on a tray beside him. His Islamabad flight was half a day away and he dozed while, intermittently, watching a cricket Test match between Pakistan and Australia on satellite. With two overs to go it looked like a win for Pakistan was likely when the match was interrupted by yet another news-flash replay. Mahmood grinned widely as the screen filled with the image of his two good friends standing in front of a camouflaged aircraft beside a Swedish freeway.

* * *

Dashka Anasovna Azarova reclined on a soft sofa in the Green Room of a television studio in Stockholm. This one would be an interview for a lightweight daytime news program. She'd become an overnight sensation and, even though she'd been in the city for no more than a few hours, had already received a dozen offers to work as a mechanic and over a hundred marriage proposals.

The monitor on the wall was transmitting images of several people being arrested in Moscow. A woman was being unceremoniously pushed into a police wagon. Dashka recognized the fur coat and the perfectly manicured crimson fingernails, secured behind the woman's back with a tight pair of cuffs.

She smiled. It had been a good day. The dishy young anchor had just moments before popped his head around the doorway with an invitation to dinner.

* * *

Cherry Davitt paced her office, illuminated by a single incandescent lamp. It was late Friday and still the television set on the wall streamed live from Moscow. She paused, head bowed, ignoring it. There was a decision to make. On the desk before her were three possibilities. A formal letter from the new President offered a high-profile position working in media liaison. A handwritten note from Charlie made a fair case for a move to Australia. And then, of course, there was the option of staying with the story.

A shadow falling across the doorway made her glance up.

'So what's it to be?' Saxon Melville asked softly.

Cherry frowned, considering his question in silence.

'I'll see you bright and early Monday morning,' she said eventually, then smiled. 'And hold the presses.'

* * *

Oskar Frederik had missed his dawn walk through the silent Oxford streets. The fog on Christ Church Meadow had lifted a good two hours ago but for once he didn't mind. He, too, sat paying close attention to the unfolding news from the BBC.

Downing Street was calling an emergency meeting and already there were, according to the reporter at the other end of the live feed, rumors coming out of Whitehall suggesting numerous arrests.

Oskar stood and turned off the set, then sighed almost inaudibly. 'I must get off to the laboratory,' he called out to his sister up the narrow stairs. 'There's still so much work to do.'

To the south of Cronin's Yard stands a fragment of
old stone wall. It points the way to the head of the
Carrauntoohil track.
On its pale face, but easily missed in the dawn
shadows, several memorial plaques bear witness to the
treacherous nature of the brooding mountain.
Near the rusting gate, a newly inscribed stone tablet has
been added.
It offers a simple message.
'In loving memory of James Michael Doyle and Gregory
Russell Carter,
who died in a place they loved. The mountains.'
Below are the dates of each birth and death.
Liam's lips brush his mother's tear-stained cheek,
he shakes hands with Zhang Liu
and then watches as the lean, grey-haired man
wheels her to the car.
He turns to Jia, kisses her on the lips, helps her on with
her pack and leads the way along the track,
towards the Hag's Glen, the Devil's Ladder,
the mountain.
A large dog appears suddenly from a fog-shrouded
hollow and lopes along beside them.
It is not a black dog.
Before they have covered more than 200 yards
they are swallowed up
by the all-embracing Kerry mist.

Acknowledgements

In an attempt to make the sections relating to the South Asian Monsoon as credible as possible I have read and consulted fairly widely. I have read the IPCC Assessment Reports from both 2007 and 2013/14 with particular attention to the following sections: AR5 IPCC Summary for Policymakers (SPM), IPCC Assessing Transformation Pathways, IPCC CH 7 Aerosols, IPCC Emergent Risks and Key Vulnerabilities, IPCC Geoengineering Ethics and Justice and The IPCC International Cooperation Agreements.

I have consulted a number of relevant papers, studies and articles, including material from the Massachusetts Institute of Technology, Lawrence Berkeley National Laboratory, Rutgers University, Universities of Reading, Leeds, Bristol and Oxford, Stanford University, the University of California, Berkeley, the Weather and Climate School of Mathematical Sciences, Monash University, the ARC Centre of Excellence for Climate System Science, Geophysical Research Letters, Earth Systems Dynamics and Science Daily. I have also consulted material prepared by Alan Robock, John CH Chiang, Andrew R. Friedman, Matt Watson, Piers Forster, Steve Rayner, Michael MacCracken, Paul Crutzen, Ken Caldeira, Philip J Rasch and many of their colleagues – too numerous to list here.

Ethicist Dr Clive Hamilton's book Earthmasters has provided important insights regarding geoengineering as has Naomi Klein's This Changes Everything.

I must also thank two of Australia's leading climate scientists who were generous enough to give me their time, assistance and advice: Dr Scott Power, the Head of Climate Research and the International Development Manager at the Australian Bureau of Meteorology; and Dr Leon Rotstayn, at the time Senior Principal Research Scientist at Australia's CSIRO, working in the areas of Climate Change, Aerosols and Global Climate Modelling.

Doctor Rotstayn's help, in particular, in guiding my fiction in a credible direction, has been invaluable.

Tim Macartney-Snape, who, along with Greg Mortimer, was the first Australian to reach the summit of Mount Everest, has kindly provided excellent advice and suggestions for the mountaineering sections of the book, for which I am deeply grateful. I hope he finds the finished product satisfactory.

I am also indebted to Dr John Newton and Scott Kelly for their generous assistance and Dr Clive Hamilton, Ron Lightfoot, Greg Devine, Trish Duncan and Noel L'Orange for their unwavering encouragement and support.

I would like to thank publishers New Internationalist, and especially editor Chris Brazier, marketing manager Dan Raymond-Barker and designer Juha Sorsa, for their commitment to this story and for their great patience.

Most importantly, I want to thank my chief advisor, confidant, soul-mate and wonderful wife, Kerry McCourt.

About the Author

Rory McCourt's background is in design, advertising and film production. After completing a graphic design diploma course and then several years of international travel, he worked with the advertising company Leo Burnett Sydney as art director, writer and eventually creative director. Subsequently he has worked as a writer, designer and film director, producing a variety of material for clients in Australia and internationally, as well as having written and directed documentaries, television pilots and some drama. He spent most of his career in Sydney but now lives in Queensland's Whitsunday region.

He has one previously published novel – *Children of the Dust* (Random House 1997) – a work co-written with Boyd Anderson under the pseudonym Anderson McCourt.